Cutting Corners
Sheila Kindellan-Sheehan

ISBN: 1-896881-66-1

Cover design: Audrey Davis, from a concept
   by JoAnn Valente
Interior design: Studio Melrose/Ted Sancton
Map from a design by Gina Pingitore

Printed in Canada

Redlader Publishing is a division of Price-Patterson Ltd.

FOR MAME
My little sister

LIST OF CHARACTERS

**On The Boulevard in Westmount
(a suburb of Montreal):**

Frank Donovan: Chris' father, corporate lawyer,
    partner at Henderson-Warren

Maggie Donovan: Chris' mother, the heart of
    the family

Chris Donovan: 26, recent Harvard MBA

Caitlin Donovan: 31, Chris' sister, author and
    professor at Concordia University

Maureen McDonough: Maggie's mother, currently
    residing in Toronto

Mireille: the cook

Friends:

Carmen DiMaggio: 28, Caitlin's best friend

Mike Halloran: 28, Chris' American friend,
    Harvard MBA

Hunter Townsend: 27, Chris' other American friend,
    Harvard MBA

**On Harvard Avenue in Notre Dame de Grace
(another suburb of Montreal, always 'NDG'
to Montrealers):**

Nicolina Pastore: head legal counsel for
    Foley Pharmaceuticals

Sophia Argento: Nicolina's boarder

Monsieur Patate: a pug with owner, bladder
    and behaviour problems

Elsa & Stephen Schreff: Nicolina's neighbours

The Suits at Station 12:
Claude Remay: lead investigator, a good guy
Jacques Lussier: forensics

Foley Pharmaceuticals:
Raymond Lecours: CEO
Jen Sexton: vice-president of human resources
Kathryn Traynor: controller, fired by Nicolina
    Pastore, recently diagnosed with cancer
Richard Walton: junior in-house counsel

Memorable characters:
Pierre Michel Beausoleil: doorman at the Ritz-Carlton
Tim Traynor: Kathryn's husband
Robert Sexton: Jen's husband
Martin Boulanger: trial judge in Traynor v. Foley
Ryan Burns: 46, an accident victim
Dave Burns: his brother

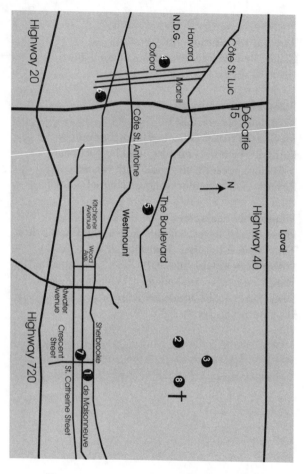

1. Ritz-Carlton
2. The Mountain
3. Côte des Neiges Cemetery
4. Nicolina's House
5. Donovan House
6. Collins & Clarke Funeral Home
7. Winnie's
8. Mount Royal Cross

CHAPTER 1

FRANK DONOVAN, IN a cashmere navy blue winter coat with its collar drawn up high to protect his ears against the wind, stood on Fort Street behind his wife and daughter waiting to join the St. Patrick's Day parade. For a moment, he didn't notice anything but the smiling face of Caitlin who laughed and jostled with her comrade in arms, Carmen DiMaggio. It was good to see Caitlin laugh. Three years of mourning the accidental death of her husband Derek had taken his daughter so far from him, he wondered sometimes if she was lost forever. Caitlin was her father's girl. Unlike many new fathers, he was hoping for a daughter, and when Caitlin came along, he lost his heart. And they both had a bond with their city, Montreal.

Every day of the year, Montreal rocks with North American pizzazz and French élan. This hotbed of political opinion and argument is a sophisticated blend of fine culture and a festive heart. Its intriguing array of haute cuisine is balanced by the succulent common taste of Schwartz's world famous smoked meat on the Main and St-Viateur's Bagel Bakery in the Plateau district, immortalized in paintings and fiction. This city lives in the grey during the long winter months, its sidewalks often slabs of treacherous ice or mounded snow. These hazards do nothing to quell a lust for speed. Its drivers are the worst in North America, and the city has the accident record to prove it.

Winning is a tradition set way back in the golden era of the Montreal Canadiens. This hockey dynasty sits as high on the sports podium as the New York Yankees. The Expos, *'nos amours'*, a bitter-sweet memory now, never had the chance to make it to the World Series in

1994 because of the baseball strike and they broke hearts every other year. Montrealers are strong and sturdy individuals who, unlike Torontonians, wouldn't think of calling in the army to help clear the streets, but the remarkable ice storm of '98 crippled the city for days. It also created a heartfelt, enduring camaraderie.

Around mid-March, with the city still strangled in the white fist of winter, Montrealers begin partying, creating their own spring with the annual St. Patrick's Day Parade, the largest in North America, that began back in 1824. On that day, green bursts upon St. Catherine Street between Fort and Jeanne Mance on shamrock-painted cheeks, top hats, banners, flags, floats, gloves, jackets and anything else that can hold that colour, all led by the Grand Marshall as the parade moves down the street. Marching bands play familiar Irish songs while young girls in short green skirts and long white legs perform traditional dances to the delight of the crowds. On the sidewalk in front of Ogilvy's department store, Montreal's most famous busker, the Spoonman, in his trusty Davy Crockett coonskin cap, clicks 'McNamara's Band', his woes with the city's anti-panhandler legislation and his new castanets tucked into his pocket for the parade. Politicians walk arm-in-arm as friendly to everyone as your corner grocer. Flag-waving fans of every culture line the street, flushed with Celtic green. Everybody's Irish!

Frank was still a hunk, Maggie often told her two children. At fifty-four, he'd lost nothing of his six-foot two lankiness, nor any of his wonderful salt and pepper black hair that crowned a round Irish face. A taller George Clooney. Frank took the time to dress well in the morning, sometimes taking off the shirt and pants he'd just donned and changing both, but he never looked in a mirror for the rest of the day. An assumed, quiet confidence and his family kept Frank away from daily temptations. Carnal or monetary, they lurked on every inch of the hardwood floors of the prestigious corporate law firm, Henderson-Warren, where he was a partner.

Frank often wondered if lawyers in the firm were hiding behind the legal walls they had built for themselves. It was a common belief that therapists tried to heal themselves in sessions. Why not lawyers with the law? His wife Maggie had seen the troubled corners in his hazel eyes and been drawn to those pools. She felt she'd known her husband well since undergrad and nothing she remembered had caused this pensive appearance. Frank must have come by the look naturally. Today, Maggie was eagerly watching the Grand Marshall and his entourage gather in the centre of the street. Frank was up for president of the St. Patrick's Society. *I don't deserve the honour,* he thought.

'Frank, are you ready to join the parade?' Maggie asked, tugging on his arm.

Looking back at his daughter, he answered, 'If we can settle these two down.'

'Carmen's getting cold feet.'

'I'm Italian, Italian and Russian. How can I walk behind the celebrated Irish contingent?'

'Here,' Caitlin countered, handing Carmen one of the two shamrocks she had pinned to her coat. 'Now, you're Irish!' With one pull, Carmen was out on Fort Street, working on her best Irish smile.

Frank took the arms of each of the women he loved and he was happy again. Conscience, like baggage, can be stored away, out of sight.

❧

Six weeks later on a sunny afternoon in Boston, he

was even better, feeling proud and secure. Christopher received his MBA from Harvard on the lawn of Aldridge Hall near the library, placing sixth in a field of ninety-four. Frank would have preferred Chris to follow him into the law, but Chris was his own man, a character like his mother, head-strong and fun-loving. His son had made it quite clear he never intended to follow in his father's footsteps. After the caps had been tossed into the air, Chris made a beeline over to where his family was standing.

Maggie grabbed Frank's shoulder, 'Frank, don't say a word to Chris about the six months he's taking off. He's made up his mind – there's nothing we can do. Anyway, it'll be great to have him home. I've missed our boy.'

'You and I never took time off – Caitlin didn't either. It's a hungry world out there. What if General Motors changes their mind?'

'They won't, Frank. They pursued *him*, and they knew of his plans. Sometimes, you talk too old, handsome. Let's just enjoy the time we have him home with us.'

'Did you forget he's bringing two friends with him?'

'Come on, Dad, enough,' Caitlin broke in, hugging her father, giving him a kiss on the cheek that did the trick.

Frank looked over at Maggie, aching for some of the garrulous heartiness that kept her soft, open. Though they were the same age, Maggie was hopping up and down like a schoolgirl, waving wildly in Chris' direction, her thick mass of honey-blonde curls, maintained with a little help, bouncing with every jump. All she needed were a few coloured ribbons to stand in for a relatively young mother nature. The rich scent of her shampoo swirled in the spring air. Maggie was the only person Frank had ever met who could cry and laugh together in a matter of seconds. Parents standing close by today smiled up at her. There was no way she was five-nine, as Maggie told everyone, even when she slouched. The few extra smile lines she'd picked up over the years stood no chance of aging the young girl in her. Waiting for Chris, swelling with infectious enthusiasm, she seemed even taller. 'Over here, Chris,' she called out, filling up the spaces, oblivious of the other parents. 'Over here, Flash!'

Frank's welcome, even Caitlin's, would seem small beside Maggie's. He rubbed the side of his chin and then scratched an imaginary itch behind his ear. He stepped closer to Maggie to feel less separate. These emotional times brought the past to mind and left Frank stiff and even distant. The parade back home was public – today was personal. Long before anything had occurred, Frank remembered stepping on his emotions. His success had done nothing to alter that. Maggie was no stranger to pain, but the jostling of four brothers and two sisters had kept her grounded and outgoing. It was the only salvation in their large, boisterous family. Frank had come to his parents late in their lives. They were quiet people, old as long as he knew them. His father never had time for his childhood or early adolescence and treated his son as a young adult from the time Frank was six. Stingy with sentences, that's what Frank recalled of his father. There had been no physical resemblance for his father, wedgy in stature, to recognize. Frank had been a stranger in the family. His mother tried as best she could to even things out. Funny, Frank thought, his appearance had always opened doors for him, but had never given him a sense of belonging. He hoped life would be better for Chris.

It was Maggie who had opened him up, reached inside and held on. Maggie who tickled his ribs till he laughed out loud. With her he was whole and good, or almost. On nights when he lay awake, he had thought of confiding in Maggie, but he was afraid of losing her. She was wired with high standards.

Chris burst through the crowd, but Frank kept his eyes on Maggie. He could even admit that he felt a tinge of jealousy at times when Maggie lavished her attention on Chris. Hell, he felt the same twitch with the band of friends that energized his wife, their celebrations, their crises, even Maggie's students, all things that invaded her heart. Frank still remembered being forced to study *The Last Duchess* in his first year of university. He felt back then that there was something to be said for the sentiments of the Duke. Even now, with Chris hugging her, Maggie was still hopping. Seeing his son today reminded him of the time he'd visited her class. The children sitting on the carpet huddled around her legs, others nuzzled under her arms. 'You smell good, Mrs. Donovan,' a little boy with marble eyes shouted. It was true. Maggie smelled of flowers.

Chris had landed in front of his family in a blur of black robes and blond hair. Sensing his father's presence, he turned from his mother and shook his hand. 'Dad, I know sixth is not the second you made in law school, but it's not bad, right?'

'Not bad at all, son. It's an achievement.' He wanted to add something about applying oneself, but didn't.

'Do you know how proud I am of you, Chris? Do you?' Maggie had tears rolling down her cheeks, but kissed Chris again anyway. 'Darn it, I've managed to get lipstick on your gown.'

'It's a rental, Ma. Forget about it.'

'Save some of that hugging for me,' Caitlin said, stepping forward.

'Sis, thanks for coming.'

'Wouldn't have missed my kid brother graduating from Harvard!'

'It's something, eh, Sis?'

'Better believe it.'

No one who saw them together could doubt the two were siblings – height, bearing, beauty, broad shoulders, clear hazel eyes from Frank, with none of the grit of age lining their cheeks. When they smiled, as they were now, a single dimple appeared on their left cheeks. But for a touch of sadness behind Caitlin's eyes, she and Chris were opposite sides of the same coin. The scramble of life was still an inviting challenge for both of them. Young and hopeful. At least that's what Frank saw when he looked at them today. He should have known better, but it didn't occur to him that grey areas could seep into their lives early.

When Maggie looked over at Frank, she left Chris immediately and hugged her husband. 'Are you thinking of your father? He's here in spirit, you know,' she whispered into his ear.

Shifting gears had become second nature to Frank and he answered, 'I guess I am, hon. Three generations of Harvard men – time passes so quickly. Dad would have been swelling with pride to be here today.'

'So let's not miss another minute of it,' she scolded gently, pulling Frank back towards Chris and Caitlin and the two graduates standing behind them.

If it's possible to swagger in only three steps, the first young man to step forward accomplished the feat. 'Mike Halloran, sir. A real pleasure, you're nothing like the ogre Chris has described.'

It took a few seconds for a thin smile to push across Frank's lips. Everyone else was already laughing, everyone except Chris. He swallowed, inched forward behind his friend and poked Mike between the shoulder blades.

'Sir, I'll step aside because Hunter is anxious to meet you.' Frank was instantly wary of this self-assured young man. Always a sucker for a mop of unruly hair and a joke, Maggie took to him immediately. Caitlin blushed, something she hadn't done since Derek died. Her pulse rose quietly as she breathed in the odour of subtle after-shave. *He's just a kid*, she thought. *But it's been too long.*

'Mr. Donovan, never take anything Mike says seriously. You've been a model for Chris. I'm Hunter Townsend and I'm nothing like Mike.' And he wasn't. He was more like an aging Anglican altar boy, young but stiff. Tall, lean with no sign of muscle, but taut with youth and resolution. Frank liked him.

'Dad, meet number one in our class! Hunter is never less than first.'

'Congratulations, Hunter! I know how much work is involved in that endeavour.'

'Thank you, sir. I appreciate the compliment.'

'Hunter and Mike, this is Maggie and our daughter Caitlin. I understand we'll be seeing you both in Montreal very soon.'

'Chris got Mike and me hooked on his stories of the city. Thank you for inviting us into your home. We won't inconvenience you or Mrs. Donovan for long. Chris is looking into finding us a place downtown. My father will cover it. Until Mike and I start work in Boston, we want to have some fun. If I can add some French to the Spanish I can speak, I feel I'd be ahead of the game.'

'Call me Maggie, boys. Stay with us as long as you want. We certainly have the room, and Frank and I look forward to the company.'

'Caitlin suggested Le Montfort on de Maisonneuve, Dad. They have suites and it's pretty central.'

'Let's wait and see how things go before you think of finding another place,' Maggie said quickly. She wanted to see as much of Chris as possible. She knew if his friends rented out, he'd probably join them. 'We're pretty central too.'

'You might not even like the city,' Caitlin said, testing the waters.

'I'm already drawn to the people,' Mike said, jumping back into the conversation, smiling only at Caitlin when he spoke.

From the moment he saw Caitlin's reaction, Chris decided to keep an eye on Mike. He didn't want his sister to be another notch on Mike's *love 'em and leave 'em* belt. He and Hunter had answered their door to many pretty girls with broken hearts. In fact, his father would be happy to know, though he'd be the last person to tell him, that he had cleaned up much of his own act because of the devastation Mike had left in his wake. Mike never meant to hurt anyone, but he did. Chris was more like his father than he ever wanted to admit. Chris liked women and their company. But more important than all that, he loved Caitlin and didn't want her hurt with a summer fling.

'Before I head home, Dad, we've planned a few days in Hyannis. I might not be back at the Cape for a while.'

Mike quickly added, 'Why not come along, Caitlin? We'll have a blast.'

'Why not!' Caitlin heard herself saying and lost the nerve to recant.

Chris did a double take.

Frank missed everything. 'Are both you fellows Bostonians?'

'Yes, sir, tried and true,' Mike said. 'I grew up in Cambridge, but the family, and me with it, now live in Back Bay. Hunter's family lives in Beacon Hill. Both our fathers are in money management, so I can tell you that I'm looking forward to conversation that won't involve business.'

'And yet, that's the field you're pursuing,' Frank felt he had to add.

'Following in my father's footsteps seemed natural. In the 'land of the bean and the cod', you can't avoid Beantown traditions, the Red Sox World Series win aside.'

'Well, Chris is his own man, and he's brave as well. My dad here is a formidable character, and I know it bothered Chris that the law wasn't where his interests led,' Caitlin threw in.

'Well said, Caitlin. Courage runs in the family,' Mike acknowledged.

'We'll look forward to seeing you and Hunter in a week or so,' Maggie said. Next to people, Maggie enjoyed good food most. 'Frank, we should let these two get back to their families. I hate to admit it, but I'm hungry.'

'See you soon then,' Hunter said, waving as he and Mike made their way back through the crowd of parents and friends.

'Dad, where have you decided on for dinner?'

'I felt on such a momentous day, I should choose an American landmark. We have reservations at Locke-Ober. I remembered you enjoy Cape scallops. I've heard theirs are nothing less than perfect. Your mother will talk for days about her duck with elderberry and ginger. Caitlin and I will stay with beef, I think.'

'Days like this, I know I chose the right man.'

'I thought I did the choosing.'

'It's healthier you feel that way, Frank. Let's get back to the hotel and shower. I'm definitely hungry. We'll wait for you there, Chris. We're staying at the XV

Beacon,' said Maggie, reaching into her purse and handing Chris the address and phone number.

'I'll grab a cab, Mom, and I'll meet you there as soon as I change.' Chris tried to get Caitlin's attention, but she turned away before their eyes met.

Frank regarded his family and spoke with authority. 'It's wonderful that we can be all together as a family. Let's remember these times.'

'Scrapbook moments,' Maggie joined in, tearing up.

A few hours later, seated in the elegant restored turn-of-the-century dining room that had fed celebrities, politicos and its share of high rollers, Frank raised his champagne flute. 'Chris, on behalf of Maggie and Caitlin and myself, I congratulate your success, I welcome you back home and I wish you hard work and the joy of accomplishment as you embark on the unbeaten path of your life. I hope you're as lucky as I have been with the partner you choose to walk with you and the good fortune of a daughter and son like the two of you that I have been blessed with.'

'Hear, hear!' enthused Maggie and Caitlin.

If Orson Welles and Caruso, both Locke-Ober patrons, had been among the living, they too would have raised their glasses to youth and its possibilities.

CHAPTER 2

THE NEXT AFTERNOON, Maggie and Frank were back home. Two and a half days later, Caitlin was in her own place on Wood Avenue, preparing her new ethics course. She had been given this course because the professor teaching it had suffered a massive coronary while walking the aisles to check up on students' work. She was trying not to think of the night she'd spent with Mike in Hyannis and failing. *What was I thinking? But, wow!*

Maggie was busy in Chris' room, preparing for his homecoming. Tomorrow, she'd be back in school. She could have had this work done for her, but she preferred to do things herself. Twice a month, she did consent, because Frank insisted, to paid housekeeping in the cutstone, 14-room mansion that sat very comfortably on the north side of The Boulevard in Westmount. Built in 1934, the home had seen more work than a Hollywood starlet. When Frank bought the mansion from his father, he had set a deadline on renovations and had brought all work to a close four years ago. He and Maggie were finally at peace from continuous noise and content with the 12,000-square-foot property. Maggie's choice of having the solid oak doors at the front of the house painted red, each adorned with large, heavy brass knockers, gave the house a heart.

There were two bedrooms and adjoining bathrooms in the service quarters on top of the three-car garage. Mike and Hunter would stay there. These quarters could not boast the fine architectural details of the main house: inlaid floors; cathedral, intricate, plaster ceilings; some original interior ironwork; four white marble fireplaces and stained glass windows. Nevertheless, the rooms were spacious and bright, each with a wonderful view of English-speaking Montreal. There was also a separate entrance for these quarters, and Maggie felt confident Mike and Hunter would stay longer than planned because of the privacy.

Historically English-speaking Westmount is a distinct society within Montreal. It is its own city and would bridle at the term 'suburb'. A suburb brings to mind cookie-cutter real estate development and there is nothing assembly line about Westmount. There may be some houses in the same style, but never more than half a dozen. And no part looks like the ranch-style developments present in most North American suburbs.

This distinct society is located between downtown and NDG. Being close to downtown keeps it close to the heart of Montreal and its commerce, restaurants, bars and festivals: there is nothing isolated about Westmount. Its relationship with NDG is more complex, perhaps like that between a rich and poor cousin: sometimes close; sometimes not. Both NDG and Westmout are largely English-speaking, but NDG is larger, poorer and more diverse. In recent years, parts of NDG have gentrified, but there is still a difference.

There was nothing subtle or reserved about Maggie, but she won people over whether they wanted to be or not. At heart, most people are a little lazy, and disliking Maggie involved too much work. Of course, Frank fit like a soft leather glove in this little moneyed city where he'd grown up. With his power in the legal world and his father's connections, the couple was often the first to be invited to any prestigious event, and there were many in Westmount. Maggie loved all these events but she was often forced to drag Frank along. Born into this life, he had become bored with the circuit. He much preferred a quiet night at home.

Expecting Frank's call, she picked up the cordless. 'Have you got it, Frank?'

'I have. I'll drive the car home and the two fellows will follow in mine. It's exactly what Chris had his heart set on, I think.'

'Don't give me details – I'll wait to see it in person. How long will you be?'

'The papers are all signed. I'm waiting for the drivers and the courtesy car. I should be home in about forty minutes.'

'I picked up the banner that we'll drape across the car, so hurry. You have me excited too!'

'Will do.'

'I told Chris to grab a cab from Trudeau. He's set to arrive at seven and he should make it home by eight-thirty tonight. I hope I've made the right choice.'

'Frank, we don't have time for second-guessing. I've never known you to make poor decisions, so relax and come on home.'

'Is Caitlin coming for dinner?'

'She can't. She's brainstorming for an ethics class tomorrow morning. It's a lot of pressure because if the head of the department likes her prep, she'll be given the course for next year. With her three Women's Studies courses at the Simone de Beauvoir Institute, another six credits means a full contract at Concordia next fall. Apparently, the stricken colleague will retire, something he should have done a few years ago. This is a wonderful chance for Caitlin; I'm sorry it's at someone else's expense.'

'I agree. I'll rush these fellows along; I want to miss the traffic.'

True to his word, Frank pulled into his driveway less than an hour later, parked the new car in the garage and waited for his own to arrive. He didn't have to worry that the dealer had driven his BMW-760Li sedan hard. Though the traffic flowed, the roads were too busy for that. He walked into the house through the garage. 'Maggie, I'm home. Come on down and let's have a look together.'

'I'm coming, I'm coming!' She followed Frank into the garage which he'd lit up like a Broadway stage. He'd left his car outside for better viewing and backed hers out as well. Maggie kept her head down so as not to ruin the surprise and stopped about fifteen feet from the car, took a deep breath and gasped. 'Oh my Lord, Chris will burst when he sees this! A red sports car, every son's dream. Of course, now I'll worry every time he drives it. Things will be okay, right Frank?'

'I considered the conservative route, but then I realized that it's Caitlin who has the lead foot, not Chris. He's the most prudent of all of us – doesn't even jaywalk. I think we're safe, Maggie. Let's go in and enjoy a glass of wine while we wait.'

'The glasses are on the table and the Chablis is chilled. I can't wait till Chris is home.' Both of them jumped to their feet when they heard a car pull into the driveway. Maggie ran to the door – Frank never ran for anything.

'Hi Ma,' Chris called out as he climbed from the cab.

'Hi yourself, let's get you inside.'

'Hi, Dad. It's great to be home!'

When she saw her men side by side, Maggie couldn't resist, 'You seem taller, Chris.'

'Ma, you saw me a couple of days ago and I stopped growing before I left for Harvard.'

So much had to be done before Chris left the campus for Hyannis that he never noticed his parents had come to his graduation without a gift. When Frank asked him to come see something in the garage, he asked. 'You haven't had an accident, Dad, have you?'

'No, son, I haven't. There is something I want your opinion on.'

'I'm behind you, Dad.'

Maggie had snuck on ahead and turned the lights back on. Maggie couldn't help herself, 'Ta da!'

Chris stopped in his tracks a few feet from a gleaming cherry red Audi TT Quattro Roadster detailed with black leather seats. 'Holy shit! Sorry, Ma, but holy shit! Wow! Dad, I never expected anything. A sports car! I feel like a kid on Christmas morning.' Chris walked slowly over to the car and ran his finger across the driver's seat. 'Wow! Thanks, Dad.'

'The car's from both of us.'

'You're the best. Who would have figured my parents would choose a sports car? Ma, I could see, but not you, Dad. I can't believe this. I have to say something more than *wow*. Is it a 3.2 litre, V6, 'cause that baby has 250 hp?'

'You nailed it, Chris. Add DSG, the Direct Shift Gearbox S-Line iteration, and I think you have an interesting car. The only thing I can think of now is that with your two friends, you may have a transportation problem.'

'Are you kidding, one of them will crouch in the back.'

'I don't suppose I have to mention rules – you're too old for that.'

'I'm not so old that I don't remember them, Dad.'

'Part of this gift is a reward for your hard work – the other is for not smoking. Mom and I feel you'll live longer and healthier now.'

Technically, that's true, Chris thought, swallowing

deep and trying to steady his Adam's apple. *I have never smoked tobacco.*

'I'm so glad we'll have you to ourselves for a little time before your friends arrive.'

'Not going to happen, Ma. You made too good an impression. They'll be here tomorrow night. Sorry. I was hoping for a week to myself, but I think they're both eager to be free. Would you like to try out my new wheels with me?'

'Take your father; I'll have dinner on the table in half an hour. I'm famished, so don't be long. Take it easy, both of you.'

'Dad, we'll save the real test for tonight. Could we drive to Caitlin's for two minutes? I want to show her the car – she'll go wild.'

'She's working on a new course, but I suppose she can spare a few minutes.'

When they reached the car, Chris was still beside himself. 'I can't believe this is mine. Dad, hop in. I didn't even notice the hands-free phone. I'll call ahead.'

In minutes, they were at the corner of Sherbrooke Street and Wood Avenue. 'Dad, I'm taking this slow. I want Caitlin to get the full effect.' The TT crept down Wood.

She was standing on the sidewalk when they pulled up beside her. 'Man about town, now Chris!' she pronounced before he could say a word. 'Aren't you the lucky bugger! Sorry, Dad, but he is. The car looks good on you. What a welcome home! Let's you and I get together tomorrow night. I'm sorry to miss dinner tonight but I really have to get back to work. I'm a little nervous about tomorrow.'

'Dad, take care of this beast while I walk Sis to her door.' Throwing his arm around Caitlin, they walked up the steps together to a red brick, semi-detached townhouse that she and Derek had bought just before real estate prices soared. 'Believe it or not, the guys, Mike in particular, wanted to hit the city as soon as possible. I think we both know the reason.'

'I'm a big girl, Chris. It's been a long time.'

'I get it. I know Mike better than you do. Be careful, Sis, that's all I'm trying to say.'

'Have you gone and grown up on me?'

'Happened against my will. Gotta go. We'll make it a group night tomorrow, okay?'

'I'll invite Carm. Like you, she's grown up too.'

'Since when?'

'Florida.'

There was no time for a follow-up question. At dinner, Chris raced through his meal so he could go back out to the garage. 'Sorry, Mom, this roasted chicken and stuffing and the oven-browned potatoes that I love are to die for, best food I've had in a year. But it's not every day a guy gets a new sports car.'

'Try to chew at least, Chris.'

'I hear you,' he looked up, but his foot never stopped tapping the floor, something he'd done as a child when he was excited. 'Ma, forgive me, I just want to sit in the car and back it out of the garage. Dad, I'll wait for you in the front. Take your time; I could sit in my car all night.' Chris was out the door before an objection could be voiced.

Frank and Maggie had not spoiled their children, until now. They wanted to teach their kids discipline and the value of hard work. Though Caitlin loved her yellow Beetle, her bike – an M-4 Specialized-Stumpjumper with its disk brakes and tubeless tires – was more important to her than her car. Chris hadn't wanted a car in Boston, and the first one he'd owned didn't merit remembering.

'Maybe we shouldn't have started down this slippery slope,' Frank said after Chris had literally run from the room.

'I'm enjoying his excitement. Do you remember when Chris was five and Santa left his red bike? He sat on it for hours. It's nice to know our little boy is still there.'

'It is. I better get out there before he starts calling. We'll be back in a bit.'

Chris took Guy Street and drove west on the Ville Marie Expressway to Highway 20. Then he let his horses gallop to Dorval. 'Slow down here, son, there are always speed traps here. You don't want a speeding violation your first night out.'

'We'll slow down on the way back, Dad. I just want to feel the power tonight – I won't be driving at this speed again. It's almost like flying! Even with the top down, I can smell the new car. I don't even feel tall in it. There's good leg room.'

'I made sure of that, son. Let's head on back; we're already in Beaconsfield. Take the St. Charles exit and circle around to get back. Mom will be lonely without us and, with your friends arriving tomorrow, this might be our only night with you.'

'You got it. Maybe Mom will want a ride.'

'She wants to spend time with you, Chris. The ride can wait.'

'Message received.'

CHAPTER 3

THURSDAY WAS A BUSY day. Maggie finished school at three, drove to her favourite food store on Greene Avenue, felt lucky to find parking on the short, busy street, popped into *Au Pain Doré* for French bread and two raspberry tortes and headed home. Chris was out in his car; Caitlin had met with the head of the department who had said new blood was just what the department needed and offered her the course to be taught in the MU building in the fall. *Full course load, full salary – I'm part of this university*, she beamed as she jaunted down the hall afterwards.

Frank was just beginning to advise on a major cross-border acquisition that would consume months – if not years – and necessitate European travel. The challenge was the best part for Frank. Work blocked out troubling thoughts.

Mike and Hunter arrived in great form and were hard at work unpacking when Caitlin arrived. Even the weather cooperated. The sun was bright, and the temperature was an unseasonal twenty-one degrees, June weather at the end of April. There are moments in life that should be frozen – this was one of them.

'Caitlin, would you go up and call the guys to dinner?' Maggie asked as they finished setting the table.

Caitlin had showered and spent extra time in front of the mirror. A cream cashmere sweater clung gently to her beige Capri slacks. She paused in front of another mirror on the landing to fluff her curls and check herself before heading to the rooms over the garage. *Chris is worrying about the wrong person*, she thought. *Control, girl, get a little control.* As she stepped into the room, Mike turned.

'Hi,' was all he managed to get out. He couldn't think of any of his knock-out come-ons.

'Hi yourself.' Heat surged across her stomach before she turned to Hunter. 'Nice to see you too. Dinner's ready. I thought Chris was up here.'

'He was but he's in the shower. It's amazing how much your parents' place reminds me of ours back home, right down to the red door.'

'Mom will be flattered, Hunter.'

'I'll see you both downstairs then.'

'Caitlin, you look great,' Mike said because he couldn't stop himself.

Caitlin thought back to Hyannis. 'See you downstairs.' She nearly bolted from the room. *Exercise a little control. That's an order!* However, her hormones, newly awakened at the Cape, refused to go back to sleep. Even with the nervous prep of last night, Mike intruded on her concentration. Chris met her on the landing.

'I hear you have the course.'

'Yup, it's mine.'

'All right, Sis! Are the guys coming down?'

'Right behind you.'

'Good.'

On Frank's insistence, Maggie had enlisted Mireille to cook and serve. She took charge and worked small miracles when Frank and Maggie hosted dinner parties. Tonight, Frank wanted Maggie to enjoy the evening and not spend most of the time in the kitchen. The dining room was a burst of sunlight. Between the beams, the walls were pale yellow adorned with original Canadian art. The principal piece Maggie had chosen exploded with bright fall colours, true reds and yellows and oranges in a background of birch. It hung over the pink marble fireplace at one end of the room. Close by, on a marble pedestal, bathed in overhead lighting, a two-foot Eskimo figure of a young pregnant girl looked out at the dinner guests with fierce, stone eyes. No one had been able to determine if she was smiling or shrieking. This piece was Maggie's favourite. Yellow roses lined the long dining room table, made brighter by candlelight. The Aynsley Empress fine china was complemented by Moser Casanova haloed-gold stemware that sparkled in the dancing flame.

Once everyone was seated, Frank raised his glass of Puligny Montrechet and offered a hearty welcome. Mireille began serving a carrot ginger soup followed closely by fresh Atlantic salmon in her gourmet cream sauce. Mike's appetites were certainly not limited to women. 'The food is great, but it's the bread! I could eat the whole loaf.'

'It's authentic French bread made with water rather than milk,' Maggie was happy to tell him. 'The bread is lighter and tastier as a result.'

'We have French bread at home, but it doesn't taste like this. No wonder the French eat it without butter.'

'I should have brought lighter clothes,' Hunter broke in. 'I'll call home tomorrow. I figured I'd need heavy clothing and that's what I brought.'

'Take no notice of Hunter, Mr. Donovan. He was surprised not to see Canada on your licence plates. Too many of us Americans are woefully ignorant about our neighbours to the north.'

'Thanks for the defence, Mike.' Then turning to Frank, Hunter added, 'I intend to brush up on this city, sir, bank on it.'

'That's good to hear, Hunter. Life is about broadening your experience and you'll be the richer for it. The weather in Boston is not that much different than what we have here in Montreal,' Frank offered. 'It can't be much of a stretch for you fellows.'

'I have to admit it's warmer than the day Hunter and I left Boston.'

'Our weather can change in five minutes. We might drop twenty degrees overnight. Montrealers seize the good days,' Maggie added. 'It's probably why we celebrate every opportunity. We know that tomorrow is uncertain.'

'Have you young people decided what you'll do with the evening?'

'Carmen can't join us because she's driving her parents to visit an aunt in Lachine, but she'll be with us tomorrow. Tonight, Chris and I decided it would be fun to walk up on the mountain and sightsee from there. Then we're heading for Crescent Street and Winnie's. With the warm weather, the street will be hopping.'

'Dad, don't worry: we're taking cabs.' Chris had an ulterior motive. Had he and Catlin used both their cars, Mike would have gone with Caitlin. He was determined to delay the inevitable between her and Mike for as long as he could, hoping his sister would come to her senses. At dinner, he had seen them look at one another, and that was enough for him to keep them apart.

'I'm glad to hear that, Chris. I won't be walking the floors,' Maggie said.

'Saturday morning, we're heading to Quebec City and we'll stay a few days. I've told the guys they're about to see the only walled city in North America.'

'Have you decided where you're staying?'

'Dad, we'll stay in a *pension*, get the flavour of the place.'

'How about one night and dinner at the Château Frontenac, on me? The view of the St. Lawrence is spectacular.'

'That would be great! Caitlin too?'

'Of course.'

'Thanks, Dad.'

'Then we're going to do our city, beginning with Old Montreal brick by brick.'

'Then you'd all better get going. It's late as it is. Chris, let yourself in, I guess that won't be before early tomorrow morning, through the service quarters. That way you won't wake your mother and me.'

'There's no doubt of the time we'll make it back home. It's been two years since I felt this free. The first night of a holiday is always the best because everything is in front of you. All right, guys, let's head out! The night is young.' Chris led the way, but not before stopping at the garage while they waited on a cab. He stood at the foot of his car and rubbed the first hint of dust from the hood with the tail of his shirt. 'See you soon, sweet thing,' he bent and whispered.

CHAPTER 4

ON HARVARD AVENUE in NDG, Nicolina Pastore was about to sit at the dining room table, set for one, and enjoy the meal she had been waiting for since last Sunday. Fresh Italian bread from *Première Moisson* lay beside a good bottle of Chianti already sweating with the early spring heat. The aroma from the oven and the salad of fresh tomatoes, cucumbers, onions, garlic and Italian seasoning caused Nicolina's mouth to water. With both oven mitts, she reached for the tray of her homemade meatballs. She had gotten the recipe from Sophia, the older woman who had rented her basement apartment last October.

Everything was in the rolling, Sophia had explained. The ingredients of bread, cheese, garlic, parsley, salt and pepper, pork and extra lean beef all seemed simple enough. But the crispness on the outside, the chewiness that hid the tender meat, could only be gotten with a little water added to the bread and a proper hand roll. She and her mentor had prepared the sauce last week. It was an aromatic concoction, its secret ingredients shared only by Sophia and her. In truth, it was a secret Sophia never thought she'd disclose to anyone, much less a woman she wasn't terribly fond of. But her life had changed dramatically since Roberto, her husband of fifty-five years, had won ten thousand dollars at the Montreal casino. In the minutes it took for the pit boss to cross the red carpet and validate his win, poor Roberto's heart stopped. Most of his life he had lost at the slots. Who could ever guess a win would kill him?

Poor Sophia lost much more than Roberto that sad night. Over the years, the house that they had bought and paid for with paltry saving and hard work had been mortgaged to the hilt. Other creditors came calling too. Roberto, it now appeared, had borrowed money everywhere. Poor Sophia paid all his debts, even using the seven thousand dollars emergency cash she had squirreled away from doing secretarial work for a doctor in Outremont years ago. She buried Roberto with a respect he didn't really deserve. She was far too proud to ask her daughter in Winnipeg to take her in. In addition, her daughter had said that days are short in Winnipeg and Sophia Argento was not looking for long, lonely nights. What she did need was a small rented apartment that her old age and widow's pensions could cover. To save money, she bagged what she could carry and hauled her belongings by bus to the basement apartment on Harvard. Much of the furniture and the accumulation of a lifetime went to the Salvation Army. What she kept, Sophia was very proud to remind herself, was driven by a neighbour's son in his father's van for only two hundred dollars. Packing her recipes was easy: those were kept in her head. Sharing them was much harder.

It was Monsieur Patate who'd convinced her she had found the right home. He was a grey pug with black markings. When Monsieur looked up at Sophia with his flat nose, bulging eyes and deeply wrinkled face, he did not bark or jump wildly. He waited for Nicolina with the serenity of an English butler. Had she encountered Nicolina first, her decision might have been very different. It was remarkable, thought Sophia, how Monsieur Patate and Nicolina so closely resembled one another, unnerving, really. But the face looked so much better on Monsieur Patate. Monsieur's wrinkles gave him character; Nicolina's, age before her time.

'Come on in,' Nicolina had said, motioning for

Sophia to move quickly. 'I'm stressed and tired. Here's the deal,' she said, rattling off the rules and price.

All the while, Monsieur Patate looked sadly at Sophia as if to bark, 'I have to live with her. Stay.'

When one of the rules was taking Monsieur for a short walk the nights madam worked late at the office, Sophia knew she had found a friend. 'Yes, I'll take the apartment,' she announced. Monsieur trotted over to Sophia and rubbed up against her leg. 'Monsieur Patate, leave our new tenant alone.'

'No, I quite like him.'

'I'm so busy with my new promotion that I'm forced to grab fast food to keep myself going. One night I had a poutine from Monsieur Patate that was cold and greasy. I shouted out loud, 'Well, Monsieur Patate, you've just lost a customer!' At the sound of that name, my new pug there came running. I left him in the dining room and walked into the kitchen to throw out the food. I called out one more time, 'Monsieur Patate.' Guess who comes running into the kitchen? The name stuck. The more I look at him, the more I think he looks like a potato.'

'I can be happy here.'

'Good. Gotta run. So many people depend on me.' That wasn't true. Behind her back, the employees of Foley Pharmaceuticals feared and loathed and avoided this 'hatchet woman' brought in by the CEO, Raymond Lecours. 'Here's the key.' As she dashed out the door, Monsieur Patate looked on indifferently. 'You'll have kitchen privileges, of course, but the hours are written on the table beside the stove. Monsieur needs his constitutional. Could you start today, like right now?'

'I have my coat on. Where is his leash?'

'On the doorknob behind you, thanks. He's been to

obedience school and graduated tops in his class. You should have no trouble.'

As the door slammed behind Nicolina, Monsieur Patate and Sophia exhaled. After the twosome returned from their walk, Sophia climbed slowly down the basement stairs, hanging onto the bannister, stopped twice and rubbed her knees. At the bottom of the stairs, she surveyed the two rooms that were now her own. At nineteen, she had married Roberto; before that, she had lived with her family. These two rooms were the linchpins of her first freedom! In the next few days, she arranged her things, took Monsieur Patate shopping with her and began cooking in the kitchen – within her designated hours, of course. Oh, how she would have loved to take long walks! She did not mourn for Roberto or the home she had lost. Sophia did not believe in looking back, but she did miss her good knees. That much longing she allowed herself, that and the half of an Ativan she now took at night to help her sleep through the pain.

Sophia had never cooked small portions because Roberto could put away three helpings without looking up from his plate. With plenty of Alcan foil, she wrapped the extra food and froze it. On the table she also left a plate of lasagna, or spaghetti, or breaded steak or meatballs for Nicolina. Soon, the busy woman stopped all fast food, ate every morsel on her plate, lost a little weight, but not her Italian hips she'd love to lose. Sophia's kitchen privileges were extended and those included more fridge and pantry space.

The next innovation was 'the listening corner'. Nicolina began to share too many of her days with poor Sophia, every detail, every imagined feat. But Roberto had taught his wife an important lesson. Those we depend on most can let us down. In another time, she might have judged Nicolina and found her wanting. But now, she listened, for Nicolina made it pretty clear that conversation was not part of their corner.

No one is all bad, she thought, not Roberto, not Nicolina. Misdirected, insecure, unhappy, lonely, but not all bad. She felt that Nicolina suffered from all four of those traits. She also had a secret that Sophia had come upon unwittingly. Four bottles of Teachers Highland Cream Scotch Whisky stood on the top shelf of the cupboard behind some all-purpose flour near the fridge. An opened bottle was hidden behind the detergent in a cupboard under the sink. *Why is she hiding these things in her own house?* Sophia wondered. Roberto had taught her that people lie to themselves most of all.

The secret did not stay hidden long. The Thursday night meatballs were the culprits that brought it out into the open. Now that Sophia had the run of the kitchen, Nicolina drank her three neat Scotches before dinner. By the third drink, her words were slurred. The old woman shook her head sadly. Monsieur Patate trotted over to Sophia's shoes. 'You cannot believe the stress of my job. I am the head legal counsel for a large pharmaceutical corporation, the first woman they've ever appointed, and I'm still stuck with all the dirty work! All my life I've worked hard and I've made certain others around me held up their end. Before I passed the bar, I worked in the education department of the government preparing courses. There was a colleague who spent his time politicking. Well, I logged the work he didn't do and had him sacked. And you know what? Nobody thanked me for saving them money. They all felt sorry for the guy because he had a family. He should have thought of them before he slacked off and had probably been doing just that for the twenty-two years he'd worked for the government. I believe if you take a paycheque, you should have worked for it. If everybody were honest, imagine how much better off we all would be.'

Sophia nodded because that was expected, but she was wondering how many children that poor man had. Monsieur Patate had fallen asleep on Sophia's shoe.

'I mean, look at this house, Sophia. I worked my butt off for every penny I used for the down payment. Nobody gave me anything. I was married, you know. I was twenty-five then; I was no kid. Joey and I went to New York for our honeymoon, and the rat had a girl-friend's letter waiting for him at the front desk of our hotel. I should have smelled something when a thirty-five year old man hasn't graduated to 'Joe'. Anyway, I went down to get an extra key, and the kid at the desk asked me to take my husband's letter up to him. Broke my heart, but I tossed the bum.'

Sophia was tired. She was almost tempted to ask for a Scotch whiskey herself to dull her hearing because Nicolina was revving up. Even Monsieur Patate felt like a hot brick on her foot.

'Dated the CEO for a while, but he was married and I lost more time out of my life. He didn't love his wife, yada, yada, yada. But I did get this big promotion because he knew I was the right person for the position. At least, that's what I feel. But nothing comes without strings. What they really wanted was a clean-up in the company, and the case I'm working on has turned the employees against me. I got the job done that I was hired to do. I fired a controller, and now the woman is suing for wrongful dismissal. Nothing ends! I'm still under pressure.'

Sophia, like Monsieur was fast asleep, but no matter. Nicolina pushed the hardened meatballs aside and reached for another scotch. All along, the Chianti had been on the table as window dressing.

'The woman has cancer. Sympathy is with *her* now! Even my boss, the CEO, is avoiding me as though he's not behind the whole thing. That's loyalty for you! I can't lose the case; my house is at stake. I borrowed money to buy a stock that did not work out, so I have my own problems. That's why I need this salary. Where could I go from here? If only the bitch…' Nicolina held her liquor pretty well; knew she had gone far enough and held her tongue.

Steadying herself, and holding onto the table, she shook the old woman. 'Sophia, get some sleep. It's late.' She bent down uncertainly and grabbed for Monsieur, but caught only his small, curly tail. He yelped when she tried to pull him up. 'Oh no, I didn't mean to hurt you, Monsieur.' She carried him to bed with her, pulled the covers over both of them and fell into a deep snore. Caught up in Nicolina's sweater, it took Monsieur a good hour to crawl out from under her arm and he woke Nicolina in the process. Nicolina sat bolt upright in bed, just before three in the morning, grungy and stale. Something she'd forgotten was gnawing at her brain. The last double Scotch had blurred the thing. What the hell was it? Vaguely, she remembered blubbering her story to Sophia, but that wasn't the problem. What the hell had she forgotten? Everything felt tight and twisted because she hadn't gotten out of her clothes. The damn controller would be the death of her! Rolling over to the side of the bed, using it for leverage, she got to her feet. Scotch rarely left a headache behind, but at this moment, a hammer banged away inside her skull. Her tongue was dry. Purposely, she didn't turn on a light in the bathroom. Once she had wiped her face with warm water, Nicolina gave her hair a quick brush and did the best she could with her clothes. 'Concentrate. Think,' she command-ed herself. 'I know there's something I've forgotten.'

The case, in its fourth day, had turned in the con-troller's favour; *that* she remembered. The *why*, was lost. With all its connections, the company would see to it that the case was won. Something else had caused Nicolina to reveal too much to Sophia tonight. Groping her way across the landing to the staircase, she held onto the banister as she came down the stairs. In the kitchen, she switched on the lights and shielded her eyes from the sting of a sudden glare. Another Scotch helped her clear her head, and she remembered what it was she had stupidly left back at the office. Her hands trembled as she put the empty glass on the table.

It was bad enough she'd already made one blunder in the case. Early on, she had accused the controller of for-gery. That breach appeared to be sufficient for termina-tion, even if the other charges proved to be unfounded. But a forensic expert who had been in the RCMP had proven that claim groundless. She stealthily shifted away from that claim and zeroed in on the other allega-tions. But tonight, a scratchy fear rose high in her throat and was not soothed by the blended Scotch. What she had forgotten at the office, if revealed, would bring devastation to the company and her walking papers.

Inside the top drawer of her desk, Nicolina had left a file, personally addressed to her, sent by courier at three yesterday afternoon. It contained one anonymous typed line. 'Will be in touch.' When Nicolina read the contents of the file, anxiety stung her ribs.

This file can't be sent to the judge. I have to get it out of the office. The embezzlement charges have to stick or I'll lose everything! Why can't that bitch just die? She's dying any-

way. What difference does it make if it's sooner than later? Why am I the scapegoat? I can't do everything myself! The gravity of what had been done to the controller never occurred to Nicolina. How could she think of anyone else when her career was in peril? She had herself to save.

Grabbing her keys from the wall peg, Nicolina slammed the door behind her. Cursing and crying, she got into her car, shot out of the driveway and tore down Sherbrooke Street to her office. Another terror seized her. Had this file originally been sent to someone else? She had to find the blackmailer. This job was her first real payday. She'd track this bastard down. She had the tools. She could be there in minutes.

Nicolina was drunk and distracted and had just made two mistakes. She had driven past her destination and she was driving without lights. Unlike most pharmaceutical companies whose operations were entirely on the West Island, Foley had its headquarters downtown at Westmount Square. Wednesday night, a security guard from the building told her the bulb in her right headlight had burned out and the left one was flickering. She was more than angry because the car was new. When she could find the time, she'd see to the problem. She hadn't planned on any night driving. When she sped past the Ritz-Carlton, she discovered her first mistake. 'Oh Jesus,' she swore, executing a full u-turn on Sherbrooke. Of course, this was Montreal, so there were no police on the street at that hour, and Nicolina sped back west along the street.

CHAPTER 5

CHRIS HAD DECIDED they should head first to Crescent Street and Winnie's before driving up for a view from the mountain. The cab let the gang out on Sherbrooke Street where Caitlin pointed out the Montreal Museum of Fine Arts and the Alcan building, explaining that Frank could arrange a private tour of the artwork Alcan was so proud to have in its possession. The 'people jam' began as soon as they turned down Crescent.

'Wow, this is great!' Mike said, getting into the swing. 'Look at the people! I'd heard that Canada was a dull place. Somebody forgot to tell these people.'

'Quit while you're ahead,' Caitlin said.

When they'd reached de Maisonneuve, Caitlin pointed to her right.

'That's where I earn the big bucks, Concordia University.'

'Wasn't there a professor from there who lost it and shot colleagues or something?' Hunter added, hoping to prove he knew something of the province. 'Wasn't there another crazed guy who shot a bunch of women, just outright slaughtered them? It was all over the news. I was only thirteen then, but I remember.'

'This place is sounding more like home,' Mike threw into the mix.

'Violence is everywhere, and that's what grabs the headlines. Yes, the professor was from Concordia, but the fourteen women were cut down at the University of Montreal,' Caitlin added. 'Neither incident is the norm. That's one of the reasons they received so much media attention.'

'Let's get on a happier plane. We'll come back to Crescent Street for the Grand Prix. The whole street is filled with great cars and loud bands and people, especially tourists. Here's Winnie's. You guys stay here. I'll see if I can grab a table.' Chris slipped a waiter some money and ran back to get the rest of the guys so their celebration could begin in earnest. The boozing buddies did the pub proud. Chris was the only prudent one of the lot. He wanted a clear head for his TT early tomorrow morning; that, and he wanted to look out for his sister.

Before they'd gone into Winnie's, Hunter had noticed a small lane on Crescent. 'Who the heck has a lane named after him?' he asked once they were seated.

'That was Nick Auf de Maur, a storied regular, who spent many a beery afternoon in this joint. He was a commentator and author who drank with some of the greats of our city, greats like Mordecai Richler. Montrealers didn't want his memory slipping through the cracks and gave him this sign, kind of like a Hollywood star.'

'All right, here's to Nick!' Mike chimed in, and the others joined in the toast.

Chris kept his eye on Caitlin and wondered about Hyannis. He could normally count on her to be sane. But maybe it was a good thing that she was finally letting go, just not with Mike. Around one-thirty, he herded the group out the door. 'Let's walk to de Maisonneuve; it'll be easier to get a cab.'

'After you, fearless leader,' Mike said as seriously as the wine permitted him. He grabbed Caitlin's hand. 'You're safe with me young lady.'

Chris walked faster so they'd have to keep up the pace.

In the cab, Mike sat beside Caitlin and Hunter, and Chris was forced to sit up front. 'It's been three years since I've been to the mountain. Monsieur,' he asked, turning his attention to the cabbie, '*Est-ce-que les tam-tams ont déja commencé?*'

'*Non, monsieur. Ils commencent le premier dimanche de l'été.*'

'That's a bummer! We won't be able to see the drummers that beat around the Georges Étienne monument. Caitlin, did you know that the tam-tams began as lessons back in the seventies at the Jazz Bar?'

'You're too sober, little brother,' Caitlin called out from the back seat. Mike felt warm beside her. She nuzzled closer to him. *I'm entitled. All my life, I've been the sensible one, just like Dad. Well, I'm lonely. What's so wrong with a little fun?* Her breathing was shallow.

The cabbie let the group out at the foot of Mount Royal, and they started walking up the mountain immediately. Chris felt he could keep the troops walking if he threw in a history lesson. 'Mount Royal Park occupies part of the mountain in the midst of Montreal. When we reach the top, we'll be standing at the highest point in the city.'

'Doesn't take a rocket scientist to get that point, Chrissy boy!' Mike laughed.

'Yeah, yeah. This is something else Dad told us, Caitlin. The park was landscaped by the same man who did New York's Central Park. Back in the fifties, to discourage immoral behaviour, the city had many trees cut down to prevent people like you and Caitlin from sneaking off into the underbrush and doing the nasty. That's why none of these trees are more than fifty years old.'

'Chris, you're getting ahead of yourself. This isn't the Cape.' Caitlin couldn't believe what he'd just said.

Mike held Caitlin's hand tighter. Caitlin was definitely in a league of her own. It might have been the first time Mike had ever met strength and passion together in one woman. This lure sapped control from him. For a few seconds, there was quiet, and the only sounds were the echoes of their feet walking on the gravel path.

'I want to see what that cross looks like close up,' Hunter announced as they walked in the direction of the lighted cross. 'It's amazing that we feel so safe. We'd all think twice about walking in Central Park.' Just then, a mounted police officer seemed to appear out of nowhere, waved at the gang and trotted on ahead.

'Except for the tragedies you remembered, Montreal is a safe place,' Chris was quick to point out. 'Well, there it is.'

'I know you want to fill us in on the history, so go ahead Chris,' Mike urged.

'Good, 'cause I have some info for you. Although it was erected in 1924, it memorializes a promise made a couple hundred years earlier. The founder of Montreal, Maisonneuve…'

'Isn't that the street we were on near the club?' Hunter asked.

'You're coming around, Hunter. If I may continue, there was a threat of a flood, and Maisonneuve promised to carry a wooden cross to the top of the mountain if the colony was spared. He kept his word. The cross is almost a hundred feet tall. Now that it's lit, it's visible for miles around.'

'On another night, I'd love to climb up the cross. The view of the city must be pretty spectacular,' Mike said excitedly.

'I'm sure it is, but you'd be arrested and fined before you reached the top. If you tried it tonight, the cop we just passed would gallop back faster than you could climb.'

'A few years ago, I wouldn't have bothered with talk; I'd have been already climbing.'

Chris was yawning. 'Yeah, well none of us are kids anymore. I think we should head back. It's after two and it's been a long day, and this is just the beginning. All in favour?'

'Take charge, young sir, and we will follow,' Mike saluted. He was standing very close to Caitlin, but his boldness had left him.

Lucky with the first cab they saw, the gang was soon driving up Pine Avenue, past the Royal Victoria Hospital on their right. They were already home when it occurred to Chris that Caitlin should not drive her car back to her place. 'Hold the cab,' he called to Caitlin. 'Take the ride home; I'll pick you up in the morning and you can get your car then.'

Mike leapt at the opportunity for time alone with Caitlin. 'I don't want Caitlin to go home alone. Enjoy your car, Chris. I'll take your sister home and be back before you know it. I'll be on my best behaviour.'

'Nothing on you, Mike, but I'd like to take my sister back. We haven't had any time to catch up.'

Feast or famine, Caitlin thought.

Once they were back in the cab, Chris said, 'I'm not that worried about Mike. I really wanted some of our own time. It's been almost three years, Sis. Are you okay with things now? You know what I mean.'

'Things will never be the same, Chris, but I'm solid now. I'm stronger than I thought I was. I guess that's something you find out when you're suddenly on your own. My book is coming out, I have a full course load, I have a great brother and parents and a best friend in Carmen. I'd like to meet someone though.'

Chris stayed at Caitlin's for a little while, and had a good talk. 'Sis, take care of yourself with Mike. That's the last I'll say about that issue. I guess I'd better call a cab.'

'Why don't you walk home? It's only twenty minutes from here. It's a beautiful, warm night. Reclaim your city, gather your thoughts.'

'That's a great idea, walk off Mom's dinner at the same time. All right then. Come over here and give me a hug,' Chris said, his arms spread wide. 'It's great to be home.'

Caitlin stood out front, waved, watched Chris walk up the street and slowly closed the front door. *Chris is all grown up*, she realized.

CHAPTER 6

CHRIS TOOK HIS time walking up Wood Avenue, pulled off his navy Polo vest, rolled it and carried it in his hand. The day had been perfect, he thought, but this time alone was the best part of it. All around him, the air was misty with summer heat and blanketed with the night. He could not remember such warmth at the end of April. Smiling to himself, he hummed his favourite song, Bob Seger's *Like a Rock*. That's how he felt, hard and strong, with doors waiting for him to walk through. Being away for two years at Harvard had given him his independence; being home had brought him to the heart of things.

When he reached Sherbrooke Street, the light was red. Caitlin would have darted across the street, but Chris waited until the light was green. *Sometimes late at night, oh, when I'm bathed in the firelight, the moon comes calling in a ghostly white, and I recall, I recall!* He was singing those words as he crossed the street and he never heard the barrelling approach of the grey Mazda 3. At the last instant, he turned to see the shadow of the car before it struck him. In seconds, there was nothing more to build on in Chris Donovan's life. The swiftness of the blow had spared him the final, agonizing moments when the knowing is everything. It would take Chris almost two hours to die as he lay unconscious behind a parked car.

Nicolina felt a thump on the right hand side of her car. The Mazda veered into the left lane, but she was able to pull it back quickly. The car shook violently for the next hundred feet. The worry about the file evaporated; keeping herself safe was paramount. Grabbing the wheel with both hands, she slammed on the brakes and came to a full stop at Elm Avenue. *Did somebody throw something at the car? What the hell happened?* Lowering her window, she looked back as far as she could, but saw nothing. *Did I hit something?* It was then that she noticed the right windshield was smashed as though someone strong had punched it. 'Have I hit a dog?' she began to sob. 'What do I do?' With a quick stab at the interior light, she caught a glimpse of herself and had her answer. Nicolina pulled out and headed back home. Slowly, cautiously, she travelled past Decarie Boulevard, past Clark's Funeral Home, past the park on her right and turned up Harvard.

Nicolina eased the car into her single garage and sat shaking for a few minutes. Then she listened for suspicious sounds. Easing the door open as quietly as she could, hunching over, peering first around the front end, she crept to examine the damage. The gaping size of the crater on the right bumper of the car, the bits of skin and the red smearing told Nicolina that she had not struck a dog. Vomit rose in her throat with a mean force and sprayed the floor and wall. Between the hurling and the moans, she screamed, 'Why does this crap happen to me? Why? Why?' A powerful terror swept over her, throwing Nicolina from the garage. She ran and stumbled across the lawn into the safety of the house.

Monsieur Patate heard the commotion and ran to the front door to greet Nicolina. She slammed it behind her and scrambled upstairs. Monsieur was at her heels. 'What the hell? Get out of my way.' Bleary-eyed, Nicolina grabbed the pug by the legs and flung him against the wall. Then she fell back against the bed and passed out. Some time later, Nicolina got herself to the bathroom. She tore off her clothes, dropped them in a heap and stepped into the shower. A sting of ice-cold water hit her body. 'God!' she screamed, reaching for the other nozzle. Washing herself with a fury, she immediately dropped the soap and, with her eyes closed, bent down trying to feel it on the slippery tub. 'Please help me, God; I don't know what to do.' Rinsing her hair and leaving soap in it, she towelled off. 'What am I going to do? I can't get rid of the car. Think! Every garage will be on the lookout for it. I know they can trace the make of the car by the paint – I'm sure I've left some behind.' The noise of the hair dryer sent Monsieur scrambling under the bed and woke Sophia. He began to chew on the toe of Sophia's left shoe. Nicolina dressed as quickly as she could, making certain she applied little make-up and no perfume. She brushed her teeth and gargled four times. She raced down the stairs and began to pace, thumping the side of her head with the heel of her hand.

Sophia stepped into her slippers, climbed the basement stairs and padded into the kitchen. 'Is there something wrong?'

'Yes, there's something wrong!' Nicolina shouted, straining for some control. 'I went out for a drive because I couldn't sleep and a dog or something ran in front of my car.'

'Have you called the police? They will help you. Are you all right?'

'I'm fine, fine!'

Sophia wanted to say, 'You should not have been driving,' but she did not dare. The frenzy in Nicolina's eyes was quite unnerving. 'You would not want Monsieur Patate lying all alone by the side of the road, would you?'

'No.'

'Maybe the dog is just injured. If you report the accident, the dog might live.'

'You're right! This was an accident after all.' Help came in the form of another idea. There was a reason that she had always landed on her feet. Nicolina could take care of Nicolina. If there was mention of a breathalyzer, she would simply say her nerves were so bad she had taken a drink to calm herself. Problem solved!

As Nicolina dialed 911, she paced, planning her script. 'Yes, hello. I must talk to the police. Thank you.' A few seconds passed; Nicolina bit her lower lip. 'Yes, I feel I should report something. As I was driving home tonight along Sherbrooke Street, I heard something terrible crash against my windshield. I thought someone had thrown something at me. When I got home, I realized I had better investigate the damage. That's when I saw the extent of it and the blood. I'm afraid I might have struck an animal. I don't want to leave that poor thing on the road if it can be helped.' Nicolina was a natural liar. In fact, there were times she quite convinced herself of some untruth.

The next question derailed her flow. 'Where?' There was always something poor Nicolina forgot. She began to cough, trying to play for time. Where in God's name had she struck something? Then she remembered, as clearly as any drunk could when pushed to the limit. She had driven past Atwater Avenue, so it was somewhere after that. 'Sir, I was so nervous I wasn't paying attention to streets, but I'm certain the accident occurred west of Atwater. What should I do now? You're sending an officer out to examine the car? That's fine; I'll be waiting. I realize now that I should have stayed at the scene, but I couldn't, not when I felt that I was being attacked. Thank you so much for your help.' Nicolina lied so well that she might have found life easier in politics. But as she waited for the doorbell to ring, her nerves began to crawl.

Her fingers drummed the kitchen table, inching closer to the bottle of Scotch. Sophia frowned. Monsieur Patate cowered behind Sophia. He forgot all his lessons, forgot the three red ribbons stuck to the fridge door. He just let go on the shiny tile that Sophia had washed earlier that day. He backed away from the yellow puddle on his tiptoes, and crouched under the table.

'Oh, Monsieur,' shrieked Nicolina, jumping to her feet. 'What have you done? I haven't got time for this now. Get over here this minute; I should put your nose in this mess! I spent four hundred dollars on his school, Sophia.'

'He has his reasons,' Sophia whispered.

Nicolina began to cry then, and her shoulders shook. 'I'm sorry, Monsieur. Please come over here. I am so tired. And I can't cry because the police will be here soon.'

Monsieur walked back to his mistress who picked him up and rocked him back and forth in her arms.

Sophia fetched some paper towels.

The phone rang and everybody in the room jumped. Monsieur leapt to the floor.

'Yes, this is she,' Nicolina answered, her face pinching with every word she heard.

'Mrs. or Ms. Pastore?'

'Ms.'

'An officer should be at your house any minute.'

'Is the poor animal dead?' she began to cry once more.

'Ms. Pastore, we need both you and the car at Station 12. A patrolman will arrive shortly, and you will follow the officer to the station. We will inform you of the details at that time. Can you still operate the vehicle?'

'Yes, the damage is to the windshield and right front bumper, but the car is drivable.'

'Are you fully capable of driving the vehicle, Ms. Pastore?'

'Of course, sir, without a doubt.'

The line went dead, and some of Nicolina's hope died with it. She grabbed her purse and car keys and stood at the front door. The Mitchum deodorant she used generously every day was not doing its job. Her armpits felt sticky, and she could feel beads of perspiration beading around the bottom of her bra. Terrible consequences, as sharp as arrows, took aim at her brain. Were there witnesses? Is that why the tone of the officer drained of emotion? Had she killed someone? She drew deep breaths; she had to appear completely surprised when the officer rang the bell. Swallow the guilt, that's what she had to do.

Sophia was back sitting at the table with Monsieur in her lap. Her head had dropped into her hand, and she was looking over at Nicolina with great sadness and the cognizance of a wise woman.

She's a witness... A tight caution laced her request. 'Sophia, would you please take Monsieur Patate downstairs with you. I want to meet the officer in peace.'

'As you wish, Nicolina.'

With that, the doorbell rang.

CHAPTER 7

AT FOUR-THIRTY, on Friday morning, Thomas Mc-
Cormick, a retired, highly regarded veteran of World
War II had another sleepless night. Sometimes, a walk
eased his restless thoughts. He rose slowly, grabbed the
bed post with one hand and stepped a little awkwardly
into his grey slacks. He tucked his white shirt neatly
into his pants, fastened his belt and reached for his navy
blue blazer on a wooden hanger. He stepped into his
loafers without his socks because bending was too difficult this early. He found his brass handled cane, stepped
outside his home on Mount Pleasant Avenue and began
walking east on Sherbrooke Street in the direction of
Elm. Only the tap of his cane disturbed the quiet of the
street.

Thomas almost lost his balance when he stepped on
Chris' Polo vest. He scooped it up with his cane and
walked closer to the street light. He saw that the
sweater was new. *What careless young people we have today!
Somebody worked hard for this, and someone else discarded it
so carelessly.* Then Thomas discovered an opened hand
that lay quietly on the sidewalk, and he recognized its
inherent supplication. He bent down and found Chris
wedged under the parked car. As the only regimental
sergeant major in his battalion, Thomas had overseen
the care of many wounded men.

He did not leave Chris to the oblivion of darkness.
He reached under the car and lay his fingers on Chris'
neck, feeling for a pulse, and found none. When he
withdrew his hand, it was red with blood, even the
palm. Taking a white handkerchief from his breast
pocket, he wiped his fingers and refolded it. The young
man was dead. The old man took off his jacket and laid

it across the visible part of Chris, gently and tenderly.
Then he stood in the street, for he would not leave his
charge. He flagged down a car, and when it stopped, the
process of recovery, and the grief that would accompany it, began.

Once the police arrived on the scene, Thomas
relayed his information succinctly. He turned away, still
carrying his jacket, and began to walk home.

The area was cordoned off, and Sherbrooke was
closed between Wood and Elm. Behind the laser, three
Montreal police cars, on either side of the beam, flashed
their red and blue lights. Once it was clearly established
by the patrolmen that the accident victim was dead,
investigators were called. They reached the scene in
minutes with their tech team. The coroner was notified
as well. The investigators worked on the scene for the
next four hours.

Shards of glass were tweezed from Chris' back and
head, paint from his clothing was scraped into small
plastic bags, the distance between the shoes and the
body was carefully measured and the damage to the
parked car was photographed. The position of the body
was lasered and its distance from the corner of Wood
and Sherbrooke measured. The absence of tire tracks
suggested a blind hit. The quiet crowd was canvassed
for witnesses. None turned up. The approximate time
of death was set at two to three hours ago. The tox
screen and the autopsy would more clearly establish the
time of death and its root causes. One of the investigators was momentarily confused about the identity of the
victim. Chris had not discarded his Harvard student
card or his address in Boston. There were more
American bills than Canadian in his wallet. The investigator knew this victim would not reflect well on the
beginning of the tourist season.

He needn't have been concerned. Under the last piece of ID, he found an address on The Boulevard. After fourteen years on the job, Claude Remay never got used to making the call home. He had three children of his own. Whenever the fatality involved the young, he thought of a phone ringing in his own home in the early morning hours. An hour after the initial investigation, the body was bagged, carried to the corner's van and driven to the morgue. The investigation at the scene continued. Choosing to be away from the noise of working voices, Remay walked over to his car, leaned against it and dialed.

The bedroom phone lay on Frank's night table because there were times, though very rare, when a client, worried about losing millions on a failed business deal, drank himself into hysteria and called the home number that Frank always gave his clients in case of emergency. It was five-forty-three when the phone rang. Frank had the receiver in his hand on the second ring.

'Are you Mr. Donovan?' the investigator asked.

'I am,' Frank answered.

'Is Christopher Donovan related to you, sir?'

'He's my son,' Frank's voice was thin and seemed to feel the pain before it reached his heart.

'Mr. Christopher Donovan was involved in a fatal automobile accident early this morning.'

'How badly is my son injured?' Frank asked, scrambling to believe that an error had been made. After all, Chris had not been driving. 'My son was not driving last night or early this morning. Are you certain you've contacted the right person?'

'Sir, the victim, Christopher Donovan, was on foot. He was struck at the corner of Sherbrooke and Wood.

The birth date listed here in his wallet is December 14, 1979.'

Maggie had awoken and she clung to Frank's shoulder.

'What hospital has he been taken to?'

'He did not survive, sir.'

'Repeat that please.'

'He did not survive, Mr. Donovan. His body has been transported to the Montreal City Morgue, located at 1710 Parthenais, on the corner of Ontario Street. We will need you or a member of your family for identification. The building is open twenty-four hours a day. In my experience, sir, the sooner someone can make the ID, the better for the family. In such a situation, there will be an autopsy. Here is a number where you can reach me.'

The line went dead – that was not unusual for Remay to lose contact when he placed such a call. The investigator made no effort to redial the number.

Frank did not throw the phone across the room; he watched his hand replace the receiver. For a few minutes, Frank did not know if Maggie was still in the room. His ears were mute to her shrieking sobs. A photo of the artificial lake up at Rawdon and their summer home behind it drew his full attention. His heart froze before the serious shakes began. He fell backwards then on top of Maggie, and together, they lay coiled in the tightening muscle of grief.

'No, no,' Maggie wailed. 'Not Chris, not my baby!'

Frank did not even try to pretend a kindness that would only inflict more pain. He did gather her into his arms in a stranglehold on the bed, pinned Maggie close, but she kicked and punched and smashed her head against his cheek in her first fury. It was almost half an hour before Maggie began to tire and whimper.

Releasing one hand, he brushed the dampened hair from her forehead. He tested her hands before he let go of her completely and rolled beside her. His legs still shook, and his eyes were wide and tearless. Grief is a dangerous affair.

'I always dreaded something like this might happen. I was one year younger than Chris when…'

Maggie was moaning, lost to Frank in of an enveloping grief. Her head was turned away from him, and she was dribbling on the white pillow case as she wept.

Planning and preparation were the snail work of the law, Frank told young lawyers articling at the firm. Without them, solid wins were lost. Looking down at Maggie, he saw that he would have to get what support he needed from a blueprint he understood. Prioritize, he tried to remind himself, but he found he couldn't move. Frank's brain dove back into the past. Unmindful of the peril, early in his life Frank had chosen a dangerous road to travel. He could not move because that road had now dead-ended. 'Why Chris?' he began to scream in a silent rage that bellowed in his brain. 'Why not me? Why not me? Take me; give me back my son!' He began to choke and cough violently. Then he sat up on the side of the bed. Work helped Frank, and he saw the job ahead of him.

His voice was flat, when he bent over the bed and whispered, 'I'll go to Caitlin's. She can't hear about Chris on the radio. Do you hear me, Maggie? Will you be all right?'

'Leave Chris alone, Frank. Why couldn't people leave him alone?' Maggie did not say another word for two days.

Frank dressed quickly, closed the bedroom door and walked to the other wing. Mike and Hunter were sound asleep and he left them that way. Back on the second floor, he looked inside Chris' room, searching for his son. The bed was still made up. On one of his dressers, Frank spotted the new set of car keys. Two pieces of opened luggage lay on the far side of the room. Neither of them had been fully unpacked. He stepped over both and opened the closet where he remembered Chris kept his sports equipment. Calmly, he walked down the stairs and out to the garage, took off his jacket and laid it across the hood of his car.

Raising the bat high above his head, he brought it down with blunt force, crashing against the TT, twenty-four or twenty-five times. Shards of glass fell everywhere. A few pieces flew back at Frank and cut him on the cheek and nose. When his damage was done, he shook his shirt and slacks, dropped the bat inside the car and retraced his steps to his own vehicle. With his jacket thrown across the seat, he backed out of the garage and drove to Caitlin's. As he made the turn down Wood Avenue, he noticed the chalk markings and empty cups on the road and sidewalk to his right. Frank could not bear to look or stop. He sped down Wood and parked on the wrong side of the road. He rang only twice. Caitlin was a light sleeper, always had been.

It was a rarity for Caitlin to sleep past seven. When she glanced at her watch on the night table, she was amazed to find it was after eight. 'The wine,' she laughed, 'I can't take all the credit.' She crept to her window and peeked out. What was her father doing here at this hour? 'Don't tell me Dad is planning his own early tour of the city!' Grabbing her white terry cloth robe, running fingers through her hair, Caitlin raced downstairs and opened the door. 'Dad, what's up? Come on in; I'll make coffee.' Her father's face was chalky and strained, and Caitlin grew afraid. 'Dad, what is it? You're bleeding! What's happened? Is it Mom? Come in, I'll fetch a wet facecloth.'

Frank stood rooted to the front hall. 'It's Chris.'

'What about Chris?' she asked, but there was some-where she already knew because tears were streaming down her cheeks before her father spoke.

'Your brother was struck down and killed last night on Sherbrooke and Wood. That's all I know.'

Caitlin began to shake her father. 'What are you talking about, Dad? He was here last night, just a few hours ago. How can he be dead?'

'Caitlin.'

'We said goodnight, and I suggested that he walk home because it was so warm out, so beautiful...'

'Caitlin.'

'I suggested he walk home. Did you hear what I just said?'

'Caitlin.'

'Poor Chris, poor Chris. He didn't even get much of a walk or exercise, not if he didn't make it past Sherbrooke Street,' her laugh was laced with regret and full of anger.

'Caitlin.'

'He was going to call a cab, but I suggested...'

'Caitlin, this isn't your fault.'

'Isn't it, Dad? Isn't it?'

'Please, be with your mother. I have to go down and identify Chris.'

'I'm going with you, Dad. It's only right that I see what I helped cause.' Caitlin was dry-eyed now, her eyes, stony.

'Your mother needs you, Caitlin. I wasn't much help. I need to reclaim my son alone. Please allow me that. Take care of your mother; she's all by herself.'

Caitlin didn't hug her father, she couldn't. 'I'll go

home, Dad.' She turned and left her father standing in the foyer.

Frank locked the door behind himself as he left. Caitlin and he might as well have been strangers. He drove to the city morgue, an uninviting, steel and glass structure. Waiting for a visitor's pass, he was told the bodies were housed in the basement. After swiping his pass across a card slot, Frank gained access through two separate electronic security gates. Frank was not bothered by the vile, stale nose-curling stench of death. The assault on him had already taken place. A coroner's assistant was waiting for him outside a blue door and he handed Frank a Ziploc bag and a list of the belongings inside. Frank immediately recognized the wallet he had given Chris before he left for Harvard. He followed the assistant across a red floor to what appeared to be a large beer fridge. Checking the nameplates, the fellow pulled out a drawer, tired and indifferent to the scene playing around him.

Frank pushed the man aside with his arm. He stood for a few seconds, measuring the length of the shrouded body, before he drew back a green sheet. He laid his hand across Chris' forehead and shivered involuntarily because his son was so cold. He hoped the heat from his hand would transfer to Chris. *He's just a boy*, Frank thought. Bringing the sheet back up over Chris' face, Frank turned to the assistant and said. 'This is Christopher Donovan, my son. Get me out of here.'

CHAPTER 8

AT STATION 12, Nicolina had stepped into her professional mode. Worries about a court case involving the
company had kept her from sleep. To clear her
thoughts, she'd taken a drive, something she had done
on other occasions, nothing out of the ordinary. Of
course, work had not affected her concentration on the
road. Alcohol? Good God, certainly not at that hour!
Of course, she did sip one Scotch when she returned
home. Speed was not on the table either; she had no
hurried destination. Was a poor dog involved?

Remay stopped questioning and tapped his thumb
on his notebook. 'The victim was a twenty-six year old
male who succumbed to his injuries.' Remay had taken
a strong dislike to the woman halfway through the
questioning. Her obvious selfishness and effrontery
were things he'd dealt with before. On principle, he
never trusted anyone who wasn't completely shaken up
after a serious accident. Those who rehearsed statements were generally falsifying information. You had to
be inside such people to weaken them, and they would-
n't let you in. Ms. Pastore did not even blink when told
of the fatality. He noticed that her eyes narrowed.

'Oh my, how dreadful,' Nicolina said, looking to
Remay for her cue.

'Yes,' he agreed. 'I am surprised you did not see him,
even at the last minute. I understand he was a tall fellow, hard to miss. Your air bag did not deploy either?'

'No, it did not. I'm upset myself about seeing nothing. The only possible answer I can think of is that perhaps the young man stepped out between parked cars to
my right. Then, of course I wouldn't have seen him. Is
that possible?'

'We'll have a more definite report tomorrow. I hope you won't mind coming in again if I have more questions.'

'When you need me, sir, I'll be here. I want to understand this terrible tragedy too.' Nicolina was feeling more confident by the minute. 'I'll take a breathalyzer as well; I hope that one drink won't affect the testing. I know something of the protocol. I'm one of those dreaded lawyers people hate till they need one.'

'All the more reason you should have contacted us immediately,' he said. 'You do understand then that you will be charged with leaving the scene of an accident and we'll need your vehicle.' He could hear her brain ticking. Remay could play her game. 'That breathalyzer would have been appreciated if you had stayed at the scene.'

'I wish I'd been braver, sir. That regret will be with me a long time.' Her mouth dried at the mention of the charge.

Sophia had lifted Monsieur Patate up beside her on the bed, but neither could sleep. Monsieur would definitely need a refresher course. He had wet the old woman's sheets within minutes of her unexpected invitation. The bed was stripped, the sheets soaked in the tub, dry sheets put on the bed, but Monsieur was not finished. As he lay on the floor watching Sophia remake the bed, he sprayed the carpet. 'Where is all this water coming from, Monsieur? You're afraid a bad thing has happened tonight, I know. And we're both afraid of what will happen when Nicolina returns to the house. We mustn't tell her about your accidents. Don't worry, Monsieur, they're our secrets. Maybe she'll forget the first one.'

When Sophia heard the front door opening, she crawled into bed and pulled Monsieur up with her.

They tried to be very quiet. With the covers over their heads, no one could hear Monsieur's whimpering on the main landing.

Nicolina was piqued at being detained, even briefly, and angry that her car was still with the police. She slammed the door when she got back home. Her expertise lay in corporate law, so she was suddenly grateful for TV lawyers on the CSI shows who had taught her the hidden menace of evidence. Regroup, that's what she needed to do. Freshen up, cab it to the office, grab the file, call her insurance at nine, take a day off and use the time to wait on the police and track the sender. Like Frank Donovan, Nicolina felt safest when consumed with work. The difference between the two was competence. Frank had it in spades, and Nicolina was sorely lacking in it. What she did have was the street smarts of a stray.

She opened the door to the basement apartment and listened, but the racket in her brain blocked out the small noise of Monsieur. Keeping Sophia's mouth shut where the police were concerned was something else she had on her docket. What she really needed was a good Scotch, so she shut the door and headed for the kitchen. Why couldn't things ever run smoothly for her? Something solid in the old woman frightened Nicolina because, quite simply, she did not have the goods on Sophia, or the weight of Foley Pharmaceuticals behind her on this problem. The opened bottle of Scotch was right on the table where she had left it. Her hand shook as she poured herself a good shot. *This is what that company and all its mess have done to me!* Grabbing the glass with both hands, seeing both of them shake, Nicolina made up her mind on her plan of attack. Walking purposefully to the sink, she emptied the Scotch. *I refuse to go down. This isn't on me! It's on them, all of them!*

Points accumulated on her 'to do' list as she waited for a cab. The file needed immediate attention. Really, she smiled thinly, how much trouble could the old woman cause her? Nicolina intended to make very certain she never found out.

CHAPTER 9

AFTER HE LEFT the morgue, Frank did not drive straight home. He parked on Sherbrooke Street near the site of the accident. His tears mingled with self-hatred and compromised his grief. His emotions were blocked by his past that had caught up with him. Turning off the ignition, he opened his door and stood leaning against the car, stealing glances at the street near the empty cups. A few feet back, he saw rust-coloured stains, and he ran over to them. It hadn't rained last night, so the evidence of dried blood was clear. Though cars were speeding past, he knelt and laid both palms protectively on the street.

A patrol car soon stopped beside him. A policeman rolled down his window and asked, 'Sir, is there something wrong?'

Frank did not bother looking up.

Cars began to detour around the flashing lights. One of the patrol officers left his vehicle and bent down over Frank. 'Sir, you cannot stay on the street like this. It's not safe. You could cause an accident.'

'I already have,' Frank mumbled sadly. 'That's my son's blood – he died on this street last night. He wasn't even driving.'

The officer at the wheel had called in and received the information about last night's fatality. He joined his partner on the street and whispered the information to him. Then he turned to Frank. '*Monsieur, je comprends que c'est très difficile pour vous à ce moment. Mais c'est mieux de retourner chez-vous. C'est trôp pénible ici.*'

They hoisted Frank up by his underarms, walked him back to his car and followed him home. When they saw his obvious wealth, one of them commented, *'On est tous vulnerable, même les gens riches!'*

Any other time, Frank would have been gracious in his gratitude, but he didn't turn around as he climbed his front stairs.

In the guest rooms over the garage, Mike and Hunter had been awakened earlier by the smashing of the car. They had showered, dressed and waited for someone to come to them. Mike hadn't heard Caitlin arrive, but he did hear a car door shut and he watched Frank enter the house as a police car, parked behind Frank's, backed out of the driveway.

'Something's up, Hunter. The cops were just here. What the hell was all that smashing in the garage? Maybe Chris and his father had some kind of argument.'

'Mike, we're not intruding on them. Chris' father is a lot like mine, demanding, but I'm not intimidated by my father the way Chris is of his. He feels he has to live up to his father's expectations although he likes to pretend otherwise. When my father unloads on me, I give it right back.'

'So you say,' Mike grinned, obviously not entirely believing Hunter's bravado.

'I'm surprised Chris hasn't come over to tell us anything. Mr. Donovan is home, so I guess we should wait for him,' Hunter advised as he began a nervous pace.

At the other end of the house, Caitlin sat on the bed beside her mother. Maggie hadn't even looked up to see who was coming into the room. The sheets were pulled up high, and Maggie lay on her side, staring at a wall. The transition from life to death was too swift for words to catch it. Language failed when it was most needed; Caitlin's quiet presence was an ointment, not a cure. When she dared, Caitlin reached under the blankets and held her mother's hand that was limp, lifeless as death. But Caitlin held on and knelt beside her mother, dropping her head onto the mattress. For a long time, she didn't move. Chris was so alive in her memory of him last night. *'Sis, take care of yourself with Mike. That's the last I'll say about that issue. I guess I'd better call a cab'. Why didn't I let him? 'Reclaim your city,' that's what I said.* A sharp, knifing pain stabbed her forehead. Caitlin drove her head into the mattress, but she didn't let go of her mother's hand. *Why can't I cry for my brother?* The only tears she had shed fell when her father told her about Chris. Since then, her sadness, flagged with guilt, was too deep for tears.

The bedroom door opened quietly for only a few seconds, and then closed. Frank stood alone on the other side of the door with his hand on the knob. He wanted to go back to the garage and smash the car till there was nothing left of it, but ten minutes later, he hadn't released the doorknob. Taking care of the necessary preparations, that's what he owed Maggie. A lethargy Frank had never felt weighted him down. His movements were mechanical when he managed to walk away. He knocked on Hunter's door first. He and Mike opened the door together.

'Last night, Chris was struck and killed by a car on Sherbrooke Street as he walked home from Caitlin's.' Frank's voice was flat.

'What?' Mike shouted. 'That can't be! Chris wasn't – they were in a cab, sir. Is Caitlin hurt too?'

This barrage was too much for Frank – he didn't want to be here. As he looked at these two young faces, a horrible thought ran through his mind. *Why Chris, why not one…?* He remembered then why it was Chris. When he began to explain what little he knew, there was an acerbic edge to his voice. 'They visited together at Caitlin's for a while. On his way back, Chris didn't call a cab. Caitlin suggested he walk, and that's what Chris did. He just didn't make it.'

'None of this makes any sense, Mr. Donovan! He didn't even finish his second beer last night. He was more interested in giving us a historical tour and talking about his car. Did a car jump the sidewalk or run a red light?'

'I don't have the particulars, Hunter.'

Hunter was raging and pacing madly. 'There's no way he could have been struck on the street. Chris followed every traffic rule that existed. For the last two years, he's driven us nuts with his caution! A street can be empty, and he won't cross against a light.' Hunter realized he had used the present tense. 'Sir, you'll have a lot to do. Give me the number of the police and I'll look into this. No bloody way it was Chris' fault! Has there been an arrest?'

The lingering trauma was dulling Frank's responses. Hunter's energy was sapping what little was holding him up.

'Hunter, I do have a number for the lead investigator, Claude Remay at Station 12, but I can't remember where I've put it. I just don't know…'

'Claude Remay, I can go from there. We can't take Chris' death sitting down. I'm sorry, but I have to do something.'

Mike hadn't yet uttered a word. He remembered that Chris had separated them last night, trying to protect his sister on his account. That was the real reason he had gone home with Caitlin. *I should have told you, Chris, that I'm falling in love with Caitlin. I would never have hurt her. Never! You've been my best friend. You should have known me better. I'm sorry, Chris.* 'How is Caitlin, sir?'

Mike's simple question was easier for Frank to answer.

'I don't know. She's with her mother. That's for the best,' Frank mumbled and turned toward the door.

'Sir, you are going to need some help, and we'd like to offer it.' Mike's sincerity was disarming. 'Count on us for anything.'

'Thank you.'

'Hunter will call in for the accident report, and I'll make the calls back home. Chris has so many friends who'll want to know. My grandmother died last year, and I know there is a great deal of work involved now.' Mike caught himself before saying funeral arrangements. He wished he could go to Caitlin, but he knew she wouldn't want to see him. *Is she blaming me? Oh God, she suggested he walk home. She's blaming both of us.*

In a matter of a few hours, the house had turned sad, lifeless, everywhere but in the visitors' quarters. Chris' friends, sequestered in their own rooms, began making calls, taking notes and questioning. Frank sat in the kitchen, staring at the fridge.

Hunter called Station 12 and spoke directly to Claude Remay. The facts he received were these: Chris had been struck on Sherbrooke Street by the right side of the vehicle, the woman driving that vehicle had left the scene because she feared for her own safety; she called the police a few hours later and reported the events. The driver had come into the station to be interviewed, the vehicle had been impounded, the case was under investigation and he expected the results of an autopsy within a day or two.

'What did she have to worry about? She was protected inside her car. Are you considering this accident a hit-and-run, sir?' Hunter's anger was palpable.

'There is an ongoing investigation, sir. Are you a member of the family?'

'No, I'm his friend.'

'Perhaps I should be talking with Mr. Donovan.'

'Mr. Donovan is taking the death of his son very hard, as you can imagine. I'm staying at his home and I'm trying to help. Be assured, I will relay all this information. I have another question. If you say the woman who struck and killed Chris Donovan took over two hours to report the accident, is it possible that Chris might have survived his injuries had she stayed at the scene and called for help? Was this woman given a breathalyzer?'

'The autopsy should give us those answers. Unfortunately, so long afterwards there was no point to a breathalyzer.'

'Do you find the woman's story credible? Once she was safely home, why did she wait so long before calling the police?'

'Sir, you are not a member of the family, and I cannot discuss an ongoing investigation. I feel I have given you the necessary preliminary information. Once all the reports are in, I will relate the findings to Mr. Donovan.'

'I will share the unanswered questions with the family. I hope you know who Mr. Donovan is. If there is any chance of bringing pressure to bear on the facts concerning this tragedy, I trust you will.'

'This case will receive our utmost attention, and that has nothing to do with who Mr. Donovan is or is not. That is just the way we work. Thank you for your call.' Remay kicked the bottom drawer of his desk shut. It wasn't that he did not feel the anguish of the family. His younger sister had been hit by a car when she was three, and his mother had been on the balcony and a witness to the tragedy. It was quite simply that Remay hated politics, more particularly, the politics of the rich. The voice on the other end sounded like money and trouble.

Remay was no fool. That bitch was probably drunk when she hit the kid, sobered up at home, took a drink to cover herself and then reported the accident. Drunks were conniving people; he'd learned that on the job. Pulling out the file, he ran her name, but nothing came up. The friend had said Donovan was a cautious kid; that was something, he supposed. Had Donovan been struck on the driver's side, Remay would have been harder on the driver. If the tox screen results showed the kid was clean, he'd solicit the help of local television stations for possible witnesses. Without them, his hands were tied. As it stood now, the kid was just unlucky. Remay was fed up with police dramas that solved crimes in sixty minutes, minus commercial time. Real police work was mostly a game of waiting and lucky breaks.

CHAPTER 10

PEOPLE ARE AMAZING when they are assaulted, battered down, winded and frightened. Up they crawl, on hands and knees, clawing at the offender, real or perceived. Closing the wound that has torn their puzzled lives apart, stapling the gaping hole, is the stuff of human life.

Nicolina paid the cabbie, marched into her office, grabbed the file and stuffed it into her purse. At her computer, she punched the search key, hunting for the employees who might have discovered the contents of the file she had received. *Bingo!* The search pointed to Jen Sexton, the vice-president of human resources. Sexton was a beautiful woman, tall, blonde, statuesque. She was also a flirt. The lunchroom buzzed about her affairs, real or fictional. Men fawned on her; women envied her. Sexton was also affable and intelligent. That was the thing; she'd understand what she'd found. Some people just had it all. Nicolina had made it her business, once taken on by Lecours, to uncover as much as she could about all the executives at Foley Pharmaceuticals. She knew that Sexton had been a strong employee representative. The woman knew the company. Sexton was one of the only people who had the gall to threaten her.

Over the past year, one by one, Nicolina had invited class one and two executives to her office, and had licked her lips a few times as one after the other 'blabbed' on colleagues and friends they had worked with for the better part of twenty years. The rumour was out that she'd been appointed to clean house, so the rats were pointing at each other. Knives are sharpened on a regular basis in the world of business. With fat wallets from good salaries on the line, the frustrated could descend to the ugliest level of petty politics. With what gossip she already had, Nicolina was quite certain of one thing. She had her woman! Nicolina threw her head back and snorted. Times like this, when her head was clear, Nicolina knew why she could depend on herself.

Unlocking the bottom drawer, she eyed the Scotch. A little celebration? Rubbing her palms together, she felt her mouth water. 'Tread gently' was a phrase that never made it into her flawed philosophy simply because Nicolina had done rather well on her bulldozer. She had not been hired to make people feel good. To her benefit, she was also a stranger to conscience. For Nicolina, morality was relative, and to be truthful, she was more and more in tune with the rest of the population. Others' disdain, she often viewed as her success. Unfortunately, she was not immune to doubt.

Grabbing a pad and pencil, she jotted down three niggling points. What if she was wrong about Sexton? Arming another enemy might be her demise. She quickly dismissed that notion. Sexton was the blackmailer. What damage could her Mazda do her? How much did Sophia remember about last night? These were dangerous avenues, and Nicolina was not unmindful of their peril. Her mouth went dry and she bent over, shut the drawer and locked it. Clicking the top of a lighter she never used on and off, Nicolina determined that not one sip of the Scotch would linger in her throat today. If she could hide her fear as well as she did, she could bloody well do without her Scotch.

Chris Donovan was as important to Nicolina as Sexton. Both of these people had come barging into her life uninvited. Hadn't she enough work with this trial without the additional stress? If only that controller would die! She'd be dead of cancer even if she won her job back. Why didn't the woman try to enjoy what life she had left? Why did her reputation matter to her at death's door? *That woman is killing herself!* If she died soon enough, the case would dead-end; and Nicolina could bring her legal skills to the other work she had been hired to do.

In the house on Harvard, Monsieur Patate and Sophia had their own problems. The plan was to take Monsieur outside to his familiar wetting grounds, to familiarize him with the lessons he had learned so well. For ten minutes, the pug sniffed the roots of his favourite maple tree, and things looked promising. Sophia extended the leash and sat on the park bench across the street from St. Augustine's Church, that like her, had lost itself. Long, long ago, she recalled that Gentlemen Ushers, that's what they were called, stood at the doors of the church and led every parishioner down the aisles to designated rows for Sunday mass. When she looked up at the steeple, she saw that the bells were gone too. Like Sophia, the stiff bones of the church were there, but the heart was gone. Waiting on Monsieur, she watched teenagers throw open the wooden doors of the storied church carrying roller blades and skateboards and was saddened. Things change, Sophia knew, but why was the grandeur and the soul of finer things so often reduced to the mundane? Sophia didn't quite phrase her idea in those words, but that's what she felt.

'Monsieur Patate, I have the bag ready. Try to remember why we've come here.'

Monsieur ran back to Sophia and nuzzled close, but he hadn't left anything by the tree.

'Go back, Monsieur. Look over there! See what that dog is doing?'

Monsieur trotted back to the tree, was excited for a few seconds, feinted at finding his position and ran back to the safety of Sophia's knees.

'Maybe you have nothing to leave, Monsieur. We will come back in the afternoon.' Together they walked past the French school, on home. Sophia dropped the white, plastic bag into a pile under the kitchen sink and Monsieur did his business in a neat little pile on the carpet in the hallway near the grandfather clock. Sophia smelled the mess before she saw it. 'Oh dear,' Sophia moaned. 'This is not good, not good at all.' Limping back to the kitchen, she reached under the sink for her rubber gloves, a square piece of cardboard she used as a dustpan, the Vim, a rag and a plastic bag. His droppings were scooped from the carpet, the area scrubbed to a sweet-smelling mist of cleanser and the bag taken out to the garbage can in the garage.

Monsieur hovered in a corner of the hall. When the old woman saw his sad, bulging eyes, almost teary, her heart broke for him. 'It's not your fault, Monsieur. This is a house of trouble and stress, but you have me now. Come here. Let's go out in the backyard and hope we can at least leave a puddle of 'number one' outside.' Monsieur jumped up and down as high as he could on his little legs, happy and forgiven. But life doesn't turn quite so easily, and poor Monsieur piddled on the kitchen floor, two feet from the door.

Sophia began to cry as she wiped up the mess. Her hands shook when she cleaned the tiles and she padded off to the washroom because her own nerves were jittery. Monsieur's loss of control signalled the wary, tentative mood that had descended on the Harvard Avenue house. The rot from the night before had infected the innocent tenants whose nervous existence might well hasten their eviction. Sophia knew her landlord had left the house and gone driving with too much Scotch in her system. The accident that had caused the death of a dog (or worse) bumped up against Sophia's conscience. She recalled the carnage Roberto had left behind for her to mop up. Now, it was Nicolina's 'worse' that was troubling her old heart.

Food helped most things, Sophia believed, lasagna more than most. Out came the pans, the parmesan, cottage, mozzarella and Swiss cheeses, the pasta, both the tomato and meat sauce and the virgin olive oil. The aromas and comforting activity would calm Monsieur and Sophia. Mostly though, she remembered how Nicolina gorged on her pasta. Since this was a heavy meal, she counted on the hope that Nicolina would not have room for Scotch. She always asked for two corner pieces because the Parmesan cheese added a crusty top to the lasagna and dripped down the side of the pan. If she felt things were getting messy, Nicolina would wipe the sides of her mouth, not with a napkin, but with the fresh Italian bread that the old woman had bought on Sherbrooke Street.

Monsieur trotted back to his corner. The events of last night had broken his trust, and trust cannot be taught in any school, public or private, to animal or human.

CHAPTER 11

IN THE LUXURIOUS home on The Boulevard, the two-legged creatures, except for Maggie, began, like Sophia, to regroup. The difference was that their persecution was real and it was permanent. Chris was not coming back, and the grit of guilt plaguing Frank and Caitlin could not be wiped away. Maggie's grief was white, innocent, and she had surrendered her heart to a sorrow that enveloped her completely. Chris' past-ness had not yet lighted on her consciousness. The only sound that pierced her ears was the ring of the phone that had brought the news. Her body was raw with anguish.

Caitlin had crept quietly from the room to make coffee and toast for her mother. On the tray, she had also left water. 'I won't bother you, Mom, but you have to eat or drink something. You have to try to keep your strength up. That's what you told me when Derek died.'

Maggie shut her eyes, crusty with dried tears.

Caitlin understood her mother, knew what it was to huddle inside a cave. She had done the same thing herself. Setting the tray on the night table, she stood for a while with her, but she knew her mother was alone, unaware of her presence. She herself was still dry-eyed. Maybe tears were parcelled out like minutes, she thought. *Have I used mine up on Derek?* There was an inner part of her that she would not open up to Chris; perhaps the tears were in those heart muscles.

Mike had walked over to the second floor in the main house, waiting for Caitlin to appear. Even as she walked towards him, she didn't see him. He saw the shock and the numbing pain that walked with her. Mike froze and wept loudly, loudly enough for both of them. Wealth and privilege had left most of his life with little responsibility. When he saw Caitlin, a surge of care and debt he'd never known overwhelmed him. He made no move towards her – all Mike said was, 'Forgive me, Caitlin. I never meant to hurt Chris or you. My bad rep was the reason Chris took you home last night. You want to hear something really funny?' Mike had trouble getting his words out between his gut-wrenching sobs. 'I never got the chance to tell Chris I've fallen in love with you. That's something, right? Isn't that fucking something?' He reached for her as she walked by.

A few feet from Mike, Caitlin turned to him, 'I told Chris to walk home.'

'I know, Caitlin,' he wept.

'How can you?' Caitlin shot back acidly. 'Have you ever lost anybody, Mike? I mean someone you really loved, have you?'

'I've lost Chris,' he wept.

Caitlin had no response and offered none. It wasn't simply his roguish ways that had drawn women to him, of course there was the money, but it was Mike's honesty that was disarming, even now. Her eyes dropped for a minute, and Caitlin was about to add, 'I'm as much to blame for the attraction as you. I acted like a school girl.' When she looked up to admit these things, Mike had already left the landing. What did any of this matter now anyway?

Frank was on the phone in the study when Caitlin found him. 'I'm calling in a favour, Stephen. I don't want any mention of the accident in *The Gazette*. Maggie would be devastated.'

'Frank, I'll do what I can, but I can't stop the news. Freedom of information and all that. We don't have to mention Chris by name. We can go with 'pending notification of next-of-kin'. What are the actual facts?'

Frank related what Hunter had learned from Remay.

'Is there any chance of finding the driver at fault?'

'We're waiting on the reports.'

'For now, I can limit the ink. Sorry, I wish I could pull more strings for you. Accept my condolences.'

Caitlin stood by the door, listening.

His mother-in-law was next on the list. 'Maureen, this is Frank. I have some very bad news...'

'I'll fly down tomorrow morning. How's Maggie? May I speak to her?'

'Maggie can't talk to you now, Maureen – she's in a bad way.'

Frank dialed the third number, the head office of a large aerospace company. 'Michel Dagenais, please. Frank Donovan here.' A few minutes passed.

'Sorry, Frank. We're caught up in a meeting. Are we still on for three?'

'I've suffered a personal tragedy, Michel. Last night my son was fatally injured in an automobile accident. Naturally, I cannot begin work on the transaction. Sometime today, my secretary will gather your files and give you the name of a very capable attorney, partner actually, one of the other partners. For the next month, I plan to attend to personal affairs.'

'Frank, my sympathies. Look, it took us three years to set up this deal; we can wait another month. Nobody's going anywhere. We approached you for a reason. If you need the month – you've got it. Stay in touch.'

After the call, Frank buried his head in his hands.

'Dad?' Caitlin whispered.

When Frank turned towards the door, Caitlin saw that his face was drained of colour. 'Come on in, honey.' He rose unsteadily from his chair and threw his arms around his daughter. 'What am I going to do?' He collapsed then, and Caitlin felt her neck muscles straining to hold her father upright. He was shaking, and she almost lost her balance. 'What are we going to do? I'm no good for your mother now. I don't know where to begin.'

'Try to sit, Dad. For the time being, we can't help Mom, but you have to pull yourself together. In the days ahead, I don't want her to feel as alone as I did when Derek died. Mom will need you, Dad.'

'Do you think he saw the car? I keep asking myself that. He must have been so afraid if he saw it.'

'He'd be alive if he'd taken a cab home. Why didn't I just let him be? Chris was so happy last night, so glad to be home.'

'Chris noticed everything – he must have seen the car.' Frank's voice was so low that Caitlin leaned in closer to hear what he was saying. 'I wonder if he called for Mom. He did that when he was afraid, when he was a kid. Always called for her.'

'I didn't have to let loose last night – that was so selfish of me. It was Chris' night after all. I was a teenager the last time I acted like that.'

'I can't bear to go to your mother. What if she asks me where he is?' Frank shuddered, 'He was so cold at the morgue, so forlorn. Do you remember if I told Chris I loved him? I must have told him at least once, but I can't recall a single time. Isn't that something? Chris survived two European trips, hitching across the States and living in Boston for the last two years where the rate of violence is much higher than our own. How could he be killed in his own backyard?'

'I want to know who the bastard is who ran him down and left him,' Caitlin said. 'I want to know what kind of monster can do such a thing, leave another human being to die alone on a street.'

Frank stared at his daughter without knowing who she was, or perhaps, who he was.

'Dad, Dad? What's wrong?'

'I don't know what to do…'

'Can I get you something to eat?'

'No, I'm not hungry. Hunter went to get some food, I think. Borrowed my car – I believe he drove to the police station. Where's Maggie?'

'Dad, I'm giving you some brandy. You have to drink it. I'll make you a sandwich and you've got to eat it, Dad.'

'Yes, yes, I'll do that.'

The night Chris died, Caitlin was seven months shy of her thirty-second birthday. Her life was just starting to take shape. Derek, her first great love, had quietly slid into the shadows of the past. Time had seen to that. Like her brother, on the night of the brutal tragedy, she too had felt the rock of strength and the firm resolve of a promising future. The appearance of Mike had only added the feeling that she was ready again for the high hurdle-jump of passion, perhaps romance. Though it seemed lost to him now, clarity was a passion Frank had passed onto his daughter. With the spreading certainty of Chris' death, with the grief it spread like a virus, Caitlin understood what she had lost for a second time. The difference now was that something else was shoving her grief to one side and taking up a strong position beside it. It was something angry and vengeful.

When Caitlin walked into the kitchen, she found Mike had made coffee and sandwiches from the chicken leftovers. 'Guys have come a long way in the kitchen. It was that or starve, living on our own. You need to eat something, Caitlin. Your father too.'

'I can't talk, Mike, not now anyway.' She filled a plate, poured coffee and went to the dining room for the brandy. When she entered the study, her father hadn't moved. After laying the food down and watching him reluctantly drink the brandy, Caitlin left him alone and went back to her room. She dialed a familiar number.

Carmen got the phone on the second ring, 'Wow! You guys must have really partied last night. It's almost two o'clock. I hope you've saved some energy for tonight.'

'Carmen...'

CHAPTER 12

SINCE HER VISIT to the police, Nicolina had tried to concentrate on the immediate issues, but she had not dared think about the most important one until now. She knew the private number but wrote it out on the pad in front of her anyway. Since the next court date for the controller's case was Tuesday, the day the plaintiff's team was set to argue, Nicolina called the CEO to assure him that the case was on track. Informing Raymond Lecours about last night's accident was harder than going to the police. She could use a double Scotch right now, but Nicolina wisely reached for a bottle of water that was on a shelf on the side of her desk.

Taking a deep breath, she called Monsieur Lecours. 'Raymond, Nicolina.'

'Rumour has it that the plaintiff's case is stronger. There is no room for error in this case. This cancer could prove costly for everyone involved!'

'Sympathy may have shifted somewhat because of the cancer. The embezzlement charges you handed me with the case will speak for themselves, I can assure you. We're prepared for them.' The file threatened everything, but truth was not her strong suit, so she kept with what had served her in the past.

'That's exactly what we want to hear. Use the weekend to further prepare.'

'Raymond, something else has occurred that I felt I should tell you, even though things will sort themselves out.'

'Something that can hurt us?' As CEO at Foley's, he made up for his shortcomings with bullying.

'An issue quite apart from the case. Last evening I took a late drive...'

'You left the scene?' Nicolina was not the only boozer in this crowd; Lecours smelled a skunk.

'I felt threatened.'

'You were in a car, for God's sake! What were you afraid of?'

'I went back, Raymond – I reported the accident.'

'How soon?'

'A couple of hours.'

'Two hours! How serious was it?'

'The young man died; I'm devastated, Raymond.'

'Ms. Pastore, consult a lawyer. Don't even consider defending yourself.'

'I've done nothing wrong.'

'This kind of publicity is very damaging to the company. With our case pending, it's a ticking bomb. Take my advice; secure a consult before the next session on Tuesday. In this case, you are on your own.'

The line went dead. Nicolina had been dismissed.

How do I find a lawyer on a Friday afternoon? The police can't prove anything. A sharp neck spasm caught Nicolina in mid-breath. Standing quickly, tilting her head to the side that wasn't constricting her airway, she tried to take shallow breaths to ease the pain. It was a full minute before she dared to breathe normally.

Frightened, shivering though it was still quite warm that afternoon, Nicolina sat in the back of a cab on her way home and she was crying. *Just once in my goddamn life, it would be nice to be treated fairly.* Not for a second, did she recall that she was speeding on a city street without lights, drunk. The kid's death would remain a mystery to her.

Monsieur Patate was on the front porch when the car pulled into the driveway. She had Monsieur. His was a forgiving nature, and he edged as close to the front step as his leash would permit. Monsieur could not tell

Nicolina that he was on the porch to prevent further accidents in the house. The bad stuff he saved for Sophia.

Anyone would succumb to Sophia's lasagna; the aromas alone were intoxicating. Nicolina realized she was famished because she hadn't eaten all day. When she was stressed, Nicolina could eat. In the Italian code, a good appetite was synonymous with strength.

'Sit,' invited Sophia. 'Everything is ready. I have a nice cold Brio for you because I knew you would be thirsty. So, sit. Enjoy!' The old woman heaped a steaming square of lasagna onto Nicolina's plate, its sides oozing with sauce and cheese. Around the edges of the plate, fresh bread soaked up the sauce. 'Don't burn your tongue, now.'

Fear fused with hunger, and Nicolina broke the pasta with her fork, blew on it, and ate the lasagna with the same determination and relish she brought to her work. Forks of pasta found their way to Nicolina's hungry mouth, as did most of the bread. When Nicolina looked up for air, Sophia was back at the pan cutting up another outside piece that went the way of the first and the second. 'I have to stop or I'll burst.'

Sophia smiled. No amount of Scotch would make it through that pasta with any effect.

'Where's Monsieur?'

'My knees were very sore today, and I was not able to take him on a walk. He needs the fresh air.' Little white lies that helped others were forgiven, Sophia believed. 'I have some lemon Italian ice for desert.'

'That sounds fine.'

'It must be difficult without your car.' This was dangerous territory, but there were things Sophia had to know.

Reality has a nasty edge. Nicolina's stomach muscles

began to work on the pasta and threatened their owner with a bad case of indigestion. Home battles were something quite new for Nicolina. It was hard to read her tenant. How could she find the truth behind such a kind face? *If I can't control this old bitch, I'm lost!*

'I'll have my car back in a day or two, probably Monday. This was an accident, a tragic accident. I'm sick about the whole thing.'

'It was not a dog then?'

'No, it wasn't. It was some poor kid who wasn't watching where he was going and he stepped out in front of my car. These terrible things happen, you know. I'm very, very sad.'

Sophia stood very still and pinched the back of her thigh to keep from laughing in her landlord's face. 'I can see that,' she said lightly. 'How bad were his injuries?'

Nicolina should have chosen the stage, for she bent her head and began to shed real tears. 'He didn't make it,' she sobbed. 'I've thought about him all day.'

'I'm sure you have. I won't bother you now. After the dishes, I will go to bed and take Monsieur with me. You will need your strength.'

Round one went to Sophia and Monsieur.

CHAPTER 13

'OH, NO, CAITLIN! This can't be happening. I'm so sorry
for Chris. God, he was just starting out, beginning his
life. How are your mother and father? How are you?'
Carmen asked, taken aback.

'Do you remember what I was like the night Derek
died?'

'I'll never forget.'

'Times that by three.'

'Can I come over?'

'Not tonight. Tomorrow afternoon will be easier.
Right now, I'm taking care of Dad. You know my father,
the man in control, the slayer of dragons. Except when
his son dies…'

'I could help, Caitlin. I want to come over right
now.'

'I can't cope with anyone else; I'm not doing well
with my parents now either. Try to understand, Carm.
Mom hasn't moved from her bed and she won't eat.
Dad is trying to make calls, but he's staring at the wall.'

'I don't want to put pressure on you, so I'll come
over tomorrow. Are Chris' friends there?'

'Hunter just got back from the police station. The
investigator said he should get the reports of the autopsy and the tests on the car that ran Chris down tomorrow. It's awful knowing that Chris is alone at the
morgue, suffering another brutal abuse. Dad said he
was so cold. I just…' Caitlin's words caught in her
throat.

'Take care of yourself, Caitlin. I hardly recognize
your voice. If you can, check the fridge and give me a
list of anything you might need. I'll call in the morning.'

'I'll try to remember, Carm. Thanks.' Caitlin folded her arms together on the kitchen table, leaned forward and laid her head across them. The room began to spin when she shut her eyes. She grabbed the edges of the table to keep from falling. Stealing a glance at her watch, she saw that it was two-fourteen. *In forty-six minutes, Chris will be dead for twelve hours, half a day.* Against the horror of that thought, Caitlin shut her eyes tightly and sought refuge in that small chamber where Chris was not allowed entry. Her mind escaped to dreams of revenge, a support that had eluded her when Derek died.

Mike had come into the kitchen and found Caitlin sprawled across the table. 'Are you all right?' He did not dare touch her.

Neither Caitlin nor her father was an idle dreamer; reality was the spine that held each of them firm. Yet the little scenario that had just played out, a harmless flight really when one considered what this woman had done, left Caitlin with the smallest smile that was almost savage. Mike's voice brought Chris back into the room and with it, the heavy sadness that hung around his death like smog.

'Yeah. I guess I nearly fell asleep.' Caitlin left her head on the table and looked up at Mike. Without his smile and high energy, he seemed shrunk, his eyes old and guilty. There was nothing she had to offer him, nothing at all. That he was sharing their guilt was small comfort. Experience had taught her that Mike would get over Chris' death, given enough time. She never would because Chris was her brother, and family was forever. 'Have you seen my father?'

'No, but Hunter is back in his room making notes. He's determined to find out exactly what happened.'

'I tried for months to analyse Derek's fall, tried to

figure out how an athletic guy could fall backwards off
his roller blades, hit his head on pavement and die. In
the end, none of that crap changes anything. Derek was
still dead, and now Chris is too. Back then, I even rented a Superman movie, the one where Lois Lane dies,
and Superman reverses time and saves her. What if I
had taken longer to speak to Mom on the phone that
day? Derek might have waited with me instead of going
out at that very minute. Maybe he wouldn't have fallen.
But none of that stuff ever brought him back, and our
guilt won't bring Chris back either.'

'Can I get you something?'

'No. I want to go up and check on my parents.'

'Have you thought about calling people here in
Montreal?'

'I know you're trying to be helpful, Mike. But Jesus,
don't you think I know what to do? I lost my husband
three years ago; I'm an old hand at this. I'll get to calling, but first I want to check on my parents, if that's all
right with you!'

'I'll get lost – I'm here if you need something.'

'No amount of kindness is going to change things,
but thanks.'

'I love you Caitlin. I've never felt this way about anybody. I want to take care of you.'

'What the hell does that matter now? My brother is
dead!'

'It matters to me, and so did Chris.'

'Look, you know what? This is not the time.'

'I can't seem to help myself where you're concerned.'

'Learn!' Caitlin walked out before Mike could
respond. Except for the water, nothing else had been
touched in her mother's room. Maggie's eyes were still
closed but she did not appear to be sleeping. Caitlin sat
beside her mother and held her. Under the blankets,

she could feel her mother go rigid against her touch. 'Try to rest, Mom. I'll get more water and fresher sandwiches. I love you.'

Her father was still in his leather chair. The only difference was that he was staring blankly at the floor now. 'Dad, you have to help me. Mom won't eat. We have to start calling people. Where does Mom keep her address book? She's changed things since I left. You have to eat too because I need your help. I can't do this alone, not again!' Caitlin began to shake Frank's shoulders, but he didn't seem to notice. 'Dad? Have you called anybody since I left?'

'I don't know what to do, Caitlin.'

'We'll probably get the autopsy results tomorrow, and that's going to be very hard. You have to decide on a funeral home. We don't want Chris spending another minute at the morgue once the tests are completed. We also have to begin calling people now. We can't put that off either. You and I have to be strong for Mom. We can't let Chris down either.'

'I don't want to tell anyone that my only son is dead.'

'The accident report will get into *The Gazette* as soon as they learn the name of the family. I can't bury Chris alone, I can't do it! I'll call your secretary; she can get in touch with your business friends. Dad, come on! Go and shower right now. I'll get more food to you. Please eat it.' Caitlin's underarms were sticky with perspiration and she had a searing migraine above her left eyebrow that stretched into her head. She barged into Mike's room and found him slumped in a chair much like her father. 'You wanted to help? Make the food then. I can't do anything with my parents. I'll find Mom's address book and start from there, but I have to shower first.'

'I'll get to work. Take care of yourself.'

'Yeah, right. Look, I know you're trying, but Chris was my brother. Isn't that beginning to sink in yet?'

'He was my best friend.'

'It's not the same, Mike. I knew him for a lifetime; you knew him for two years.'

'I'll get to work.'

In the shower, Caitlin stood without moving, allowing the water spray to hit her face full force. The names of friends she had to call bounced against her brain until she felt sharp pain on both palms. Her fists were so tightly clenched that her nails had drawn blood. Purposely, she poured shampoo into the cut on her left hand and did not wince with the sting. Caitlin scrubbed her head with a vengeance and made no attempt to protect her eyes from the soap. Small inflicted pain felt good, until the fury in her brain pulled her back to Sherbrooke Street. When she felt the thud of the car as it struck Chris, she fell back against the marble wall inside the shower. *Come back, Chris. Please come back!* Her frantic appeal was thin and dry.

Recalling the bargains she'd made on Derek's behalf, even when she knew they were too late, cut off a refuge she saw now was of no avail. Still, Caitlin could not cry. It was as if she were saving the energy lost to tears for some use later on. With her arms folded around her ribs, shivering naked on the bathroom floor, Caitlin began to panic that she might forget the names of friends to notify. Once she was dressed, she raced downstairs and began looking for the address book that she finally found in the third drawer under the cutlery in the dishtowel drawer. In happier times, Maggie would have given her a logical reason for choosing such an unlikely place.

Mike had made a batch of grilled cheese sandwiches and a pot of hot coffee. Caitlin brought the food to both parents and then sequestered herself in her bedroom and began making the calls, first to her parents' friends, then, much later, to her own. 'Hello, Mr. Preston. This is Caitlin Donovan; I have some very sad news…'

'Mrs. O'Reilly, yes, they're fine, but…'

'Mr. Sullivan, I hope I'm not disturbing you this late, but…'

'Mr. Patterson, I'm glad you remember me. No, I'm calling about my brother Chris…' Caitlin kept the calls up until midnight, and then she stopped. *In three hours, Chris will have died one day ago. A whole day passed since he was alive.*

CHAPTER 14

A SOBER NICOLINA discovered the jagged edge of fear, but she also found that a clear head worked faster and more accurately than she remembered. From a Google search, she learned that bloodstain splatter analysis and crash indents determined speed or lack of it, strong evidence for culpability. She regretted now she had not gotten more information from Remay at Station 12. If witnesses had come forward, she was reasonably certain she'd have been arrested, and that had not happened. When and if charges were filed against her, Nicolina would seek counsel, but not before. Contacting a lawyer at this early stage was suspicious. The only witness that she knew of rented her basement apartment. For the time being, her apparent sadness and regret about the accident seemed to quiet the old woman, but Nicolina would carefully monitor the homefront.

Friday evening, she had her own phone call to make. The venture was risky, but Nicolina saw no other options. *Damn them all!* If there were additional errors made in this case, they'd be her own. She punched in the numbers. 'Good evening, is Jen home tonight?'

'Just a sec,' answered a teenage voice that lost interest as soon as it realized the call was not for him. 'Mom, MOM! Some lady wants you on the phone.'

When Jen picked up the hall phone, her husband Robert walked up beside her. 'Yes?'

'This is Nicolina Pastore. Do you have a few minutes? I know this is Friday night, but I do need to speak to you.'

Jen mouthed the words *the bitch from Foley's* and shooed Robert from the room. Not a single executive spoke to Nicolina without a sense of threat. The rats had jumped from the controller's ship for good reason. The prevailing thought, unshared naturally, was that only a few of them would survive close scrutiny. Terrible and unjust ideas travelled the company corridors. If you were an executive and heavy, you were a booze hound. If you dressed well, you were a thief. If you were a hunk or a beauty, you had slept your way to the top. Score two of the three, and you were fried. Jen was the bravest of the lot. At this moment, she did not feel brave at all, but she knew a command when she heard one. 'I have some time, Ms. Pastore. How can I help you?' Jen did her level best not to choke on her feigned civility.

'On second thought, I think a face-to-face is a better idea. This won't take more than an hour. I haven't eaten yet. How about the Second Cup on Monkland Avenue in thirty minutes?'

'I'll need forty-five. I'm in Beaconsfield. Second Cup on the corner of Old Orchard, right?'

'That's correct; I'll be waiting.'

Jen felt it was just a matter of time before she made it to Nicolina's hit list. Well, she'd make moves of her own. It didn't much matter that she'd done nothing. Pastore's house cleaning had dropped dust on everyone. She had almost pulled off accusing poor Kathryn of forgery. In this witch hunt, anything could happen.

'Robert, I have to go out. She wants to meet with me in NDG tonight. This must concern the case. Court reconvenes on Tuesday. She wants information from me. Something stinks! If it didn't, I'd be hauled into her office on Monday morning, not ordered out on a Friday night. I won't testify against Kathryn. She's being railroaded; we all know it.'

'Jen, we have two children here. Get off your horse. We need both salaries.'

'I'm just saying there are things I can't do. Does Ryan still have his small recorder?'

'Ryan, we need you downstairs, right now!'

'In a few, Dad, I'm busy.'

'Now, mister, get your butt down here.'

'All right, but you're to blame if I don't finish this essay tonight!'

'This is Friday night, Ryan,' Robert shouted up the stairs.

There was a loud thundering on the stairs. 'I'm here. Now what?'

'Do you still have the tape recorder?' Jen asked.

'Somewhere, I guess.'

'Find it, now! I need it tonight. What about batteries?'

'Only in my Game Boy.'

'Grab two batteries from it, Ryan. This is an emergency.'

'What am I supposed to do then?'

'Survive. On the double, get upstairs, find the recorder and take out the batteries.'

'All right, Ma. Chill out.'

'What did you just say to me?'

'I was only kidding, Ma,' he laughed as he bolted up the stairs.

'Be patient, Jen. He'll find it in that mess somewhere.'

'I'll give him five, but then I've got to go.'

'Got it, Mom!'

'You're set then, Jen. How do you plan to operate the recorder without her knowing it?'

'I'm working that out. The guys who've been called in to see her all say she lies about their statements. Regardless, the company has to throw their support behind her because of the trial and all that involves. I'll bring my briefcase and run the recorder inside of it.'

'Doesn't it make some noise taping?'

'Gees, Robert, I don't know. I'll figure it out. I sure as hell can't get caught taping her.'

'Be careful.'

'You don't have to tell me. See you, Robert.' Driving along Highway 20, Jen tried to figure out how much Pastore knew. How much could she prove? It was one thing to help other employees with work-related problems. It was not quite so easy when the problem might be hers. Reaching across the seat, she grabbed the recorder and pressed the play button. There was noise. If the Second Cup coffee house had other patrons sitting at tables nearby, she might just get away with this caper. The tape might not be admissible in court, but the executives would have no problem listening to it. By the time she drove across Cote St. Antoine Road, her bladder needed a tap, but there was no time. She'd have to hold everything. Finding parking on Monkland wasn't easy. The trendy area was mobbed with shoppers and gawkers.

Jen cursed the city parking permits and meters that had sprung up a few years ago like dandelions. Overnight, visitors from the suburbs could not find parking in the city. Monkland village was the latest hot spot to make restaurant eating next to impossible for visitors. If she was forced to cross Girouard Avenue, she'd be late for sure. As she approached the traffic lights, someone pulled out of meter parking on Monkland itself. Jen slammed on the brakes, the driver behind her gave her the horn and Jen drove up on the sidewalk and backed up neatly to a coveted space. She reached for the loonies she knew Robert kept in the glove compartment and fed the meter. As she ran the few blocks back to the café, Jen passed an arts and crafts shop, a state of the art electronics shop, a pastry shop, a bakery and a Multi-Mag. She mumbled to herself trying to prepare for the onslaught.

When she reached the door of the café, she spotted Pastore sitting at the back table and gave her a small wave. Two empty tables stood beside hers. Once she was seated, she laid her briefcase on the floor. 'Sorry I'm late, Ms. Pastore. Parking was difficult.'

'Coffee?'

'Please.'

Nicolina had prepared herself as well. 'It's been a long day and I'll get to the point,' she said as she took the file from her briefcase and handed it to Jen.

'Do you recognize this, Jen?'

Jen took her time reading it. 'Why?'

'Answer the question.'

'Yes.'

Nicolina knifed her next question with precision. 'Did you send me this file?'

We *have two kids. Get off your horse. We need both salaries.* She leaned back on her chair, trying to see if the tape was still recording. She couldn't be sure.

'Anyone could have sent it, Ms. Pastore. My office is not locked.'

'Answer the question, Jen.'

'Yes.'

'Why?'

'I could say to give you pertinent information that might protect you in the long run. But the real reason was justice for Kathryn.'

'Listen to me very carefully, Jen. Understand this salient point; I cannot afford to lose this case.'

'I'm listening, Ms. Pastore.' There was no way Jen wanted to be informal with this woman.

'Do you have solid proof of these allegations?'

'I will within the week.'

'Do you understand the broad implications of these claims?'

'I'm more interested in the immediate implications for Kathryn and the cause of her cancer.'

'Most whistleblowers have ruined their own lives and accomplished very little. Have you informed anyone else of this?'

'That may be true. No one else is aware this file. I'm waiting for the final results.'

'What you have now is dangerous supposition. Go forward with any of this and your career is history! Your reputation is folklore, you know. There's a lot we can do with that alone.'

'I have no doubt you can.'

'Are you being impertinent?'

'Not at all, Ms. Pastore.'

'I can reward loyalty, and punish betrayal. Life isn't fair for many of us. Had this file reached me in time, I would have handled this case very differently. I'm asking you to hold onto the information you have. Mrs. Traynor's condition is deteriorating every day. She might not have the strength to attend the trial to its conclusion. For all I know, another delay might put off the proceedings. If that occurs, anything can happen.'

Right, Kathryn might die and let you and Foley off the hook.

'Do I have a promise on that, Jen?'

'I have to think carefully about this, Ms. Pastore. I'm asking *you* to settle generously with Kathryn. Allow her to end her life without the humiliation and stress of this case. I'll bet my life that the embezzlement charges are groundless. She was set up to get rid of her.'

'You're on dangerous ground without solid proof, Jen.'

'I am fully aware of that, Ms. Pastore.'

'Be sure that you are.' Nicolina shot her last words at Jen as she rose and stomped out of the café.

Jen made a beeline for the washroom, grabbing the briefcase as she ran. Lucky for her, she made it to the toilet before she suffered the fate of Monsieur Patate. Then again, she was older and had more schooling. Her cream blouse was soaked with perspiration and she was unsteady as she reached into the case for the recorder. She pressed rewind and play. Nothing! Not a goddamn sound. In her haste, she hadn't depressed both the play and record buttons! *Shit! Damn it to hell!*

CHAPTER 15

ON ALL FRONTS, Friday night was bad.

On Harvard, Sophia lay in bed holding both knees. Half of an Ativan was not bringing the coveted sleep that usually relieved her for a few hours from the misery of arthritis. Taking a whole tablet was out of the question because Sophia had a fear of all medication and addiction. Old people who took too many pills lost their balance, and worse. The clean-up after Monsieur's dumps and puddles had robbed her of the one pain-free hour she so needed during the day. She worried about the tragic death of the young man and she knew the repercussions of the accident did not bode well for the house. With so little money, how could she move again and start house hunting? Monsieur could sense Sophia's fretting, but he did not dare to climb up beside her, not with the mistakes he was still making. He lay shivering at the bottom of the bed on a blanket of old newspapers, just in case.

Nicolina sat slumped in the back seat of her cab, stunned by the turn of events. The meeting had resolved nothing. It mattered little that Sexton had sent the file; she was unflappable. What might she do with her information? Thinking about things did nothing to quell Nicolina's stress. Did Sexton not understand the ramifications to Foley, herself included, if the plaintiff got hold of her findings? Couldn't Sexton see that? The woman was supposed to know something about company politics. *People are expendable, for God's sake!* Nothing was going to change the fact that Traynor was dying.

What did the cause of her cancer matter when the fate of the entire company was in jeopardy?

Now that she fully realized what was at stake, Nicolina suddenly remembered her own blunder in the case. Everybody knew she had made a fool of herself. Had she taken the time and done her work with the signature, she would not have accused Traynor of forgery. Usually, Nicolina paid close attention to details; that was how she'd survived. Pressure had been brought to bear on this case. Lecours wanted it closed quickly. He'd set her up as well; she knew that now. At all costs, she had to win the case.

Adding to all her woes, Kathryn had decided to play hardball by not dying. Her death would make life so much easier for Nicolina and the company, but the woman was hanging on. Who knew for how long? Buying her house on the strength of this temporary position, with the goddamn loan still outstanding, had not been Nicolina's greatest move either. She stood to lose everything.

The accident on Sherbrooke Street was another source of terrible grief for Nicolina. The evidence from her impounded car itself could destroy her. Tomorrow, a witness might turn up who saw more of the crash than Nicolina even remembered. Would the police then come to her home, perhaps interview Sophia when she was at work? Nicolina leaned her cheek against the back window of the cab and saw the city passing her by. A single tear fell from her left eye and parked itself at the side of her nose. *What if the accident is reported in The Gazette and my name appears? Everybody will know about it. How did all this happen to me? God, please, just this once in my life, could you give me a pass? I don't deserve any of this; you know I don't.* Hot tears threatened to streak her mascara, but Nicolina hoarded them in the corners of her eyes, the same way she hoarded her gripes. What would the cabbie think! The dead kid made a short cameo appearance. *Why didn't you see my car that night? You should have taken better care of yourself. Now, look at what you've done to both of us!*

When the cab pulled up, Nicolina threw a bill on the front seat of the passenger side and stalked up the front steps. The house was as quiet as a tomb. The basement door was closed, but she opened it and called for Monsieur. He scuttled up the steps. 'You can't abandon me too, Monsieur.' Nicolina leaned over and picked up her pug. Such an unexpected show of tenderness released more than a few loving licks. 'Oh God, have you just peed all over my slacks? What's wrong with you?' she screamed as she threw Monsieur down.

Sophia hobbled up the stairs with a wet rag. 'I will clean up after him. Since Thursday night, Monsieur has suffered some anxiety. There is food for you in the kitchen that I hope you enjoy after you change from your slacks. I will care for Monsieur.'

'Get him out of here. Take him with you downstairs and he's to have no water after six from now on. What next?'

Sophia wiped up after Monsieur and, with all the practice, she had a routine down. The dog padded back to his newspaper pile in the basement.

Nicolina closed the door behind them, changed, eyed the food, opened the cabinet above the sink, grabbed the bottle and plunked herself at the table and poured herself three fingers of Scotch. 'What the hell,' she wailed, 'I need some support. I sure as hell am not getting it anywhere else.'

Up in the tony neighbourhood around The

Boulevard, things were just as dismal. Frank had begun bargaining. If Chris received justice, he would go to the police soon after the funeral. An arrest would not bring Chris back to the family, but it might help Maggie to know that the driver who left her son to die on the side of a street was held to account. With this decision came a certain order. Frank found the strength to shower, even eat. Maggie needed him now. He crept into their bedroom, but before he reached the bed, Maggie raised her hand, barring him from any contact. His wife had never shut him out before, but her grief was inviolate, a barbed wire fence around her broken heart. Frank stood alone on the sandy carpeting, needing the closeness of Maggie. Then he turned and left as quietly as he had entered.

Maggie felt Frank leave and shut her eyes tighter against the reality Frank brought closer every time he entered the room. She recalled hearing on one occasion that as much joy as children bring, they can double the sadness. *Only when they die*, Maggie wept into her sheet, *only when they die*. Replaying the wish, over and over, that Chris had jumped from the path of the car at the last second had drained the illusion of its pretended comfort. The skin of her heart had torn, and she felt the bludgeoning pain deep in her womb, where she had carried her son. *Chris was so strong; how could he die? How could he die?*

Caitlin lay dressed on her bed, her shoulders stiff and sore from the burden of her words, the last ones she'd spoken to Chris. She wanted to go to her father, but grief separated them now. How she longed to sit on Chris' bed, to pull him back. She wished now that she had asked Carmen to come to the house, for her friend would understand what she intended to do. It was after three in the morning when Caitlin dialed a familiar number. 'Did I wake you, Carm?'

'No. I couldn't sleep. Feeling a little left out too, I guess.'

'Could you come over around four-thirty?'

'I'm there. I'll park at your front door.'

'I'll meet you at the entrance of the driveway.' For the next hour or so, she lay on her bed with her arm across her eyes.

Hunter and Mike were talking quietly together. Neither one had gone to bed. 'Mike, I'm not giving up, but I didn't get much.'

'You just started looking into things. Give it some time.'

'The cop knew I was an American and I think he might have been stonewalling me. He even recognized the accent.'

'So what?'

'I'm a foreigner here is what. I thought of my father, but he can't pull strings here in Canada. Don't you feel like we're intruding? The family should be alone at a time like this. I mean, I saw what Frank did to the car. I don't think Chris would want us to stay here. A few days after the funeral, I'm going home.'

'You're tanking, is that it?'

'Mike, he was my friend too. Squatting. That's what we're doing.'

'I'm staying.'

'Jesus, stop thinking of yourself, just for once.'

'I can't leave, not now.'

CHAPTER 16

WHEN CARMEN PULLED up in her blue Mini that she'd be paying off for years, Caitlin was sitting on the curb. Without a word, she rose and climbed into the car. Her grief was a second skin, and Carmen choked back tears when she saw her friend. 'I'm so sorry,' she whispered, pulling her friend into her arms.

'Drive to Sherbrooke and Wood; I couldn't go alone. Let's not talk; what is there to say?'

The warm air was thick with sadness as they drove to the scene of the accident.

Once Carmen had parked on Sherbrooke Street near the remnants of the discarded debris, illuminated by her headlights, Caitlin surprised her by not leaving the car. Instead, her eyes bore down on the street and she did not blink back one tear, not for the silent half hour they sat together. When Caitlin finally spoke, her voice was thin and distant and bloodless. 'This time yesterday, Chris was already dead. Can you believe that? I asked to see you for a reason, Carmen. I've been thinking that there's something I've never told you. Even in your worst times, I've always admired your spunk and your impulsiveness, your fearlessness. In Miami, you dared, even when you were dead wrong and you knew it. That's where we're different. All my life, I've been the good girl, the person who thought things out. I'm like my father. We chew on a thought until there's nothing left but the splinters.'

'I always admired those qualities, Caitlin.'

'When Derek died, I fell apart and broke, but I did-n't do anything. Every day, I was scared of being without him and of dying.'

'What could you have done?'

'I have to tell you some things. I thought my father would be up half the night calling colleagues, but he's falling apart. He's even blaming himself. My mother hasn't gotten out of bed and hasn't spoken one word. I can't reach her. She reminds me of myself when Derek died. So, that leaves me.

While I was waiting for you, I was wondering where you got the balls to go for the money we found on the beach in Miami. When we opened the bags and saw all the large bills, I was scared shitless, but you needed cash and you went for it. Later, when I discovered you'd gone back for the bags we'd buried even though you were risking your life, I wanted to throttle you, but I envied you too. You could have died alone in some hole we'd dug together, and you still went back for the money. That's chutzpah.'

'I wasn't brave; I was stupid. I learned that lesson in Miami. Are you forgetting my foolhardiness scared a homeless man and he lost his life? I was seconds from losing mine if you hadn't pulled me from the lake. How can you not remember the truth about something that happened in February?'

'I remember the truth, but you're missing my point. You have to take risks in life.'

'Caitlin, why are we talking about these things now? Why aren't you crying about Chris? I know how close you two were.'

'My point is about Chris. I can't cry and I won't until his death means more than a human life splashed across a city street. I'm not taking his death lying down, beaten into shock by grief. I have to stand up for my brother. In Montreal, probably in most cities, no one does anything about auto fatalities. Do you recall the two women who were killed by a drunk driver in Pointe Claire about four years ago? He supposedly boasted he'd get off because he had the best lawyer in the city. I remember their deaths because I cycled out there last summer and happened down Cartier Avenue. There are still flowers left for the women on the side of the road. Remember that Olympic swimmer, Victor somebody, who was allegedly purposely run down in St. Anne de Bellevue?'

'Davis, Victor Davis.'

'I don't think there was any jail time in that case, or little if there was any. Chris will not be another statistic. It was a woman who struck Chris down and then left him on this street for two hours before calling the police. If she had called in time, Chris might be alive.'

'What are you going to do?'

'If this woman is not arrested, I'll bring her into court myself. I'll find out where she lives, where she works, what kind of a driver she is and if she drinks. I'll search for witnesses and learn what other people think of her. There won't be a part of her life I won't know about. I'll follow her home and back to work.'

'You've heard of restraining orders, right?'

'That's where you come in. We'll work as a team.'

'If nothing turns up, are you going to throw your life away? Do you think that's what Chris would want?'

'I won't back down or break, not this time.'

'Your book launch is coming up. Didn't you put three years of work into it? You'll have a full contract next year, something every professor covets. You'll chuck it all?'

'If I lose along the way, I'm ready. Are you with me?'

'You'll feel differently tomorrow. I'm listening to a stranger. Let the police do their work, Caitlin. At least give them a week.'

'And if nothing happens, are you with me?'

'You know I am.'

'Thanks, that's what I needed to hear. I won't forget this.' Caitlin's attention was pulled back on the street. 'Would you wait in the car for a few minutes? I have to see the place where Chris died.'

'I understand. Go.' Carmen watched as Caitlin walked haltingly along the sidewalk as though she were in a cemetery stepping on graves. When she stopped and knelt, Carmen looked away.

It was not terribly long before Caitlin was back in the car. 'Come to my place for a little while. I'll stay with Mom and Dad for a bit but I have to pick up clothes and other stuff. I'm glad you're with me, Carm. I couldn't do this without you.'

'You won't have to.'

As the C's left the car together, Carmen slowed her pace and walked behind her friend, trying to fathom Caitlin's aggressive fade to this angry grief. When she saw Saturday's *Gazette* already lying on the stoop, she ran on ahead and picked it up.

'Give me the paper, Carm. If there's something on the accident, I want to see it. Maybe the driver is mentioned. Don't think I'll ever go back to my old self. Back there on the street where Chris died, I promised him that woman would pay for what she did to him. There is no way,' Caitlin shouted, 'that Chris crossed on a red or jaywalked. So you know what that leaves, right?'

The sun was just a promising glimmer, rising in east Montreal at five thirty-six in the morning. Caitlin snapped on the hall lights, took the first section of the paper, threw the rest on the floor and sat on the carpeted stairs leading to the second floor. She went directly to page four, *FastTrack,* and found nothing about Chris listed with the two motorists killed on Friday night. Two columns to the right on the same page, she found a small piece. The by-line read: ***Witnesses sought to*** *fatal crash*: *Montreal police are seeking witnesses to a fatal crash that occurred early Friday morning at the corner of Sherbrooke Street and Wood Avenue. Christopher Donovan, 26, of Westmount, died after he was struck crossing Sherbrooke Street shortly after three a.m. Motorists and pedestrians who saw the accident are asked to call the Montreal police who are investigating the case at (514)555-8970.*

With her eyes, Caitlin traced each letter of Chris' name and caught her breath at the number twenty-six. *A few years past being a kid,* she whimpered, and began rocking back and forth with the section held against her heart. 'Chris can't stay like this, Carmen. A statistic, six lines for twenty-six years! He merits more than that. He had a life, and that woman took it and left him to die alone at the end of my street. You'll help me, right? Promise me you won't back out. I'm not losing it; I'm more focused than I've ever been in my life.'

'I'm with you, Caitlin. You're going to need me.'

'Oh my God, Dad can't read the paper alone. I've got to get back to him, to both of them. We haven't even thought of writing an obituary for Chris. My parents won't be up to the task, so I'll write it, but I want my father at least to see the obituary before I email it to *The Gazette*. I'd like to have a photo of Chris too. Seeing Derek's face softened the painful facts under it and brought a measure of humanity to his death.'

'I need the name of the driver!'

'I know exactly who can help us. Michel from Club One. He's home from Miami now. If anyone can help us find the name of the driver, he can! He's a retired police officer.'

'Get on it, Carm!'

CHAPTER 17

GNAWING ANXIETY WAS enough to block half a bottle
of Scotch from smoothly coiling its fingers around
Nicolina's nerve endings. She grabbed the banister and
lugged one foot after the other up the carpeted stairs.
She was always good in the dark and didn't bother groping for the light switches, preferring to feel her way
along the hall to her bedroom. Between that door and
the bed itself, all that remained to negotiate was the
throw rug beside the bed. Nicolina lunged for the bed,
not seeing in the darkness that the rug was a good two
feet from its usual position. As she lunged, the rug slid
across the floor like a piece of ice.

The slick ride came to an abrupt stop. Nicolina
crashed, ribs first on her left side, into the fruitwood
night table. The silver lamp, with its cylindrical white
shade, crashed into the back wall with the clock and a
handful of white shells that were gathered together
inside a fishnet. The table bounced into the wall with a
dull thud, shook a little and landed on its sturdy four
legs. Nicolina herself fell backwards, a foot or so, and
crumpled on the rug in a heap of pain. Unable to
breathe, she got on all fours, as Monsieur Patate might
do, managing a gasp, breathing thinly. For a good five
minutes, she dared not move and used her strength
wisely to lean towards her good side, turn her head
away from the cutting pain and concentrate on small
breaths. In this situation, the Scotch provided a buffer
between her and the knifing pain in her ribs.

For a full minute, she lowered her head, breathed in,
raised her head slowly and exhaled more deeply with
every manoeuvre. Righting her back, anchoring her fingers on the carpet, she stretched her back forward and

then her rib cage. She gave a very tiny snort. A smile broke through her teeth when she managed a timid, but deep breath. *I didn't break my ribs! If I had, I wouldn't be able to breathe in deeply. Thank you, God!*

With her right arm wrapped around her side, she reached for the night table and pulled herself to her feet. She bent over gingerly and lit the lamp. Stepping off the rug, using her foot, she kicked it against the far wall. When she was there, she flipped on the overhead light and pulled off her sweater and blouse. Unfastening her bra, she held her breath. Walking to the mirror on the dresser, she raised her left arm and inspected her rib cage. The bruise was already evident and it was a solid twelve inches that began under her armpit and snaked its way down her side. *At least, nothing is broken.* Even as she spoke those grateful words, her shoulders began to tighten as though they were caught in a vice. Rotating her head was difficult from the internal bruising. She'd brainstorm from bed.

Downstairs in the basement, although the door to the main floor was closed, both other residents shook when they heard the awful thud. To his credit, Monsieur was not a barker, not like some of the annoying little friends he had met in the park. He scampered up the basement stairs and pawed the door for a while. Sophia shook her head from side to side but did not let go of her sore knees. She had propped two pillows behind her because on nights like this she got no sleep at all. *Maybe tomorrow will be a better day for me.*

It might have been the clarity of pain that helped Nicolina come up with an idea she had never thought to use. Retreat seemed inevitable with the trial on Tuesday looming above her, even in her bedroom, with the ominous threat of Jen Sexton and the police report on her car. Retreat, not for Nicolina! Hand in her resignation and slither away with her pride between her legs? Never! Ambush; that was the ticket. Hit Lecours with the truth! My God, why had she never thought of using the truth before? Every other way now seemed lengthy and circuitous. The truth was the only way to go.

First though, before she walked the steady path of truth, she'd take a short detour. Moving her head as little as possible, she strained to see the time from the clock on the night table. It was well after four in the morning. She'd try to rest until dawn and then call one of the junior lawyers attending the trial, whose presence on Tuesday was necessary for the court proceedings. Contact the most obsequious of the lot. The company needs extra time, she would inform him. New evidence had come forward. Would he please call in ill on Monday and delay the case to the next date, which she knew was eleven days away. What Nicolina could do with eleven long days! This delay, however, must not be attributed to her. The fall in the bedroom must remain a secret. That information could not get into the hands of Remay. He might already be of a mind that alcohol played a part in the accident on Sherbrooke Street. Evidence of a new injury would only strengthen that thought.

Now, on to the winning card, the truth! With years of practice, Nicolina could push the Scotch to the side of her head and think coherently. Practising her speech aloud, Nicolina edited as she went along. Formality would serve her best. *Raymond, I've uncovered new information you should be made aware of immediately. Jen Sexton, the vice-president of human resources approached me with potentially explosive allegations. She sent me the file and I've met with her.*

My prime concern is the good name of Foley Pharmaceuticals. This new evidence is very damaging. Sexton is sug-

gesting that Traynor's cancer might have been caused by
exposure to the ingredients of the new drug, Comitrixin.
She's waiting for final confirmation of her findings. We have
no time to lose. I suggest we call Kathryn Traynor to a meet-
ing as soon as possible, without her lawyers present. In good
faith, in a show of compassion for Kathryn's grave illness, we
offer her a generous settlement. If we proceed quickly, Jen
Sexton might back off from her threat of disclosure. I hope
you feel this solution is in our best interests.

This wonderfully sculpted oration and the Scotch
parked at the side of her brain brought our weary, crafty
thinker into the land of heavy snoring. With the excep-
tion of a few choking coughs, Nicolina lay on her back
the rest of the night, sawing at the air. She did not hear
Sophia open the front door to pick up the paper and
leash Monsieur to the railing on the small grey and
white wood balcony. The coffee aroma woke the lady of
the house some time later. Sleep caked in small piles at
the side of her eyes, fur had grown on her tongue,
cracks had opened at the corners of her mouth and the
two bruised ribs had laced themselves around her chest
like a tight straightjacket.

Just before eight Saturday morning, Nicolina did
not at first recall her fall, but it had not forgotten her.
Usually, she wore flannel pyjamas, but on Scotch
nights, Nicolina wore clothes to bed, or nothing at all.
This morning, naked, chilled as soon as she kicked off
the sheet, she reached over for her pyjamas that lay on
the empty side. 'What the hell is this?' A little slower
this time and tentatively, she tried again to grab her top.
'God almighty, what happened?' Rolling like a sausage
to the side of the bed, easing herself off, she manoeu-
vred her body into a standing position. When she saw
the rug up against the wall, Nicolina remembered the
fall.

For most drunks, the night before is a blur, but Nicolina was far from your average drunk. The night of the accident, she kept her Mazda 3 on the road and did not crash into other cars parked on the street. Once she had dispatched Chris Donovan to the oblivion of the dead, Nicolina drove her car back home without further incident. Had she taken her car to the dealer to fix the light problem, Chris might have been home today planning with the gang to feast on a wood burning oven pizza at La Pizzaiolle on Hutchison Street in Outremont. Instead, he lay on a steel bed under bright lights suffering the cut of a scalpel.

With a full day ahead of her, Nicolina dressed as quickly as she could with the band of pain across her shoulders. While she could not recite that logical oration from a few hours ago, she could certainly tell you that even before coffee, she'd call the junior lawyer. She never forgot necessities. Sitting on the side of the bed, she reached for her black book, found the name and punched in a number. 'Richard. Glad I got you. We have a new strategy....'

'Ms. Pastore, the judge will not look favourably upon us if I miss a court date because of a cold. Mrs. Traynor has terminal cancer and she is attending.'

Dammit! 'Well, Richard, come up with some family crisis. We can't meet on Tuesday!'

'Actually, my mother is at St. Mary's Hospital.'

'Good, use that.' Nicolina hung up. Another admirable quality of our drunk was steely concentration. Because it was such a novel idea, the answer presented itself to Nicolina. *I've got it. The truth!* Had it not been for her ribs, she would have jumped for joy. But things being what they were, she inched down the stairs as flexible as an old wooden clothes pin.

What she desperately needed was hot coffee, lots of

hot coffee. She went into the den and rehearsed before making her call to Raymond Lecours. He would not be pleased with the intrusion, but it was necessary.

The kitchen was unusually quiet. Monsieur was nowhere to be seen. Sophia was sitting at the table with *The Gazette* opened in front of her. As Nicolina entered, Sophia turned and handed her the page that had drawn her attention. Nerves in Nicolina's back went into tiny spasms as she took the section and read the article Sophia had circled in red ink. 'It was an accident, a regrettable, tragic accident. Sophia, you know how badly I feel, don't you? Investigation? What are they talking about?'

Sophia had read the call for witnesses, but she knew enough to say nothing and she rose to fetch her land-lord coffee, for the sorry state of this woman was obvious. Yesterday's make-up was caked on the sides of her cheeks, her pupils were large and her face was pinched.

Everybody will find out about the accident! Nicolina broke then and began to cry real tears. For these awful heaving moments, wincing with pain, she forgot that the witness the police were seeking was right here in this house, standing at the kitchen sink pouring her coffee.

CHAPTER 18

AT TWENTY-EIGHT, Carmen was three years younger than Caitlin. The age difference and Caitlin's usual caution had safely piloted their friendship, past even the deadly chase Carmen had gotten them into in Miami. In the last few months, true to her word, she had put schemes aside and now worked two jobs to pay off credit cards and perhaps save for another vacation with her friend.

They were an odd couple to this extent. Carmen, the dark-eyed beauty of her large extended Italian family of aunts, uncles, cousins, nieces and nephews and copious food fests, had left the safety of that nest for the friendship of an Irish shamrock from Westmount with whom she shared very little. Yet, the impulse of one and the caution of the other worked and had forged the bond of sisterhood.

Early Saturday morning, the compass of that friendship shifted. Carmen would be the first to tell you that people could change. Hadn't she in these past few months? Yet, as she drove back to her apartment on Samson Boulevard in Laval, Caitlin's eyes, red from the tears she couldn't cry and the rage that she had begun to hoard, unsettled Carmen and deeply disturbed her. Would Caitlin ever mourn for Chris? Her grief was anger, Carmen knew, but she did not want that wrath to suffocate the natural sadness she should be feeling for her brother, for then she would suffer a deeper loss.

Carmen worried too about her new role as comforter. She never thought about her extra job that she might now lose by helping her friend. Once she was home, though it was still very early Saturday morning, Carmen did not go back to bed. She got out her Miami phone numbers and found Michel's. He was a decent

friend and she hoped he would understand her calling
him at this hour. He was groggy for a minute, but in the
next, alert like a cop. 'Present yourself at Station 12
with the time, date and location of the accident. Ask for
a copy of the accident report for insurance purposes.
Normally, the driver's name should be blacked out.
However, three times out of ten, it's not. Get back to
me if you don't get it.'

Carmen decided not to tell Caitlin until she had
results. She headed for Station 12 and walked out with
the report. Outside, she read it and blew an imaginary
kiss to Michel! At home, she began the grunt work of
going online, calling up the listings for Nicolina
Pastore. In only the second search, Nicolina's name,
jumped out at her. A search of Canada 411 pulled up the
home address on Harvard Avenue. Carmen did a
MapQuest and saw that the house was located in NDG.
It was a start.

When Caitlin walked through the front door carrying the paper no one had picked up, the house was as
quiet as a grave. The door to the study was closed, but
light from inside had spilled out onto the floor. Turning
the doorknob gently, not wanting to wake her father in
case he had fallen asleep, she peeped inside the wood-
panelled room. On the right wall, leather-bound law
books, with green and red coloured jackets, lined the
recessed custom-built shelves. They were Frank's pride.
The other wall held the books Frank had chosen to read
for education and pleasure. Among these books were
fourteen first editions. Surrounded by such wisdom,
Caitlin had loved this room best in the house since she
was four. The first story she remembered was one her

grandmother had read to Frank when he was a boy, *The Littlest Angel.* But that was a long time ago.

This morning, she found her father in his chair behind the desk. His head was thrown back against the top of his chair, so Caitlin could not discern if her father was sleeping. Tip-toeing across the floor, she could not help the groan of a single line of wood that always sent up a whining grievance when it was stepped upon.

Frank's head jerked up, and his eyes were weary from thought and tears. 'Caitlin, it's you.'

Caitlin went to her father and threw her arms around his shoulders.

'I guess I was hoping it was Mom. She hasn't come down, and I don't know how to help her, Cait.'

'Dad, you have to try to be strong yourself. Mom needs you to be. I don't think she has any comfort to give anyone.'

'Of course, you're right, but I've always depended on her.'

'Mom needs us now and we have to give her the time she needs.'

'All right. I've replayed my time with Chris. Mostly, I remember lecturing him, directing him, setting goals for him, but I don't remember a single time I told him I loved him. Not a single time.'

'You've told me many times, Dad. Maybe fathers don't tell their sons.'

'My father never told me, but I wanted to be different with my children. Like everything else, we only see our failures when the chance to correct them is lost to us. Have you been up to check on your mother?'

'I came to you first. After we talk, I'll go up to Mom, but I want you to shower and shave when I do go. *The Gazette* is here, and there is a short article on the accident. Mom can't read this, but you should. Are you listening, Dad?'

'I'll follow your lead, Cait.'

'I need you beside me, Dad, working with me. Hunter didn't get much from the investigator, Claude Remay, but he said he'd talk to you. Call him at nine. Though it's Saturday, you should be able to connect with him and find out where he is on the case.'

When Frank got up from his chair, he was stiff and sore and stale and stubbly. 'I'll go up and shower as soon as I read the article. You're a good girl, Cait, always.'

Caitlin kissed her father when she handed him the section. 'I'll make some toast and coffee for Mom. Then I want to meet you down here as soon as you're up to it and we can compose Chris' obituary.'

Frank's head fell back as though he'd just been punched in the face. 'I don't think I can help you with that, Cait. I just can't.' When Frank broke down again, Caitlin's heart tensed because she had never seen her father cry before.

'All right, I'll compose it and you can check it.'

'Thank you.' Caitlin waited for her father to read the article. He followed her up the stairs.

Hunter had finally fallen asleep, but Mike had crept to his door and saw Caitlin and her father from a distance as they climbed the stairs. Mike was beginning to feel the currency of guilt and he walked back and dropped onto his bed. He wished he could be as generous as Hunter and leave Caitlin to her family. Where women were concerned, he'd always skipped out at the first hint of pressure. Whatever it was he felt for Caitlin held him in this house and would not let him leave. Hunter had mentioned that calls to the house would begin today. That's how he could help; field the calls for the next couple of days.

Caitlin looked into her mother's room and found nothing had changed. It was funny, Caitlin thought, she had never felt she'd taken after her mother until now. Yet she understood her mother for she herself had lain in bed, without eating, when Derek died. Caitlin brought the untouched tray back to the kitchen, made toast and coffee and brought the tray back up to her mother. When she had put it on the night table, she whispered, 'I love you, Mom. I know nothing I say will help, but remember that I love you.' This time, Maggie did not freeze when Caitlin kissed her cheek, but she kept her eyes closed.

When she was back in her old room, she found paper and pens in the side drawer of the desk she had used. It seemed so long ago. Amazing, she thought, how these unimportant things had withstood the passage of the years, and Chris had not. Her room was long and rectangular; really it appeared to be two rooms in one. The walls were painted her favourite colour, pale blue bordered in white. The desk where she sat now was white as well. Caitlin could have gone down to the study and used the computer, but she wanted the human touch of paper and pen for the words that would bracket the life of her brother in a single page.

Early Friday morning a cold, heartless woman killed my brother, and I will hunt her down for that crime. That's what she wanted to write, but she began the last précis of Chris' life with the same words she had written for Derek. 'It is with the deepest sadness….' Once she had included the necessary facts, she saw there was so little room for Chris himself. Her parents would not want to expose Chris' memory to the emptiness of words. She bowed her head and held the pen so tightly in both

hands that it split in two. She and her father would have
to choose the funeral home, but Caitlin knew Chris
would be brought to the church her parents still attended, The Ascension of Our Lord on Kitchener Avenue.
At the end of the draft, she wrote, 'Chris, Dad and
Mom and I thank you for the life you brought into our
family. This is not good-bye; it is only farewell.'

Caitlin pushed her chair back from the desk and
stood quickly as though the sheet were on fire. Mike
had come into her room, and her nerves jumped when
she saw him.

'I won't bother you, Caitlin, but I'll stay close to the
phone downstairs and take the calls and make note of
the names, so you and your father can see to other
things. I guess that's it.'

Before he turned and left, Caitlin said forlornly, 'I
need a photo of Chris and I don't know how I'm going
to find the right one.' Until this moment, Caitlin had
stood firm on her anger. In front of Mike, she folded in
two.

'I took some digital photos at graduation. Does your
father have the software?'

'Yes.'

'Take me to his computer and I'll run them off. I
have a couple of Chris alone.'

Caitlin began to tremble. 'I want to see them; I'll
stay with you.'

'Good.'

Photography was Mike's hobby. Once he had insert-
ed the Kodak paper, he took little time printing the
photos he'd taken of their family.

Caitlin could not breathe as they came through on
the tray, for the photos stabbed like knives, each a
reminder of a lost happiness and a past that was so close
and gone forever. When the two of Chris were printed,

Caitlin turned her back on them for she could not bear
to see them.

Mike studied them and chose the one he thought she
would treasure. In the photo he had chosen, Chris had
blue sky behind him like a halo, the blue of it reflected
in the sure gaze of his eyes. His smile was strong and
proud and close. He put his hand on Caitlin's shoulder,
gave her the photo and left the study.

Caitlin walked to the window, breathed deeply and
held it up to the early morning light. 'Oh, Chris, forgive
me.'

Carmen called with the identity of the driver.

'Find out where she works, Carm.'

'Count on it.'

When she was alone, Caitlin went to the computer,
typed out the obit, attached the photo to an email,
found *The Gazette's* email address and sent it. There was
no reason for her father to see this now. He had his own
difficult calls to make. Her head was light, but her eyes
felt like rocks inside the tender skin of a balloon. When
she closed them, the room turned in a nauseous spin.
Without intending to retreat from the charge she had
taken on, her head fell back on the chair, and Caitlin
surrendered involuntarily to sleep.

CHAPTER 19

NICOLINA, LIKE FRANK, began to bargain as she paced back and forth in her den like a cornered fox. She knew enough not to delve into the contents of the file with Lecours. Nicolina felt bad, for herself, for Kathryn Traynor and, when she bent a little to her left side and the injured ribs fired back, she felt bad for the young man she had struck.

In a magnanimous thought, she wondered about Kathryn Traynor who knew tomorrow might not come for her. She climbed inside her ribs when she thought of the swift, sledgehammer blow of her car that had struck that young man. Nicolina was sorry for both of them. Stopping at a framed print of Mont Tremblant encased in cheap glass, she did not recognize the woman reflected back at her. Scurrying and scratching at life was not what she had wanted for herself.

At an early age, she knew she wasn't pretty. Her mother had told her often enough for her to wonder why. Develop a personality, her mother had said. What kind of personality could she build when kids teased her in elementary school; when boys shoved her into lockers in high school? Her grades were mediocre; gym was her best subject. Back then, girls hated gym, so that didn't work for her either. Her mother had looked at her medals in track and field and said, 'Those things are not important for a young girl.' Once when she was seventeen, something she'd said sparked the ire in her mother. Nicolina remembered her mother's parting salvo. 'It's no wonder you have no friends.'

The fact was that Nicolina worked harder than anyone she knew. What success she had, she'd bloody well earned. 'Nicolina will stay late, Nicolina can do this on the weekend, give that to Nicolina, 'Get the dope on so-and-so', 'Smell him out on that', and on and on. She'd been a gopher, a brown noser; name it, she'd done it. In this case, hadn't Lecours told her to move on things, show those entitled executives she meant business, and get it done? Hadn't he told her to fire Traynor on the best grounds she could find or invent? Now that this file had appeared, the speech she'd rehearsed for him did not sound as compelling as it had a few hours ago. The call would have to wait.

If I get through this and the accident report, I won't touch another drop of Scotch. To make her point, she checked first to see that Sophia was out back with Monsieur; then she went on a hunt through the entire house scooping up every bottle of Scotch, full or empty, or somewhere in-between. Nicolina never forgot the many hiding places. In record time, she'd piled twenty-nine bottles on the floor in the kitchen. In the basement, with sweat dripping from her chin, she cackled when she lifted a full bottle of Teachers Highland Cream Scotch from one of Sophia's empty suitcases. She'd stashed it there in case the old woman had embarked on a rescue mission. All the yellow Scotch went down the kitchen drain; the empties were bundled in orange garbage bags and taken out to the blue box in the garage.

Finally, there was nothing to put between her and the call. She stood alone in the den and dialed the private number of Raymond Lecours, the CEO, and followed a procedure he had taught her to use. 'Raymond, Nicolina. Forgive me for disturbing your Saturday morning. The information I have is urgent and could not wait.'

'Have you seen *The Gazette's* article on your little accident this morning?'

How could she have forgotten about the paper? She had not even begun and he was on the attack. Lately, it didn't matter what legitimate point she had to discuss with him, Lecours would derail her. 'Yes, I have, but that is not the reason I've called.'

'This publicity is not good for the company, not good at all.'

'I appreciate what you're saying, Raymond.' The friendship between them had evaporated. 'It's a tragedy; I haven't slept since it happened. I've called on a different matter. We have a problem with the case...'

Nicolina could hear Lecours' asthmatic wheeze. When it came down to it, powerful bosses weren't often brave or fair. As long as Lecours chewed on the cigar he never lit and gestured orders to the sky with his short arms, he looked the part. When trouble sat beside him, Lecours left the room.

'Are you quite finished, Ms. Pastore?'

'Yes, that's the problem we face. I've asked one of our representatives to ask for a delay and I should know by late Monday. If we get it, we have eleven days.'

'What's your read on Sexton?'

'I was hoping you might know. She's been the vice-president of human resources at Foley's for fifteen years.'

'Do you think I have the time to know these executives? I run the company!'

There was panic in his voice; she could hear it. 'I'll contact her again. What about my plan to call in Kathryn Traynor and lay out the truth?'

'Is this something you concocted in the wee hours? Where is your sense, woman? I am having grave reservations about your appointment. You and I both know the reason I gave you the job in the first place.'

'I've done my best, Raymond. How could I possibly have known about this?'

'*Merde!* Right now, I'm thinking about your forgery claim.'

'I accept full responsibility for that. I thought I'd found something and I was wrong. This file is a different matter.' *I'm not going down alone, you fucker!*

'This is your case, Ms. Pastore. You're our lawyer!'

'You wanted a rush job, Raymond.' Nicolina began to scratch back at her boss.

'You were adamant the controller had forged a document. Slam dunk, I thought.'

'I admit my error.'

'Does us no good now.'

'What about the file?'

She could hear Lecour's rasping breath.

'None of this can come out. Get something on Sexton. Meet with her again; shut her up. Work on the delay. Do not call my personal number again.' Lecours dropped his head into his hands. Foley was on the verge of an IPO (initial public offering of shares on the stock market). That meant money for him, the executives and the owners who'd now be able to sell their previously illiquid shares to any member of the public. The IPO was predicated on Comitrixin. It was the company's hot new drug. Evidence that the drug caused cancer would nix the IPO, might kill the company and expose it to a negligence lawsuit by Kathryn Traynor. As an ex-scientist, he felt he could fix the problem with Comitrixin. But Kathryn Traynor had to go away, or die.

Nicolina noted that Lecours never said 'good-bye', even in their good times. This morning he had brushed her off like dirt on his shoes. Nicolina thought about tossing the phone, but throttled it instead, walked around the room, trying to break up the fire in her ribs.

She dialed her gopher and reminded him to call the judge first thing Monday morning.

Her next job was Sexton. Rifling through her briefcase, she found her number and called. She had no choice.

'Hello,' Jen's cheery voice answered.

'Jen Sexton, please?'

With caller ID, Jen knew it was Nicolina and she sighed before she spoke again.

'Yes, Ms. Pastore?' Jen kept their exchange formal.

'Find a quiet place to talk.'

'All right,' she answered, handing Robert the receiver. Then she took the stairs two at a time.

'I can talk now, Ms. Pastore. Just wait a second.'

'Robert, hang up.' They both heard the click.

'Jen, I'm going to play my cards straight up. Send the evidence to the plaintiff and both of us go down. That's the word from Lecours. You have another fifteen or twenty years; think about that. Even if you decide to leave and seek employment elsewhere, the company will smear you. When the company turns its attention on you, how well do you think you'll come out? I'm trying to get us both out of this mess. If Kathryn Traynor is not physically able to continue with the case, hold onto to the evidence. I promise to do my best in her regard. What's the benefit of destroying us both?'

'Are you going to try to wait her out with delays?' Jen's words sounded braver than she felt. Much of what Pastore said was true.

'Actually, I felt you needed more time to decide what you were going to do, but that was before I spoke to Lecours. Now, I have to know your intent. Have you already sent the evidence?'

'No.'

'Get back to me in forty-eight hours, at home on my

private line. Take down my number. Call me at home
Monday night, Jen.'

CHAPTER 20

FOR THE NEXT few hours, everyone played a waiting game. Jen Sexton lay on her bed beside the phone, wishing she had never sent the file in the first place. Few believed that Kathryn was guilty of forgery or embezzlement, but no one was absolutely certain. Like most of the execs, Jen had a family to think about. Yet, could she abandon her dying friend?

Raymond Lecours lit his cigar, and ten minutes later his wife was running for his inhaler. His cheeks burst into a violent red, his nostrils flared and his forehead sweated patches of perspiration. Like poor Monsieur, his eyes bulged. In fact, his head looked liked a fat grenade ready to explode. He had two impending heart attacks crouching in his restricted arteries. Firstly, Lecours had hired the bitch and touted her abilities to his staff that had looked askance at his bold political muscle flexing. Now that was looking like a bad decision. Secondly, the underlying Comitrixin issue could spell bankruptcy. With these dumbbells on his thoughts, he now had to worry about the accident Pastore had caused and the implications of that as well.

Nicolina stood in the kitchen, wishing she'd saved one bottle. She could hear doors slamming on her. In the backyard, Sophia was talking to Monsieur. Her tone seemed serious. *What am I going to do about her? Push her down the basement stairs?* Nicolina laughed at that tempting thought. *In three days, I run a kid down and kill him. Then my tenant falls down my basement stairs and dies in a bloody heap. Too much CourtTV! Proximity of events would nail me. For God's sake, I'm not a killer, but Sophia's fall would save my ass. The problem is, with my sore ribs, we'd probably both go down the stairs.* She saw her hands tremble when another thought occurred. What if there was a witness on Sherbrooke Street? To relieve the stress of withdrawal, Nicolina bit the tips of her fingers. She walked to the bathroom, raised her blouse and saw the bruising was a bright red and purple. Back in the kitchen, she grabbed a water bottle from the fridge and, tight with pain, walked slowly out to the yard to join her tenant and her dog, both potential traitors.

Sophia sat on the edge of the picnic table that had taken a beating from the winter. She was not adding to Monsieur's anxiety attacks by confiding her dilemma with him. It was the second time today that Nicolina had read a situation incorrectly, first with Lecours, now with Sophia. She had been trying to explain to Monsieur that he could be calm again, she would protect him, but the accidents had to stop if he wished to stay in this house because his mistress was not in a forgiving mood. Monsieur had nodded wisely.

However, as Nicolina approached them, Monsieur backed up, away from her, till he felt the warmth of Sophia's legs. No one had ever hurt him like Nicolina had done. Sophia was a quiet woman whose cooking and kindness spoke loudly for her. She was a thinker, the sort of person who accomplished things without a fuss; Roberto had given her much to ponder over their years together. Yet, Sophia was alert and moved her black shoe away from Monsieur's yellow spray before it hit the one pair that gave her good support for her knees.

Be nice to her, Nicolina was telling herself. *Make her feel needed until I decide what to do about both of them.* 'Good morning, Sophia. Thank you so much for taking care of Monsieur. I am so upset about that young man who stepped in front of my car; I just can't take on Monsieur's problems right now. I haven't got the money

for obedience school as I've already said before, so I
really need your help with his problem. We don't want
to be forced to give up on Monsieur because he's one of
the family, like you. We both need you and trust you,
Sophia. I know you can work your wonders with him.'

Sophia knew a ruse when she heard one. Yet, it was
also good to be needed. Time to come to a decision
about the events of last Thursday. Courage of conviction was a behavioural code she respected and practised
when the situation called for it. Yet, worry and age were
the twin potholes that could bury a conscience, and
Sophia knew that too. Things seemed easier when she
was younger. One thing was certain – Sophia would not
abandon Monsieur Patate. He was her only friend.
Once she determined her course of action, she would
not delay. For now, on the chance that Nicolina was
telling the truth about the accident, she would be
patient and quiet.

The phones began ringing in the Donovan home
just after nine, giving credence to the adage that bad
news travels quickly. Mike fielded the calls on a single
ring. Hunter had joined him and took note of the
callers' names. From time to time, they stole glances at
the door, hoping for a member of the family to make an
appearance. Hunter's decision to leave after the funeral
seemed more and more the right move. The family
needed time alone to recover.

Hunter hardly recognized Mike. His face was pale,
sunken even. He dared not broach the subject of leaving with him a second time, for Mike's eyes were burning with passion and dread. He would not have figured
Mike with so stiff a conscience. There was a depth missing in Hunter, and Chris' death had fingered the shal-

lowness. After his initial outrage of early Friday morning after arguing with Investigator Remay, he'd slipped into acceptance. He envied Mike but he had no desire to hurt like him either.

Mike longed to go to Caitlin, but he stayed with the phones. He felt alone himself. He knew he was a thorn in Caitlin's side, but she'd left it there because something of Chris survived in the guilt they shared. If she asked him to leave, well, he could not allow himself to even ponder that possibility.

Carmen rang Caitlin's cell, and it played *'take me out to the ball game'* in the pocket of her slacks. In the nanosecond between unconsciousness and first thought, the happy tune blotted out the reason Caitlin was asleep in a chair. A simple thing like opening her eyes brought her brother's horrible death back. Her stomach was empty and her grief was ravenous. Reaching into her pocket, she grabbed her cell. 'Hello.'

'It's me.'

'I know.'

'I have addresses, home and work. Have you gotten any reports?'

'No. I can't believe I fell asleep. I mean, how could I? I don't know what's happened.' When she looked at her watch, she swore. 'How could I have left my father alone?'

'I'd like to come over.'

'I could use the support, Carm. I could really use the support. I don't know if I can get up from this chair.'

'Have you eaten anything?'

'No.'

'Go to your mother and father. I'll take care of the

food when I get there. Give me an hour for showering and stuff. In the meantime, get some coffee into you.'

'Yeah, all right.'

The study was closer, so that's where Caitlin went to find her father. He had showered and shaved and looked smaller but human in his blue slacks and his rolled up, white cotton Izod shirt, open at the neck. There was a boyish vulnerability Caitlin had never seen when he turned from the window as she entered the room. 'What did Remay have to tell you, Dad?'

'I didn't call, Cait. I was waiting for you.'

I was waiting for you. Caitlin knew instantly she could not scold her father; that would be cruel. Instead, she hugged him and she could feel him relax in her gentleness. 'I'll dial and stand beside you, Dad. Is that okay?'

'I don't know what I've done with his number.'

When she saw the yellow sheet on his desk, she said, 'It's here, Dad.' Clenching her fist, she dialed. 'Claude Remay, please. Yes, I know it's Saturday, but he's expecting our call. My name? Caitlin Donovan, but it's my father who wants to speak to him. Yes, I'll hold.' A good few minutes passed.

'Remay.'

Caitlin quickly passed the phone to her father. 'Frank Donovan here. Have you received either report, sir?'

'I have the medical report, Mr. Donovan. Since there were other auto fatalities this weekend, the report on the vehicle will only be ready some time this afternoon.'

The structured conversation brought Frank back into the kind of world he understood and strengthened him. 'Have any witnesses come forward?'

'Not yet, but sometimes, witnesses call a week later, so don't give up hope. Not everyone has time to read the paper Saturday morning. The article ran also in *La Presse* and *Le Journal de Montréal*.'

His strength dissolved with his next question. 'What have you learned about my son's death?'

'The tox screen was negative and, while alcohol was detected, the level was very low, below that required for impaired driving.'

'We already knew that, sir.' Before his next question, perspiration fell freely from Frank's temples, and his breathing was shallow. 'Would my son have survived his injuries if the driver had called for help immediately?' That was the question that had haunted the family, and some deeper part of Frank did not want to know.

'Mr. Donovan, death resulted from severe trauma to his right side. The immediate cause of death was acute subdural haematoma in the brain. There were other internal injuries as well.'

'You haven't answered my question.'

'According to the pathologist, a craniotomy, if carried out soon enough, forgive me, sir, but I'm reading notes here, might have allowed for a full recovery.'

'Oh my God, oh my God! My son did not have to die? My son is dead because the driver left the scene?'

'I'm relying on my notes. The pathologist did say that your son might have succumbed to his injuries even if help had come quickly. But, barring complications, there was a chance for recovery.'

'What you're saying is that this woman struck my son and took his life a second time by leaving the scene, leaving him to die by the side of the road.'

'There is a chance of that, yes.'

Caitlin picked up a beaten brass wastepaper basket and threw it hard against the closed door.

'Sir, are you all right?'

'Call me as soon as you get the report on the vehicle.' Frank had completely forgotten his own past action because Chris' death had taken up all the space in the room.

'Cait honey, I need you to be strong. Please stay strong; I couldn't see things through without your help.'

'Jesus Christ, Chris didn't have to die. Oh, Dad. We didn't have to lose him. That bitch murdered him, murdered him.'

Frank grabbed his daughter and didn't let her go until she stopped struggling against him.

'Dad, we can't let this woman get away with killing Chris.'

'I have friends who practise criminal law and I'll make those calls. They sometimes hire their own investigators and I'll look into that. Cait, your mother can't know about this, not now, not ever. She'd be lost to us then. This isn't a case of medical help arriving too late. It's a case of deliberate and monstrous negligence.'

CHAPTER 21

ONCE FRANK FELT Caitlin had regained a measure of control, he released her. She threw herself into her father's chair and rocked back and forth, cupping her mouth to keep from screaming.

'I have to call Remay again. I don't know how I could have forgotten to ask if we can take possession of Chris' body, now that we have the autopsy results.' Caitlin kept rocking as Frank dialed the investigator. This time, the wait was longer. Finally, he recognized the voice on the other end of the line. 'Frank Donovan again. Will the morgue release my son's body today?'

'Yes, sir. The funeral home you choose will transport the body. Was there anything else?'

'Are you maintaining the current position of not filing charges?'

'That opinion stands, but I'm waiting for the second report, Mr. Donovan. I haven't given up on witnesses, but I have to operate within the law. I cannot violate the rights of the driver in the process either.'

'That's rich,' Frank laughed. 'But my son's rights seem non-existent. One other thing! There's something puzzling me that you can help me through. My son was struck on the right side of his body. Correct?'

'Yes, sir.'

'Where was the damage to the vehicle?'

'On the far right passenger side.'

'That's the problem I've been trying to figure out because that's what I thought you told me. Tell me again what the driver remembers. I want to be clear in my mind.'

'She doesn't recall anything clearly. She reported to me that she felt someone had thrown an object at her vehicle, said a kid had done just that during the ice storm. Frightened, she left the scene of the accident. Two hours later, she said she worried she might have struck an animal. That's when she called us. In retrospect, she thinks your son walked out between cars into the path of hers, but she's not certain. She was adamant about the last point.'

'It's all very convenient, isn't it? The ice storm hit the city seven years ago. Surely she would have gotten over her fear of flying objects by now.'

'I have my doubts, Mr. Donovan, so I ran the complaints from back then and I did find hers. At least that story was true.'

'Fine, but I see another problem with her story. On what side of the street was my son struck?'

'The accident occurred on the north side of the street. Your son was struck by the vehicle and propelled into a parked car a few feet away.'

'Give me a second, please. This is very difficult for me.' Caitlin was very alert to this conversation and rose and stood beside her father, leaning into the receiver so she could hear.

'I know that he was crossing to the north side of the street. That means at some point he passed in front of the vehicle. It makes no sense to me that the damage occurred on the right side of it. How did he pass in front of the vehicle without being struck, or seen by the driver? Does it not make more sense that he would have been struck by the left side of the vehicle or the front of the vehicle?'

'I see your point.'

'Even if he was the fastest sprinter in Montreal and was struck at the last instant, that fact negates the driver's story that he stepped out between parked cars.'

'The driver doesn't recall seeing anything or anyone; she only remembers hearing the crash.'

'Selective memory protects her interests. My first point is that Chris did not walk into the path of her vehicle from between parked cars. He couldn't have because he was crossing to the north side of Sherbrooke Street. Chris incurred injuries on the right side of his body, so he was obviously going north. How could the driver not see a man over six feet walking in front of her vehicle? I wonder as well, how come my son did not see the vehicle either? You know now, as the family already knew, that my son was alert and sober. Do you believe this woman?'

'Sir, in my business, people lie convincingly to me every day. That's why I rely on facts, like the vehicle report and, even then, facts can be inconclusive.'

'That's not very reassuring, sir.'

'I appreciate that, Mr. Donovan. I will get back to you this afternoon with whatever facts I get from the report. I hope there was one witness out there that night who will contact us.'

'That's my desperate hope as well, sir.' Frank put down the receiver, shaking his head.

'Nothing, right Dad?'

'Nothing conclusive, Cait. I'm sorry. For now, let's get Chris out of that morgue. Where do you think your mother would want him?'

'Home.'

'You know that's not possible, Cait. For the burial, we have the family mausoleum in Côte des Neiges Cemetery. I thought it would be years before I had to think of opening it again, can't even believe I'm talking about these things.'

Caitlin saw the sad confusion in her father's demeanour, but her tears stayed in the back of her head.

'Chris hated being closed in, Dad. He never shut his door at night. I think he'd want to be buried naturally, in the ground.'

'How could I have forgotten that? We own three lots beside the mausoleum. We'll bury Chris on the grassy hill beside his grandparents.'

'Dad, I think we should call Collins and Clarke on Sherbrooke Street because Chris and I used to cycle to the park across the street when we were teenagers. I'd stay outside, guarding the bikes, and Chris'd buy fries and cokes from the Chalet B-B-Q. He'd go in by the back entrance because he got a charge out of watching the chefs, if you can call them chefs, cut up the hot chickens, faster that you could deal cards. We'd cross the street and sit on the grass eating junk, enjoying those greasy fries, imagining one day we'd cycle to Ottawa. All that seems like yesterday.'

Caitlin wanted to start tracking down the driver this very minute, but she would not leave her father. If Pastore were standing beside her, Caitlin would have killed the woman. 'I'll call the funeral home and send the information to *The Gazette*. Go and sit with Mom, so she knows she's not alone. Oh my God, we have to think about bringing clothes for Chris to the funeral home. This isn't happening! None of this is real.'

'I keep thinking Maggie will walk into the study and take charge. She'd know exactly what to do, where to go.'

'Mom can't be here to help us, Dad.'

'I know that, Cait. Funny you know, sometimes over the years, I envied her affection for Chris; I wanted her all to myself. It's a good thing she loved him with all her heart. He was hers for only twenty-six summers. Those memories will have to last for the rest of her life.'

'Chris didn't have to die, Dad.'

'That's what's eating my heart. Swear to me that you'll never tell your mother about this. We'd lose her for sure.'

'You can trust me, Dad. Neither one of us can hurt Mom, any more that she's hurting right now. It's awfully quiet without her voice in the house.'

'Come and get me when Remay calls.'

'I will. Try to get some rest.'

Caitlin wondered as she watched her father climb the stairs, how someone could age so much in a couple of days. Her father had grabbed the banister as he mounted the stairs because he needed the support; that was something he'd never done before. When she made the calls, Caitlin closed her heart and followed the common, bruising road in the ritual of burial. These preparations numbed her guilt, but did not touch a hatred that grew each time she punched in another number.

As she approached the kitchen, she was surprised to smell something other than coffee and toast. Mike was working at a furious pace. On the table was a full plate of egg salad sandwiches, two loaves, at least.

'I hope you don't mind,' he said, his eyes swollen and tired. My grandmother believed egg salad sandwiches could cure a cold, put hair on your chest and lighten a spirit. She used to say, "No one can turn his back on egg salad." Cholesterol wasn't a big thing in her day. I didn't want to leave the house. Hunter's taking the calls, and I felt we all needed more than toast.'

Caitlin was about to say she wasn't hungry, but she'd reached for a half sandwich before she had a chance to respond. A full sandwich had been devoured and, she was reaching for a second one, before she was able to say anything. Because she'd gulped the food, Caitlin sat quiet, for a minute, surprised. 'I guess I was hungry; I wasn't till I saw the food.'

Mike didn't smile, but he felt needed and good for Caitlin. Hunter produced sheets of names. 'I didn't tell any of these people we'd call back. There are too many of them, but I did say I'd extend their sympathies to the family.'

'I've sent Chris' obituary to *The Gazette;* our friends can get the necessary information from the paper. If other calls come in, and I'm not in the room, you can say the family will receive condolences on Monday and Tuesday at Collins and Clarke on Sherbrooke Street. We will bury Chris in the Côte des Neiges Cemetery, Wednesday morning at eleven. Here, Hunter, let me write that down for you.' Her hand shook as she wrote out the information.

Mike did not approach Caitlin, but stayed working at an island in the centre of the kitchen. 'Can we do something with the car to help your father out?'

'What's wrong with the car?'

'When your father heard the news, he took a baseball bat and smashed it to bits. I thought you wouldn't want your mother to see it.'

Caitlin ran out to the garage. When she saw what was left of the car, Caitlin thought of Chris' fatal injuries. She slammed her fist onto the mangled hood until Mike, who had run after her, grabbed her arm.

'Stop, stop. You've cut your hand, Caitlin.'

'My mother can't see the car like this. Get it out of here Mike.'

CHAPTER 22

THE WAITING GAME continued well into Saturday, each of them caught in a blizzard of nerves. On the West Island, Jen Sexton had confided in Robert. At the moment, they were arguing ethics. 'Jen, you're a moral person, but our family needs you working. Losing your job because you want Kathryn Traynor to know the truth before she dies is admirable, but where does that leave us? I don't remember you mentioning her very often; she's not even a good friend. We're your family. You have obligations, three children, one of them only three years old. Aren't we more important to you than a colleague?'

Jen didn't blink or lose eye contact with Robert. Like Frank Donovan, she was learning that the past has a long arm. For Jen, it was nine years ago. She and Kathryn had attended a three-day conference and had driven to Toronto together. On the second night, they sat talking in the car, and neither could explain what happened next. Smell and the need to touch it drew them together. Without a word, Jen leaned forward and brushed Kathryn's cheek with her lips. Kathryn trembled when the moan she heard was her own. She turned and the women kissed, tentatively at first, discovering, lingering for a few seconds with the newness. Jen remembered that Kathryn smelled like peppermint. Then the kiss was deep and searching; then insistent and wet. 'I can't do this, Jen. Tim is the only man I've ever been with and I've wondered sometimes what I'd missed. I better go before I can't live with myself.'

That's what Kathryn had said and meant, but on the last night, she had gone to Jen's room to explain, or so she thought. Yet, when she sat beside her on the couch,

Kathryn couldn't speak. Her shoulders tingled; her breasts were hot. Jen reached for Kathryn's hand, and Kathryn felt that all of her was under its warmth. She heard her breath and Kathryn's. For an instant they were connected only by the grasp of hands. In the next, they melted into one another, into the softness of breasts and the demands of release. The safety and the abandon and the fluid ease surprised them both. Kathryn dressed in the darkness without a word and left quietly. Jen followed her to the door and watched Kathryn run down the hall back to her room. Jen wanted to go after her, but she was afraid. She felt unsteady. When she wiped away the tears, her hand smelled of peppermint.

'I work with her, Robert, that's all. What you're saying makes sense, and you're right. Yet, I keep thinking, if I were dying from cancer caused from exposure to the company's drug, wouldn't you hope the one person who knew the truth would reveal it?'

'Of course, I'd want the truth to clear your name. If we had no kids, I'd say support her, we'd get along, but we're not in that position, are we? We're not in our twenties either. Can you sacrifice your family for a colleague? How ethical is that?'

'I have to figure things out.'

'I can't believe what you're saying. Don't betray us, Jen.'

'I hear you.'

Robert watched Jen walk from the room. His wife's wild, wacky independent spirit, her need to still go on every ride at La Ronde, the city's amusement park, had left him sometimes unsteady in their marriage. Marrying a beautiful woman left a man doubtful.

Kathryn Traynor was sadly reduced from the woman grown men followed with their approving nods as she walked down company corridors. Most of the time, she lay at home on the couch in the den, rose with help and walked with crutches. Clothes, watches and jewellery were all too heavy for her to wear, so she had borrowed Tim's flannel pyjamas. That didn't work with the weight she'd lost after the radiation and chemo. When the Victorian Order of Nurses relieved Tim during the week, he'd gone shopping at the first opportunity and found pyjamas that fit. In an odd way, she was glad she and Tim had chosen not to have children. Kathryn could not imagine putting them through her cancer and her case. Tim wanted Kathryn to forget about the court case. 'It doesn't matter, now, honey.' Kathryn had pushed herself up from the couch. 'It matters more than ever, Tim.' Saturday afternoon, he got the call about the delay. 'They're hoping I die before we go back to court. Well, I hope to surprise them all.'

Nicolina discovered one bright spot in her life. The case and the accident had so preoccupied her thoughts that she'd forgotten to check her insurance policy. She discovered she was entitled to a rental and it would be ready for her before five. Until then, she began to clean the upstairs, working on her hands and knees, first in the bathroom, then in the hallway and finally in both bedrooms. Lecours, Traynor, Sexton and Sophia, she thought of all her enemies as she scrubbed the bathroom tiles with Lysol, wishing with all her might she could scrape them off her back with something stronger than disinfectant. If Sexton backed off, she had a chance, but she loathed waiting and depending on anyone else. What the hell was wrong with her? She was supposed to be politically astute. Lecours would wait in the shadows while the trial proceeded and make his move if she lost the case. She was thirsty as she cleaned and Nicolina began to scratch her arms and legs, drawing red lines everywhere she scratched. As long as she played the Monsieur card with Sophia, the old woman posed no immediate problem, or so she felt. Remay had appeared to buy her story, but it was hard to tell because he showed no facial expression that she'd been able to read. Nicolina willed the phone not to ring. When it did, she winced, but this time the caller was not Remay.

While her landlord cleaned the upstairs, Sophia worked on the kitchen. Monsieur Patate stood on the back balcony, sniffing at the door. Sophia had made little diapers from the worn T-shirt drawer that Nicolina used for polishing and cleaning, but there were only three of them, and they were for tonight. Sophia had cut the article from the paper and had hidden it behind the toaster. As she was putting the lunch dishes back into the cupboard, she noticed that the bottle of Scotch, hidden behind a stack of dishes, was gone. She quickly checked the laundry room, another familiar hideout, with the same result. No bottle was found at the bottom of the hamper in the hall bathroom either. *Strange*, she thought. Laying down her mop, she joined Monsieur on the balcony. Together, they sat side-by-side like the odd couple they were, conversing. Sophia was whispering; Monsieur nodded or threatened a bark. 'Yes, Monsieur, how good it is to find the liquor gone, but why has Nicolina done this? Is she afraid the police will come to her house?'

Claude Remay sat at his desk, clearly disappointed. 'Is there nothing more definitive we can do on this investigation? How will Monday be any better? Lussier is the best analyst? All right then, I'll call the family. Something stinks on this case. Why would an adult run in front of a car like that? I know that's my job, Jacques, and, you can be sure *mon ami*, I will do my best to find the answer.' If he were a politician, Remay would work 24/7 trying to add sharp teeth to the penalties in the law where auto fatalities were concerned. If he got any kind of handle on this case, he'd go after the driver. He opened his desk drawer, reached far in the back of it, till he felt what he was looking for, an old, stale pack of cigarettes. He lit a torch, choked on the first drag because he'd quit four months ago, and cursed. *Fuck the rules!*

As Caitlin took in the damage to the car, she thought of her brother. So little of his homecoming survived that night. The car would be towed, and the space left empty, as though he'd never come home from Harvard. He was so proud of this gift, so cautious not to drive that night. Mike stood behind Caitlin, and when she turned, he reached for her, but she ran past him without seeing him. *I wish Carmen would get here. I want to start planning.* Caitlin ran out to the front of the house and waited for her friend to arrive.

Carmen was late through no fault of her own. Construction had begun, and the city's rite of summer was worse than snow for motorists. Highway 13, both north and south, had been reduced to single lanes. Forty minutes after leaving Laval, she was bottlenecked in traffic and angry horns. To her left, she could see the signs for Samson Boulevard. She was exactly five minutes from her point of departure. *Thank God, work on the Decarie Expressway is finally completed.* Montreal road workers were legendary for beginning construction of main thoroughfares that could last for six or seven tortured summers. Her plan had been to buy pizzas for the family, but, because she was running late, ordering in was a better option. When she pulled into the driveway, one hour and forty-minutes later, she almost missed seeing Caitlin sitting alone on the bottom step. She walked over and sat beside her friend and hugged her. 'I'm glad I'm here.'

At five to five, Claude Remay made an official call.

CHAPTER 23

'FRANK DONOVAN, PLEASE.'

Hunter took the call. 'At the moment the family is indisposed. I will gladly take your name and message and pass both on to them.'

'This is Claude Remay, of the Montreal Police Department.'

'This is Hunter Townsend, sir. We met yesterday. I know Mr. Donovan is waiting for your call. Just a moment, please.' Hunter jumped up from the table. 'Mike, do you know where Mr. Donovan is?'

'Upstairs with Chris' mother. Just a sec, I'll get Caitlin. She's outside with her friend.' Mike made a mad dash out the front door. 'Caitlin, Remay's on the phone.'

Caitlin ran past Mike, back into the house and grabbed the receiver. 'Sir, this is Caitlin Donovan. Chris was my brother. My father is anxious for your call. He's finally resting, but I'll go up and get him for you.'

'Ms. Donovan, I don't have the complete results; I'll have them only on Monday. What I have now, I can give to you and you can relay the information to your father.'

Caitlin closed her eyes tightly.

'All significant parts of the vehicle have been investigated: weight, height, tires and their tracks or lack of, indents, windshield, and the temperature that evening. Unfortunately, there were no tire tracks which are good indicators of speed.'

'That means that the driver struck my brother and didn't even try to apply the brakes.' Caitlin was spitting her words out in disgust.

'It also indicates the driver never saw your brother. Our greatest problem is the front bumper and the point of impact. The right front struck your brother. That part of the bumper, on either side, has more reinforcement than any other part. Had Mr. Donovan been struck by the centre of the bumper, we would have conclusive evidence of speed.'

'And now, you don't?'

'Please, allow me to go on.' Remay wished now that he had asked this young woman to get her father. 'We know that the car was travelling in excess of thirty kilometres, but how much faster, we have been unable to ascertain.'

'This means you have nothing, right? This woman will walk away from killing my brother. Is that what you are trying to tell me? All the forensic information you have now amounts to a walk!'

'What I began to tell you, Ms. Donovan, is that we have inconclusive evidence from the first investigation, but, on Monday, the head of the department will do a second testing. We can hope he might find something the techs might have missed.'

'Are you insinuating the techs that did this work aren't up to scratch?'

'I understand you're very upset...'

'You're damn right about that. You're telling us you don't have much.'

'The department head might find something on Monday. I have also decided to approach radio and television stations in a call for witnesses. The media have been of great assistance in difficult cases. There is still hope, Ms. Donovan.'

'Not for my brother.'

'Tell you father I will get back to him on Monday.'

'I will, sir.' Caitlin slammed the receiver back on the

phone. 'Chris didn't get a single break, not one! We have to hope for witnesses now. I guess it's something like waiting for a kidney. If Dad is asleep, there is no point waking him for this.'

Mike, Carmen and Hunter looked on helplessly as Caitlin slumped into a chair. 'Not a single, fucking break...'

Hunter took another call. 'I'm sorry, Caitlin, but I think you should take this. It's the funeral home.'

'Yes?'

'I'm calling from Collins, Clarke, MacGillvray and White Funeral Home. We wanted the family to know we will have the remains of Mr. Christopher Donovan in the home this evening.'

'I'm Caitlin Donovan and I called you.'

In a blur of sympathetic words that meant nothing to Caitlin, she listened for the barbs that tore her heart. 'Yes, I have everything. We will receive friends Monday and Tuesday in the evenings, from seven to ten, followed by a celebration of mass at The Ascension of Our Lord Church on... Just a minute, I have the address somewhere.'

'We know the church. It's on Kitchener Avenue in Westmount.'

'That's it.'

With the next point, all colour drained from Caitlin's face.

'We will need clothes for your brother and at least one member of the family to select the casket. Have the notices been sent to the paper? We can do that work for you as well.'

'I've notified *The Gazette*, but thank you for the offer.' Caitlin had a hard time believing she was the person on her end of the line calmly arranging the last rites for Chris. For a minute before she hung up, she hated

Derek for dying, for stealing a layer of grief she felt she was missing for her own brother. She left her friends and headed for her father's study. Was it possible, she wondered, that, like the brimming emotions of first love that could never be repeated, the absolute pain of first grief so emptied a heart that it never felt so deeply again? It would not allow itself to be hurt so grievously a second time.

For Derek, her grief had been pure and generous. For Chris, Caitlin was unable to see that her guilt and the retribution she planned for the driver blocked the tears she should have wept. In another sense, death was no longer a surprise for Caitlin. After Derek died, at twenty-eight, she knew that anything could break. It was only since her return from Miami that she had begun not to be so afraid. Since early Friday morning, Caitlin knew no one she loved would ever be safe again and she would be afraid forever. She laid her head on her father's beautiful wood table and thought. *This is the first time Chris has ever been alone. When he went away to school, he lived with friends. There were always people around him. He must be so lonely and scared.*

Caitlin didn't even sense she had fallen asleep, did not know her tears fell and smudged the desk, because her attention was somewhere else. Chris stood on the stage and received his diploma and turned her way and smiled. Over the heads of parents, their eyes locked. *Well, I did it, Sis. I'm all grown up. Dad won't have to worry about me anymore. Move over now; I'm coming home! I'll walk back to the apartment, you guys meet me there.* Caitlin pushed her way towards the stage to get to her brother. Chris was walking off to the far corner, away from her. *Don't walk home, Chris. Come with us!* When Caitlin finally reached the foot of the stage, Chris turned to her a second and looked into her eyes. Then he walked away as though he knew. When Caitlin woke, the dream stayed with her.

Mike and Hunter did not dare follow Caitlin, but Carmen did. From the door of the study, she approached quietly, but spoke when she saw that Caitlin's eyes were open. 'Why don't you go up and check on your parents? If they're resting, take a break yourself. We'll take care of things down here.'

'I had an awful dream.'

'That's normal right now.'

'It was so real, Carm.'

'But it wasn't.'

'Chris just walked away from me. I told him not to walk home, but he did anyway.'

'Caitlin, Chris didn't do any of that. It's a dream; it's your dream.'

'I know, but it's the feeling behind it that hurts so much. Nothing will happen with the police; I feel it. Don't think for a minute that I'm backing away from Pastore.' Caitlin spoke these last words with the numbing authority of one who will not waffle on the issue.

'I told you I'm with you, all the way. You saved my life in Miami. I owe you.'

'You don't, but I'm glad you're with me.'

CHAPTER 24

THE STORY WAS quite different in the brick house with the wood balcony on Harvard Avenue. Most significant, was the progress of Monsieur Patate. With Nicolina sequestering herself on the second floor out of Monsieur's path, he had just passed four hours without incident. He sniffed all the corners that had been off limits during his days of exile and he scampered around Sophia's legs as she cooked, his tail curled tight with glee.

It was dinnertime, and Sophia was busy preparing her Italian sausages. The radio was turned low, but Sophia had good ears and was enjoying *Cinq à Six* on CBC 88.5. First, she fried the peppers and onions in a little oil, took them off the burner and set them aside. Then she fried the fresh, sizzling sausages that spit back at her as she rolled them across the pan. Once they were cooked, she picked each one up with a tong and laid it inside a fresh bun. On top of the meat, Sophia dropped mozzarella cheese that melted on the hot sausage. She spooned the peppers and onions on top of the cheese. On the table, which she had set, sat a plate of sliced, oiled tomatoes and diced garlic. But the dinner was still cooking when the news came on the air. Just before the traffic and weather, Sophia turned off the radio and called Nicolina down to dinner. There was a particular announcement from the Montreal Police Department that Sophia had just missed hearing, but it would repeat, of course, and Sophia wasn't going anywhere.

In between the vacuuming, while Nicolina sweated from every pore in her body, a new idea popped into her head. Out came the black book. When you were on your own, you had to depend on yourself, and that's exactly what she did. There was one employee in purchasing who seemed to enjoy ratting on his colleagues. He actually thought he might win her favour, and she had enjoyed toying with him. All the others confided in her because they were afraid for their jobs. Saturday or not, she dialed his number. 'Is Stanley home?'

'Stan, phone,' shrieked a voice on the other end of the line. No wonder this man wasn't happy.

'Hello.'

'It's Nicolina Pastore, Stanley. I must apologize for calling you on a Saturday night. What you have confided in me during our previous meetings has been most helpful. I know the questioning of these past months has been difficult. Believe me; this process has been hard for me as well, but the company does want the right people in the best posts for next year. The information you volunteer will be strictly guarded, I can assure you. However, Raymond Lecours and I have a question about Jen Sexton because there have been so many rumours about her. A scandal is the last thing Foley Pharmaceuticals needs right now. Do you actually know the name of anyone with whom she's had an extramarital affair? That behaviour is not the purview of the firm. We have no interest in the shenanigans of our employees. However, we want our leaders to be of the highest moral calibre. It wouldn't be fair to Sexton if we relied on unfounded rumours. That's why I've come to you.'

Stanley did not want to lose his shot at impressing Raymond Lecours or Pastore. This confidence might mean a promotion for him. 'I don't know fact from fiction where Sexton is involved because there has been so much of both. I can only think of one, but I hesitate to mention her name.'

'I understand, but you have to realize our quandary. It's not easy when we don't know the players.'

Stanley did not feel very good, even tried to convince himself his intentions were honest. He wanted his wife Eileen to be proud of him, but he could not pass up this opportunity and, in fact, he did not owe Jen Sexton anything. 'Well, if you say this information will be kept private...'

'You have my word.'

'Well,' Stanley hesitated again. His wife Eileen had come into the room, motioning for him to hang up and get down to dinner. He held up his *gimme me a minute* finger and walked over and shut the door. 'Well, we all know she and Kathryn Traynor had a thing. For years, they were inseparable. No one has first-hand information, naturally, but we knew what was going on.'

Nicolina licked her lips. 'Kathryn Traynor and Jen Sexton?'

'Yes.'

'Thank you for your trust and confidence, Stanley. Go and enjoy the evening; I'll get back to work.'

Ha! This is better than a good Scotch! These idiots despise me, but they should be much more wary of each other.

Nicolina noticed she had stopped scratching her arms. *I'm going to get through this; I just have to keep plugging.* She wanted to call Lecours. Who cared that it was after six on Saturday? *No, I've made mistakes by jumping at things too quickly. What the hell did Raymond say? Oh yes, the company would be held liable because it had deep pockets. I'm sure Sexton's husband would love to know about the other woman in his wife's life!'*

Nicolina had not felt good about anything in a long while. Before she went down to dinner, she jumped for joy, not dangerously high, but higher than Monsieur could jump. She hurried down. 'Doesn't that smell good! How do you do it, Sophia? Hello, Monsieur,' she said, bending to cuddle her pug.

'Nicolina, do you mind if I keep the radio on? It's company.'

'How about some quiet music instead? I'm famished. Everything looks so good.'

At dinner, Nicolina devoured the sausage subs, the same way she intended to devour Jen Sexton. Once CBC Radio was turned off for the night, Nicolina herself did not realize she had dodged another bullet, but the magazine was far from empty.

CHAPTER 25

LONG AFTER CARMEN had gone home, and the others were up in their rooms, Caitlin could not allow herself to sleep. It was strange to be back in her old room, strange because it no longer felt safe. Derek's death had wounded the core of her, but losing Chris broke the heart of the family and threatened them all. The illuminated numbers on the vanity clock flipped minute after minute, measuring time past. Much like her mother, Caitlin lay on her side and watched the numbers. At three, she lay stiff, with her fists clenched, as the minutes flipped by, indifferent to the distance they were putting between voice and memory. At three-fifteen, she whispered into the darkened room, *Chris died seventy-two hours ago.*

After seven on Sunday morning, Hunter and Mike were back in the kitchen, but didn't intend to stay long to give the family some time together. Caitlin showered very early and planned to go to the funeral home with her father. Frank crawled quietly from the bed he shared with Maggie and showered in another guest room. Caitlin waited for him in the hall. 'Dad,' she whispered into the room.

'Coming, Cait.' He'd forgotten to bring fresh clothes with him, so he walked out in his blue shirt and boxers.

With the morning light behind him, Caitlin thought, *He looks so much like Chris.* She changed her mind when he drew closer. The circles under his eyes were dark and his cheeks were colourless and gaunt.

'Did Remay call?'

'Yes, but we'll have the full report only Monday.' They walked back towards the master bedroom. 'Dad, the funeral home called. I guess you know we have to bring clothes for Chris today and choose his casket. Should we tell Mom? I don't feel right about going into Chris' room.'

'I don't want anyone in Chris' room.'

Frank and Caitlin shrank in surprise to see Maggie standing in the doorway. Her hair was matted to one side; her eyes were tired but fierce. 'I heard you. I'll choose my son's clothes. I brought Chris into this world and I want to be there to take care of him now that he's leaving it.'

'Maggie, are you sure you're up to this?'

'No, I'm not, but I won't abandon my son either.'

'Mom, would you like me to help you with Chris' clothes? You were such a support to me when Derek died.'

'I need to be alone in his room,' Maggie said softly. As she pulled her hair back, trying to pin it behind her ears, she felt its flatness and tangles on the one side. 'I'm a mess. Chris would never recognize me. I'm going to freshen up first.'

When Maggie turned back to the master bedroom, Caitlin grabbed her father's arm, and whispered, but not softly enough, 'Go with her. She's not steady, Dad. Mom might fall. She hasn't eaten in two days.'

'Leave me alone, both of you! I need time to think and I can't do that with you two hovering behind me.'

'We'll wait out in the hall, Maggie. Be careful, honey.'

In hushed tones, Caitlin told her father about Remay's call.

'It doesn't really surprise me that they have nothing. The minute the driver left the scene, she took our strongest evidence with her, principally, the sobriety test. She's a lawyer; she knew exactly what to do. I'll make those calls, but cases involving traffic fatalities rarely see the inside of a court. Unless this investigator finds something substantial on Monday, or a witness appears, we'll have little with which to prosecute.'

'Why can't they charge her with leaving the scene? Is Pastore bluffing Remay?'

'What could the police do? She presented herself at the station with her defence story for leaving the scene of the accident.' When Frank talked about Chris' case and liability, his own guilt crawled back onto his shoulders. Even he was surprised by its weight.

'I wish Chris had never come to my place. I should have walked back with him to Sherbrooke Street. Maybe I would have spotted the car. I still don't understand why he didn't see it. Dad, you know he never would have crossed before looking in both directions. If only…'

'I have my own guilt, Caitlin.' The words slipped out before Frank heard them.

'What are you talking about, Dad? You didn't tell Chris to walk home. What kind of guilt can you possibly be feeling?'

Had they had more time together, Frank might have told Caitlin what he was hiding, but Maggie was back, faster then either of them expected. Their conversation ended.

Maggie smelled like flowers again when she stopped beside them, but her face was haggard and her eyes, dark craters. Without a word, she walked past them, but she stopped at the door to Chris' room and looked back their way. She rubbed her arms, steadying herself before she opened his door, and disappeared into the room.

Caitlin heard her moan. 'Dad, we have to stay here.

I've never seen Mom like this. She can cry over a commercial, but she hasn't shed a tear for Chris, not one.'

'Mom's in shock, Cait, and she's going through the motions. But, she'll break in two when Chris' death reaches her heart. Right now he's only in her head, so it's still unreal for her. When she needs me, I'll take care of her.'

Once Maggie was inside the room, she froze on the blue carpet as soon as she closed the door behind her. She wasn't certain she could move, until she saw the luggage. *Chris was such a neat freak; he wouldn't want his bags out on the floor like this.* Maggie walked towards them mechanically, opened each of the Ralph Lauren bags she'd bought him for Harvard, emptied the clothes and quietly opened drawers and closets. Laying the garments on the bed first, she ran her hands over the slacks and shirts, and crushed them when she pulled them tightly to her heart. Reluctantly, she followed Chris' lead and stacked the socks and shirts the way he would have done himself. When she came upon the suit she and Frank had bought him for graduation, Maggie buried her face in it and breathed as deeply as she could. In the threads, Maggie smelled Chris, the soap he used and the Armani aftershave that was his favourite. *Chris looked so handsome in this, so handsome. Now, where's the shirt that goes with it?* Terrified she might have lost it, she tore open the drawers and threw wide the closet doors with such angry force that they slammed against the walls. *I can't find Chris' shirt; I can't find Chris' shirt.*

Frank and Caitlin heard her bewildered screams of panic and ran to the room.

'Stay out of here! Don't you understand, I have to find Chris' shirt. How can we bury him if I can't find the shirt? Oh my God, what have I done with it?'

'Mom,' Caitlin had to shout at her. 'It's right there

on the pillow. You must have taken it out first and for-gotten about it. It's right there, Mom.'

Maggie ran for the light beige shirt as though she'd found Chris himself. Once she had it in her arms, Maggie fell against the bed. 'We needed this shirt; don't you both see that?' she wailed. 'We can't lose another thing that belonged to Chris, not another thing!' Maggie's face was as hard as stone when she challenged Frank and Caitlin. 'How can you both be so calm? How can you stand there and make sense of anything? Frank, you've lost your only son. Caitlin, you've lost your only brother. I don't understand either of you. How can any of us let Chris go?'

Frank took Caitlin by the shoulder, signalling she should leave them alone together. 'Maggie, I'm coming into Chris' room.'

'Leave me alone, Frank. Go back to the business of burying our son because I won't. Why, Frank? Why did this have to happen?'

Frank got on the bed beside Maggie and held her tightly. 'Curse at me all you want, Maggie, if that helps you. There are no answers as to why Chris died, not for you, or me, or Caitlin. I know you don't mean to be angry with us. Cait does too.'

'If Chris had pushed someone out of the path of the car, or saved some small animal, but he died for noth-ing. He was hurt and dying and he was all alone. I'll never forgive God for taking him from us.'

'You don't have to, Maggie. You can stay here today where you'll be safe. Caitlin and I will go the funeral home.'

'Don't you understand anything, Frank? I can't *not* go. Chris has to know I was there.'

'All right then, you can come on one condition.'

'Don't start setting rules, Frank.'

'Only one. You have to eat something solid because, right now, you're too weak to go anywhere. The afternoon will be very hard on you and me.' Frank got up from the bed. Maybe Maggie needed this terrible task more than he realized. 'I'll get the tie; I know which one it is because I chose it for Chris. I'll use my overnight bag for his things. First, let's get some food into you and me too, I guess. Take your time; I'll prepare something for both of us.'

'Are Chris' friends still here?'

'They've been very helpful, taking the calls for us and making food.'

'It's too painful for me to see them today.'

'I'll make sure we're alone in the kitchen. I'll see you in a little bit.'

Caitlin had waited for her father around a corner of the hall. 'How is she?'

'Coping as best she can.'

'Is she up to the funeral home?'

'Whether she is or not, she's determined to come with me. Would you go and ask the fellows to stay out of the kitchen for a little while? I think I heard them down there. Your mother is not up to seeing them. I'll change and then head down.'

Caitlin knew exactly what she'd do with a few hours on her own. At the bottom of the stairs, she called Carmen. 'Hi, how quickly can you get here?'

'Soon. I surfed the net for info and have a few details.'

'Good. Don't speed; I need you around.'

'Not to worry.'

'OK then.'

When she walked into the kitchen, a rather large,

square room that comfortably housed two separate meal tables and an island, she saw immediately that Mike had done a wonderful job of cleaning everything up. Hunter was arranging his notes. 'Hi, thank you for all this work. Mom is coming down very soon. I know it will be too hard for her to see you both right now.'

'We'll get out of your way.'

'Thanks. Hunter, do you remember if anyone from the university has called? I should have contacted a few people myself, but I couldn't.'

'Yes, they did. I arranged these lists. You have a separate one and your parents have their own. Your grandmother is arriving this afternoon at five from Toronto, but she insisted on taking a limo from the airport.'

'Thank you both for all the work.'

'I know,' Mike responded. 'Take it easy; we'll get out of your hair.' It was only when he spoke that Caitlin saw the darkening circles under his eyes. 'Chris was our friend; we thought for a lifetime. We'll get back later tonight and we'll come through the side entrance.'

They disappeared almost immediately. Caitlin grabbed her purse from the foyer as Frank came down the stairs. 'Take some time with Mom. I have to get out for a while. Carmen's coming over. I need to pick up a few clothes and my car. We might just go for coffee, nothing special or long.' That was the first time Caitlin had looked her father in the eye and lied.

By ten-thirty Carmen reached the house, then they drove together back to Caitlin's. 'What's up?'

'I want to drive to Harvard Avenue to see exactly where Pastore lives.'

'I thought you agreed to give the cops a week.'

'Changed my mind when I learned Remay has nothing.'

'We have to be careful, Caitlin. No one can remember us if we're going to do this properly.'

'You're more devious than I am, so you can make the rules.'

'What about your parents?'

'They'll be busy at the funeral home.'

'First thing, we can't be noticed or remembered by some neighbour who's out walking. We'll drive by the house only once. Then, we should park on Old Orchard or Marcil Avenue. With your yellow Beetle and my blue Mini, someone might remember seeing one of them parked too close to the house.'

'Makes sense. Let's get out of my place; I can't stay away too long. What have you learned?'

'I have the numbers for the executives and managers at Foley's. I can call a few up myself, pretending to be a member of the press and try to get information that way.'

'No one will talk to the press, but I'm just thinking we can pretend to be one of Pastore's friends and see what we can dig up.'

'Sounds like a plan. Are you forgetting about Chris, Caitlin? I'm worried about you.'

'How can you ask me that? I will not allow his murderer to walk away!'

CHAPTER 26

IN THE BASEMENT on Harvard Avenue, Monsieur Patate waited quietly at the side of Sophia's bed. He had just come through his first dry night and he was sniffing loudly near Sophia's ear, as close as he could get to it from the floor. When she was much younger, Sophia loved to give herself a good stretch before getting up from bed. But age had taken away that small pleasure. Any extended stretching could well aggravate the dull ache in her knees she woke up to everyday. Sometimes, she tried to recall a time when she was pain-free, but that was so long ago, it did not much matter.

'Good morning, Monsieur. I'll be with you after I rub my knees.' First, Sophia gently lowered one leg to the floor and pulled the other one across the bed to join its partner. Then she hoisted herself off the bed, lowering her weight carefully onto her legs. She took a few steps to loosen the stiffened joints. Monsieur watched all these machinations with a loving patience and a sage understanding. There was no doubt Monsieur was nobler than his name. When Sophia turned her attention to him, he jumped. 'Oh Monsieur, not a single drop, how wonderful! Let's let you out.'

Monsieur ran up the stairs, and poor Sophia moved much faster than she wanted. She pushed the basement door open and hobbled to the back door in the kitchen and opened it too. Monsieur dashed between her legs and scurried down the four back stairs.

Monsieur is safe again, and so am I. In celebration, Sophia made freshly squeezed orange juice and prepared fluffy, blueberry pancakes that were as large as a dinner plate and just as heavy. The sweet scent of a renewed harmony and brewing coffee wafted up to the second floor and circled around the nose of Nicolina. She had reason for a little jubilation herself. Her night had been restless because it was the first without even a drop of Scotch in a long time. Noticing that her hands were shaking less, Nicolina figured she'd managed some rest at least. That police officer had not called her again. That had to be a good sign. As soon as she thought of the accident though, her stomach muscles tightened into knots. With this problem, she'd have to live minute to minute. When she shifted her attention to Jen Sexton, she exhaled and felt a whole lot better. She'd call her today, but not before a set strategy. Right at this minute the pull of Sophia's pancakes threw all caution to the wind. She grabbed her robe and made a beeline for the food.

'Sophia, you've made my favourite breakfast. The pancakes are huge, but I want two of them. I'm famished!' Nicolina flopped into a chair, laid her palms on the table like a kid who was waiting on her mother to do all the work. 'All night long I thought of that poor young man and how terrible it must be for the family. How is my Monsieur this morning?'

Good news displaced Sophia's misgivings and anxiety. 'He has gone a whole night without a single mishap!'

'Isn't that wonderful! This might be a decent day for all of us. Pass the syrup and butter, please.' Nicolina cut the pancakes in squares until they almost formed a pyramid. She daubed the tops with chunks of butter that slid down the sides and melted. Then she poured half the bottle of syrup on top. The gooey plate looked like an ad for Aunt Jemima. Had Nicolina looked better, it might have been quite a photo. However, into her second day of withdrawal and stress, she didn't look any better than the grieving family on The Boulevard. Her eyes were stretched and the corners red from lack of sleep. Her skin was pasty. Yet, though chaos was circling her chair, her appetite was something to see.

She bit into the sugary mound, and her fork never stopped for a rest until the pancakes were safely piled inside her belly. Syrup dripped from the corners of her mouth, and she wiped it away with her sticky hands. 'Would you get me more coffee, Sophia? I don't know if I can stand up yet. I feel as though I've eaten the house.'

Sophia watched this show in awe, the same way she had when Roberto ate. A smile trickled across her cheek. She was always happy to see people enjoying her food. Nicolina rubbed her stomach and pushed her chair away from the table. Sophia felt satisfied and secure. 'May I turn on the radio?'

'After a breakfast like this, you can do anything you please. You're such an important part of this family.'

It was five minutes before the hour when Sophia turned on her favourite CBC station.

'One favour, Sophia. Let's hit 92.5 FM for some music. I think we may have turned a corner today. I'm so thankful for everything.'

Sophia wanted her CBC Radio, but she complied. This house did not belong to her. In a few minutes, the news came on the air, then the traffic, then the weather. The top of the hour was followed by a police announcement that threw a hushed pall into the tentatively happy room. The announcer's voice was as steady as a small drill. *Montreal Police are seeking any witnesses to a fatal accident that occurred on the corner of Sherbrooke Street and Wood Avenue early Friday morning. If you have any information, please contact…*

The sugary goop in Nicolina's digestive tract was having a hard enough time. When nerves gripped the mess, some of it, heavy and confused, backed up. Nicolina grabbed her mouth, trying to keep it closed, but some seeped through her fingers. She jumped up and ran for the toilet.

Sophia held onto the counter, shaking with obligation and what that involved.

When the pancakes were flushed, Nicolina hung her head in the toilet bowl. When nothing remained of the breakfast but bile, she stood, took a few steps to the sink, wiped her mouth and cheeks with a cold facecloth and began a frenzy of dry coughing. *The old bitch can't rat on me now! There is no goddamn way she's going to bring me down! I have to get back in there and do something.*

Sophia looked her landlord squarely in the eye. 'The police are still looking for witnesses.' Every word was an arrow, sharply tipped.

Too bad, Sophia was nowhere near the basement stairs! It was one thing to be defeated by your enemies; one might expect that eventuality. It was quite another to fall victim to a tenant under your own roof! Her mind began to thump. The one thing she regretted telling Remay was that the young man must have stepped out from behind parked cars. When she lied, Nicolina followed a simple rule: Don't fabricate with fact that can be disproved. *What do I say to the old bitch? What the hell do I say?*

'Do you think this is easy on me, Sophia?' Her voice was shrill with menace. 'Do you think I haven't gone over things a thousand times? The young man is dead! He will haunt me for the rest of my life.'

Roberto used to holler at Sophia when he was lying about the money he'd gambled and lost. 'Am I not the man of this house? I can afford to enjoy myself a little. How dare you look at me that way?' It was never a little with Roberto; of course, it was less and nothing at the end. The truth never came out until he died. Now, here was this woman hurling lies at her, just like Roberto.

'I hope someone saw the accident because that person will clear me of any fault. It will change nothing for that young man, I am fully aware of that. If he made a terrible mistake, he has certainly paid the ultimate price. Fate intervened, I guess.'

You could not walk without falling when you left this house... The truth is mostly something people with choices and strong walls can afford. It is a particularly rare event when those with everything to lose step forward with the truth. These people are the backbone of courage.

'Did you hear what I just said, Sophia?' *Was the old bag losing it, standing there in front of her in a blank daze?*

'I hope a witness calls the police. That might help everyone involved.'

The old bitch was not going to give anything up. *Is she trying to threaten me? Does she have it in her?*

Nicolina was discovering that Sophia was difficult to shove aside. The hair on her neck bristled as she watched the old woman hobble to the back door. Miscalculating the distance to the doorknob, Sophia stumbled and grabbed the side counter before falling to the floor.

Nicolina saw the mishap without making any attempt to help Sophia before she fell. *It would be so easy. A single fall, a quiet end.* Purposely late, she conveniently caught up to Sophia and took her arm as they walked down the back stairs. 'You have to be careful. The last thing you need is a bad fall. I don't want to have to call your family and friends to tell them you've broken a hip, or worse.'

Sophia's courage began to shake like her knees. She

had a daughter in Winnipeg, but had not spoken to her in four years. She had a good friend, a neighbour, but she had passed away two years ago. And worse, she had told Nicolina all of this.

Sophia nodded, but felt very much alone until Monsieur rubbed up against her ankle.

'I'll leave you two because I have work that needs my attention.' Once she was back inside the house, Nicolina ran, unplugging the two phones. For the time being, there was no point giving Sophia the opportunity to make a call to the police number. She'd use her cell.

Sophia took Monsieur up on her lap and hung onto him. How much could she risk for a young man she didn't know? Where would she find an apartment for three hundred dollars a month? What would happen to Monsieur? She was not entirely sure what time Nicolina left the house last Thursday. What troubled her was the idea that perhaps this was an unavoidable accident after all. Yet, what if the police were waiting for her evidence? What if they needed it to solve the case?

CHAPTER 27

CARMEN HAD CHOSEN to drive for their first stakeout. Wisely, she took de Maisonneuve Boulevard to Kensington Avenue to get back onto Sherbrooke Street. The pain was still too raw on the corner where Chris was struck. It was better that Caitlin did not have to see it again. It was enough that her friend would have to walk up to the area every day for a long time.

The warm weather was hanging on, and the sidewalks on either side were dotted with couples and baby carriages, older folks with shopping carts and a few bikes needling their way in between pedestrians and cars. Everywhere, the newness of spring winked its bright light through boughs loaded with green buds. Without snow, the streets and sidewalks looked wider, and the city softer. It was difficult to believe that a young man had lost his life on such a calm night when the city was just beginning to bloom again.

As they approached Marcil Avenue, Caitlin covered her eyes. 'Dad and Mom must be in there now. I don't know how Mom will get through it.'

'I'm sorry, Caitlin. I should have taken Côte St. Antoine Road. This must be so hard for you.'

Caitlin did not look at the red brick funeral home; she turned to her right and focused on the park. 'Chris and I came here a few times when we were younger.'

'Are you sure you want to go through with this? I can drive you back, and you could help your parents.'

'Don't keep asking me that, Carm. Here's Harvard Avenue; take a right.'

'Remember, we're not stopping, not if we intend to come back here. I'll drive slowly, but not slowly enough to attract attention. We're in the two thousands. It's an odd number, right?'

'Keep going, we're looking for the fours.' A block later, Caitlin rose in her seat and whispered, 'There it is.' Her cheeks flushed white with anger. She had wanted the house to stand out, to menace with intent, but it didn't. It was a two-storey brown brick house with oak doors, centred with thick glass in a pinwheel design that must have come with the eighty year old structure. The windows, with stained wooden frames, were relatively new. The blue and white wooden balcony, soft in tone, bothered Caitlin. 'It's benign. I wasn't expecting that.'

'Exteriors don't reveal much. You should know that. We can't stop, but we know exactly where she lives.'

'See the car in the driveway?' Caitlin, lowered her window and stuck her head out.

'The police have the car. That must be a rental.'

'I want to come back tomorrow.'

'How can you leave your parents? Isn't Chris going to be waked tomorrow?'

'Not till seven. Is there any chance you can take a day off? Pastore will be at work.'

'Because of Miami, I have no holidays, but I haven't taken a single sick day. I could call in sick. What can we do here? Shouldn't we be on our cells, collecting info? We have to plan this very carefully, Caitlin.'

'Her neighbours might help us. People see a host of things. I also want to get inside the house. If she's a boozer, we'll find lots of evidence.'

'And do what with it? That's a B-and-E, for Christ's sake.'

'All right, maybe I'm going off the deep end. Let me think about this. We can decide tonight. If I don't change my mind, you won't be guilty of anything. You'd act as a lookout.'

'I say we should brainstorm; visit the house Thursday or Friday. Turn your full attention to Chris for the next few days.'

'I can't. That would be letting his murderer off. You have no idea how much I want this woman.'

'I'm beginning to.'

A few blocks away, Frank and Maggie sat in a sombre office listening to one of the owners, whose name they had not even heard, explain the service they had chosen for Chris. Frank sat in one of the chairs that faced the desk. He was holding Maggie's arm. Her hands were locked tightly together around the handle of the black overnight bag that held Chris' clothes. Frank could see her white knuckles. She neither blinked nor nodded as the director spoke, so he turned his attention to Frank. 'I hope you will be pleased with everything. We'll do our utmost for your family at this difficult time.'

All that moved on Maggie's face were her lips. Her jaw was sore from clenching.

'I want to know if I can bring these clothes to my son.'

All easy, practical mechanics failed the director who looked to Frank for help.

'That's not a good idea, honey.'

'Why not? I don't want a stranger dressing my son. Can't you understand that, Frank?' He rose to put his arms around Maggie. 'Don't try to mollify me.'

Frank remembered the autopsy. Before he said anything, the director had regained his composure.

'Mrs. Donovan, how about coming a little earlier tomorrow night? It's against regulations to allow an unlicensed person to come downstairs. I know you want a closed casket, but I can open it for you and the family at six-thirty tomorrow night.'

The fight went out of Maggie. She smiled sadly at the bag, handed it across the desk, turned and left without a word.

'Sir, I need your signature before you go. I was also wondering about flowers.'

Frank scribbled his name. 'I'll call McKenna's.' He ran out of the room, frantic to find Maggie. She had not gone far. He found her folded in two, a few feet down the hall. 'Let's go home.'

'I wish I didn't have to.'

'I know.'

CHAPTER 28

NICOLINA DID NOT notice a blue Mini drive slowly by the house that represented everything she owned. No, she was busy trying to get her mind off the idea of murdering her tenant, the woman who cooked her meals, cared for her pug, picked up after her and paid her three hundred dollars a month to live in a makeshift room in her basement. However, with a single phone call, this aging angel with bum knees could set in motion a humiliating end to a life she had fought to salvage.

Would it be murder if she were to leave a shoe on the second from the top basement stair, and the old bat tripped over it and fell to her death on the cement floor? Nicolina wouldn't have pushed her, not really; she'd have fallen. Shouldn't older people check things like stairs before taking them? Isn't it even possible that Monsieur might drag a slipper up the stairs and leave it on a step? How long did she have before Sophia realized the phones were unplugged? The problem with her tenant was her independence and strength. Where were all the frail, old women, afraid of shadows, who took beatings from family and never reported them? Why hadn't she rented to one of them? Sophia had nothing; yet the old bitch was proud. *Of what?* she wondered. *Who does she think she is?*

If only Nicolina knew what Sophia had on her from last Thursday. Life is not easy for a drunk. Nicolina wished she could confide in the old bitch, offer to cut the rent and assure her she had this home for as long as she needed it. Yet, if she acknowledged any responsibility in the fatality, she might as well dial the cops for Sophia.

Nicolina was enjoying herself. Why not make an

extended death list while she was in this mood? Raymond Lecours merited the harsh sentence for callously abandoning her. Jen Sexton, she'd throw in as spice. The only player she would not murder was Kathryn Traynor, a real victim like herself.

These turns of fancy extricated Nicolina from the stress that hobbled her every minute, but once they ended, she deflated like a tired balloon. Rolling off her bed, she walked over to the back window. *What the hell can she be doing with the dog? They've been out there*, she checked her watch, *for over an hour. I loved that dog and she's taken him from me as well.* A good thought came her way. *Something is holding Sophia back from making the call, more than just the dog, I think. That's what I have to keep in mind. Look at her out there in my yard, with my dog. Anyone would think she owned the place! I think I can afford to wait a little longer with her. I'm no murderer, for God's sake! Jen Sexton is my main problem.*

She was going to stay with her game plan, the truth. If Sexton sent the file, she'd be out of a job before the end of the year. Nicolina had to be firm, but not so hard as to lose her. From what she learned, Sexton was an optimist. It took her longer time to admit defeat. Beautiful people felt entitled. If only Nicolina could be assured that Sexton would destroy the evidence, she might pull through. Then Nicolina could give her full attention to Sophia.

This was a game point call, and she could have used a good Scotch before punching in the numbers. It was just before dinner, and Jen answered. For that, she was grateful. 'Jen, Nicolina Pastore. I know it's Sunday, but I have information that I feel you should know as soon as possible. After dinner, is there a chance of us getting together? We need to talk. I'm willing to drive out to the West Island.'

The change in Pastore's tone was more alarming for Jen than the pit bull she'd come to expect. Had she lost what little leverage she had? Did someone else have a copy of the file? Yet, Pastore wanted something from her and Jen had little choice but to discover what that was. 'How about we meet at Chenoy's on St. John's Boulevard? It'll be quiet, and we can have a booth to ourselves.'

'What time is easier for you?'

Jen could feel perspiration trickle inside her bra. 'Eight o'clock?'

'I'll be there.' Nicolina felt like a boxer in the first round, feeling her opponent out.

After she hung up the phone, Jen stood motionless and scared. Then she ran outside to the backyard and hollered. 'Gotta go out for a few minutes, Robert.'

'Where?'

'New batteries. I have to meet with her tonight. No choice.'

'I thought you had till tomorrow night.'

'She's changed her mind; something's up.'

'Bad for us?'

'I don't know.'

'Just go.' All the doubts, all the nights of waiting up late for Jen to get home had left Robert with a vein of hatred that now throbbed and ached with this news. It never seemed normal to Robert that Jen was out more than he was. She was a good mother and wife, but throughout their marriage, Robert never fully trusted her. At times, it wasn't easy loving a woman most other men wanted. Jen lied about stupid things. He remembered once asking her to mail a letter because he was bathing the kids and she was going out to a meeting. When he asked about it, she said she'd mailed it. A few days later, together in the family car for weekend shopping, he'd found the letter on the floor.

Jen herself began to do a hurried inventory of crimes and misdemeanours as she ran for the car keys. She had time when she got back to call her connection for the job in Laval. With her background, she wasn't worried, but how did she get herself into this mess? There was a title from one of her books in college that she never forgot, *A Woman Killed with Kindness*. More often, it was the other way around, she thought.

Kathryn Traynor lay resting on the sofa in the living room. Tim was preparing omelettes with shallots and Emmenthal Swiss cheese grated on top. As a side dish, he boiled carrots and turnip that he'd later mash together, adding butter and brown sugar. A few times, he crept into the living room, hoping Kathryn was awake. For the last two days, she hadn't said much of anything, and even when she was awake, Kathryn was despondent. The steroids, the antibiotics, the Empracet, all the meds and the court delay had all taken their toll. The cancer and the trial had been the daily focus of their waking hours. Tim felt he wouldn't lose Kathryn as long she fought the court case. He wasn't certain why he felt that way, but zeroing in on the end of her life stole what living days and hours Kathryn had left. He did not believe she would die, no matter what the doctors had said.

'Hey, you. That smells good!' Kathryn opened her eyes, smiling. 'What will I do without you?'

'If you eat everything here, you won't have to worry about that. I made you vegetables the way you like them.'

'I'll do my best, but I'm not very hungry, Tim.'

'Eat what you can.'

Before placing the dinner on a pull-out tray, Tim gathered pillows and bunched them behind Kathryn and added two others on either side for better support. As Kathryn slowly slung her legs down from the sofa, Tim saw that both feet were very swollen. When had that happened? Tears welled in his eyes. He wanted to gather Kathryn in his arms and run away with her, as far as they could get from cancer.

In a sitting position, Kathryn felt nauseous. All she could do was push the food around her plate. She took a spoonful of the vegetables, gagged, but swallowed. She took another mouthful, and, though her stomach recoiled, she finished the carrots and turnip nonetheless. The smell of the eggs was too much for her and she told Tim to take them away. Then she fell against the couch, her head falling to her left side as though it was too heavy to hold upright.

Tim ran to the kitchen with the food and was back at her side in seconds. 'It's the meds, honey. They'd fuck up anyone's stomach.'

'I've been thinking, Tim. If I can't make the next court date... What I'm trying to say is that I don't want you to continue with the case if I'm not around.'

'This is just a bad day; you've had them before. Tomorrow will be better.'

'Tim, listen to me, please. I want to spend my time with you and not with the case between us. In a few years, no one will mention my name. The case won't matter at all.'

'Kathryn, please don't give up.'

'Tim, I promise you I'll be there if I'm feeling better, but I was thinking last night that they've probably planned more delays. I have no worries about the people who know me. Why should I care about those who don't? Right and wrong don't seem important now. Not being able to eat that omelette bothers me more.'

'You'll feel better after a night's sleep.' He shouldered Kathryn into the bedroom, helped her into bed and crawled in beside her. In minutes, Tim was asleep; Kathryn smiled, comforted by his warmth, but she stayed awake, afraid to sleep, afraid to let go. She began silently to recite the rosary, using her fingers to count the Hail Marys.

Once again, Jen slid the recorder inside her briefcase, and made a quick call to her connection in Laval. 'Dave, glad I caught you. It's Jen Sexton. Quick question. Is there any chance you know now if there will be a place for me next year?'

'We'll have the numbers only in June. If there's a place, it's yours. Things that bad?'

'And worse.'

CHAPTER 29

IT WOULD HAVE been difficult to say who was more nervous driving to Chenoy's delicatessen. Jen got there first and set the case beside her in the booth, opened it and pressed both the play/record buttons. She ordered a coffee, but did not have long to wait. Nicolina arrived minutes later.

Though Nicolina sat across from her, Jen could hear the hum of the cheap machine. She pulled her sweater across the top of the case, but she could still hear the damn thing. In a panic, Jen shut the case.

'I'll order a coffee and cheesecake. Can I tempt you?'

'We've just eaten.'

'Thank you for coming, Jen. When we last spoke, you told me you wouldn't send the file without first advising me and waiting to see if Kathryn Traynor was well enough to attend the session. Correct so far?'

'Yes; you gave me till Monday for my reply.'

'Something has come up. To reiterate, if you send the file, we're both out of a job.'

Jen did not want to give Pastore the satisfaction of an answer she already knew, so she said nothing.

'Jen, I have another reason you might want to hold onto your information. I've just learned that you carried on an affair with Kathryn Traynor that everybody at Foley's knew about. The words 'common knowledge' came up frequently.'

There was a buzzing behind Jen's eyes and her throat went dry.

Nicolina allowed herself a little snort.

'Who said such a thing?'

Let her squirm like I have since she sent me the damn file.

'Kathryn Traynor and I are friends.' *How did she find out?*

Pastore was drooling unintentionally. Her nerves were fraying as well. 'How old are you, Jen?'

'Forty-six.'

'Do you know what I find amusing? I almost believe you.'

'I'm telling you the truth.' Jen knew she had to lie.

'So what? Lecours is not going to give a rat's ass either if you bedded this woman or not, as long as he can use the affair to shut you up.'

Words, and what's behind them, can throw knock-out punches. Jen went down for the count. 'I've had the odd affair over the years. Many people married for twenty years have slipped a few times. But never with Kathryn, never!' What more would Kathryn have to endure?

'Here's the thing, Jen. If you produce this evidence, Kathryn's husband will hear of the affair. Whatever time the Traynors have left will be ruined, and her husband will hurt long after she dies. I hear he's on sick leave himself. How much care will he want to give an unfaithful wife when she's broken his heart and made all their years of marriage suspect? I'll also make it my business to inform your husband. Your own marriage might never recover, especially when he finds out about you and Traynor.'

'You'd do this?'

'Bank on it. You snivelling hypocrite! You're sorry for yourself even though you admit to cheating, just maybe not in this instance. Your husband works, right?'

Jen nodded.

'Well, I have only myself and I need my job. Life's that simple. If you'd given me the file at the outset, we wouldn't be sitting here now. Don't flatter yourself that you're any better than I am. When I'm finished with you, no one will think so either.'

'I didn't falsely charge Kathryn with forgery. That's on you.'

'I've made my share of blunders; so have you.'

Nicolina and Jen sank back in their booth, exhausted, spent.

'What do you want?'

'The file and a signed affidavit that there are no copies.'

'Once you have them, you'll get rid of me.'

'Not if I keep my job.'

'Right.' Jen's mind was racing, but she had not lost all sense. 'I give you my word that I won't produce the file. I won't give it to you because it's all the protection I have now.'

'You're playing a dangerous game.'

'Aren't we both?'

Nicolina's cheeks ballooned with fury, but she had her promise. At least that was something. 'I'm the only one who knows about both issues, the file and the affair. Remember that.'

The bout ended in a draw.

Jen threw money on the table and headed for the door with Pastore's words stinging her ears.

Nicolina sat bristling, stabbing her cheesecake with a fork. How she hated any form of litigation! Nothing was ever decided in a single meeting. Progress or lack of it moved ahead by centimetres, or back the same way. Just when you felt you could apply the right pressure, you found yourself back at square one. Trouble spots appeared out of nowhere. The worst part of all court proceedings was a lack of control.

Like Sexton, she didn't bother to wait for the waitress, but rose and left cash on the table as well. One good thing came out of this. Stomping towards the front door, Nicolina noticed stress had taken her attention off the pain in her ribs, or they were healing well. On Highway 20, Nicolina never entertained the thought that Sexton might have lied to her about not sending the file. It was odd that a woman familiar with deceit could fail to detect it in others. Driving past the Dorval Circle, Nicolina saw she was doing 125 km and slammed on the brakes, slowing down. All she needed now was a speeding ticket!

CHAPTER 30

CARMEN WAS UP in Caitlin's room, going over the information she'd found on Pastore. 'Here's a list of the people at Foley Pharmaceuticals and a list of the executives. We can't call all these people, but we can try a few, as you suggested, pretending to be her friend. If we find one or two people willing to talk about her, we're ahead.'

'I'm beginning to worry that we'll look like idiots asking her colleagues to tell us something about a friend we're supposed to know. I don't always have the greatest ideas.'

'That's where I come in, the sly one. I've been thinking we'll say that we are very worried about her since the accident and ask if there is anything they can suggest we can do to help her. Have they noticed her great stress? If they like her, of course, they'll want to help us out. If she's unpopular, we can pick up on that from their tone and brush-off.'

'You should have been a criminal!'

'Think I coulda been a contender; been a somebody?'

'Not when I flash back to Miami.' Then feeling guilty, Caitlin got very serious. 'I want to get back to Harvard Avenue.'

'We have to check the place out before you try any of your own criminal ideas. I think Friday is the best day. In the meantime, you should be home with your parents. You need time for Chris in the next few days. I can make a few calls, so we'll have a better plan.'

'There's got to be a reason she left the scene of the accident. Alcohol, other violations, whatever, something forced her to abandon Chris. I have to remember to tell Dad to ask Remay if he's checked her record. If the accident had been Chris' fault, she would have stayed. We have to find out what's going on in her life that made her leave Chris to die needlessly and alone.'

'That's why we need the time to learn more about her.'

'I think Mom and Dad are back; I can hear them downstairs.'

'I'm going to go. Call if you need me, anytime.'

'Thanks, Carm.'

As soon as Frank parked the car in the driveway, Maggie headed for the front door and almost had a collision with Carmen. She was taken aback by Maggie's haggard appearance. Caitlin's mother had always seemed like a tall kid to Carmen. The curls, the energy, the easy laugh, the garrulous nature all denied a woman in her fifties. Chris' death had extinguished her exuberance. 'I'm so sorry, Mrs. Donovan.'

'Please understand I can't talk to anyone.' Maggie said and headed to Chris' room as though a magnet were pulling her back.

Outside, Frank had just opened the garage door to find that Chris' car was still there. *I thought Mike was seeing to this.* He closed the door and went looking for Caitlin and found her in the kitchen looking at the lists Hunter had made. A self loathing for his own past and a biting anger at the woman who took his son's life had come together when he had stood beside Maggie in the 'showroom' at the funeral home. Caskets, illuminated with soft light that pretended to ease the passage of a loved one from the world of light to the dark of oblivion, flanked the couple on both sides. The battered car was another casket as far as Frank was concerned. He wanted to shout at Caitlin, demanding why the damn thing was still in the garage, but he couldn't because she was alone at the table and had buried her head in her arms. 'Cait, are you all right?'

'No, but that doesn't matter. There are so many people here, so many of Chris' friends from Boston are coming for the funeral. Apart from Carmen, I can't bring myself to call anyone else. Is Granny here already?'

'She must be. I saw the umbrella she uses as a cane in the stand down the front hall. I'll bet she's unpacked and is probably upstairs waiting for Maggie. We'll leave them alone for a while. Cait, I thought the car would have been towed by now.'

'Mike made the calls but, after taking a better look at it, he felt it was best to have the dealer come for the car. It's to be towed first thing tomorrow morning. According to Mike, the car is salvageable, so there was no point, he felt, in just giving it to a body shop.'

'Well, you have to make sure your mother doesn't go out to garage before tomorrow morning. She can't see it.'

'I know, Dad.'

'Keep your grandmother out as well. She means well, but…'

'I'm on it, Dad.'

'What about Chris' friends?'

'They won't be back till later tonight.'

The familiar heavy footsteps of Maureen McDonough had Frank and Caitlin turn in their direction before they actually saw her. Maureen did not look any better than her daughter. Frank threw open his arms and she collapsed, and he knew that she was broken inside.

'Why did this have to happen to our Chris?'

'Frank, Maggie won't talk to me. She's up there alone in Chris' room. She needs me.'

'Maureen,' Frank tried to explain, 'Maggie wants and needs to feel close to Chris, and we can't be around her.' Tears ran down his cheeks when he next spoke. 'At the funeral home, she said, 'I have only three days left with Chris, and then every part of my son is gone forever.' We have to give her the time, Maureen. Could I possibly prevail on you to help us out with dinner? Caitlin and I are bone tired.'

Feeling needed, Maureen's spirits rose a little. 'Leave that to me.'

'Nothing fancy, something to keep us going.'

'I'll call you when the food's ready.'

Later, Frank took Maggie by the arm and led her to the table. He wanted to be sure she ate. No one remembered what Maureen had made, but everyone, including Maggie, ate.

Caitlin stayed alone in the kitchen reading the names of people who knew her brother, people she had never met. When she felt a buzzing on her hip, she reached for her cell and answered because it was Carmen.

'I have a few things. Made calls to three people at the company; dug out their home numbers. Here's the summary: Number one: *I have nothing to say about Ms. Pastore.* Number two: *I can only say that she has a lot on her plate with the case and now this terrible accident.* Number three: *I'm retiring in a month and I will not say anything that might interfere with my pension. I will tell you that I hope Ms. Pastore gets everything she so rightly deserves.* We now know, she's disliked, is involved in a case which we will make it our business to find out about and is despised by the guy retiring.'

'That's very good work, Carm. I wonder if I dare take the chance of calling that third person back and telling him who I am. Do you think he might reveal more to me?'

'Let's sleep on that, Caitlin. Let's see what we can discover without identifying ourselves. Why take a chance at this stage? The guy, the man, whatever, has another six weeks before retirement. He's not going anywhere; he'll probably tell us more the closer he gets to leaving.'

'Get some rest; I'll keep working on home numbers.'

Caitlin was still downstairs when Hunter and Mike came through the side entrance. Having left the house for the first time, they felt more like intruders coming back into it. Hunter gave Caitlin a nod and headed up the back stairs. Mike walked into the kitchen. 'Can I talk to you for a minute?'

'A little later, okay?'

'I'll be in my room.'

Though the house was not empty, it was as silent as a tomb. Caitlin rested her head on the table and fell into a nightmare. She then woke with a sudden jerk.

She did not know the time when she climbed the stairs and remembered Mike, but it was dark. Without knocking, she opened his door. 'Are you awake?'

'Yes,'

'Leave the lights off.'

Mike felt his way over to the voice. He was standing so close to Caitlin, he could feel her breath against his mouth. 'If you want me to go back home after Chris' funeral, I will. I love you, Caitlin.'

'Chris will always be between us. He brought us together. I might have loved you…' It was Caitlin who reached out in the darkness and pulled Mike to her, roughly and without any pretence of tenderness.

Mike tried to hold her back because he sensed a doom, an end in her desire.

Caitlin swallowed the salt from his tears, and her tongue bore deep into his mouth. He could not fight his own desperation and carried her to his bed. Together, their bodies fused into a single passion, stiff and hard and forlorn. Not a word, not a guttural sound escaped. The trembling and the savagery were all inside, too visceral to share. For a few seconds, Caitlin held onto Mike so tightly, she left bruises. Their bodies were slippery when they finally lay hot and spent beside one another.

Caitlin turned and whispered, 'Mike, after the funeral, I never want to see you again.'

'You love me, Caitlin.' His words fell into empty spaces in the darkness because Caitlin had left the room.

Hunter had not been sleeping and had heard Caitlin and Mike speaking to one another. When all he heard was the silence, he knew what had gone on. 'Figures,' he said to himself. He waited for an hour before knocking on Mike's door and announcing himself. 'It's Hunter.' He opened the door himself because he was pretty sure Caitlin had left.

'I didn't invite you in,' Mike said through the darkened room. 'Don't turn on the lights. What the hell do you want?'

'You're a piece of work. You couldn't leave her alone, even in this situation. You make me sick. You were Chris'…'

Mike had grown used to the darkness and he knew exactly where Hunter was standing. He landed a solid right to the solar plexus and heard the wind fly from Hunter's mouth as he fell against the wall. 'What the fuck do you know about this?'

Hunter couldn't answer because he'd doubled over and was trying to breathe.

'Don't you ever accuse me of not being Chris' friend. Do you hear me, you sanctimonious piece of shit?' Mike bent and grabbed Hunter by the hair and pulled his head up. But the fight was out of him as suddenly as it had erupted. 'You know what's really funny, a real laugher, I told her I'd leave if that's what she wanted. I was doing better on my own without interference and advice.'

'All right,' Hunter whispered, because that's all he could do. 'I didn't know.'

'She never wants to see me again after the funeral. That was her answer. Fuck! Well, you know what, I'm not going. She loves me.'

Hunter knew enough to get out of the room.

'I think she loves me,' Mike repeated as he fell back on the bed.

CHAPTER 31

SUNDAY NIGHT, NICOLINA lay uncomfortably on her back. Her ribs had begun to ache as soon as she lay down. Well aware that Monday could be the day the police might call, she was trying in vain to recall any of the events of Thursday night. At work tomorrow, she could count on colleagues gloating and wishing her the worst. Lecours might call her to the office for another dressing down. When she'd gotten home after the meeting with Sexton, Sophia had already retired for the night. She'd hoped to get a better read on the old bag, but barging downstairs did not seem the best route to take. The fact that she did not have to worry about the damn file was something. It was a significant point that let her fall asleep after midnight, that and the fact she was still sober. Nicolina was holding her own.

Monsieur squirmed at the foot of Sophia's bed, rubbing his bum against the bottom of it, trying his best to wiggle out of his diaper. If he could think, Monsieur would have said emphatically that putting diapers on dogs was not natural. He had not sprayed, pissed, peed or piddled since his mishap earlier in the day. He tucked his back leg up against his rump and gave another tug. The diaper fell to his legs and Monsieur, with as much dignity as a pug can muster, stepped out of it. He kicked the diaper off the newspaper and settled in for the night.

Sometimes, a simple fall can be as painful as an awful one. A muscle in her right shoulder had been strained when Sophia had grabbed the counter before falling. She could find no position that relieved the hot, stabbing needles in her shoulder. When she was quite certain Nicolina had gone to bed, Sophia turned on her

lamp and reached for the section she had saved from
Sunday's *Gazette*. She was the only one out of all concerned parties who had thought to look at the obituar-
ies.

With her magnifying glass, she read every notice.
On page seventeen of *Section H*, the second page of the
obits, she found a photo of a beautiful young man, far
too young to be listed in this section. Sophia felt connected to him. She read that Christopher Donovan had
died tragically early Friday morning. For a long time
she looked at the smiling face of this poor young man
and discovered he was the family's only son. Putting a
face to the events of last Thursday redoubled the mag-
nitude of the tragedy and dropped another layer of obligation on Sophia. This young Christopher appeared
loving and warm. How his mother would miss him!
Sophia thought of her own daughter. *I will call Sandra,
just to tell her I will always love her. Maybe, she wants to
know where I am living. Perhaps, she has thought of me. I
will call Winnipeg, but not from this house. I will walk to the
bank and ask for a lot of change and I will use a pay phone.*
Sophia knew exactly where she had the Winnipeg number. For most of the night, pain and urgency struggled
with one another.

Jen Sexton leaned over and was glad that Robert was
asleep, secure their family was safe. She lay on her back,
guilty and small, remembering the times she had put
herself and her family in jeopardy. The thing was, she
loved Robert and their kids, but she'd made the mistake
of thinking marriage was adventurous. A long time ago,
the first affair had brought her back to life. The danger
of it was part of the appeal. She never thought of leaving Robert and she never once thought he might leave

her. She was stupid; selfish and stupid. *I never wanted to
know myself, never felt I measured up to Robert's black and
white world. In the end, I never did, and now I could lose
him.* In spite of this awareness, she still wanted Kathryn
to know about her discovery, learn the truth before she
died. What would Kathryn do with the explosive information? Disclosure of the affair would destroy both
families. Jen loved challenge, adventure; the prize was
secondary, except when it came to Kathryn. All her life,
Jen had sidestepped love and commitment because she
couldn't trust either of them. Kathryn had brought with
her the threat of love. That's why Jen had been afraid on
that last night. It was close to four in the morning when
she finally fell asleep.

Some fathers, who had lost their sons tragically,
might wonder how such a thing could happen. These
tragedies occurred in other families, not theirs. Frank
Donovan had no such arrogant thoughts. Frank liked
tradition and its structure. As a Catholic, he'd be the
first to admit he lost his altar boy faith when he stopped
serving mass for Father O'Rourke. However, at twenty-
two, his world was still black and white. All that
changed on a Tuesday night, one month into his twen-
ty-fifth year. From that point on, he was a fervid believ-
er in *stuff catches up with you*. And now it had, with a
vengeance!

Frank had not only lost his son, he had also surrendered the pure grief that washes over you and fills you
up with love and pain and loss, a grief that breathes
inside the heart. It is for those, like Maggie, who grieve
purely, a penultimate human experience. For Frank,
riddled with Judas guilt, the grief is grey and jagged. As
he lay beside Maggie, he thought of the brass casket, of

how it would in time suffocate Chris' memory. He tried to see Chris flicking a little dust from his new car, but the photo that he saw was the gurney at the morgue. When he squeezed his eyes shut, he was looking back at a boy lying on Dorchester. Frank wrapped his fist against his forehead, more than once.

Maggie could not turn to Frank because she was clutching a dream. In it, she was fast asleep and her eyes were crusted shut from dried tears. She knew Chris was with her before he knelt beside the bed and laid his palm on her cheek. She did not dare move and frighten him away. Maggie relaxed against the warmth of Chris' hand. For a long time she felt the heartbeat through his palm and Maggie knew Chris was not lost. Then he bent very close to his mother, kissed her gently on the forehead and whispered, 'It's not so bad, Mom.' 'Thank you for telling me, Chris.'

'Maggie, are you all right?' Frank asked when he heard her mumbling.

She turned to him then and buried her head in his chest. The rhythmic steady beating of Frank's heart and Chris' words that echoed softly in her ears soothed Maggie into the short reprieve that sleep allows.

Caitlin did not shower after leaving Mike's room, but threw herself on the bed and buried her head in a pillow. She rolled onto her back soon after and covered her face with her hands. Mike had left himself all over her, on her hands, her arms, her cheeks, her breasts and her stomach, everywhere. If Caitlin's idea had been to hurt him, to walk away feeling less guilty, the plan had failed. She pounded her stomach with both fists until she was worn out. While she punished herself, because there is relief in pain, she could not admit that there had been no plan, just a force beyond her reason, a hungry heart she had been powerless to deny.

When the truth was too painful to admit, even in the dark, Caitlin's thoughts turned to revenge. What Carmen had warned her of did not matter, that she would regret not living the grief when it was close and present. Caitlin would not allow herself to think only of Chris. She did not deserve to mourn for her brother, not when she had played a part in his death. Once Pastore was behind bars, then she would devote herself to losing Chris. Once Mike no longer mattered, Chris would be hers to grieve. For now, passion and revenge blocked the valves of her heart.

However, for most of her life, Caitlin was an organized human being, and habits are not easily broken. In the midst of her warring thoughts she remembered she hadn't bothered to look at the morning's paper. Throwing on her robe, she ran downstairs and into the study. When she shut the door and switched on a light, she saw *The Gazette* lying on top of Saturday's papers. When she picked it up, it was obvious that it had not been opened. Caitlin sat at her father's desk and turned to the obits. When Chris' smiling face appeared, she covered it with her hand and read the notice, editing what she had written. *So little for twenty-six years.* She bent and kissed his eyes. Inch by inch, she drew her hand from the photo. *What will I do without you?*

She took the paper with her, but before she'd left the room, Caitlin gasped. *No one's mentioned a eulogy. Someone has to speak for you, Chris. Mom and Dad won't be able to. I can't write about you; that will mean you're gone.* Like the night her father told her Chris had been killed, though she would not allow herself to weep, tears fell on her cheeks. She booted up the computer and stared at the blank screen, but not for long. Memories of

Chris, past and present, burst before her, and Caitlin felt their close companion and leaned against the chapters of the past. Words flew onto the screen, *my mother's little darling smearing grape jelly on the yellow kitchen walls, the bow my father couldn't bend, 'I want to be like you, Dad, I have to choose my own way. That's what you taught me.' 'Sis, stop borrowing my sweaters. They don't fit me after you've used them. I don't have breasts!'* Then she came haltingly to the last sentence. *Chris was my friend, a younger brother who looked out for his sister. You are my angel now, Chris.* Caitlin made copies, carried them back to her room and was soon asleep.

Kathryn Traynor dreaded the night. Alone in the darkness, she was able to identify the areas of pain in the kidneys, the lungs, front and back, and the stinging headache in her forehead behind the lesions that had developed in the brain. Tim had prayed with her first and then had tucked her gently in, on all sides of the bed. In her prayers, she asked for a miracle, to sleep without pain this one night. She knew Tim would tiptoe into the room to be sure she was asleep before he lay down on the couch in the den. By now, she was adept at fooling him. He deserved to sleep without worrying about her. For each new day, for more time with Tim, for a chance to leave the bed, for the wonder of a wheelchair ride in front of the apartment with the wind against her cheeks, Kathryn lay alone and gave thanks. The case seemed far away; what was close and urgent was a need for confession and a certain absolution. Kathryn had the rest of the night to examine her motive for telling Tim about Jen Sexton. One thing Kathryn knew was that secrets get told, even by people you trust. What purpose would the knowledge serve Tim? If he knew the truth, if she had the courage to tell it, he had its protection against loose tongues. The moon was full Sunday night; a shaft of light shone between the verticals and caught the edge of her pillow. And there was some comfort in that.

When Tim felt that Kathryn was asleep, he lay on the pull-out with secrets of his own. Two, in fact. The years had passed and Tim had felt he could leave the past behind, because it was a done deal, or, to be accurate, two done deals. To Tim the *why* was not the reason he thought of them tonight. *We were young back then, and the pickings were easy.* Tim remembered the details, but what bothered him was the time he'd taken from Kathryn, time he wished he had back. *I thought we'd be together forever and I'd have the time to make things up to Kathryn. Now, it's too late.* He had a single wish for his wife. *Take her in her sleep, so Kathryn's not hurt any more.* Tim let go and fell asleep because he had cared for Kathryn all day long. He also slept because he wasn't the one dying.

CHAPTER 32

ALTHOUGH IT WENT against the accepted protocol, Remay punched in Jacques Lussier's private number. If there was something to find on the car, he was the investigator Remay wanted on this case. 'Jacques, Claude here. Forgive the pressure, I need to know what you've found; the family of the victim is very influential, and I don't want the perception to be that I've dragged my feet.'

'I was about to call you. My guys didn't miss anything, because there is nothing here that will hold up in court.' Lussier was not correct. He had not checked the front lights. Lussier assumed the initial investigator had taken care of that, but he hadn't. A problem with his son at school had forced the initial investigator to leave early from work, so that check was never made. 'This driver is one lucky bitch. Had the victim been struck as much as an inch either way, we'd have our trace evidence. To have made hard contact with all the reinforced points is almost unheard of in our business.'

'Dammit!'

'Is there any chance you can bluff her at the next interview? It's worth a try.'

'There are persons of interest, I enjoy this new way of referring to them, who have rehearsed their lines and I can see the nerves through the lies. Bluff works well with them. But this driver is a natural liar; she was baiting me, for God's sake!'

'This bitch would probably ace Russian roulette. Shit like this happens. All part of the job, Claude.'

'I'll get her back in here; try my shtick on her anyway. She doesn't have a DUI record, so I'm running on empty.'

'Is there a chance she's telling the truth? Stranger things have happened.'

'She's dirty. I knew it from the moment she walked into the office.'

'Give it your best shot!'

'I will.' Before Remay called the Donovan house, he made one call he enjoyed. Intruding upon a dirty suspect at his place of work was a measure of revenge for Remay. 'Ms. Pastore, please.'

'I'm sorry, sir, Ms. Pastore's in a meeting at the moment. Who shall I say is calling?'

'The Montreal Police Department.'

'Oh.'

'Please call her from the meeting.'

'Yes, sir.'

Remay allowed himself a smile while he waited.

Before Nicolina Pastore's meeting in the boardroom had begun, not a single person had asked her how she was doing. Instead, they stood around in small clusters whispering and gloating; some even smirked. Lecours had walked right past her without as much as a nod and called the meeting to order. When it was her turn to present a report, Nicolina could feel eyes boring into her brain. Towards the end of her presentation, she gave notice of the delay in their court case. Once more there was smirking, they all knew the game and how it was played. Outside, Nicolina sat stiffly, perspiring in a black cotton shirt and grey tailored slacks. Inside, she shrivelled.

When the receptionist knocked on the door, Lecours waved her into the room, over to him. His face turned stony as he flicked a finger towards Nicolina, and the receptionist crept over to her. 'Excuse me Ms. Pastore, the police are on the phone and wish to speak with you.' She made certain she whispered loud enough for people around Nicolina to hear.

Nicolina rose while her heartbeat spiked to high levels and walked as steadily as she could from the room. Her legs were rubbery as she made her way down the hall to her office on the first floor. Closing the door behind her, she stood in place and took ten deep breaths. If she had harboured the slightest hope that Lecours might decide it was in his interest to support her, that wishful thought died when he flicked a finger in her direction as though he'd already dismissed her. She hadn't had to fold yet, and she sure as hell was not about to walk away now.

First, she rubbed her eyes; then she picked up the phone. 'Ms. Pastore speaking.'

'This is Claude Remay, Ms. Pastore. You were in my office a few days ago.'

'Of course, I remember.'

'I'd like to meet with you today.'

There was something in his tone that led Nicolina to believe Remay had made this case personal. 'I'm in a meeting now, but it should end by noon.'

He cut her off before she could suggest a time. 'One o'clock then, Station 12. Ask for me at the front desk.'

'I want to offer as much assistance as I can,' she answered sweetly before he had the chance to hang up on her. To her surprise, she felt better and in control.

In a fit of fury and nerves, Lecours had ended the meeting abruptly. The last thing he needed was the arrest of their legal counsel. The fallout would be disastrous for the company. He still needed time to work on Comitrixin. He lit a cigar and stood fuming. Lecours rued the day he met the bitch and worse, hired her. Terminating Pastore was out of the question. Heat from this case had to fall on her! As he stomped down the hall, he saw her coming out of her office. How had he ever found her attractive? One too many cognacs, that would do it. There was something feral about Pastore with her narrow head and thin face and beady brown eyes. She disgusted him, especially when she smiled.

'What did the police want?'

'Raymond, this visit is routine, nothing to worry about.'

'Did you seek counsel as I suggested?'

'I gave it a lot of thought, but I decided against the idea. I've done nothing wrong, Raymond.'

'You do know a call for witnesses is all over the media.'

'I'd welcome a witness, Raymond. All this will be cleared up very soon.'

'It better be!' He turned and left her standing there, much as he had the last few times they had run into one another.

I hope you have a stroke! Nicolina walked back into the office with her head high and her fists pumped. Until she left for Station 12, she quizzed herself on things Remay might ask. After twelve, her bravado ebbed, and a band of dread began to snake around her heart. She paced her office to keep herself fluid; no way would she cave to this cop, or any other for that matter. Nicolina was far away from shutting down. Twenty minutes later, she was driving to the station. Getting to the station early would indicate her desire to help in any way she could. The steering wheel was wet from the sweat of her hands. No matter; she was ready!

Remay purposely kept her waiting. Standing at the front desk kept witnesses on edge, and that's when he had his best interviews. He came for Ms. Pastore at ten after one. 'Sorry to keep you waiting. Follow me, please.'

'I understand, Monsieur Remay.' He pointed to the chair he wanted her to take, the more uncomfortable of the two in front of his desk. Nicolina took the better chair. The confrontation began.

Remay opened a manila folder and extracted the reports, pretended to reread them, placed an empty pad in front of him, picked up his pen and was ready to take notes. 'Well, I have everything here. Would you please recount the events of the accident as you recall them?'

Nicolina repeated her story slowly so as not to give the impression she'd memorized it. The only angle she omitted was the suggestion the victim had walked out from between parked cars. How she wished she could erase that lie.

As she spoke, Remay checked his notes. 'You did say last Friday morning that the young man had walked out between parked cars.'

'That was a supposition on my part; I should have stuck with facts.'

'I see. I'm wondering why you made it in the first place.'

'At the time, and it was very late, it just seemed obvious to me that that's what he must have done. When I got back home, I realized I hadn't seen anything. You wanted facts and I offered a theory.'

Remay intended to surprise Nicolina with his next point and he did. He read from a report. 'According to our forensic investigators, your vehicle exceeded the speed limit at the time of the accident.'

'I assume you've run my licence plate and you've discovered that I've had only one speeding violation, and that was over ten years ago. I'm not a speeder, not with the price of gas today. I might have been doing forty kilometres, but not more. Police don't ticket at that speed, we both know that. It was dark and late and there was no one around, so I might have been clocking forty. I'll 'cop' to that, as you police say.'

'Ms. Pastore, Christopher Donovan was around; that's the young man you struck and killed.'

'I meant no disrespect. I was referring to other vehicles, sir.'

'You are aware that we are seeking witnesses.'

'A witness could certainly clear things up. I hope one shows up.'

Pastore was good; he had to give her that. 'I want to give you the opportunity to reveal as much as you know about this case now. If a witness comes forward and contradicts your version of events, things will go very badly for you. Obstruction of justice is a felony, and I would push for the limit in this case, jail time, because you were not forthcoming, given two separate opportunities.'

'I would expect no less, sir.'

Remay had met his match and he knew it. 'Thank you for coming in, Ms. Pastore. Remember what I've just said. Things will go much easier on you if you cooperate now.'

'That's exactly what I've been doing, sir.' Nicolina got up from her chair and walked out of Remay's office. Sweat from her armpits had trickled down to her elbows. Nicolina walked briskly to her car and drove back to the office for only an hour before heading out. Something had to be done about Sophia.

On the way home, Nicolina observed the rules of the road. As she drove onto her driveway, she noticed her neighbour Elsa, sweeping her front walk. It wasn't a minute too soon to begin preventative measures. Walking across her brown grass, she called out to Elsa. 'Isn't this remarkable weather?'

In more than a year, her neighbour had never offered

more than a cursory wave. *Things change*, Elsa thought. 'Yes, if only this run could last!'

'You're ahead of me with your clean-up; I must get to it.'

If this was a friendly gesture, Elsa could jump in. 'It must be good to have your mother with you.'

'Actually, Sophia is not my mother. Mine passed three years ago. Sophia was going through a rough period, so I'm doing my best to help out. The small rent she pays is welcome too. She's been a godsend, cooking, cleaning, caring for my pug and good company to boot. But she has me concerned.'

'Is she ill?'

'Heavens no, she's strong as a horse! Her arthritic knees are beginning to affect her balance. Yesterday, she did fall but she was lucky enough to save herself from the worst of it. I worry because I'm away a lot.'

'I know it's hard to say anything, though I worry about Mom too.'

'Sophia is very proud and independent, so I don't want to interfere.'

'I feel the same way.'

'Well, have a great day! Nice chatting with you.'

'You too.'

Plan B, the last resort, groundwork laid.

Nicolina found Sophia in the kitchen rolling meat-balls. As she limped to the sink, an obvious result of the fall, Nicolina thought, *she's making things too easy for me.*

Monsieur had stationed himself by the back door. That's where Sophia had told him to stay, and he was beholden to her for wiping up so many puddles, he did not dare stray. She had also given him two wooden spoons to save her shoes, and he had managed to get his teeth around both of them. Nicolina rushed over to her pug. He needed help to extricate himself from the spoons. 'How's our little guy today?'

'He has been a good boy so far. Is this a holiday?'

'No. I see what you're getting at, Sophia. I took a few hours off today; it's about time. *Why can't I trust her? Why can't I just say, 'Promise me you won't go to the cops; you don't know what happened; you weren't even there. You're in my house, under my roof, you owe me!' If I say that to her, and I sense I can't trust her, I have to go to Plan B and that would fuck up my life in yet another way.*

She had to begin somewhere; Nicolina couldn't leave things as they were now. 'Actually, I was at the police station.'

Sophia surprised her, by wiping her hands in a dish towel and sitting down at the table with meat ball pans in front of her. 'Why?' It was a simple question, but the seconds stretched wide between the women before there was an answer.

'I was there to assist them with the facts and I learned more about that awful night too. The young man was struck at the side of the road, not in the centre of it. Naturally, I couldn't see him. From their reports, the experts have verified that there was no excessive speed on my part. I'm saddened, but relieved. I knew I wasn't speeding.'

In her state, Sophia knew Nicolina couldn't recall anything she did that night. Stubbornly, she threw out a challenge. 'Again I heard the police on CBC and CJAD looking for witnesses.'

'I guess they will keep that up, but they seem satisfied with their reports.'

Why is Nicolina telling me these things? I can see she is angry with me; there is wrath behind her eyes. She is afraid I will go to the police. If no other witness presents himself, I know what I must do.

Sophia remembered the photo of the young man. 'The family cares only that their son is dead.' As a personal safeguard, because Nicolina's confidence seemed to threaten her, Sophia changed her mind about something. 'I called my daughter today.'

'I thought you weren't talking to one another.'

'We spoke today.'

Christ! Anger pinched Nicolina's brow.

CHAPTER 33

CLAUDE REMAY CALLED Frank Donovan after his meeting with Nicolina Pastore. Earlier, Frank had spoken with a colleague who worked criminal cases and had done his own investigation over the weekend with nothing of substance to report. In Remay's voice, Frank heard sincerity and regret. 'Sir, I came as close as I could to accusing Ms. Pastore, I'm sorry for you and your family. The outside hope is a witness. In one of my previous cases, a month after an accident, a woman came forward and testified at trial.'

'How long can you maintain this media blitz?'

'Another ten days.'

'That's something. I wish we had more.'

'I'll keep you updated, sir.'

'Thank you.'

Caitlin had stood close by as her father spoke with Remay, and the gist of the conversation was not difficult to figure out. Well, she had Thursday with Carmen. 'Nothing?'

'Afraid so. Is Mom still upstairs?'

'With Gran.'

'The boys?'

'They've gone out somewhere. Dad, I wrote something for Chris last night; I didn't think you'd be up to it.'

'That's so good of you, Cait. Everything seems so rushed, the funeral parlour, the church, the burial, the florist, everything. It's all so organized, so scripted, like a three-act tragedy. I guess that's what Chris' death is, dramatic and tragic. I'm very tired but I have to make another call. I wonder how anyone survives the death of a child.'

'There's little choice, Dad.'

Back in his study, Frank checked his Rolodex and dialed a friend. 'Bruce Strong, please.'

'Strong, here.'

'Frank Donovan. Sorry to be a bother. I've been wondering how many hit-and-run auto accidents occur in Montreal. How many drivers are eventually apprehended but slip through the system without prosecution?'

'All that information's in police computers.'

'How far do the records go back, Bruce?'

'I've done searches for my own cases. I believe it's twenty-five or thirty years.'

'How difficult would it be for you to run a check for me?'

'How far back?'

'All the way.'

'Give me a couple of days; I'll email the results to you.'

'Places and dates included?'

'The works. I won't forget this, Bruce.'

'This information might not help you through your grief, Frank.'

'Chris' death is like cancer. It's remote until it strikes at home, and then you want to find out everything you can about it.'

'I understand. Mary and I will be there tonight, Frank. Hold on.'

'Thanks, Bruce.' When Frank put the phone down, he shuddered. In a few days, he'd know the extent of the damage he had caused twenty-three years ago. Till then, his conscience, etched for so many years with self-loathing, would sit rigid, waiting for judgment. In

Chris' case, Remay suspected alcohol; in his own, he did not even have that excuse. It's funny, he thought, all the charity work, the donations, the decent life he'd led since, his own guilt, none of that ever erased one cowardly act. Through the years, he remembered what his father had drummed into his head. *Words are weightless; it's what a man does in this life that marks him.* If his father was correct, not even a confession would absolve Frank. He was a coward and that might never change. In a terrible way, he knew why this Pastore had run. Like him, she'd been afraid. Chris had deserved better. All victims did.

Frank felt his time was running out. If Bruce was true to his word, Frank would bury his son the same day he'd come face-to-face with his past. Frank's faith was hope, at best. Yet, he believed Chris knew now what he had done, and it would be Chris' death that would force him out into the open. Frank was glad Maureen was with Maggie because he felt unworthy of her love. In the past, so many times, he had envisioned the look on Maggie's face when he told her of the hit-and-run. If he had thought she might forgive him, pardon him, all of that evaporated last Thursday night when Chris was struck and killed. Like him, she would draw the parallels. He would watch respect drain from her face. He'd even felt he knew exactly what Maggie would say to him before she turned away and left the room. *How could you, Frank? How have you been able to live with yourself?*

Caitlin had stood outside Chris' room, listening to her grandmother's soothing words to her mother. She listened behind the closed door, but her mother was not responding. 'Maggie, we have to get dressed soon and you have to eat something.' Caitlin heard her mother say something, but she could not discern the words. Once her grandmother spoke again, Caitlin understood. 'You have to come, Maggie. Frank and I and Caitlin will stand beside you, but you have to be there. You have to say goodbye.' Then Caitlin heard her mother's strangled moan, so pitiful that it jarred her from the side of the door. She ran to her room. She would mourn for Chris, but she would not allow herself to break before she went after the woman who killed him. On her bed, she plugged her ears with the palms of her hands to keep the sound of her mother's anguish from tearing her apart.

During the next hour, the family ate at odd intervals, each alone, filling their bodies with the rations that would see them through the night. As Frank dressed, his body was not his own. He buttoned his shirt, but he could not feel his chest beneath. His legs were as stiff as a mannequin's, bloodless and hollow, as he pulled on his pants. His face was white with grief and disbelief. When he sat on the side of the bed, his shoulders ached. When he spread his hands, he saw they were shaking. Sweat was the only part of Frank that sadness could not extinguish. He felt its sticky rivulets running down the insides of his arms. He went downstairs and waited for Maggie and Caitlin. Remembering the car, Frank checked the garage. Like Chris, it was gone. Only a few shards of glass that Mike had missed in his sweep-up twinkled in the light. Frank bent and picked up a sliver of glass and crushed it in the palm of his hand.

Maureen and Caitlin, with Maggie between them, left by the front door and got into the car with Frank. During the relatively short ride, Maggie stared out the window, silent and far away. She had left her heart back in Chris' room. Caitlin consoled herself with the possibilities of Thursday. When they reached Decarie Boulevard and Sherbrooke Street, Maggie pressed the shell of herself against the seat as though she had just been struck and covered her face with her hands. Frank pulled into the parking lot before six. Together they walked through the wooden door of Collins and Clarke funeral home. Frank put his hand on Maggie's back to support her. 'I'm with you, honey.'

They were greeted at the front door by one of the owners and led to the large room at the back of the building. Before they reached the room, Maggie pulled back and fell against Frank. Above her was a simple black sign with white lettering, *Christopher Michael Donovan*. Maggie's eyes traced each letter and every letter cut into her flesh, every one. 'Frank, this can't be Chris. We never used his middle name.'

'Hold on to me, Maggie.'

Maureen stepped back a few feet, permitting Frank and Caitlin to hold Maggie under each arm and lead her gently in a wooden walk across the green carpet to the end of the room. Inside, Maggie dissolved, but her body pulled her forward to her only son.

There is a life that the young take with them into death. Tonight, Chris was himself, beautiful and young. He lay in a garden of flowers, hundreds of white and yellow roses. His graduation suit looked as new as it had a few weeks ago. The hint of a smile, easy and natural softened the brass bed that held him down. Hair fell over his forehead to cover a wound that makeup could not hide, but it looked as though Chris himself had fussed with it.

Maggie stepped close to the casket, bent and kissed Chris on the cheek. Then she rubbed her lipstick off and laid her palm under his chin. Frank and Caitlin stood transfixed. 'He's so small, Frank.'

Frank reached for Maggie and held her up.

'May I say a decade of the rosary, Frank?' Maureen asked.

'Of course.'

Together, they prayed for an angel and they kept a silent vigil with Chris until seven o'clock. Frank took Maggie from the room when the casket was closed and the flowers laid on top of it.

Before seven, dozens of people walked in one after another like a black wave to pay their respects. Maggie sat beside Chris, but she never once turned or noticed the room overflowing with young men and women who were still alive and had their lives ahead of them. How could she when her son was gone? Many times, she put her hand on the casket and whispered. Sometimes, she rested her head against it. Her mother sat beside her, but Maggie was unaware of anyone but Chris.

Frank and Caitlin took turns standing at the door to greet the mourners. There were no smiles as there are at some wakes, no casual exchanges. Chris' friends were in shock. They were polite, shook hands with Frank and Caitlin, but they too were numbed with grief and left quietly. Frank and Maggie's friends knew that words failed at such a time. Most patted Frank on the shoulder and left. Caitlin's friends wept openly and hugged her. Carmen had come early and stayed in her car for a long time before joining the mourners. She stood behind Caitlin. She left her side only once when she threaded her way through the throng to say goodbye to Chris. Though people left the room quickly, it never appeared to be empty. When one black wave ebbed, another took its place, well past closing time.

Mike came with Hunter. Frank shook their hands. Mike made no attempt to be strong or stoic. His eyes were red and sore-looking when he extended his hand to Caitlin. He recognized the hurt in her eyes. He wanted to scream, 'Forgive me for loving you.' Yet, he stood rigid with remorse. It was Caitlin who leaned forward and kissed his cheek. Mike turned away, sensing the finality in her touch. He made no effort to stem the flow of tears. Hunter was taken aback and finally admitted the depth of Mike's emotion. He led Mike by the arm to the casket. 'Don't give up hope. I was wrong about you.' They both knew enough not to approach Maggie when they knelt in front of the casket. The photo Mike had taken of Chris stood on a small table, illuminated by a single light, surrounded by white roses.

Throughout the entire evening, Maggie sat, like a stone sculpture beside her son, blind to the human wave behind her.

The following night was a repeat of Monday. Frank and Caitlin walked back to the room where Chris lay when Maggie and Maureen waited in the car for them.

'I hope Chris is not afraid. He hates being closed in.' Caitlin took deep breaths, some for Chris.

CHAPTER 34

FOR KATHRYN TRAYNOR, Monday night was a minor miracle. She slept without the usual pain and coughing. That morning, buoyed by rest, her thoughts did not carry with them the weight of pain. She even managed to climb out from all the cushions that Tim had set out around her, step into her slippers, reach for her crutches and walk into the den. She stood quietly a few feet from the sofa, leaning on her supports, smiling down at the man who had shared her life and was supporting her as she was leaving it. How much protection did Tim really need? He didn't work at Foley's. Her funeral would be the only place he'd run into her colleagues. Hopefully, Jen had spoken to no one about what had taken place between them. Sometimes, confessions are better delayed.

Tim sensed Kathryn's presence and opened his eyes. 'Well, don't you look beautiful!' He rolled up his blanket and sheets into a huge ball and dropped it on his pillow, picked up the whole thing, opened the louvered panels and deposited his stuff into the empty hamper. 'Let's go into the living room. I want you to see something. I looked at the paper after you were asleep and I came across something you might be interested in. I called on one of my golfing pals at Foley's and heard the news.' He helped Kathryn to sit on the blue leather sofa and reached for *The Gazette*. He'd marked the article, opened the paper and handed it to her. 'This is our Pastore.'

'Would you get my glasses, Tim? The steroids have done a number on my eyesight.'

'Sure.' He ran to the kitchen and found them on a side counter next to the battalion of medications that he carefully monitored and administered. 'Here you go, beautiful.'

Kathryn read and said, 'Oh, my God. Pastore is not content to ruin what's left of my life; she's taken another one. This is dreadful, just dreadful. Imagine what his family must be going through. He was just a kid.'

'Now that I think of it, I heard the police appeal for witnesses on 940 AM, and this must be the case they're talking about! I hope they find grounds to arrest the bitch.'

'The way I feel this morning, Tim, I know I could make court today if we had a session, so I hope there are no further delays. I don't mean to be so selfish, but my reputation matters to me.'

'You've no idea how glad that makes me to hear you talk that way.'

'I wonder if alcohol was involved in the auto accident.'

'Why?'

'I hate to repeat rumours, considering what's happened to me.'

'Indulge yourself.'

'Teachers Highland Cream Scotch Whisky.'

'How do you know this?'

'Apparently she keeps a couple of bottles at work. She's tried, and I hear failed, to be one of the big guys. You should see some of our bosses at parties. They're often three sheets to the wind and a few of them are quite obnoxious.'

'I wonder if the cops know she drinks.'

'They're rumours, Tim.'

'What if they're not and she drives her way into another fatality?'

'I can't swear to the fact that she drinks.'

'I could leave an anonymous tip; the number's right here. Let the cops investigate.'

'Tim!'

'I'd like to crucify her for what she's done to you, to us! I hope she's shitting her pants. Excuse the language, but for her, it's appropriate.'

'Tim!'

'All right. Hungry?'

'I could eat; I feel better. These damn steroids keep me hungry and bloated.'

'You're beautiful. Before I start on breakfast, let me put some lotion on your arms and legs. Keep you soft for me.'

'Sounds like a plan. Stay off the phone.'

'Yes, ma'am.' *Till after the next court date and then all bets are off.* Tim knew he could wait for awhile before making the call. He was already planning to use a pay phone. Even cells were traceable. He was sure the cops could use the fact that the bitch was a hard drinker. When Kathryn had a good day, Tim felt he could take on the world.

For Nicolina, Monday night fired up the threat within her own home. All she really needed now was for Sophia to announce that her daughter was planning a visit. She tried to focus on the barbarians she had held at the gate. Remay didn't have the evidence to nail her, not yet anyway. Sexton had said she would not send the damn file, but Nicolina had her doubts. Cheaters can't be trusted. That much she knew from experience. No witness had answered the police appeal. Her immediate problem was Sophia. She was an imminent threat and a credible witness if she called the police. Yet, what did she know? The bottles of Scotch were long gone if the police appeared with a search warrant. The old crab knew something; Nicolina could see that in her eyes. The ripple effect was the risk. If Sophia called the cops, and they in turn interviewed her colleagues, she was toast.

Meetings after hours were the culprit, not Nicolina. Often, when the upper echelon held these boring, long, useless sessions, the food did not arrive till after ten. To get herself through these marathons, she'd popped back into her office for another Scotch. Because she was sober tonight, Nicolina suddenly remembered a devastating debacle that many of those old boys knew about. *If that were to come out...*

Ask a drinker how many he's had, and the truth is, after a certain point, he can't tell you. One night at the end of September, Nicolina sat beside Lecours at another late night meeting in the boardroom. When she turned to listen to what he was saying, he began to spin. She felt she was falling backwards. Forcing her mind to interact with her limbs, she rose from the table and stumbled to the washroom where she promptly fell sideways onto the cold tiled floor. On all fours, Nicolina had crawled to the toilet, but not before someone had come to check on her. From the doorway, he saw the bottom in the opened stall and heard the retching, full and furious, and gagged at the stench.

'All you all right, Nicolina? Do you need help?'

Slurring her words between retches, 'I'm fine.' She knew immediately that he'd go back and offer her up to the room, even though most of them had drunk too much as well. After she'd put her head under a faucet, tried to wash the vomit from her mouth, rinsed it, brushed off her dress and headed back twenty minutes later, Nicolina saw from the smirks that everyone knew.

Add last September to what Sophia could tell and

she wouldn't stand a chance with Remay. She could throttle the old woman for the trouble she had brought into this house. *There is no one to watch over me*, she thought. God, she was thirsty tonight. A dry house had never been her plan. Then she remembered the Chianti, the show bottle, sitting on the kitchen table.

It's my house; I can damn well do as I please. Tonight, it pleases me to have a glass of Chianti. It's not the hard stuff; I'm not breaking my vow. I'm not! I promised no Scotch. Flare-ups from injuries often occur under stress. When Nicolina rose too quickly from her bed, her ribs fired up like a V-8 engine. *Dammit! Whew! I need the Chianti for pain. At least I don't take pills.* Stealthily, she crept downstairs and into the kitchen. With a corkscrew in one hand and the bottle in the other, she quietly headed back up the stairs. Why dirty a glass? Once the bottle was opened, Nicolina had some misgivings. After all, she was into her third sober day. She ran the bottle under her nose and breathed in the sweet smell. When she envisioned herself out of a job, even behind bars, she downed a long swig. And then another...

When the tiny plan came back to Nicolina, she marvelled at its simplicity. Tomorrow, she would leave the slipper on the second to top stair of the basement steps, loosen the single light bulb at the top of the stairs and hope for the worst for poor Sophia. *Why not do it now*, she thought? Her nemesis could just as easily fall backwards down the stairs as forward. Getting out of the bed was not quite as easy as it had been a few hours ago, but her ribs felt better, or the pain seemed farther away. She swerved over to her clothes closet, bent awkwardly to pick up a slipper, but she was sober enough to realize that the murder weapon, the slipper or shoe, should be Sophia's. If she used one of hers, she might as well print up a sign with an arrow pointing back at herself. How would she get the old bag's slipper tonight? Nicolina planned to be out of the house when she fell; that was a given. She threw down the shoe she had scooped up from the closet and stumbled back to bed. She needed her sleep for work tomorrow. Then she remembered the empty bottle on the bed. Sometimes, Sophia braved the stairs and freshened up her room. Worse case scenario, the police question Sophia. It wouldn't do at all for her to report an empty bottle in her bedroom. Once Nicolina located the bottle, she tramped over to the back window, raised it, and tossed the Chianti bottle as far as she could towards the side fence. A popping burst told her it had smashed on something down there. In the morning, before the old crow got out to the back yard, Nicolina intended to pick up the pieces.

Before she fell into booze's short, snoring sleep, she thought of another trouble spot. Lumbering out of bed yet again, she checked the phone; it was still disconnected, just as she had left it. How the hell did the old bag call her daughter with the phones unplugged? Did she have access to another phone?

CHAPTER 35

WHILE NICOLINA WAS busy choosing a possible murder weapon, Mike and Hunter worked ceaselessly on funeral plans. Mike spoke with the local pastor who kindly gave him the personal number of Father Kevin Egan. He had married Maggie and Frank, baptized both Caitlin and Chris and married Caitlin and Derek. He assented to the plans of Chris' friends. 'Michael, is it?'

'Mike, Father.'

'What a fine tribute to Chris! Get to the church early and I'll have everything ready for you. Our organist will supply the sheet music if it's needed. At the end of the mass, Chris' three friends will speak before Caitlin, his sister. I think we have everything covered; I'll be happy to meet with you Wednesday at ten.'

'Thank you, Father.'

When they were back in the car, Hunter sat back and rubbed his eyes. 'On TV and in films, death is commonplace. In the flesh, it's real. I keep thinking Chris will stick his head in the room and say, "Enough of this, let's get back to living." 'If Chris can die, any of us can. That's frightening, you know. We just graduated; this isn't supposed to happen.'

'Do you believe in fate?' Mike asked.

'No. Accidents are everywhere. If they were providential, there would be something special about Chris' death and there wasn't. Random acts scare the shit out of me. Death is the absolute loss of control. That's why I want to get out of here right after the funeral.'

'I can't say I have faith, but I still have hope of something. Chris deserves something better than a hole in the ground.'

'You mean *deserved*.'

'Hard to pronounce.'

Hunter was uneasy and changed the subject. 'Mike, are you packed?'

'Almost. I'll leave Thursday morning. I rented an apartment at Le Montfort on de Maisonneuve Boulevard and Fort Street, the same place you are I were going to check out. I know one thing. Caitlin isn't random; she just isn't.'

'I'm going home. This is such a desolate house. It's hard to breathe here.'

Caitlin wished for rain on Wednesday but that didn't happen. The sun rose and gained absolute dominion, as if a warm hand had been placed on the forehead of the city. Everywhere, Montreal sparkled with spring and dazzling light, everywhere but the house on The Boulevard. There, the family and two friends dressed in silence. When Maggie walked to the top of the stairs, she did not even resemble a version of herself. On some people, black is elegant; on Maggie the dress was a shroud. Her curls hung lifeless; her face was a shadow. Behind the spectre that was Frank, there played a distant sound of retribution that he carried on his shoulders. He went to take Maggie's hand, but she pulled it away. Caitlin's eyes were raw and angry, for she knew that grief, even justice for Chris, could not bring her brother back. Mike and Hunter had left the house early to meet with Father Egan.

Frank drove his family and Maureen to the funeral home for a last goodbye. The three women sat in the black limousine while Frank stood by the door. He wanted to see Chris being carried to the hearse. Like heavy, black sharks, they rode silently east on Sherbrooke Street to Kitchener Avenue. No one spoke. Two streets west of the church, there was a mammoth traffic snarl. Police lights from three squad cars swirled red, white and blue. Maggie moaned, 'Don't tell me there is an accident so close to our church.' She began to shake and sink further into her seat. When the limo inched forward, Frank saw that the cops had cordoned off a couple of streets and were directing motorists to parking.

'It's not an accident, Maggie. These people have come for Chris.'

Maggie closed her eyes and crumpled forward. Frank laid his hand on her back. Maureen reached over and took Maggie's hand.

The Ascension of Our Lord was one of the many inspiring greystone churches, in neo-gothic style, that populated Montreal. Its chime perched at the top of the enormous square tower. The interior of the church was elegant, simple and sober, the framework of the nave reminiscent of Montreal's basilicas. The oak doors were opened for today's mass.

Father Egan was standing outside the front door, quietly waiting for the family to arrive, nodding to the stream of mourners passing him on their way into the church. Mike and Hunter stood beside the old priest. Five minutes passed before their driver got out of the limo and walked around to the side door. Chris' casket was lifted from the hearse as the family stepped out of the limo. Frank stood directly in front of Maggie so she could not see the pallbearers making the arrangements for Chris' body.

As they proceeded slowly up the stairs, Maggie and Frank walked in the middle. Caitlin held her mother's arm on one side; Frank took the other. Maureen walked beside Caitlin. They waited outside the church for Chris' body to be carried up the stairs, and watched numbly as the two mass servers lifted the white roses from the casket and laid a white, gold-trimmed satin shroud on top of it. A server then replaced the flowers. Mike and Hunter took the place of two pallbearers at the front of the casket. Father Egan, with the two young servers on either side, led the small procession. One of the boys carried an elevated cross.

Behind the family, not a single seat was empty, mourners without seats stood against the side walls. Each of the pews in the centre aisle bore five white roses gathered together with a bright yellow bow. Past the first fifty feet, on either side, young friends of Chris, male and female, held white candles to light the way for their fallen friend. Father Egan stopped and turned to Chris and his family. He wore a small black microphone. When he spoke, he was heard by the congregation. 'Chris, we welcome you into the arms of Christ. When you came into this world, apart from your mother and father, you were alone. Today, as you leave us, and I look around, I see all the lives you have touched in the short time you were loaned to this earth. What a wonderful, rich testament! Come with Christ now and join him in eternity.'

Accompanied by a single guitar, a young voice, strong and sure, sang 'Be Not Afraid'. Within seconds, hundreds of voices joined the lone singer as Chris was brought to the altar of his baptism and first communion. Maggie saw no one but the casket as she followed stiffly towards the front of the church. She sat in the aisle seat, as close as she could to her son.

The older mourners comprised a list of prominent Montrealers. Two senators sat together with the mayor of Westmount. Behind them, the mayor of Montreal and three members of parliament took up another pew. Hospital directors, museum directors, four society presidents, with the Saint Patrick's Society the most evident, joined the battonier of the bar association and influential bankers. Frank was grateful to them all, but these events were not new to any of these dignitaries. One cannot reach a certain age without suffering the loss of a loved one. Chris' funeral would soon be forgotten or filed away in mental filing cabinets.

What amazed Frank most was the number of young men and women who filled the church. Not a single candle holder was dry-eyed. Chris was the first of their own to be lost, and their sense of immortality vanished with the death of their friend. These young people would remember Chris the way we remember our first love. For the Donovan family, they were also images of the son they had lost. In that sense, seeing them was painful, especially for Maggie. Off to their left, near the organ, the singer, a friend from Harvard, bore a resemblance to Chris. Frank tried not to look his way, but he did. Maggie looked over at the casket during the entire mass.

Since the weather was beautiful and still unseasonably warm, the front doors were left open. A broad shaft of light shone down the main aisle. Everywhere in the air around the mourners, there was the strong, potent smell of youth. Aftershave, gel, shampoo, the light perfume of girls, all of these things protested the inappropriateness of death to one so young and well loved. Chris had not even found a steady girlfriend. He was still on the first step when he was struck down.

The communion lines were long and the singer sang 'Eagle's Wings' and then 'Ave Maria'. No Donovan sang with the congregation. Carmen DiMaggio sat in the family pew and she began to comprehend the anger in Caitlin. Her fury was not only for Chris' death, but also for the devastation that it had brought on the family. She was thinking how unfair it was that death had come so often to them. Caitlin had just found herself, and now she wanted to risk everything to bring the driver down.

At the end of the mass, Father Egan said that Caitlin would say a few words for her brother, but before she spoke, a few friends wanted to say farewell. In all, three offered words of tribute. Mike was the last to speak. He was the only one whose voice broke. Crumpling his speech, he looked out at the people in the church. 'In your life, the best friend you can have is one who, through his example, forces you to be a better person. For me, Chris was that friend.'

Caitlin spoke from the heart. She took her eyes off the casket only once, when she looked at her mother. 'Chris modeled himself after you, Mom. You were strict, you'd have to admit that, but you also managed to be his best friend.' Not a sound broke into the flow of her thoughts; no one in the church wiped away the tears that fell liberally. Caitlin recalled the small events in their life together; the things that cause us to laugh and cry years later when they come to mind. For these few moments, Chris lived again through the vivid photos, coloured by a sister's love. Before Caitlin had returned to her seat and Father Egan had come to give the final blessing, the singer began a haunting version of 'Danny Boy'. This time, because the rafters resounded with the plaintive lyrics, no one joined in. The final procession walked from the church surrounded by the words of the song that broke all Irish hearts.

Frank had stipulated through Father Egan that the family wanted to be alone at the cemetery with their son. The Donovan family returned their only son to the hallowed earth and stayed with him long after the cemetery workers had hoped to be home. Frank compensated both young men, and they stood by the side of the grave and told the family to take as long they need-ed.

An hour later, when Frank whispered to Maggie that it was time to go, she protested. 'How can we leave Chris here? What if it turns cold tonight, Frank?'

Carmen waited a few hours before calling Caitlin. 'I've been thinking about tomorrow.'

'Carmen, you're not backing out, are you?'

'No, of course not. But I have a plan to suggest. We want our visit to Harvard to count, right?'

'Keep talking.'

'I think we should put off our stakeout till Friday.'

'Go on.'

'I have the number of the guy from the company who's retiring. I think, if you're up to it, come to my place and we can call him, identify ourselves and try to get more information about the trial and possible alco-hol link. Then, we can head out to Harvard Avenue with some facts to work with. The neighbours might help even more, if we know something about her. How does that sound?'

'Like a better plan. I'll be at your place by seven.'

'See you then.'

CHAPTER 36

MERCIFULLY, THE DONOVANS had not watched the news, but Sophia had, on a small TV that lay on top of the fridge. The segment lasted only eighteen seconds, but it was long enough for Sophia to pick up the name and recognize it. She was also able to catch a quick glimpse of the family and hear the police appealing for anyone who knew something of this fatal accident to contact the police. When Sophia heard the front door opening, she turned off the TV.

At night, Sophia prayed that a witness would go to the police. She was forced to allow herself time for her shoulder to heal. If she had to pack her things yet again, Sophia needed her strength. Finding another basement apartment was also on her list. If only she had her old knees, she could walk the neighbourhood checking out nearby streets: Wilson, Melrose and Draper. If she found nothing there, she'd try Marcil, Old Orchard, even Prud'Homme. Her arthritis precluded such searches. The problem with basement apartments was that the landlords did not want to spend the money to post ads for a three-hundred-dollar room. These people looked for students and posted their apartment listings on university bulletin boards. For Sophia, these venues were out of reach.

Her greatest fear was not for herself, but for Monsieur Patate. He was still on probation, and his problems were not all behind him. He had now chewed most of the toe off her good shoe. Sophia saw how he trembled when Nicolina came close to him. He might be sent to the SPCA and locked in a cage. Oh, he'd try to put his best face forward to little children who were looking for pets. But the trouble was, Monsieur left lots

to be desired in the looks department. What chance did
the pug stand against a cocker spaniel, a miniature poo-
dle or a Scottish terrier? Sophia did not want the pug to
be given the needle; like herself, there was a lot of
punch left in Monsieur. How could she take him with
her? Who would rent a basement apartment to an old
woman and a dog that was incontinent and destructive?

When Sophia heard Nicolina slam the foyer door,
fear replaced her worried musings. She hated when her
landlord was in a bad mood. Everybody suffered. For
dinner, Sophia had defrosted leftover lasagna and she
had made a fresh tomato and onion salad. The food
might help Nicolina's bad mood. When she didn't come
straight for the food, Sophia sensed a black and ugly
temper. How she hoped Nicolina had not brought
Scotch home with her tonight.

Upstairs in her bedroom, Nicolina tore off her good
clothes and threw them on the bed. She stepped into
the shower to wash off the day's grime and insinuation.
Throughout her entire day at the office, she met a
secret glee on the faces of all Foley's employees. Her
secretary hadn't the nerve, but she saw *The Gazette* on
numerous desks, purposely left opened with the section
of Chris' obit and photo, some even highlighted. All of
them were anxiously waiting for her arrest. She could
hear the voices behind her back. *It's only a matter of time
now. Who would have thought we'd get rid of her this way?
She deserves everything she gets! I'd give anything to be there
when she's arrested. It's a real shame she was ever hired.*
Nicolina had not one friend she could go to for help.
Lecours had not bothered to come into the office. Even
her pug had dumped her.

As she towelled off, Nicolina had two things on her
mind. Finally picking up the shattered glass in the backyard was one of them. Sneaking down to the basement

to retrieve a slipper was the other. Tonight, she'd set the trap on the stair. Sophia would blame herself for her fall. If only she had seen that Nicolina needed her loyalty, things could have been so different.

Once she was in her blue sweats, she headed down to supper and ate two servings and two dollops of ice cream for dessert. Nicolina would miss Sophia's food. When she was quite stuffed, Nicolina asked Sophia a favour. 'I know the basement is your apartment, but I think I've left some of the original case files down there. Would you mind terribly if I checked?'

'The house is yours, Nicolina. Take the time you need.' The landlord's gentle mood was unnerving.

'Thank you, I won't be long.' In a flash, she was rummaging through Sophia's closet. *Doesn't everybody own two pairs of slippers?* No one would ever accuse Nicolina of having a soft touch. Trying not to leave traces that she had gone through the old bag's things took real work. *Ah ha! There they are.* Nicolina carefully reached into an old paper bag and took out a single slipper. For a second, she was deep in thought. Better to leave the bag open. The closet door was already ajar when she came to it, all the better! Fingers would point to Monsieur as the culprit. *Who needs a friend? Could murder be this easy?* She moved to another closet and retrieved two folders and headed back upstairs. 'I found what I needed. Thanks. Listen, why don't you relax in the living room? I'll take care of the dishes. This trial has made my nerves jittery; I have to keep active.'

'Thank you, Nicolina. My knees are very sore. I first must take Monsieur out to the yard.'

'I'll do that; you've done enough for him. It's my turn tonight.'

'He does his business by the bench.' All this kindness caused Sophia to have gas and spiky nerves.

'That's where I'll lead him. Thanks.'

Twice Sophia looked behind her as she limped to the sofa in the living room; she was afraid, threatened by Nicolina's kindness.

Her landlord was not about to pounce; she was out in the backyard, scooping up the remnants of glass and dumping them into one of the bags she had brought outside.

Monsieur made quite sure he kept his distance and cowered under the picnic table.

When Nicolina found Monsieur's leavings, she was rather pleased. Things might just work out for her pug and her. 'Excellent, Monsieur! Good work!'

The dog had every right to be cocky. Monsieur chased his tail and Nicolina laughed, in spite of her murderous intent. The poop and the glass shards from the Chianti bottle went into the same bin.

Tonight, which was Wednesday, Nicolina would creep down the stairs, without making the slightest sound, open the basement door and lay the old slipper on the middle of the second step. Loosening the light bulb might not be the way to go. If the old bag fell to her death, and by some quirk of fate a neighbour found her because Monsieur was barking, that bulb could nail her to the murder. The light wasn't the best to begin with, and Sophia would not be looking for obstacles on the stairs. She had learned that the old bitch often came up the stairs without holding onto the banister. It was pride and her unwillingness to surrender to the travesty of time. *Well, that pride will be the death of you!*

No alcohol tonight for Nicolina; tonight she'd be on her tiptoes.

Though so much of Sophia's body ached and pulled with age, and she did not trust the sudden change in Nicolina, she was grateful for the time away from the cleanup in the kitchen and the limp out to the yard for Monsieur's pickup. She went to bed early and lay thinking for a while, waiting for the Ativan to kick in. *I am afraid because I am alone, and Nicolina is not a good woman. My food has not changed that. Even Monsieur is afraid. Please, Roberto, give me a good night's sleep.* Sophia slept through the night and without bad dreams.

Nicolina had no time for a conscience tonight. In her mind, self-defence was the name she used for this particular scheme. When life began to play fair with her, she'd begin to think of the welfare of others, not before. Accordingly, she mapped out her movements for later that night and early Thursday morning. On cue, at three, she reached under her bed and grabbed the slipper. She crept through the dark of night to the murder chamber. It took Nicolina a good two minutes to ease the door open without a single complaint from it.

On her knees, Nicolina reached down to the second step and left the slipper in the middle of the stair. She pushed the slipper an inch over the side of the stair so that Sophia would lose her footing as soon as she stepped on it. There must be at least twenty stairs, dropping straight down to a cement floor. She got slowly to her feet and closed the door with the same care she had used to open it. On her way back up to her room, a nasty thought raised its head. What if Sophia survived the tumble? Broke both hips, fractured other bones, but survived? What then? Nicolina could not leave her on the floor to starve to death, too easy for a forensics pathologist. A plastic bag? A whallop that could be attributed to the fall?

Staying on track was uppermost, she reminded herself. *Deal with one thing at a time.* Tomorrow, she'd take *The Gazette* in from the front balcony and leave it on the small table in the foyer. *Don't break patterns*. She had to be out of the house before Sophia fell and get home from work at the usual time. *Hope for the worst!* Nicolina slept well and operated on schedule.

Sophia could not believe that it was already seven-twenty when she opened her eyes. Added to her good fortune, not a single body part ached! Not a one! *Thank you, Roberto. Thank you for this good night.* What a difference to feel no pain, what a boost. Everything looked better in the morning. She was almost afraid to move a muscle for fear she might start up the usual cycle. However, hunger had Sophia up and dressed in short order. First, she would tend to Monsieur who himself had enjoyed a dry night. As she began to mount the stairs, she felt young and strong. *'Come on, Monsieur, follow me.'*

As high as the seventeenth stair she still felt pretty darn good for an old woman. Sophia took the eighteenth with extra gusto. *Roberto would be proud if he could see me now!*

CHAPTER 37

FOLLOWING CHRIS' FUNERAL on Wednesday morning, Caitlin had not gone back to the cemetery with her parents. Instead, she called Carmen. 'I've been thinking that we shouldn't delay things. Claude Remay is interested in Chris' case now. Let's call tonight.'

'I'm home by five-thirty. We can order Domino's pizzas and call after we eat.'

'To avoid the traffic, I'll get to your place early. I have a key.'

'Are you thinking of Chris at all?'

'I can't allow myself to; I need all my energy for Pastore.'

'I can't believe this is you talking.'

'Neither can I, but it is.'

'Two small pepperoni pizzas?'

'At least we're still on the same page there, mine with thin crust and pepperoni on top.'

'How could I forget? You always order the same thing.'

After the call, Caitlin changed into navy cotton slacks, a white t-shirt and open-toed sandals. She carried a linen blazer and a small purse. On the landing, she met her grandmother.

Maureen was carrying a photo of Chris. 'This must be so hard for you, Caitlin. You two were best buddies from the time you were toddlers.' Caitlin could see that her grandmother wanted company, and she had a little time.

'Do you want coffee? We can go to the kitchen.'

'Water would be better.' Before they had reached the bottom of the stairs, Maureen began to voice her concern for her daughter. 'Maggie has always been so strong. I've never seen her like this and so angry. I am worried about her.'

'Chris was her favourite. That never bothered me because I was Dad's. It's such a cliché, but Mom needs time. Whether you want it to or not, time dulls the pain and blurs the memories. Right now, Mom needs to be angry and devastated. We have to support her and not try to heal what she's feeling. The truth is that you can't lose one of two children and ever be the same. None of us will be.'

'You seem so strong, Caitlin.'

'I'm not. I'm angry. I can't talk about Chris.'

'Nobody in this house wants to talk about Chris; I don't understand any of this.'

Caitlin didn't know what to say so she hugged her grandmother. 'I have to go, Gran. Tell Mom I won't be late.'

'Are Chris' friends coming back to the house?'

'I think their stuff is still here, so they should be back. Mom and Dad will be back soon. Bye.'

'Goodbye, dear.'

The last thing that Caitlin wanted to do was talk about Chris or run into Mike. In minutes, she was heading north on the Decarie Expressway to Carmen's. When the photo of Chris played before her eyes, she strangled a moan. Caitlin recognized she was off the normal tracks of her life, and she knew if she succeeded in having Pastore arrested, Chris would still be dead. A force of gut-wrenching anger, far out of control, was directing her actions. Her thoughts were scattered as well. One idea was steel, immutable. Chris' life had to amount to more than a cipher. If it didn't, nothing would ever matter again.

Inside Carmen's apartment, Caitlin found refuge. She looked closely at the memorabilia, laminated on the

white walls, or poised on wooden boxes she and Carm
had bought together at Pier 1. A netted bag of seashells,
a blue and white lighthouse, a wooden carving of a bird
they'd bought on St. Denis Street in a nautical shop,
and Snoopy and the gang in various places in all sizes
and colours. How Caitlin respected Carmen! What little she owned, she'd bought for herself and treasured.
With a single salary, Carmen lived happily and survived.
Her lotto tickets were another issue. Here was a friend
who was willing to risk everything for her though she
had so little. While she waited, Caitlin curled up on the
couch. Her eyes fell on a familiar stack of magazines,
old issues of *People Magazine*, *The National Enquirer* and
Paris Match, all memorializing the life and death of John
F. Kennedy Jr. and his wife Carolyn Bessette. Whenever
Carmen proofed her work, Caitlin reread these old
magazines, still fascinated. Today she looked away and
buried her face in her arms.

When she heard Carmen opening the side door that
came in from the driveway, she jumped to her feet.
'You're early!'

'My boss was surprised I came back to work after the
funeral and got a couple of hours in. I also snagged an
account he wasn't expecting. He took one look at me
and said I could make up the time next week. So, here I
am, ready for duty. We'll eat first and try him before
dinner.'

'Let's order and pick up the pizzas ourselves. They're
on me tonight; don't give me an argument.'

'I won't. Here's the number; I know it by heart.'

The C's made quick work of the pizzas. Then Caitlin
made the call and wasted no time. 'Sir, I apologize for
imposing on you. I'll get quickly to the point, so as not
to keep you from your dinner. My friend Carmen spoke

briefly with you, pretending to be a friend of Ms. Pastore. In fact, we are not her friends.'

'I was lied to?'

'We saw no other way, sir. I'm Caitlin Donovan, the sister of the young man Ms. Pastore killed last Thursday night. Please, give me a few minutes.'

'Two.'

'The police believe alcohol may have played a part in the accident, but no witnesses have presented themselves, and Ms. Pastore left my brother to die alone on the road while she drove home and waited two hours before notifying the police. My brother might have survived had she remained at the scene and called for help.'

'How can I help without jeopardizing my position at the company?'

'We would never identify you by name or ask you to testify.'

'Continue.'

'Do you know if Ms. Pastore is a heavy drinker?'

Without hesitation, he recounted the famous night Pastore got drunk and fell at a meeting. 'She goes for the hard stuff.'

'We heard about some kind of case she's involved in…'

'You'd be referring to the wrongful dismissal suit filed by Kathryn Traynor.' He summarized the case for them. 'I should add a few important points. She accused our controller of forgery, a charge later disproved by an RCMP forensic. But that didn't stop Nicolina Pastore. You should also know that if Ms. Pastore loses this case, she's out of a job. Kathryn Traynor is also in stage four of cancer and is not expected to survive. When I see this company unjustly going after a dying woman, I get sick to my stomach.'

'You feel her dismissal was a witch hunt?'

'So does everyone else, but no one will admit it. Ah yes, I've forgotten something else. From what we heard, the case has turned in Traynor's favour. That's the reason for the delay, orchestrated by Pastore herself, I believe. They're hoping Kathryn dies before the trial resumes.'

'So, she's under a lot of stress.'

'To say the very least. I have no idea what happened the night your brother was killed, but if she was drinking, it would answer the question of why she took so long to inform the police. I wish you the best of luck, but you have your work cut out for you. Pastore is as sly and as devious as a cobra.'

'Thank you for your help, sir.'

'I wish we were going tomorrow,' Caitlin said when she hung up the phone.

'Friday is better; let's plan out a strategy. You need to spend some time with your mother.'

'I will. In Miami, you were the one in the deep end. Now, it's my turn.'

'You don't have to tell me.'

CHAPTER 38

FOR THIRTY-ONE YEARS, Pierre Michel Beausoleil had been a fixture in Montreal as the doorman of the Ritz-Carlton hotel. The sixty-five year old was fit and wore his black pants, white shirt, blue vest, trimmed in gold, wide blue tie, and blue jacket with pride and distinction. Returning guests remembered him. He was a master at directing traffic in front of the hotel; his silver whistle was his baton on busy days. Montrealers who passed by the hotel stopped, and often asked him if he was related to the hockey legend Jean Beliveau. Nevertheless, he had caught wind of a plan to 'retire' him.

Around three, when everything was quiet, he stood on the north side of Sherbrooke Street. Pierre was about to cross the street and call a cab from the hotel because the busses and metro stopped running at one in the morning when he heard a car. In seconds, it sped past the Ritz, braked and pulled a u-turn in the middle of Sherbrooke Street. Pierre noticed, for his job required that he be observant, that the car was a grey Mazda, the new one you saw everywhere on the street, and it was travelling without lights. He could have written a book about the moves he'd witnessed cars attempt and sometimes fail to execute over the years.

He forgot about the grey Mazda, until Thursday morning when he picked up a copy of *La Presse*. He read that a grey Mazda had been involved in a fatality, and police were searching for witnesses to step forward. The date and time of the accident fit Pierre's recollection. He counted backwards on his fingers to be sure. Then he picked up his phone and dialed Station 12.

Nicolina's hopeful mood was dashed the minute she walked into the office. Someone had had the audacity to pin the call for witnesses and the obituary to the bulletin board in the main corridor. As she approached the clippings, she began to shake with rage. If she squeezed through this mess and the damn court case, she'd sack the lot of them. Talk about persecution; the cops were determined to destroy her or manufacture evidence that could. If they weren't cops, she'd have filed a harassment charge against Station 12. She took the time to read the article and scan the photo. *I am just not lucky. Why couldn't this kid have been a drunk? Then no one would have cared.* She marched into her office and slammed the door. *What if the old bitch hasn't fallen and has read the paper? Jesus!* How she longed to speed back home and help the project along! But she didn't dare. Nicolina sat at her desk, took calls, signed papers and paid numerous trips to the washroom. Nicolina watched the steel clock on her desk all day long.

Frank sat in his study and checked his e-mail every fifteen minutes. All these years, he had felt that his own self-condemnation had been severe punishment; but he was about to experience the blunt forehand of public exposure. He reminded himself that he had promised to come forward if the driver who had killed Chris was brought to justice. What if nothing happened to her? That was his dilemma now. Once Frank saw what he had done in print, would he not be compelled to confess, to honour the memory of his son? He checked his e-mail again; nothing yet.

Caitlin could think of nothing else but Friday.

Pastore was a drunk. She was a fiend who could prosecute a dying woman to keep her job! Naturally, she left the scene; she could not take the chance of having her name linked with Chris' death. Yet, it was now anyway. Imagine if she found a huge stack of liquor bottles hidden in her house? Circumstantial evidence was a potent legal tool. *I'll get her, Chris. That's a promise.*

To calm herself, Caitlin went to her mother's room. At least her mother was dressed today, but she was lying on the bed, staring at the ceiling. 'Hi, can I come in?'

'Not if you're looking for company. I haven't any to offer.'

'That's okay, Mom. I'd like to be with you.'

'I drove my mother from the room a little while ago. Your grandmother thinks prayers can work miracles. I couldn't play along with her today.'

'That's all right. Religion is her way of accepting this tragedy.'

'His name was Chris, Caitlin.'

'I haven't forgotten.'

'I don't know why you and my mother want me to talk. I have nothing to say.'

'You don't have to say another word.'

Maggie turned on her side, away from Caitlin.

There is some comfort to be found in the presence of another human being and some in silence. Maggie felt a little better, knowing Caitlin was beside her and demanding nothing of her. When Caitlin put her arm around her, Maggie did not pull away. A few minutes later, Maggie whispered, 'I love you, Cait.'

Frank was beginning to think Bruce Strong had forgotten him. He tried again and found mail from him and numerous attachments. The note was short: *The*

'works' are all here. Hope this info helps. Yesterday's service
was memorable, Frank. Again, sympathies. Bruce. The
truth was finally at Frank's fingertips. He could erase
these files easily, get up and walk away, but he didn't.
Frank wanted to know the facts as much as he did not
want to know them. He drew deep breaths and opened
the first attachment. The collator had done a fine job.
All pertinent information had been carefully document-
ed. Names, dates, the accident account given a full para-
graph, ditto for the follow-up, the prosecution or lack
of it duly noted. Frank read the first two reports; then
he began to scroll slowly, searching for a particular date,
October 17, 1976. He had an outside hope he'd discover no report had ever been filed. Maybe the kid had
walked away cursing with only minor abrasions.

He was wrong.

On Tuesday, October 17, 1976, Ryan Burns had
been the victim of a hit-and-run at the corner of Bishop
Street and Dorchester Boulevard. (René Lévesque was
the name assigned to the boulevard today.) According
to the account, a red Ford Mustang ran a stop sign and
struck the victim. A few hundred feet ahead, the driver
pulled over to the side of the boulevard, left his vehicle,
acted as though he were coming to the aid of the victim,
changed his mind and drove off. The driver appeared to
be in his twenties, tall, with brown hair. Ryan Burns
sustained a broken collarbone, multiple fractures to his
right arm and a broken ankle. The driver was never
located.

At least he survived, Frank thought and was grateful.
In his mind, the victim's account was not entirely accurate. Along the boulevard today, there were traffic lights
at every corner, but back then, there were four-way
stops. Frank remembered pulling an American stop,
maybe worse than that. This Ryan Burns, cycling down

Bishop, had not even attempted to make a partial stop but had shot out across Dorchester in front of him. But the fact was that if he had come to a full stop himself, he would not have struck Burns.

Frank was twenty-five back then, rushing to an interview. His life was ahead of him. He had a young wife, a baby daughter and a career in law. This accident might have destroyed his career, so he ran. That day, when he had looked back, he saw the victim getting to his feet. Would he have rushed back if Burns had lain unconscious on the road? Today, Frank could not answer that question. Confronted with the loss of our future, how many of us would surrender ourselves to the law if we had the opportunity to flee? Frank didn't hate Pastore any more than he hated himself.

He came to one decision; he would locate Burns and send him money. Finding Burns after twenty-nine years was another matter. From these notes he did have his address in 1976. Frank would work from that point. The money he'd send would be untraceable cash.

CHAPTER 39

IN EXACTLY ONE hour and forty-one minutes, Nicolina could leave the office and drive home to reclaim her house and her dog. Sophia had not shared her daughter's number with her, so she had no obligation to inform the police about next of kin. She rubbed her palms together, itching to leave. The minutes ticked away.

Jen Sexton, left the office, sat in her late-model Beemer and called the Traynor home. Tim answered.

'Hi, my name is Jen Sexton, one of Kathryn's colleagues. We are all thinking of her and not calling to give you both the peace you need.'

'We've appreciated that.' Tim's tone was not especially friendly. These were the colleagues who had offered nothing in the way of help to Kathryn. *Cowards, all of them*, he thought.

'Is there any chance I might speak to Kathryn for two minutes? I have some information I feel she'd want to hear.'

'Jen, is it?'

'Yes.'

'Not today or tomorrow. Kathryn has come down with pneumonia and the antibiotics have levelled her. She's sleeping at the moment. Is there something I can tell her? Is it about the case?'

'I'd like to speak to Kathryn first, if that's possible.'

Tim bristled at the rebuff. 'Well, I can't give you a time. I'm her husband and I know all about the case.'

'Can I leave you my cell number?'

'Shoot.'

Sexton had the distinct feeling that she'd just made another mistake. She tossed the cell on the driver's seat and repeatedly punched the steering wheel with both palms. 'Now, they'll both be edgy.' *Why the hell did I call? Shit, shit, shit! How the hell could I tell her husband? Now, I've just added extra stress to her life. Way to go, Jen!*

Tim put the receiver down more slowly. Walking quietly across the parquet floor, he peeped into the bedroom and found Kathryn asleep. He'd bet his life that she had never kept secrets from him, but he wondered about Jen Sexton's call, just a little. He had his past, but was it possible that Kathryn…? Either way, he didn't want to know. Then he remembered that he wanted to speak for her at the service when the inevitable happened. The palliative physician had told him to begin preparations in that direction. Maybe Tim would just ask Kathryn, straight out. There was nothing to worry about.

Claude Remay lost no time getting back to Beausoleil, the doorman at the Ritz. 'You are certain it was a grey Madza 3?'

'Of course, I watch people and cars all day. I like cars, always have.'

'Did you note whether the driver was male or female?'

'No, I did not. I often see this sort of thing; sometimes much worse. At times, I have notified the police.'

'Do you remember anything else?'

'Of course, the car was definitely speeding and driving without lights.'

'You're certain of that, sir?'

'Absolutely.'

'Please give me your home number. I appreciate the help. How old are you, sir?'

'Young enough to recognize a grey Madza.'

'Good enough.'

Pierre Michel couldn't wait to tell the manager he had assisted the police in the case featured in *La Presse*. Let them even think about replacing him now. He was a man who noticed things young guys would wave off.

Claude Remay had the first answer in the case. Christopher Donovan never saw the car that struck him because it sped down Sherbrooke Street without lights.

Nicolina picked up her briefcase, said goodbye to her secretary who nodded back because she needed the salary that went with this job, and headed for her rental. For a minute or two, she sat in her car. *Have I really killed somebody?* Time suspended itself as she started up the engine. Blood drilled through her veins, sweat curled around the corners of her nose. Yet, amid the regret and disbelief, Nicolina was buzzed, really buzzed. Dammit, this was a high!

I have to get control of myself. What do I do when I find her? Run to the neighbour. What the hell is her name? Belsa, Melsa, shit! Nicolina was good with facts; with names she got the sounds, but not the names themselves. *I don't have to call her anything. I'll be upset; I am already. Poor Sophia! It didn't have to come to this.* Nicolina was ten percent sad for the old bag; ninety percent relieved.

The house seemed unnaturally quiet when she pulled into the driveway. She remembered to take her purse and briefcase. All she wanted to do was run down the basement stairs. When her neighbour waved, Nicolina waved and smiled. Elsa! That was her name. 'What wonderful weather!' she called over.

'I'd like to package it,' Elsa called back.

'Me too!' Nicolina unlocked the front door and walked cautiously into her house. It was very quiet. The door to the basement was closed. The paper was still on the table. She forgot for a second that Sophia always put it back there for her after she had read it. 'Sophia?' she called gently. Wanting to check all quarters before the basement, she went upstairs, in case the old bag had survived and was up there cleaning. 'Sophia?' she called into every room. *Good so far!* Back downstairs, she called again, 'Sophia?' No sound came from the kitchen.

Shock and glee bumped against her heart, each vying for her attention. Murder is control, dominance. Nicolina was revelling in both. Her palms were sweating as she inched toward the basement door and opened it. Just for a second, she closed her eyes. Then she flipped on the light and froze. The slipper was gone. Sophia was not lying on the floor in a mangled heap of blood. *Oh, no!* Her throat constricted and Nicolina grabbed the railing to keep from falling herself. She still had hope. *Maybe the old bitch had crawled back to her bed.* Step by step, Nicolina descended the stairs, her cheeks oily with sweat. Nothing!

'Damn, damn, damn,' she howled as she ran up the stairs. *Where the hell is she? I can't shoot her, for God's sake!* She remembered a place she had forgotten to look. Nicolina ran to the kitchen and opened the back door. Sophia was sitting on the bench, tossing the old slipper a few feet, and Monsieur was retrieving it for her. What a lovely pair they made, for anyone but Nicolina.

'Hello,' Sophia called to her. 'Monsieur got into my cupboard and found this,' she said, holding up the murder weapon. 'I have had a wonderful day! I'm sorry dinner will be a little late. The day is so beautiful.'

More bad news for Nicolina. She was ravenous.

CHAPTER 40

CAITLIN HAD A plan for Thursday night. Her parents and grandmother were together in the living room, and she could not be with them tonight. She might lose her focus. She met Mike and Hunter on the landing.

'Hi, Caitlin. I can't imagine how hard this is for you and your parents. I'll be getting out of your way tomorrow morning. I'm heading back to Boston.'

Mike stood behind Hunter.

Hunter reached into his pocket and withdrew a note. 'I've rearranged the lists, but I have something separate for you. Your publisher called and expressed his sympathy, but he hopes to hear from you next week. It's kind of urgent. Let me read my notes. He says you have a launch date at the Double Hook on June 21. He's also snagged you an interview with the anchor of the late news of CTV and one with a noonday host of CBC.'

'I don't care about any of this right now.'

'I have notes on the back too. He's very excited. He says you will be one of the last authors at the Double Hook because it's closing and you can't miss these interviews.'

'Give me the note. I'll get back to him next week, not before. Thank you for your help, Hunter.'

Hunter shook Caitlin's hand, gave her a quick hug, and left Mike alone with her.

Mike shifted from one foot to the other. 'I'm out of here tomorrow too, but I'm not leaving Montreal. I found an apartment where we had originally planned to stay. I won't give up on us. I'd also like to visit Chris' grave, say a proper goodbye. My grandfather was kind of a cemetery man, visited all his family and friends often. I take after him, I guess.'

'Chris would like that.' Caitlin walked by him and down the stairs.

She didn't blow me off! Mike felt better.

Once she was in her yellow Beetle, she backed up past what appeared to be a white Chrysler of some kind, probably Mike's rental, and drove to NDG. If she was about to throw away her career, Caitlin first wanted to scout the Harvard house, see as much as she could of the backyard or side door. A high fence or hedge, either one, could mask her entry. The neighbours and their houses were also on her list. Caitlin was an athlete, a strong cyclist, swimmer and runner. If anyone could get in and out of that house quickly, that person was Caitlin.

Mike never intended to stalk Caitlin, but he ran down the back stairs, out to his car and followed the yellow Beetle with the black Turbo decal on the side doors and Tweety decals on the back tinted glass window. Mike wanted to protect Caitlin; that's what he told himself. Caitlin turned right on Sherbrooke Street. Mike was five cars behind. *Jesus, I hope she's not going back to the funeral home. I wouldn't be any help; I'm still bummed out from Monday and Tuesday.* Mike started to worry about Caitlin when she turned right on Marcil Avenue and parked.

Caitlin did not walk back towards the funeral home, but up to Côte St. Antoine Road and turned to her left. She began sprinting, realizing she had to take full advantage of the remaining light. Mike was careful not to run. He knew if he did, she'd be sure to turn and pick up the tail. When he was partially hidden behind cars, he bent his head and ran like cops in movies, except he wasn't carrying a gun. *When she moves, she moves!* Twice, he almost tripped and fell forward on the sidewalk because of the way he was running.

At the corner of Harvard, Caitlin abruptly stopped her sprint and began to walk up the street. She now wished Carmen was with her. Taking note of the house numbers, Caitlin's nerves began to hop as she got closer to her target. Judging by the numbers, she still had a good block in front of her. *Chill out, and remember why you're doing this!* She began to breathe easier.

'Caitlin? Caitlin Donovan?' A voice from a front door on her right rang out.

Caitlin tried to swallow her surprise before she turned to answer the intruding voice.

'Caitlin, I am so sorry to hear about your brother.' Sandy Patterson threw her arms around Caitlin. 'All of us at work were just devastated when we heard the news. You spoke very well at the funeral mass yesterday.' Sandy was a metaphysics professor at Concordia. Caitlin rarely saw her, but by all accounts, she was tough and well-liked by the students. The kids in her classes often rated profs and generally were fair and hit the mark.

'Thank you for coming to the funeral, Sandy. People are a comfort.'

'Well, what are you doing in my neck of the woods? You're in Westmount, aren't you? I only know because it was my turn to help out with the staff directory.'

'It's so sad at home; I needed to clear my head.'

'Are you up for coffee?'

'It's the talking I'm not up for. I wanted to be alone.'

'Here I am disturbing you. Listen, it's good to see you, and I'll say good night.'

'Sorry.'

'I understand.' Sandy kissed Caitlin's cheek before leaving her.

Caitlin walked up to NDG Avenue as casually as she could, leaving Harvard as soon as she could and doubled over in shock. *I almost blew the whole thing! I should never have come here without Carmen. What the hell was I thinking of? What a bloody idiot I am! But, shit, who would have thought I'd run into Sandy Patterson, who's young enough and alert enough to remember that I was here? Some of the old profs at Concordia can't remember what class they're heading to. What are the odds?*

Caitlin was not thinking clearly. The fact was that many older professors had long ago bought old homes in Westmount, didn't have the money to do much renovation, but were very happy with their creaky wooden floors, drafty rooms, cathedral ceilings and Westmount address. Younger profs, like Sandy, bought in NDG, which had come back from a drought in the early eighties and was the 'place to be' in the city if you weren't a millionaire. Hundred thousand-dollar homes were selling for half a million today.

Once she'd recovered, Caitlin ran like a gazelle back to her car and drove home. She did not dare tell Carmen about tonight. If things went well tomorrow, she would.

What spooked her? Clearly, the woman had. He guessed she was going home. He had better get back and pack the rest of his things. *I could get pretty good at this! One thing I'm going to do tomorrow is change this car. Mike Hammer would do the same. Caitlin's seen it. She sure as hell would recognize the car parked near her house tomorrow morning. Caitlin was looking for something on this street and it wasn't that woman. That means she's going to be back! And so will I. Sooner or later, she will need me.*

In her room that night, Caitlin laid out clothes for Friday's break in, non-descript stuff that no one would remember. Friday had to go well; it had to!

If Caitlin had come upon the Harvard house, she would have seen Pastore in the flesh, backing out of her driveway. At the SAQ liquor outlet, she'd make up her mind if she wanted the Scotch or not. Her mood was foul. She didn't want to lie on her four-poster bed cursing her fate without a buzz if she needed one. The old bag had served leftovers that had lost their zing. Seconds before she turned on Monkland Avenue, she was jarred by the buzz of her cell. When she saw the caller ID, she pulled over. 'Yes?'

'Claude Remay, Ms. Pastore. Forensics has released your vehicle. I tried to reach you at home, but the phone there is out of order. We may have a witness.'

Nicolina was stunned. Her heart began to hammer.

'Are you still on the line, Ms. Pastore?'

'Yes, I am. I'll be down in an hour to get my car and take it to the dealer. My dog chews on phone lines and shoes; I'll look into that.' Now, what should she say? *Are you arresting me?* She recovered because she had no other choice. 'Was the witness on the scene?'

'Apparently. I'm calling him early tomorrow morning. Naturally, I'll keep you informed. Good night.' *Let her sweat this out.*

He, not her, as in Sophia. Definitely, no Scotch, stiff or otherwise tonight. Nicolina drove home, parked the rental, called a cab and took possession of her Mazda. An hour and a half later, she was sitting on a grimy chair in a no-name mechanic's shop. The Mazda dealer would have left a paper trail that spelled reckless endangerment causing death if her light problem was discovered. Here she was anonymous. 'You had no lights because the clips weren't catching properly,' the mechanic had said. 'Happens sometimes. Easy to adjust.'

When the Mazda had been deposited at the dealer's

for the other repairs and she had been driven home, Nicolina sought asylum in her bed on top of her one extravagance, Pratesi sheets. Somewhere, in the frantic jumble of her nerves, legal sense was telling her she'd have been arrested tonight if the evidence this witness had on her was compelling. Remay would not be waiting until tomorrow morning to contact his witness. But their witness had something, that was certain, or the cops would not be interested.

What this witness had, plus Sophia's info, was a clear and present danger for Nicolina. She began plotting Plan C.

CHAPTER 41

MIKE WENT BACK into the house on The Boulevard the same way he had left it. Except for Hunter, no one saw him. In minutes, his things were packed. 'Are you leaving tonight?' Hunter asked from the doorway.

'I figured it might be easier this way. Are Mr. and Mrs. Donovan downstairs?'

'I guess. Are you really staying in Montreal?'

'Haven't changed my mind about anything I told you.'

'Like Chris, I can't believe the change in you either. You're not the same guy who left Boston.'

'I met the right woman; I have six months before I begin work.'

'What about Caitlin's *I never want to see you again* comment?'

'Case closed, Hunter.' Mike picked up both bags. 'Keep in touch; here's my number.' Mike reached into his pant pocket and handed Hunter a small white sheet.

'All right, good luck then.' Even though what had happened touched him the least, Hunter Townsend would feel better when he was home. He didn't deal well with change.

As Mike came down the centre stairs, he heard voices. He laid his bags on the floor near the foyer door and followed the sound. He peeped into the room. 'Excuse me, I just want to say good bye. Thank you both for everything.'

'I thought you and Hunter were here for the night,' Frank said as he rose to greet Mike.

'Sir, I'm staying in Montreal for a while.'

'I see. Well Mike, thank you for your help. I wish we had met…'

'I understand, sir. It was nice to meet you, Mrs. Donovan. Take care of yourself. Good-bye Mrs. McDonough. Sir, I'd like to leave my number with you. If you need anything, call.'

'That's very kind of you.'

'Goes for Caitlin too. Please give her my number as well.'

'Thank you for the offer, Mike. I'll go up and get her. I think she's in her room.'

'We kind of said our good-byes already.'

'Well, be safe.' Frank shook Mike's hand.

When they were alone, Frank said, 'Maggie I think we should call Mireille and have her back cooking for us. I don't want you more tired than you already are.'

'I'd rather we keep to ourselves for a while.' Turning to her mother, 'Mom, are you still going home on Sunday?'

'I'll stay if you need me.'

'I want to be alone, for a while anyway, especially tonight.' Maggie got up and left Frank and Maureen alone. 'I'll let you know, Mom, if it's too hard by myself.' She crept up the stairs to Chris' room.

'If it is, I'll be on the next plane, Maggie,' her mother called after her.

Twenty minutes later, Mike was at the rental agency, loading his bags into a blue Sebring. First step completed, he thought. *I'll be back on The Boulevard by nine tomorrow. She's going to need me; I feel it.*

Caitlin was unaware that Mike had left because she was talking to Carmen.

'I have Kathryn Traynor's home number. We have to be careful before we even think of intruding on her husband and her at this time. I'll pick you up at nine-thirty tomorrow. We have to give Pastore time to leave the house and get to work. I've been plotting things out. Before you even consider breaking into her house, I think we should try talking to the neighbours.'

'If they can't give us anything?'

'Then we go for it.'

'All right.'

'I feel like I'm back in Miami. Are you bringing tools like a screwdriver, hammer, gloves…?'

'Hadn't thought of those things. I've only pictured myself in her house, finding liquor bottles.'

'I still don't get what that proves, Caitlin.'

'Shit, Carm, don't get me down. If I find a lot of liquor, it might help us.'

'Let's concentrate on one step at a time, the neighbours.'

'I just want to go meet that bitch face-to-face and shake the truth out of her. That's what I really want. That and a confession.'

'Get some sleep. See you tomorrow.'

'You were just as stupid and foolhardy in Miami as I am now.'

'If you hadn't pulled me from the water, I'd be dead. I've got your back.'

'I know.'

Tim Traynor was happy to see that Kathryn was awake. 'Hi, honey.' Sometimes when Tim looked at his wife, he saw clearly that part of the woman he loved was already gone; the other half was fighting to stay with him. Maybe tonight, after she was asleep, he'd get to work on words he wanted to speak for her at her funeral. *I never want tomorrow to start without you, Kathryn.*

'Hi,' Kathryn answered, managing a smile. 'I feel

better. I'm thankful for another day. It's probably the antibiotics.'

'In a day or two, you'll be more yourself.'

'You look so worried, Tim. Is there something on your mind, apart from me?' Every word was an effort for Kathryn.

'Maybe, I can wait.'

'For what?'

'I was talking to your mother while you were asleep and she asked if I would prepare some words for you when…'

'When the time comes…'

'I shouldn't have brought this up.'

'Why don't we keep the service simple; then you won't have anything to worry about?'

'Let's get off this topic.'

'I don't think I'll escape reality, Tim.'

'Well, you have friends, a lot of them. I don't want this goddamn case forcing us to hide even after you…'

'I know, Tim.'

'I almost forgot; Jen Sexton called and wanted to tell you something.'

Kathryn winced; Tim noticed the change in her.

'If she calls back, and you're up to it, you can find out what she wants. I have so much I want to say about you, Kathryn, so many good times. You always made me feel good about myself. That's something I want to say.'

Kathryn smiled on top of her fear.

'My true and faithful friend… stuff like that, you know.' Tim's brow constricted with lines that would one day stay permanently. 'Can I say that Kathryn?'

CHAPTER 42

BEFORE SHE WAS able to fall asleep, Nicolina came up with an idea. The old bag had dry skin and slathered her arms and legs with baby lotion each and every day. Her stash stood on the floor near the cupboard downstairs, eight or nine of them, like pink plastic flowers. What if she spilled some lotion on that second stair before she left for work? The pug couldn't pull Sophia out of that one. The lotion was a lot more slippery than a stupid slipper, more deadly even. Should she put the project in motion tomorrow or Monday morning?

The witness that Remay was about to speak with Friday morning could be worse for her than a slipper or lotion. Her project would have to wait till Monday. From the moment she was asleep, Nicolina felt she was falling off the bed and jerked most of the night. In the morning, her ribs were aching. She showered and made every effort to appear calm and concerned at the same time. Truth was, she still looked as bad as Maggie Donovan, but that might win her sympathy points. She'd take anything she could get.

Alone that night, Mike walked over to Crescent Street from the Montfort and spent a long time looking up at Winnie's, remembering. Then he grabbed a burger and beer at the Hard Rock Café and headed back. This city was such a live wire. Crescent Street was crawling with people of all ages, and it was only Thursday night.

Mike was parked four houses away from the Donovans by nine the next morning. He didn't have to wait long. Carmen's blue Mini passed his car and turned into Caitlin's driveway. Mike put on his shades and the Sox cap he often wore, but Caitlin hadn't seen. Then he waited.

From one look at Caitlin, Carmen knew she'd had little sleep. Then she remembered that last night was Thursday. Caitlin, unlike her usual style, wore nothing that remotely matched. She carried her sunglasses and cap. 'Hi, you're right on time.'

'Left Laval early so I wouldn't be late. I see you didn't bother with the tools of the trade.'

'I haven't hit bottom yet. When I couldn't sleep, I began to think that Pastore probably has a spare key under a mat or something. I might even find it. That way, there won't be any damage.'

'Good thought! All right, let's do the deed.' The C's drove to Oxford Avenue, turned left on Côte St. Antoine Road and parked behind another car. They both wore the caps they'd brought and the shades as well. They did not notice a blue Sebring drive past and park closer to Sherbrooke Street. Why would they? What had their attention was behind them.

'Let's walk up Oxford to Monkland and then down Harvard; you know, change our routine a little.' Caitlin did not dare tell Carmen that a colleague lived a block from Pastore because that might have put some sense into her, and Caitlin didn't want that.

Ten minutes later they were standing across the street from the target, pretending to be talking to one another. Mike wasn't far away. 'Listen, Caitlin. I brought a whistle. If and when you go around the back, I have an alarm system. If I blow once, stop in your tracks. If I blow twice, get the hell back over to this side of the street.'

'Sounds good to me; pardon the pun. The lane across the street is shared by Pastore and her neighbour. Before we do any scouting of the people around here, I'm going to run over there and peek in the garage door to be certain her car isn't locked up. Then I'm going to check the back to see if I can find a key.'

'Fine, but don't even think of going inside until we talk again.'

'Deal.'

Caitlin walked nonchalantly across the street, faster down the driveway.

Carmen kept guard. When he was twelve and thirteen, Mike had snuck into many neighbours' yards. He quickly figured out what the C's were up to. *Wow! She's as brave as a kid.* Everything Caitlin did impressed Mike. No wonder Chris had loved her as a sister and friend.

Sophia was into her second good day. She took Monsieur's leash, and the pug himself had come running as fast as he could. He knew he was up for a walk. Sophia lugged her heavy brown purse that held just about everything she owned, opened the front door and led Monsieur outside to the veranda.

Carmen's mouth fell open. She fumbled with the whistle, couldn't catch her breath, finally did and whistled.

Monsieur gave an unaccustomed little bark and pulled on his leash, threatening Sophia's shoulder. She herself didn't catch on to what was happening. She reined the pug in, grabbed the white banister and slowly descended the stairs. The twosome began their walk to Monkland Avenue.

Carmen walked to the other side of the street and blew the whistle twice, as softly as she could.

Caitlin sprinted back, eyes sparkling, afraid but triumphant!

'Caitlin, her mother lives with her. She just came out of that house, for God's sake! Are we even at the right place to begin with?'

At that moment, Elsa was back with her broom and rake to continue the work she had begun earlier in the week. 'Can I help you? You look lost.'

Caitlin thought quickly. 'Hello. Nicolina didn't tell me her mother lived with her. We were passing by, looking for homes. I was surprised to see someone else coming out of Nicolina's house.'

'She never told you because that's her boarder, not her mother.'

'There you go. How is the neighbourhood by the way? It appears so friendly. We were just realizing there was nothing for sale. I guess everybody's happy here.'

'Are you friends of Nicolina's?'

'Colleagues.'

'Ah,' Elsa nodded.

'I gather, being on a first name basis, you're a friend of hers.'

'That's a strange thing. She's been my neighbour for over a year and yesterday was the first time she's ever spoken to me. Took me by surprise actually.'

'I understand. Nicolina is not terribly friendly sometimes. I can say that because I know her,' Caitlin added.

'Oh, there's Stephen. Gotta go; he's impatient. Men and their retirement! He's on a kick to give me shopping lessons. I had no problem for thirty-one years. Listen, would you like me to tell Nicolina you were asking for her?'

'I hate to admit this, but I want to surprise her. She's popped in on me unannounced, so I figure it's my turn.'

'You sound like a devil.' As a brand new beige

Bronco backed up rather close to the women, Elsa turned and climbed up onto the front seat. 'See what I mean, girls? Good luck with your surprise; my lips are sealed. Bye now.'

The C's waved as innocently as two break-in artists could. Then they feigned walking away from their target until the Bronco had turned off the street. 'I found the key! There's no car in the garage and the boarder's gone.'

'This woman Elsa would recognize both of us.'

'That won't be a problem. I won't disturb anything; I'll count the bottles, not take them as I planned.'

'OK then. Let's synchronize our watches. I have eleven twenty-eight.'

'Me too.'

'Six minutes is the absolute limit you should be inside that house. I can spot the boarder walking back. She's not young, and it will take her more than six minutes to get back here from either end of the street. Run to the front of the house at least three or four times. Open the mailbox slot, an inch or two. That way, I'll know you're OK. If you don't, this whistle is bloody useless.' Struck by an afterthought, Carmen reached into her pocket and pulled out thin, hospital plastic gloves. 'Wear these. I got them at work from the first-aid room.'

'You are a pro!'

'Remember to look everywhere. My grandfather drank and my grandmother told wonderful stories of his hiding places. The best was a bottle of gin in the toilet reservoir.'

Caitlin walked to the backyard as though she owned the place. In seconds, she was inside the house. Her first near mishap was Monsieur's water bowl. 'Shit,' she whispered as she jumped over it.

At his post, pretending to read the morning paper, Mike had a strong urge to go after Caitlin, help her out. He also knew better. Scanning the street for the old lady was the best he could do at the moment.

Nicolina had been at work for a little over two hours when Remay called. 'I'd like to see you at twelve in my office.'

A flood of perspiration ran down from her underarms; some of the sweat ran around her back. Could she use a stiff one now! 'Of course, I'll be there, sir.' She hated how Remay made short shrift of her and hung up on her abruptly each time he called. Raising her right arm, she took a small whiff and realized there was no way she would walk into Remay's office without a shower. Grabbing her briefcase, she ran out of the office and drove home.

When Nicolina turned up Harvard Avenue, she was behind a cement truck. They had popped up around the city during this horrid year of construction. 'Move your ass!' Nicolina shouted, checking her watch. At a snail's pace, the driver took his time. The longer he took to get to the site, the fewer his deliveries.

Mike didn't notice the car because he had never seen it before.

Carmen was looking up towards Monkland Avenue. By the time she spotted the rental, it had already pulled into the driveway.

The woman almost leapt from the car and ran up the front stairs.

Carmen turned sideways and blew hard twice on her whistle.

Nicolina turned around furiously at the sound of the whistle's shriek, took a quick look at Carmen, thought she was calling her dog, quickly unlocked her front door and disappeared inside the house.

Caitlin was upstairs in Nicolina's bedroom, looking behind the toilet, when she thought she heard the whistle. Then she was certain she heard the front door slam. She replaced the toilet top as quietly as possible. She noticed the closet was open; she couldn't hide there. The mattress was lying on a pedestal, so hiding under the bed was out. However, the bed itself was on a slant to make the room appear larger. Caitlin ran to the far side of the bed. Without a sound, she lay on her side, flat against the pedestal, as close to the headboard as she could get. She did not dare bring up her knees; they'd be seen for sure. The white duvet hanging over the side of the bed was camouflage, provided whoever didn't walk over to that side of her room. She heard Pastore storm up the stairs.

When Caitlin heard the thud of her shoes on the wooden floor, she held her breath. Thud, carpet, thud, carpet, thud, carpet, all the noise was on the other side of the bed.

'I have no time for a shower. Fuck!'

Caitlin heard the splash of water, more swearing. Then silence. 'What the hell is this? I didn't put the Kleenex on the side of the tub. I have to tell that old bitch to stay out of my goddamn room.' She stole a fast check of the time. 'I have exactly twenty-two minutes to clean up and get out of here.'

Caitlin drew shallow breaths. Why had she ever come up with this stupid plan? Getting out of Miami with their lives had been amateurs' luck. The next second, Caitlin heard the sharp smack of breaking glass from the bathroom.

'Shit! That goddamn Clinique moisturizer cost me seventy-one dollars, plus tax! I should hand Remay the bill. I'm not going to make his office on time; I can't do it.' Nicolina kicked the broken shards of glass mixed with the gooey moisturizer against the wall. 'Why is this happening to me?'

Caitlin regained her conviction. She wanted desperately to stand up and shout the answer, 'Because you killed my brother, because you are a murderer. That's why this is happening to you! You don't deserve to live!' Her wrath was raw; she was in the same room as the driver who had struck Chris and left him to die.

Whipping her damp hair across her face, Nicolina slammed the bathroom door shut, rushed to the closet and began throwing clothes across the bed. 'What can this witness know? Will there be a formal arrest? What should I wear? Oh God, I hope he hasn't called the media! That's all I need.'

There's a witness! Maybe an arrest! What if she finds me and I ruin everything? Caitlin hunkered down even closer to the pedestal. Her shoulder began to ache; the arm supporting her was falling asleep. In her spine, she felt a prickly panic.

Nicolina was circling the room in front of the bed, coming dangerously close to Caitlin's side. 'I have seven minutes to get dressed. Shit, I'm sweating again.' Nicolina ran back to the bathroom, wiped her armpits with a facecloth, reapplied Mitchum and hurried back to the bed. She chose a light grey pant suit and a black round-necked camisole. 'Goddamn it, even my feet are perspiring!' Once more she ran to the bathroom, almost slipped on the mess she'd dropped, ran back with powder, flopped down on the bed and threw the white stuff on both feet.

Caitlin could hear her breathing.

Outside, Carmen was sweating bullets. She had walked away from the house and sat on the curb behind an old Volvo. She was praying Pastore would leave soon, before she found Caitlin. She hadn't noticed the old woman and the dog slowly making their way down Harvard.

Mike had. He left his post and ran towards Carmen. 'Remember me?'

'What are you doing here?'

'Never mind that. I know what's happening. Look up there.'

'Oh no!'

'Let me take care of this; hope Caitlin gets out in time. If she doesn't, the dog will sniff her out.'

Mike closed the distance between him and Sophia as quickly as he could without alarming the old woman. When they were about to pass one another, he stopped. 'Good morning! What a cute dog! I had one just like him when I was a kid. He was a loyal little guy. When I got home from school, he was always at the front door waiting for me. I called him Shorty because of his legs. Had him till I was a teenager.'

Monsieur did not know this young man so he stood between Sophia's legs.

'I'm sorry, my name is Mike. I'm here visiting a friend. What a beautiful city you have! The people are so friendly.'

Sophia was a woman. In her day... She broke her rules. 'My name is Sophia; this is Monsieur Patate.' If Sophia hadn't been close to home, she would never have spoken to this young man. Nevertheless, she hung more tightly to her purse. She had heard the stories of young men who struck up conversations with old ladies to distract them. Sophia was too smart for that.

'That's a French name, right? How did he come by it?'

'Good, keep her talking. I should have seen that. Me and my whistle…' With little else to do, Carmen sat on the curb and waited. She thought of running back to get the car, but that was just something else someone might remember.

'Help me though this, God. You're the only one I have left. I'll deal with Sophia later.' Nicolina left the bedroom with the same bluster.

Who's Sophia? Caitlin did not make a single move until she heard the front door slam. She rose slowly to her feet, grabbed her left arm with her right hand and gave it a good shake. The needles left. She moved quickly down the stairs, out the back door, locked it, replaced the key and walked beside the neighbour's lane as though she didn't have a care in the world.

Carmen saw Pastore's car back out of the driveway and tear off down the street. She stood and waited for Caitlin. When she saw her, she pointed up the street and waved her across.

Caitlin fell into Carmen's arms. 'That was too close!'

'The whistle didn't do much, sorry.'

'Actually, I heard it, but I was in Pastore's bedroom when she opened the front door. Thank God, she's loud.'

'Look back there.'

'Is that Mike?'

'Yep.'

'What the hell is he doing here?'

'Saving your butt.'

'That's the boarder!'

'Yep, and he's kept her talking to give you time to get out of the house.'

'He's forgiven.'

When Mike looked back and saw the coast was clear, he said good-bye. He waited for the C's. It would be suspicious if he walked back down the street. As Caitlin got closer, he saw the sheepish look on her face. No matter what she did, Caitlin looked good to him.

'Before I chew you out, I want to thank you. Now, what the hell are you doing here? Are you stalking me?'

'Guilty.'

This was the first time Mike had seen Caitlin smile since the night Chris was killed. She was radiant!

'Did you find anything?' Carmen wanted to know.

'I scoped the place. Couldn't find a single bottle. Doesn't make sense from what we heard.'

'Does, if she got rid of the evidence after the accident.'

'I just don't have a criminal mind.'

'That's why you have me.'

'Remay has a witness! I learned that much because she talks out loud. There's a problem with somebody called Sophia she has to take care of. Who's Sophia?'

'I know.' It was Mike's turn to smile; it was also his ticket in, and he knew it.

CHAPTER 43

A GOOD LIFE rule to follow is never ask a question you wouldn't want to answer. Tim Traynor wished immediately he could pull his words back. But he couldn't because Kathryn had heard them. 'I shouldn't have asked you that, Kathryn, not now.' Tim thought if he kept talking, he could shelve the question.

'After your mother spoke to me, I lay awake for a long time, thinking about us. I came up with answers, rolled into short paragraphs. I've felt loved and supported. We've shared. We're friends who've enjoyed doing things together. We've gotten through the rough times. And, we like one another. That's all I need to know, Kathryn. You're a part of me, part of who I am. I haven't been the easiest person to live with. What I'll treasure most is finding someone who's made me laugh, even in the worst of times. You always made me feel good about myself.

Remember when we were in that doubles' tennis tournament in Dennisport on the Cape? We swore to one another we wouldn't fight. We had made it to the semi-finals. We could play singles for two or three hours and not fight, except to win. You had the strokes and I had the power. But we turned into villains in doubles. We were ahead 5-1. I was volleying every ball that crossed the net, every ball. I missed only one. You did too at the base line. "Can you not get one ball back, Kathryn?" I hissed at you. "If you stopped hogging everything, I'd be better prepared. I didn't realize I've been in this match!" We never won a single game after that, and we stomped off the courts. I forget who spoke first.'

'You did,' Kathryn reminded him. 'You threw your

arms around me, and we laughed at ourselves all the way home. How could I forget?'

Tim suddenly changed the subject because he could tell she had not been taken in by the aside. He tried something else. 'Do you want me to call Jen Sexton for you?'

'I'll wait till I feel better.'

'Tim?'

'Yes.'

'I'm ready to answer your question.'

The phone came to Tim's rescue. 'I better get that.'

'Let it ring, Tim.'

'What if it's the results of your scan?'

'All right. I'm not going anywhere.'

'Neither am I,' he sighed as he ran to take the call.

CHAPTER 44

ONCE NICOLINA GOT to Girouard Avenue and turned right, she drove very cautiously. The unwanted attention and the glare of eyes that followed her every move at Foley's had infected Nicolina with a touch of paranoia. Now, she felt the cops were poised on every side street, waiting to nab her for some infraction they could add to the circumstantial evidence against her. *What's the freakin' probability that there's a cop on Northcliffe or Marlowe?*

Driving cautiously in Montreal is a violation of the driver's code. Those who dare to make that attempt often discover there is more danger in safety than they ever imagined. Nicolina was given the horn, routinely passed in the right lane on Sherbrooke Street, tailgated into whizzing through a yellow light, and narrowly missed by cowboy truck drivers who barrelled down the busy street and made turns or sudden stops without signalling. At Victoria Avenue, she got stuck behind a truck that was making deliveries. It took her four minutes to pull back out into the left lane, risking her life in the process.

When Remay led Nicolina back to his office, Beausoleil was hidden in another interview room. Today he sat with his blue cap on his knees. His white hair glistened under the ceiling light. He didn't mind getting back to the Ritz early for work. He'd have great stories to tell. Even the manager had come around.

Remay did not bother with warm-up questions. 'Ms. Pastore, please sit.'

Shell-shocked, certain their witness was close by, Nicolina slumped in her seat and couldn't muster the energy to get up and take the better chair.

Remay got up and left her alone for a good five minutes. If only she could remember something, she'd come up with better lies to defend herself. Seeing things from the right side had never been Nicolina's strength. *It might be more convincing that I can't remember a damn thing. The blackout might just be the better ticket.* Nicolina got up and took the other seat.

Remay opened his office door, making certain Nicolina heard him. 'This is a very important case, sir. Thank you for your assistance.' He walked back inside and sat behind his desk. 'That was our witness, Ms. Pastore.'

Nicolina gave only the slightest hint of a nod.

'The witness saw a grey Mazda 3 speed east on Sherbrooke Street, past the Ritz, pull a u-turn in the middle of the street and drive back west.'

'Was he able to get the licence number?'

'The interesting thing is that he says the vehicle was driving without lights.'

'That suggests your witness couldn't get the numbers on the plate.'

'Before we get to that, I have a point to make. We've had trouble all along trying to understand why Mr. Donovan did not see your vehicle approaching. He was not under the influence of any substance that might have rendered him less alert. Now, I have the answer. The Mazda that struck Mr. Donovan had no lights he could have seen.' Remay had called Jacques Lussier immediately with this information, but he'd been told that the techs had found no problem with the lights. Remay did contact the dealer, but got nowhere on the lights. He said nothing to Nicolina for a full minute.

The air in the room was thick with accusation.

'Ms. Pastore, not many investigators do this, but I like to lay my cards out on the table, so here goes. I believe you drove that Thursday night under the influence and struck Chris Donovan. You managed to get home, sobered up and then called the police. I know what a conviction would do to your career, not to mention disbarment and prison time. But I'm telling you my supposition because the pieces are falling into place. In these fatal hit-and-run cases, we wait for witnesses to call. That can take three or four weeks. In this case, we have our first witness in a week. Somebody in the city saw what happened that night. Someone else may have evidence that you were intoxicated that Thursday. It's just a matter of time for the last piece to fall into the puzzle. At the moment, you are guilty of not stopping, identifying yourself and helping the victim as the law requires you to do.'

Nicolina rode out the silence. She was not about to repeat her defence story. Why should she? Both her headlights were working; they couldn't prove anything in that direction. When she thought of Sophia, her stomach knotted. That was a problem for home. Offer Remay nothing, she reminded herself. When he was suddenly silent, waiting her out, she understood that Remay had shot his best bullets at her and she was still there.

'Did the witness manage a description of the driver? Did he make the plates?'

'Before we go to the next point, Ms. Pastore, remember what I said to you about coming forward with the truth and things going easier on you if you do.'

'I know the procedure.'

'No doubt. Well?'

'Well what? You have the make of the car, but no plate number. You have a witness who can't make an ID. Am I correct so far, Monsieur Remay?'

'We know your vehicle struck Mr. Donovan. We

know why he didn't see it. We can put you close to the
Ritz at the time of the accident. What are the odds that
another grey Mazda was speeding west along Sherbrooke Street at exactly the time of the accident?'

'The same odds that put three grey Mazdas on my
street in a radius of one city block! It's the most popular car in the city this year. Come see for yourself. I also
invite you to check the invoice on the repairs to my car.
I read nothing about lights. Now, if you have no further
questions, I have to get back to work. My offer to
appear at your office at a moment's notice still stands.'

'See yourself out.'

And she did.

CHAPTER 45

ONCE THE TRIO had gotten off Harvard Avenue safely, Caitlin lost it. Even after everything she had just risked, she felt she was running in place, going nowhere. 'I must have been out of my mind.'

'You are. I've tried to tell you,' Carmen said with a straight face.

Mike was thinking it might prove more difficult than he had first thought, breaking into the inner circle of this friendship. He listened for an opening.

'Don't give up, Caitlin. You and I are never down.'

'I could be in handcuffs right now!'

'But you're not. I have an idea I think we should work on now.'

'Does it involve weapons?'

'I'm serious. I think we should call the Traynors. You weren't the greatest in the trenches today, but you are one hell of a talker. That's why you teach.'

'What do I say?' This last stunt had seriously dented Caitlin's resolve.

'Make it brief; tell the truth.'

'Listen, you guys, my car is down the street, my cell too. We can call from there.' Without a word they walked to the new rental.

'Why did you change cars?' Caitlin wanted to know.

'For stalking purposes.'

'Makes sense. We're all criminals at heart!' Caitlin could not believe what was coming out of her mouth.

Friday afternoon was suddenly grey and forlorn.

Mike stayed in the front, while the C's opted for the back seat.

'Just a sec, I'm carrying all the numbers. OK, here it is.'

'I feel badly disturbing the Traynors at a time like this.'

'Caitlin, keep it brief.'

Tim Traynor picked up the phone on the fourth ring, a nanosecond before the answering machine engaged. 'Hello.'

'Sir, please forgive me for disturbing you at this time. I only need five minutes of your time. I'll get to the point quickly.'

'Are you a telemarketer?'

'I'm Caitlin Donovan. Nicolina Pastore struck and killed my brother eight days ago. Had she not left the scene, my brother might have survived. I know something of the unfounded case against your wife as well. I'm trying to amass circumstantial evidence of Ms. Pastore's drinking habits. One person from Foley Pharmaceuticals was brave enough to tell me of an episode at work. We will not use his name, or yours if you can help me out.'

'Just a minute. I'll ask my wife.'

'Thank you.'

Tim was grateful for this interruption, relieved as well that he wouldn't have to make the call himself and go against Kathryn's wishes. He found Kathryn deep in thought, still caught in the vice lock of his question. 'Honey, I have something to tell you…'

'I don't want to spread rumours, Tim. I've told you that already.'

'How can this be a rumour when the people who work with Pastore know she has a stockpile at work and they know her brand? What if I just admit that what I'm giving them is a rumour?'

'Semantics, Tim.'

'Why do you think she didn't bother to stop? It stands to reason she couldn't take the chance of a DUI.

This is a young kid who didn't deserve to die, and this tragedy might even help us in the long run.'

'I trust your judgment.'

'I have to get back to the sister. I'll tell you everything later.'

'I hope we're not going to regret this.'

'We won't.' Tim ran back to the phone. 'Hi.'

'I'm still here,' Caitlin added hopefully.

'My wife is very ambivalent about disclosing this rumour. That's what it is. However, she's a better person than I am. Pastore has put us through hell. Apparently, she's a hard drinker, specifically Teachers Highland Cream Scotch Whisky. Keeps a stash at work; that's how the brand name got out. Kathryn said most of the execs are heavy drinkers at their after-hours meetings. Pastore drinks like an old boy. That's all I have.'

'Thank you for taking the time to talk to me. I wish you peace during this difficult time. I wish I'd had one more day with my brother. Cherish what you have.'

'Get Pastore out in the open. You'll help us both. My sympathy.'

'Thanks.' Caitlin handed the phone back to Mike. 'Everything is so sad. It's always the innocent who get hurt. People like Pastore get to walk away, but Chris and Kathryn Traynor don't.'

Carmen and Mike let Caitlin vent.

'All right, you two, I'll get back to our investigation. According to Kathryn Traynor, Pastore is a boozer, whisky. She keeps a stash at work. She probably did dump the liquor at home, so the cops would find nothing if they paid her an unwanted visit.'

'We know now that she drinks, keeps stashes, was falling down drunk one night at work, is apparently unjustly going after a dying woman, is openly loathed by her colleagues, struck Chris and left him to die at the scene,' Carmen summarized.

'Wanton disregard for others and narcissism come to mind,' Caitlin threw into the mix.

'What do we do with this information?' Carmen asked.

'We need hard evidence to tie her to booze the night of the accident. What we've got is background material, nothing Remay can really use. I should call him to find out what he learned from his witness. Maybe he has something that can tie into what we know. His number is burned into my brain.' Caitlin punched it in, connected with the front desk and was told he'd get back to her.

'Are you both forgetting something *hard* we do have? Who's Sophia, Mike?'

'Get this. Sophia is Pastore's boarder, the woman with the pug I was stalling to give you a chance to get out of the house.'

'Holy shit!'

'And Pastore said Sophia was a problem she had to take care of! Oh, my God, Sophia might be the witness who can tie Pastore to alcohol that Thursday night.'

'Or a tenant who's behind in her rent. Let's not jump to conclusions too quickly,' Mike cautioned.

'Mike you're on probation, remember? I need to hear only positives from you, understand?'

'Look Caitlin,' Carmen defended Mike, 'we can't rush into this. If she knows something, why hasn't she called the police? We can't go back to Harvard Avenue for a couple of days. We can't take the risk of that neighbour spotting us. Let's be honest; we don't want to be arrested.'

'I wasn't seen on the street,' Mike said. 'She shops. I can wait Sophia out and she won't be afraid when we meet up again. I can call you, Caitlin, once she's left the house, and we can meet her together. She must go out around the same time and with that dog, she's as slow as a snail. Most of us are habit junkies.'

'You're both ganging up on me! I think Sophia is our witness; I think she's probably afraid to call the police.'

'I did find out the dog's not hers, but I could tell she loves it.'

'That could be the reason she didn't call the police; she'd lose the dog if she has to move.'

'His name's Monsieur Patate.'

'Only in Quebec!'

Mike's cell played a short segment of the Sox winning the World Series. Caitlin had left Mike's number when she'd made her call and grabbed the phone immediately. 'Yes?'

'Claude Remay, Ms. Donovan.' In précis, he recounted Beausoleil's statement and left the salient point to last. 'The Mazda Monsieur Beausoleil saw was speeding on Sherbrooke Street without lights.'

Caitlin dissolved into the seat. 'That's why Chris never had a chance, why he never saw the car that struck him. But, you have no ID on her or her plate.'

'Progress is slow. I have never come across a suspect who has an answer for everything.'

'I have something for you, sir.' Without divulging anything about Sophia, because Caitlin wanted Pastore so badly herself, she recounted their findings.

'How are you coming up with this information?'

'Desire and ingenuity. Actually, my friends and I have made calls and surfed the net.'

'We can work on that from our end. Don't give up hope. Somebody out there knows something pertinent. It's just a matter of time.'

'I know it is, sir.' Caitlin switched off the phone.

'The bitch was speeding along Sherbrooke Street without lights. That's why Chris never had a chance.'

'Caitlin,' Mike whispered over the seat, 'Sophia is the link to that night. We're going to nail the bitch, but we have to take our time. We can't afford to scare her off, and lose her.'

'I know, but I hate waiting.'

CHAPTER 46

FRANK WAS SURPRISED at how quickly he was able to find the whereabouts of Ryan Burns. Computers made everything so easy today, he thought. Burns had relocated to the West Island on Norwood Avenue in Pointe Claire. He did a quick addition and realized Burns would be forty-six today and probably had a family of his own. *How quickly time has passed! Chris won't even make it to thirty.*

Frank knew retrieving the money from the bank was not the easy transaction one might think. Cashing in a bond and cutting a cheque for the whole amount was out of the question. Successful lawyers have great connections. Frank called a partner he trusted and discussed the money transaction with him. The quickest and least complicated debit was a cash transfer to the Bahamas. Bruce Strong could supply the account, and Frank could expect the cash delivery by Tuesday. Frank could pick up the money from a safety deposit box his friend leased year round. 'There should be no problems, Frank. The merchandise will be available to you by four o'clock.'

'This is a godsend, Bruce. I still find it strange that it's so difficult to get your own money and dispose of it as you will.'

'That's why mattresses were the thing for so long!'

'I guess. I owe you big time!'

'This is routine. Glad to have been of help.'

Frank sat back and began wondering what he'd say to Ryan Burns when they met one another. At this late date, would Burns even care about his selfish explanation, his cowardice? Frank would cab it out there, dress casually, and be honest, for himself as much as for his son. Before he made the trek, however, he wanted to talk to Caitlin. It was time for him to share the guilt for losing Chris. He needed her home with Maggie Tuesday night while he was out. Frank shut the door of the study. He need not have taken the precaution.

Maggie was resting on Chris' bed. A stack of photo albums lay beside her. It was amazing how short any life seems when one looks back. Maggie was recoiling from that shock. With the myriad of photos, she had scanned, touched, held to her heart, kissed and dropped her tears upon, Chris was with Maggie closer, perhaps, than he had been in life. His childhood, his adolescence, his early adulthood, the bruised knees, the torn football jersey, the good-bye waves, all of these faces and smiles of Chris for twenty-six years comforted Maggie. And she held on tight. Frank could have shouted fire, and Maggie would not have moved. What was missing was Chris' future. Chris' past and his near present kept him close to his mother.

After a deep breath, Frank punched in the number. 'Ryan Burns, how can I be of help?'

'Hello, Ryan. You and I met by chance many years ago. I was hoping we might reconnect.'

'Who is this please?'

'My name is Michael, but I don't expect you to remember. I'll be in the West Island Tuesday night. Is there any chance you could give me five minutes?'

'If you're selling, the answer is no.'

'You have my word this is not a pitch. Five minutes.'

'Does outside work for you? I cut the lawn that night. Chores, we all have them. My teenage sons tell me they've outgrown lawn-cutting.'

'Outside works for me. I'll be at your place around seven-thirty.'

'Do you have the address?'

'Yep.'
'You have me guessing.'

CHAPTER 47

TIM KNEW KATHRYN well enough to know he'd run out of stalling time, so he grabbed a chair and pulled it in front of her and sat down less than a foot away from his wife.

'Tim, I want to leave you and my life with a clear conscience. It's time.'

'Doesn't have to be, Kathryn.'

'Has to for me. Don't look so worried.'

Tim couldn't tell her what was bothering him. He tried to relax and took Kathryn's hand.

'In all our years together, I was unfaithful only once, very briefly. Nothing else ever followed it. Nothing.'

Tim felt the prick, but he said, 'Can I ask who? Does that really matter?'

'It might.'

'OK, who? Don't tell me one of our friends.'

'It was Jen Sexton.'

Tim let go of Kathryn's hand. 'Jen Sexton, but she's a woman!'

'I know that, Tim.'

'Wow! You wild adventurous thing! I don't know what to say. I mean, were you happy with me, Kathryn, in that area?'

'You know I was, Tim.'

'Why did it happen then?'

'I never really understood the *why*.'

'I'm curious. I never would have thought in a million years… How long did it last?'

'Two nights at a conference in Toronto. I thought about you and what I could lose. That's the God's truth. We stayed friends, period.'

'Jen Sexton, isn't she the notorious Jen that you've mentioned the odd time?'

'Yes.'

'What is there about this woman that's so special?'

'It's hard to explain. She's daring and funny, with just the hint of the bad girl about her. I guess everybody wants to be wild once.'

'What was it like with a woman?'

'You want specifics?'

'I'm taken aback. I still can't believe it. Do you love me?'

'With a passion that I'll take with me when I die.'

Tim bent over and held Kathryn as tightly as he dared without hurting her. 'You are an interesting woman, Kathryn Traynor, and you're very brave.' His heart was thumping.

'I guess I have to close the brackets. Have you been a good and faithful mate, Tim?'

Kathryn could feel Tim tremble and she smiled, 'You're forgiven.'

'It was only twice, both short and tawdry.'

'Did you ever think of leaving me, Tim?'

'Not for a second. Thank you for the truth. I don't feel so bad about Jen. We're still the same people, aren't we Kathryn?'

'We are.'

'Believe me, I have nothing exciting to share any-way.'

Tears brimmed in Tim's eyes and Kathryn's too. It was hard to know close up that they had each hurt the person they loved most.

'We never gave up on each other, Kathryn. Look at all our friends who have.'

'Then, I think we're better now than we were a half hour ago, cleaner.'

'We were never far apart.'

Tim held Kathryn's hand through the night. He never let go, not once. Yet, he couldn't get the image of Kathryn and Jen Sexton out of his mind.

CHAPTER 48

NICOLINA DROVE BACK to work, made a beeline for the bulletin board, ripped the article to shreds, spent two hours alone in her office, rechecked the court date, tried to find another patsy for a second delay and left for home. As she drove, she was twitchy and jerky on the road. Remay's threatening words repeated in her brain, *someone out there, someone knows…*

When she pulled into her driveway, she swore and it wasn't pretty. *Is that bloody witch with the broom spying on me too? Is Remay thinking about someone like Elsa?*

'Hi! Isn't this a glorious spring?' Elsa was in fine form as she invaded Nicolina's property.

Nicolina tried to get away with a wave, but the broom was walking towards her car. *Shit!*

'You had company today!'

'Company? I wasn't expecting anyone,' Nicolina said warily.

'Two pretty young women. They said they were looking to buy in the area and they knew you lived on the street. Apparently, they worked with you. I think they said before you got this job, something like that.'

'Did they leave their names?'

'They're still looking and said they'd try you again.'

Likely story! Probably cops. 'I've worked with so many people, but I'll be on the lookout for them.'

'Nicolina, isn't it? I'm not sure.'

'Yes, it is.'

'My husband was wondering if you're the driver in that tragic accident written up in *The Gazette*? He saw your car and put two and two together.'

The moan Elsa heard was real. The mask was back at work. 'Yes, sadly I am. I haven't had a decent night's sleep because the young man and his family haven't left my thoughts. I wish with all my heart he were still alive.'

'My Stephen doesn't miss much.'

'I can see that. Elsa, have a good, safe weekend. Good talking with you.' Nicolina slithered away.

As soon as she opened the front door, the cooking odours of cheese, meat, pasta, garlic, olive oil, tomatoes, onions and whatever else Sophia had going in the kitchen wafted down the hall and into her nose. It wasn't easy plotting the murder of such a cook! Sophia's busy hands were stained with tomato sauce and her fingers glistened with olive oil.

Sophia looked over smiling, 'I have a large pan of lasagna and we will have many leftovers.'

All the better for me! 'What a feast, Sophia! Were you up in my room cleaning yesterday?'

'No, Nicolina, I was not there. I worked upstairs only last week.'

Was she losing it, or had someone else been in her room? Nicolina wondered with dread. She left the kitchen to run upstairs and investigate. She opened drawers, both closets, checked the linen closet in the bathroom and threw herself on the bed. *I have to calm down – deal with one problem at a time. Nobody was up here. I'm imagining it. But dammit, there were those two women around. Could they have been in my house? Forget this shit! Concentrate on the old bag! If I can get the better of a police investigator, I can get rid of one old woman!*

Pulling herself up off the bed, Nicolina ran to the linen closet, felt under some towels and found the pink plastic bottle of baby lotion. *Tonight's the night! I'll go shopping early in the morning, so I won't be around when she falls.* Once that issue was settled, Nicolina relaxed and thought about food. She fully intended to enjoy her dinner and went down to the kitchen. 'What a wonder you are, Sophia. You outdo yourself with every meal. I'm going for my camera; I'd love a photo of the table and you behind it and Monsieur too, the family. I can set the camera and run back and stand with you. Just a sec, I'll be right back.' What a cosy group stood smiling behind the steaming pan of lasagna, salad, and fresh bread! Nicolina was on her best behaviour. After all, she had to show respect. This was Sophia's last supper.

CHAPTER 49

'WHY DON'T WE grab something to eat?' Mike suggested, mostly because he wanted to be around Caitlin.
'Before you nix the idea, we might want to sit together
and talk about Chris. There has been so much going on,
we haven't had the time. Didn't you say something
about a favourite pizza place?'

'We ate pizza a couple of nights ago,' Caitlin said.

'I could eat pizza every day of the week; I'd like to
go,' Carmen said, adding her two cents.

'We could plan how best to approach Sophia. It's
Friday night; we could all crash at my place and plan
strategy. I have two bedrooms.'

'Do I look like Red Riding Hood, Mike?'

'Better!'

'Let's go for pizza; we can talk there.' They rode in
Mike's car.

One small step, Mike thought.

Unfortunately, Sherbrooke Street was part of their
route once again. Caitlin dropped her head and closed
her eyes when they passed Wood Avenue. They took a
left on St. Laurent Boulevard, a left on Laurier and
snagged the first meter they could find after Park
Avenue. From there, they walked to Hutchison Street.

'Is that the mountain up there?'

'Yep,' Carmen said proudly.

'This city reminds me of San Francisco, hills and
neat streets.'

They peeked in at Patisserie Gascogne, Anjou
Quebec, the charcuterie with its daily array of fine
French food, designer clothes shops, custom-designed
condos and enjoyed the well-heeled of Outremont

ambling slowly down Laurier Avenue. Mike was enjoying himself.

'After the pizza, we can get some hot bagels on
Fairmount; it's only one street up.'

'Do you ever think of anything but food?'

'I'm Italian, that's what we do best!'

'Let's get to the pizza.' They all enjoyed the Caesar
salad, one of the best in Montreal. Caitlin tried to eat
her parmesan with sun-dried tomatoes, but guilt
blocked her appetite. Carmen made short order of her
clam pizza, sprinkling every bite with spicy oil. Mike
was on his second pepperoni pizza before they began to
talk.

'There's not much to these pizzas, but they're fan-
tastic. I could go for a third.'

'Don't. I couldn't stand it,' Caitlin said, laughing.
'You remind me of a garbage truck.'

'In my defence, I haven't eaten much this past week.
This is the first time I feel less edgy. Now, I feel guilty;
I meant no disrespect.'

'I was kidding, Mike. Lighten up! What do we do
about the boarder?'

'I promise to be on Harvard Avenue tomorrow
before nine. Give me your cell number and I'll call you
if she leaves the house.'

'What if I get there too late?'

'That's why I suggested my place; we could go
together. We can't scare her off; she's our main hope.
She has to trust me. We also have to understand that
she might not have seen anything.'

'If Sophia stays up till at least nine, she probably saw
Pastore drinking,' Caitlin said.

'She's afraid to call the police or she has nothing to
tell them. I'm certain she listens to the radio and prob-

ably reads the newspaper. She knows about the accident.' Mike felt he had the facts.

'Mike, we're not staying at your place. Carm, do you want to bunk with me at Mom and Dad's tonight? Then we can all meet on Harvard early tomorrow.'

'Actually, I'd prefer to shower and do my stuff at home. I can still be at your place by eight-thirty. I'll stay over Saturday night if nothing happens tomorrow.'

'That's fine.'

'You understand, Mike, right?'

'Yeah, I do.'

'Before I head for home, I'd like to go alone to the cemetery.'

'Call me.' Carmen said.

When Caitlin arrived, her mother was sitting alone on the grass. The palm of her hand rested on the mound of earth and small rocks. Caitlin noticed the blue hydrangeas her mother had laid beside the plaque Frank had left to mark the grave. Maggie did not hear Caitlin approach.

'Hi, Mom,' Caitlin whispered, but Maggie jumped with surprise all the same.

'It doesn't seem right to leave Chris alone. I know he wasn't big on flowers, but he loved the Cape and the hydrangeas remind me of it.'

'Why are you so busy, Caitlin? This is your first time here since the funeral, isn't it?'

'Mom, I'm trying to have the driver who killed Chris arrested.'

'That's small comfort. Chris is gone. Remember him because everything fades.'

'You don't understand, Mom.' Caitlin got to her feet and began to shake and weep hysterically. 'Chris would be alive if it weren't for me!'

'Why are you saying that, Caitlin? You didn't run him down.'

'I told him to walk home that night from my place. He wanted to call a cab, but I suggested he walk home. That's why I have to get the woman who killed him!'

Maggie backed away from Caitlin as though her daughter had punched her in the face. Caitlin felt her mother withdraw.

'What was Chris doing at your place that night?' Maggie's voice was thin.

'I'll tell you. Mom, I'll tell you everything!' Caitlin wept as she spoke and shouted through a flood of tears. 'Chris was trying to protect me; isn't that a big laugh?'

Without a word, Maggie stepped forward and pulled Caitlin into her arms. 'We're a lot alike. In your place, I would have told Chris to walk home too for the exercise.'

'Oh, Mom, I love you and I'm so sorry.'

Forgiveness is a state of grace.

CHAPTER 50

ON THE BOULEVARD, the closeness of the family, the repetition of dinner together, the comfortable routine that Mireille had brought back with her, restored a layer of tranquility, but it was no match for the fact that Chris' place at the table was empty. From time to time, each family member glanced at the chair, remembering that Chris had sat there eight short days ago. Was it only eight?

'Dad, did Remay call you?'

'Yes, things are moving, but it's a slow process.'

'If you two will excuse me, I can't hear about this driver. It all hurts too much. Don't worry about me, I'll be fine.'

Confessions, like suicide attempts, are laced with doubts, sallies and retreats. Tuesday, the pickup and the meeting with Burns, weighed heavily on Frank. When he glanced at Caitlin, he trembled. What would this truth do to her? Was he using her as a test case, desperately hoping she'd tell him that Maggie could never know? Someone in his family had to know the truth. Wasn't he coming clean for Chris? Frank wasn't certain of his motives, now that the time had come for him to step forward.

'Dad, what's wrong? You look terrible. Mom's noticed the change in you too.'

There it was! The invitation to step up.

'I have something to tell you, Caitlin. Let's talk in the study.'

Caitlin saw the tightening lines around her father's mouth; she didn't want to talk; she didn't want to hear more misery. She hardly recognized her father, hadn't really since the night Chris died. *He seemed to be coming around. What's happened to change that?* 'Okay, Dad.' Caitlin walked behind her father into the study.

Frank had his file on the desk under a manila folder. For the time being, he left it there. Frank dropped his head into his hands. Then weary from years of concealment, he said, 'I don't know where to begin.'

'Start where you feel most comfortable. You can gather the pieces as we go along.'

Frank rose and began to pace behind his desk. He took one last look at the daughter who idolized him and memorized the love in her eyes. 'Do you recall one night when you were blaming yourself for Chris' death and I said I had my own guilt?'

I don't want to know. Keep your secret. 'I remember.'

'Twenty-nine years ago, something happened, and I've tried to make up for it ever since. What good I did doesn't really matter. What does is that I never forgave myself and I believed all along that one day I'd be punished. I never thought for a moment Chris would pay the price.'

'What are you saying, Dad?' Caitlin had begun to cry. 'What are you trying to tell me?'

'I was twenty-five that night; you were three.'

'So?'

'I had an interview and I was running late.'

Caitlin clutched her stomach and rocked back and forth on her chair.

'I ran a stop sign. A kid on a bike cycling from the opposite direction ran his too. He crashed into the back of my car.'

'Was the kid okay?'

'Yes, broken bones, but he survived.'

Caitlin felt relieved. 'Well, Dad, you were both at fault, right?'

'Cait, I was so scared, scared of losing my family and career.'

'But you stopped and…'

'I drove away. I stopped a few hundred feet down the road, got out of the car and saw that he was trying to stand up.'

'You went back then, right?'

'I drove off.'

Frank saw Caitlin's love and respect drain from her eyes. She turned away from her father.

'I've told you this, Cait, because if anyone is to blame for Chris' death in this family, it's me.'

'How could you do such a thing? The kid might have tried to get up, that's a natural thing to do, but he might have fallen again and died on the street, like Chris,' Caitlin was shouting.

'I was afraid to lose what I'd worked so hard for. It was a split-second, cowardly decision.'

'Do you think your confession has helped me, Dad?'

'I don't know anything right now.'

'I was so in awe of you growing up; you always did the right thing. Just not the one time when it really counted, right?'

'I don't expect you to forgive me, Cait.'

'You're no different than Pastore. The only difference is that you were lucky the kid survived.'

Frank dropped into his chair and said nothing.

Caitlin wasn't a priest, but she knew her father was looking for some kind of absolution. 'Look, Dad, I'll always love you, but…'

'You just won't trust or respect me again.'

'I didn't say that.'

'It doesn't much matter. It's time to pay up.'

'What do you mean?' Caitlin's voice was shrill.

'Don't even think of telling Mom! This would destroy her! Be a man. Don't go dumping your life on Mom.'

'You have my word.'

'That's something at least.'

'I found him.'

'The kid you struck?'

'He's forty-six now; has his own family. That's how I learned he'd suffered only broken bones.'

'What are you going to do?' Caitlin was talking to a man she hardly knew, and he had begun to frighten her.

Frank told her.

'Dammit, Dad, why are you putting yourself in this kind of jeopardy now? Mom needs you. What if he has you arrested? Have you thought of that? So what if you're taking a cab. He can jump into his car and follow you.'

'I'll handle this, Cait. I have to meet him. I thought I was doing this for Chris.'

'Maybe you are, but I'm going with you.'

'You're staying with your Mom! I don't want you involved.'

'All right, all right! You can never tell Mom. Promise me that again.'

'Never tell me what, Frank?' Maggie walked into the study. 'What's wrong now?'

'Hi honey, it's nothing. Cait said not to bother you with bits of information about the driver of the car that struck Chris.'

'Caitlin's right. I don't want to know Frank. Let's all turn in early – you both look terrible.'

'Let's call it a night, then,' Frank said mostly to Caitlin as he joined Maggie.

Before Caitlin left the study, she suddenly remembered Steve in Miami and stopped in her tracks.

CHAPTER 51

NICOLINA DID NOT look any better than the Donovans. Her eyes were strained and her cheeks were drawn. The one good thing was the weight she'd managed to lose despite all the food she continued to wolf down. Late this afternoon, she'd driven into her driveway and found Elsa talking to Sophia out back. Monsieur was attentive, his head tilted to one side as though he understood every word.

Nicolina wasn't in the right mood to murder Sophia tonight. One had to be up for something like that! Her *tête-à-tête* with Remay had been nerve-wracking. She would have preferred to lie in bed after dinner. To get her thoughts off the trouble points that were choking her, she'd rather replay her part in getting the better of a cop. But no, Nicolina had to work into the wee hours tonight a second time. Sophia had to take her tumble. Elsa had sealed Sophia's fate.

Butting into the backyard conversation was a must. 'Hi Sophia. How's everything?'

'We're just fine,' Elsa cut in. 'I've been telling Sophia, that I just must have at least one recipe. The aromas that I've enjoyed coming from your home are mouth-watering! I thought you might be the cook, Nicolina, but I've discovered it's Sophia. I'm having trouble getting her to give me a single recipe.'

'No doubt. They're her well-guarded secrets. Speaking of food…'

'Yes, yes, I must go, Elsa.'

'Not one…'

'Not today,' Sophia smiled, but she was piqued at Elsa's insistence.

As they walked into the kitchen, Nicolina whispered.

'Got you out of that one, Sophia. Do you need help with dinner?'

'I work alone, well, Monsieur is with me.'

'See you both later. I need a shower.' Nicolina bounded up the stairs and threw herself on the bed. Nicolina checked both hands and found not even the hint of the shakes. *Something good has come out of all this! But dammit all, I have to get up at three again and murder the old bag. Cooperate, Sophia, I need my sleep. I can't keep going through this.* Nicolina got a good snort out of that one.

At ten after three, she crept down the stairs with her baby lotion. Only the best for Sophia! The stair was duly oiled. In fact, Nicolina laid her hand on it to verify she had put enough down and almost took a tumble herself. She added more for good measure.

Monsieur raised his head for just a second and fervently hoped Nicolina would lay off her sleep-walking. He needed his rest just like anybody else.

Sophia never came up to the main floor before eight. She wanted to freshen up her room and dress before taking the stairs. Nicolina was out by eight and driving to the Atwater Market. For an alibi, if she ever needed one, Nicolina made sure to select vegetables and fruit that only Sophia wanted. It was normal that she bought herself apples and cantaloupe. Sophia preferred yellow melon. Nicolina loved the market, couldn't wait for June when it blossomed with colours and scents. This place was almost as good as the fudge store Nicolina loved.

While she shopped, she entertained delicious thoughts of food and dead bodies of old people. At nine forty-five, she drove back to the murder scene on Harvard Avenue.

At the set time, Mike was parked behind a cobalt blue Jetta on Harvard Avenue. The C's walked briskly up the street and slipped into the back seat of his car. 'All quiet on the eastern front.'

'If you two don't mind, I'll rest my eyes while you scope out our house. I've had one busy week,' Carmen told her friends.

'We're on it,' Mike assured Carmen. 'We'll wake you at the first sign of promising activity.'

Caitlin had been quiet, even driving with Carmen to their stakeout.

'Tired?' Mike whispered across the seat. He noticed Carmen was already asleep.

'Weary more than tired. So many things are changing.'

'You've lost me.'

'And myself too. I'll try to concentrate on the house.'

From nine to nine forty-five, there was no outdoor activity they could see. At five after ten, Mike spotted a car driving slowly up Harvard. 'Check it out!'

Mike's voice jarred Caitlin from her grim thoughts, and six eyes watched the grey Mazda turn onto the driveway of the target house. Caitlin's eyes were pinned to the right front bumper before the car made its turn. The repair work had erased any trace of Chris. The Mazda was as good as new; that's what the dealer must have told Pastore.

Caitlin felt worse when Pastore emerged from the car. In fiction and film, villains were big, stocky people who often wore black, bullying sub-humans even children could spot. Pastore wasn't tall or imposing. She wasn't fat or bulky. She was ordinary. Everything about her looked brown: brown hair, brown clothes and brown shoes. Brown. From what Caitlin could see, she was someone you'd pass on the street and not even notice. Her innocuous non-presence diminished Chris somehow, and Caitlin hated her for that. If Chris had to die, he deserved better than this woman. At that second, she saw her father's image; then she recalled her own. Human failure was generous and did not discriminate.

'What do you think?' Carmen asked.

'She's not what I expected,' Caitlin answered.

'It's what she had inside that mattered most that night. That, none of us can see. Let's wait and hope Sophia shops today.'

'We might be out of luck. Pastore was carrying grocery bags. Maybe she shops on the weekend for both of them.'

'Can we stay till noon?' Caitlin asked Carmen and Mike.

'I have an idea. We stay till twelve; then we have lunch at the Orange Julep because we can be back here by one-thirty if we want to be.'

'Sounds good,' Mike said. 'But, older people are better in the morning. By afternoon, their arthritis kicks in.'

'How do you know?'

'Grandmothers.'

'We'll go with that,' Caitlin agreed. 'Thanks for all this time, you guys. Let's take Mike to Schwartz's deli instead. Sophia won't be going out later today, not when Pastore just bought food. Let's eat and call off the stakeout for the day.'

'Good by me,' Mike said.

'Ditto,' Carmen agreed.

Nicolina laid her bags down, unlocked the door, and

crossed her fingers. Every hope she had died when she heard Sophia weeping and found her at the kitchen table. Her first impulse was to throw her bags on the floor and run to the utility drawer for a hammer. What the hell was it with this woman? Why couldn't she kill her? Donovan, she knew the name now, had been easy. Nicolina did none of the horrid things she wished she could do. Instead, she walked into the kitchen as calmly as she could.

Monsieur was standing on the table, on three legs! His fourth was wrapped in what looked like a diaper and knotted around his belly. The stupid pug appeared to be enjoying the attention.

'What happened, Sophia?' Nicolina said under a camouflage of concern.

'I usually walk up the basement stairs first. With Monsieur's short legs, the wooden stairs are difficult for him. But today, he was in a rush to get outside and he climbed them first. Before I understood what had occurred, Monsieur tumbled back down the stairs. I am so sorry that I was not able to catch him before he landed on the floor.'

'How did he trip?'

'Please forgive me. I must have dropped some lotion on a step. I do not know how, but the fault is mine. I have bandaged his leg; it is not broken and will heal. I will take good care of him.'

Slouched on the kitchen chair, Nicolina had to admit that murder was a hands-on task. In the roll and jerk of her real life, she'd probably have to push the old bat down the stairs. With her luck, Sophia would land on the pug and they'd both survive. She could actually visualize them both in plaster casts and crutches. Nicolina was beginning to tire of the whole thing.

CHAPTER 52

THEY OPTED TO leave two of the cars at the Donovans. Caitlin forced Mike into the back seat of her Beetle. Carmen took the passenger seat. 'Parking is a bitch on St. Laurent; be patient. Carmen, do you have change?'

'I thought the new meters were everywhere.'

'I can see the old ones that eat loonies are still around on this street.'

'You know me. Change I have; it's the paper I have trouble collecting.'

'There's Schwartz's.'

'Where?' asked Mike, clearly looking for something larger.

'We've passed it. I should have told you not to blink.'

'Funny.'

'No, true. Carmen, keep your eyes open.'

'To your right! There's a place, grab it.'

'Great!' In seconds, with three tailored moves; she backed in perfectly, centred the Beetle and turned off the ignition.

'There's the red and white sign!'

'Let me try my French, Charcuterie Hebraique.'

'Not bad, Mike.'

'There's a line-up.'

'Always.'

'Is this it?' Mike asked, staring through the window over the slabs of smoked meat and between hanging chickens. 'Is there a back to the deli?'

'Told you it was small; you should have listened.'

'I come from the land of *big*.'

Ten minutes later, they were inching their way through the front door, under a red awning into a long rectangular white-tiled deli with photos and reviews, framed on the walls. 'The wait is never long.'

'Smells good so far.'

Seconds later, they were grabbing seats at a long narrow table that was being cleared faster than you could switch off a light.

Just as quickly, two more small twosomes joined their table.

'Tight,' Mike whispered. 'Wow! Great photos and reviews on the wall.' He began to read, "The best place in the Milky Way to sample smoked meat sandwiches!" *Time Magazine*. 'That's something.'

Caitlin and Carmen ordered together. 'Two lean, two fries, slaw, two pickles, Cherry Coke, Coke, water.'

Sounded good to Mike. 'Same order, drop the Cherry Coke.'

'All for you?' the waiter asked.

'Lucky me. That pretty woman is footing the bill.'

'*Tant mieux,*' the waiter said, before taking their neighbours' orders. As it is with Schwartz's, the drinks arrived first, the fries second, the meat last.

Mike ate quickly and finished his first instalment. 'Wow! This is exactly what smoked meat should taste like! These are the best fries I've ever had. I'd live in Montreal for the smoked meat and bagels!' He winked at Caitlin.

She'd put so much Heinz ketchup on her fries that each time she picked up a fry it dripped the red stuff. 'You like your ketchup.'

'I do, but not this much. It came out too fast. You can generally see my fries. How is it, Carm?'

'Good, good, good. I should take my parents again. They love Schwartz's and it's been over a year since they were here.'

The trio beat their neighbours to the finish line.

Caitlin left six dollars, and grabbed the bill. Single file, past the stools at the counter on their left and waiters carrying smoked meat sandwiches down the single aisle, Carmen and Mike followed her to the front of the deli, waited while she paid the bill and were back on St. Laurent in forty minutes.

When the threesome was back on The Boulevard, Caitlin excused herself, saying that she wanted to talk to her father. 'I haven't spent much time at home lately.'

'Do what you have to do,' Carmen was quick to add. 'Caitlin, you know I have a hard time taking care of *moi*!'

'Do you want me on Harvard tomorrow?'

'I haven't decided yet. I'll call you both tonight.' Caitlin watched them drive away. *The past is never over, not for Dad, and not for me.*

CHAPTER 53

NICOLINA YANKED AND kicked her fine sheets. She still felt she might get the hammer and visit the basement. Elsa was a talker and nosey. Obviously, she was trying to befriend Sophia and maybe not simply for recipes. Adding to her misery, small facts about the accident were taking bites out of her. Remay wouldn't close the case until he brought her in. It was never a wise move for a woman to get the better of a man. Nicolina knew that going in, but hell, what was she supposed to do in this situation? Hang herself?

She had almost forgotten about the case. In the dark hours, stiff and sober, Nicolina remembered it resumed in a matter of days. When she thought about things, she had to admit eleven days wasn't a long period of time. How could she discover if Kathryn Traynor was well enough to make it to court? There was no point bullying another aide to get her a delay if the woman was too ill to leave the house. Did she dare call Jen Sexton a third time? Even if Sexton kept her mouth shut and the trial proceeded, there was no guarantee she'd win the case. Once she had seen the truth in Sexton's file, she figured the embezzlement charges Lecours had given her were a pretext for firing Traynor and false to begin with. How could she get around that?

Raymond Lecours was suffering from heartburn that Saturday night. He'd been puffing on his Cuban *Cohibas*, two a day, since his last encounter with Pastore. Though no one suspected, blood did run through his veins and it had been running hot and hard. If the problems with Comitrixin ever came out … That their arthritis wonder drug caused cancer... He brought his fist down on the arm of the chair. He could not bear to entertain that possibility. Across from him in the living room, his wife knew exactly what Raymond wanted. 'You're not having another cigar!'

Ryan Burns had been curious about the call, but hadn't told Lindsay. It would probably amount to nothing, and she'd kid him for the rest of the week. The guy who contacted him might be in the area, and he might not. Still, he phoned his brother Dave and told him about the call. 'The guy's selling something. What else could it be? Don't get conned. Some of these guys are good. Could be a pyramid scheme. That's probably what it is.' Anyway, Dave said he'd drop by Tuesday, and that was fine with Ryan as long as he didn't crowd him. 'I'll stay in the car.'

Friday night, Ryan had gone to a class reunion, a small one of about eleven people. The evening amounted to chucking their lives, families and all, renting a couple of apartments downtown and partying till they dropped. At forty-six, nothing was what he had thought it might be. It wasn't that Ryan was unhappy; he just wasn't happy, not the way he'd been in high school. Freedom was what the group had decided they'd lost after years of wife and kids, mortgages and routine. Lindsay was a good wife; his kids were decent. He was luckier than most. He knew that. But no life examined comes off with high honours. Most of all, the monotonous regulations in his life chewed him up. *Don't forget the lawn, the bread and milk, my parents are coming for dinner, Pat and Mary have invited us for a B-B-Q, and on and on.* That's why the mysterious call had Ryan curious. He needed something in his life. Ryan was looking forward to Tuesday.

Mike drove to Old Montreal on Saturday night and walked the cobbled streets. With the wonderful new lights, he was able to fully enjoy the charm and beauty of the many grey limestone façades that lined the streets of the Old Port along the St. Lawrence River. St. Paul Street was his favourite street and Notre Dame de Bon Secours, a jewel he would never forget. Perhaps that was because he said some prayers at the church. When he saw the small, wooden statuette of the Virgin, that had survived three hundred years, three fires and a burglary, he found what he was looking for. He needed a miracle because Mike felt he was off centre again. Had Caitlin moved him from lover to friend? That wasn't where he wanted to be. He wanted her friendship, but he wanted more than that. He didn't even recognize himself. He wasn't the person who had left Boston. Maybe Hunter had been right that he didn't belong here. That's what he needed to know. By ten, he was in bed, punching his pillows. He wasn't just horny because he didn't relieve himself. Mike was in love.

Caitlin called just before eleven. 'Let's take a break from Sophia tomorrow. I want to go with my mother to Sunday mass. Sophia will be alone on Monday; we'll have a better chance then.'

'Take care of your mother. I'll go tomorrow.'

'Take a break, Mike. I'm feeling bad tonight, out of it.'

'Makes two of us. I'll be on Harvard anyway.'

Was Caitlin pulling away again? What more could he do? When she hung up he gave into his urge and was his own best friend Saturday night.

Sophia had taken Monsieur to bed with her. She was that contrite. How had she managed to spill so much lotion on the stair? She had applied her daily lotion in the kitchen because the light was so much better. The whole thing was a mystery. Monsieur was squirming, trying to find a comfortable spot on the bed. Sophia was weary, too tired to solve mysteries.

Elsa Schreff was the only happy person in the bunch. She spent the night plotting to poach Sophia. Elsa had had it with cooking daily meals. She had the extra space, not in a basement, but in a large, bright room upstairs. What if she offered Sophia the room for two hundred dollars a month? The money could cover a couple weeks of food. To have Sophia cook for Stephen and her would be heaven! *How can I get Sophia to leave the damn dog? I have to put on my thinking cap.*

CHAPTER 54

THE DONOVANS WERE up early Sunday morning. The reality of Chris' death and the silence that came with it left a gaping hole in their family. When it appeared no one's appetite would improve, Caitlin turned to her mother. 'I'll go to mass with you if you want me to come.'

'I couldn't bear to see the inside of that church so soon,' Maggie was quick to answer.

'You know I'm not a church person, but I went for a year after Derek died because I felt close to him there.'

'Not this Sunday; it's too soon. I would like to go to the cemetery around two. Would you like to come with me?'

'Sure, I would. Dad, come with us.'

Frank did not look at Caitlin when he responded. 'You and Maggie should go alone. If I change my mind, I'll join you.' He got up from the table and left the room.

'Mom, I've put the sympathy, mass and flower cards into two baskets and the lists of the people who've called in the guest room beside mine upstairs. I'll take care of these dishes. I thought you might want to go through them.'

'I don't know if I'm up to that either. I want to keep Chris close in my thoughts; I don't want to share him with cards or anything like that. I just can't.'

'I'll write a note of thanks to send to *The Gazette*. Don't worry about anything else.'

Caitlin made quick work of the clean-up, made certain her mother was upstairs and went looking for her father.

As usual, she found him in his study. He was reading

the accident report on Ryan Burns. When she walked quietly into the room, he stood and handed her the sheet.

'Here's the hard evidence; take a look.'

Caitlin took the paper and read it. 'It's what you said it was, except I see Ryan Burns didn't mention he had ridden through his stop.'

'I can understand that. He was zeroing in on his injuries, not his error.'

'I suppose.'

'Caitlin, I won't tell Mom. Trust me on that, at least.'

'That's not why I want to talk to you. I'm sorry for the way I acted when you told me. You caught me off guard. As soon as you left the room, I took a good look at myself. Something happened in Miami last February.'

'Cait, you don't have to make the Catholic grand confession because I have. It's not necessary. I know what kind of daughter I have.'

'No, you don't.'

'If you want to talk, let's get out of the house, and keep our secrets to ourselves.'

'Good idea. I'll grab a sweater.'

They didn't speak until they turned down Aberdeen Avenue. The sun was already warm in this city of hills. A few walkers with leashed dogs passed them. Otherwise, they were alone under tall poplar trees.

Caitlin told her father about Florida and their role in Steve's death. She made no excuses.

'Does anyone know about this apart from Carmen?'

'No one. I've told you, Dad, because I have no right to judge you. I know first-hand when you're really frightened, ethics don't occur to you. Like you, I live with regret, but that doesn't change a thing for Steve. He accidentally killed himself, but he'd still be alive if we hadn't hidden under that deck that night. So, I guess we're some pair, you and I.'

Frank threw his arms around Caitlin. 'Thank God, you're safe! Never even consider telling your mother any of this.'

'She'd throw us both out. Now, about Tuesday...'

'I don't want you involved.'

'Listen to me for a second.'

'Cait!'

'Just listen. Do you want to go to the police as well?'

'No, I'm not that brave and I can't face disbarment at this stage in my life.'

'I didn't think so, not to mention losing Mom in the process.'

'That, most of all.'

'Okay then, where are you meeting him?'

'On Norwood Avenue in Pointe Claire; it's near the Lakeshore General Hospital. I checked my city map.'

'I know the area. I have a friend who lives at the Southwest One Complex. All right. You can't meet him at his house. That's too dangerous. There's a park that I've walked around with Linda. What's the name of it? Let me think. Yes, yes, it's called Seigniory Park. That's where you meet him. You'll be able to see that you're both alone.'

'I don't intend to be long.'

'Do you want him to know your identity?'

'No.'

'Well, we have to prevent him from finding out. I'll drive you.'

'I told you I don't want you involved.'

'I am involved. You're my father. I'll drive you, park on the east side of the mall and wait for you there. When you leave, walk back through the way you came, and I'll be waiting. He won't be able to see what car you're getting into after you leave. He'll be checking out the money. Then we head for home. It sounds more complicated than it is. You meet him, give him the money and we leave by a back door. Doesn't that sound better than using a cab?'

'I have to admit it does. I guess Miami taught you something.'

'Yeah,' Caitlin laughed with self-reproach. 'It taught me escape is everything. Do you have the money?'

'Tuesday afternoon.'

'Do you have bags for it?'

'That's being taken care of.'

'Call Burns with this change. Here's my cell.'

'Honey, I haven't his number with me.'

'Then, let's get back and get it. I want you to call. He might not be home tomorrow.'

Caitlin drove to Sherbrooke Street, and Frank directed her to a pay phone.

'Is this some kind of cloak and dagger?' Burns asked excitedly. 'Do I owe you for something?'

'Nothing like that, Ryan.'

'Same time?'

'Just a different venue.'

What kind of a guy says 'venue'? 'See you at seven-thirty.'

'I'll be there.' Ryan thought of calling his brother, but he just might just save this adventure for himself. He had a day to decide.

CHAPTER 55

JEN SEXTON DROVE to a mall. There was no way she'd call Kathryn from home. The trial resumed next week, and Jen had to know if Kathryn was well enough to attend. If only Jen could count on her answering the phone. Not too many things frightened Jen, but this call did.

Tim answered.

'Hello again. This is Jen Sexton, Tim. I apologize for disturbing you once more. Is there any chance of speaking with Kathryn?' She could immediately detect a difference in his tone.

'Right now, she's napping. She's much better, but I don't want to wake her. She needs every bit of rest she can get.'

'May I try tonight?'

'Whatever you have to say, you can tell me, Jen. A few days ago, Kathryn and I confided in one another. For the rest of our time together, and I hope it's not as short as we've been led to believe, we'll have no secrets between us.'

What could Jen say to that? When her heart stopped banging, she managed to say, 'That's very rare. I envy you.'

'Maybe nothing would have come out if our time wasn't limited. Absolute truth is a first for me too. It's sobering but liberating.'

'You must love one another deeply.'

'I know about you and Kathryn if that's what you want to talk about.'

The reason Jen was in human resources was her keen ability to read people, solve problems and understand sticky politics. Right now, the contours of her plans began to fade. If Tim already knew about them, Kathryn had nothing to fear from Pastore announcing the affair. The only family in jeopardy would be hers.

'Tim, I instigated the affair, and Kathryn ended it.'

'That's in the past; I'm over it,' Tim lied. 'Was this what you wanted to talk to Kathryn about?'

'Only partially.'

'What's the rest?'

Jen's mind was racing. 'It's something to do with her case.'

'What do you have, Jen? We could use the support.'

Times like this, Jen wished she weren't a risk taker. 'Tim, it's imperative I see Kathryn. I have to speak to her first. Please understand.'

'You don't trust me?'

'I do, but all litigation is a crapshoot. I want Kathryn to hear firsthand what I've found. The decision has to be hers. She's owed that much.'

'Are you in love with Kathryn? Is that what this is all about?'

'No, Tim. For God's sake, the affair was years ago.'

'To me it was yesterday. I want to be in the room when you talk to her.'

'That's for Kathryn to decide.'

It was one thing for Kathryn to surprise him with her indiscretion, even titillate him. Tim feared the whole company might learn his wife had cheated on him with Jen Sexton, a woman for God's sake! He knew many of the executives, played golf with one of them. When he lost Kathryn, she'd escape the mess; he'd still be around to face the knowing smirks. His affairs had stayed under the radar. For the first time, since Kathryn fell ill, Tim was angry with her.

'Does Pastore know about the affair?'

'I don't know.' Jen was not about to bandy the words

'common knowledge'. Let Kathryn tell him she did. 'Tim, my discovery is far more important than the affair.'

'All right.'

'Look, I'm more sorry than you know, but Kathryn should get an opportunity to weigh my information. I don't want to lose my family or my job. That's why I'd like to talk to her, Tim.'

To his complete dismay, he found himself liking this woman. She had spunk and she was taking a risk with this call. He admired that.

'Leave this with me.'

'Here's my cell number. Please don't call me at home.'

'I'll be in touch.' Tim stared out the back window before he walked down the hall to their bedroom. It appeared Kathryn was still asleep. But Tim wasn't sure; he wasn't sure about anything any more.

Jen drove home asking herself if she was single-handedly trying to destroy her family. If that was her agenda, she was doing a crack-up job at it. *I didn't give Tim the actual evidence. Robert and I are going to be around for awhile, truth-bearing isn't an option, no matter how liberating it is. We'd both go down.* She saw no point in going through an inventory of possible worst scenarios. Positive thinking, that's what Jen had to maintain.

CHAPTER 56

BY THE TIME Mike was back at his post on Harvard
Avenue on Sunday morning, it was close to ten o'clock.
Caitlin was probably right when she said that nothing
would happen today. He slumped in his seat, impassive
and lonely. His window was down, and he noticed that
the wind had picked up. The Harvard house was quiet;
the whole street was quiet. He perked up a little when
he thought that Caitlin said she'd be back here Monday
morning. Carmen had to be back at work, but that
might not be such a good thing either. That meant he'd
have Caitlin to himself. What if she was planning
another *get outta town* monologue?

He was quick to see Elsa Schreff come out her front
door with a rake in hand. The woman made certain she
worked very close to Pastore's property. Every minute
or two, she glanced quickly at the house, waiting or spying on someone. Mike saw her walk up the driveway
and look out back. It was obvious she was hesitant to
knock, but she was planning to see somebody in that
house. He didn't have to be a rocket scientist to realize
it was Sophia or Pastore the rake lady wanted to see. As
she walked back out front, Mike ducked down. He did-
n't want to ruin tomorrow for Caitlin by being caught
on this stakeout.

Earlier, seven o'clock actually, Sophia was washing
the basement stairs. Monsieur was hobbling beside her
on his three legs while she worked on the first few
stairs, but he stayed put when she worked higher up.
The mystery of the oily stair was a knot of concern in
Sophia's stomach. Was it possible? No, that idea was

too terrible to contemplate. It was time for Monsieur's walk, and Sophia took him out back. Could she herself have been so careless? She had found one bottle of lotion open, and she remembered there were times she forgot to snap it shut. She would be more vigilant in the future.

Sophia stepped out on the back porch and walked into the yard to clean up after Monsieur. Elsa's wait paid off. She ran out back in a flash when she heard a door close. 'Good morning, Sophia,' she said, waving her best hello.

Sophia nodded and began to worry about her recipes.

'We are still so lucky with another beautiful day, windy but lovely all the same. I felt badly all night when I thought about asking for your recipes. Please, forgive me. They're your treasures and I won't ask you to share them with me again.'

'Thank you, I am glad you understand.'

'I will go on enjoying the wonderful aromas that escape this house when you work your magic. Oh my, what's happened to the little dog?'

'Monsieur took a tumble, but he will be fine.'

Monsieur came hobbling at the sound of his name, showing off his prowess on three feet.

'He doesn't look the worse for wear. He's very lucky to have such a caretaker! I don't mean to be nosey, but it was my husband Stephen who realized it was Nicolina who was involved in that awful car accident on Sherbrooke Street. As I was lying in bed last night, I was thinking it must be so difficult for Nicolina to absorb the shock of such a terrible tragedy. It doesn't matter much what happened. He was such a handsome young man! I saw his photo in *The Gazette*.'

The recipe question had left Sophia wary, but the

woman had apologized. That was to her credit. Sophia knew well that everyone made mistakes. She herself might even have killed Monsieur Patate! To be truthful, Sophia had been very much alone with her thoughts on the tragedy and that was not always easy. Roberto, like Nicolina, rarely had conversations with her. He never listened, but spoke at her. A nodding assent was all they were seeking. Sophia had spent a lifetime of keeping her ideas to herself.

'I don't want to pry, but if you need a good ear, I'm always around. A long time ago, before Stephen and I moved to Harvard Avenue, a young boy was struck and killed by a city bus. The bus driver lived on our street, Benny Avenue, below Sherbrooke Street. That man was never the same; had to give up his bus. I think they put him on a desk job. He was destroyed, and I never remember him speaking to another neighbour for years.'

'I know a little of what Nicolina is going through. I know she has a lot on her mind. She also told me she was worried about you falling. Remember, I'm just next door if you need help. My Stephen remembers the night of the accident. He's not certain, but he thinks he might have heard Nicolina going out that night. I told him he was imagining things. He sleeps like a hog.'

A shiver travelled up Sophia's spine. 'When did Nicolina tell you that she was worried about me?'

'The day after you almost fell in the kitchen. How are you, by the way?'

Sophia's muscles relaxed. 'I'm very well now, thank you.'

Nicolina spied the women talking in the backyard. 'Sophia, will you please bring Monsieur in now? I'd like to take a look at his leg.' *I can't trust anybody! I should never have said a single word to that witch! Bad mistake on my part.*

CHAPTER 57

MIKE HALLORAN SPENT the afternoon on St. Denis Street. He parked at an ESSO station on the corner of Sherbrooke Street and paid an attendant ten bucks for the afternoon. For over half an hour, he'd tried to find a place to park. Deciphering the parking signs and their regulations was tying his head in a tight knot. He should have taken a subway, the Metro, as it was called here. Using a guide book, he walked north from Sherbrooke Street into the Plateau Mont-Royal.

On warm, sunny afternoons in spring, throngs of couples, hand in hand, amble up the crowded street window-shopping and hunt for chairs in the tiny terrasses that explode along the street with the first sign of warm weather. The long winters have made all Montrealers desperate to sit outdoors. The Café Cherrier that Mike had found in his guidebook was too crowded to even attempt. Of all the streets in the city, St. Denis Street was the lovers' domain. It was not the place for a handsome guy pining for a woman he might never win. By the time Mike reached Duluth Avenue, he was more depressed than when he'd started out.

He'd call Caitlin tonight to be sure that she'd join him at the stake-out. What if she bailed on him tomorrow morning? All his dating life, he'd had more than enough women fall for him. With Caitlin, he really did not know if he was up to her standards. He knew Caitlin was attracted to him; he could feel it. All these lovers had put him off. He headed back to his apartment and ordered in. Late that night, Caitlin said she'd find him on Harvard Monday morning.

On her end, Mike's call opened a need. Trying to get him out of her hormones, she concentrated on Tuesday and her father's meeting with Burns. Why couldn't her father simply drop the money off and make a clean break, send an explanatory note if he wanted. Why was he putting the family in harm's way so soon after Chris? Steadying herself, she remembered she'd better call her publisher, Geoffrey Smyth, tomorrow after the stake-out, thank him for the good work and tell him she'd hold up her end of things and attend everything. Mike's voice unnerved her, made her belly burn. Why couldn't he have been a flirtation? Why had she allowed him to get inside her?

Frank Donovan had heard Caitlin's concerns and he began to hold out a slim hope that the money wouldn't arrive on time. He could do the anonymous thing that Caitlin had suggested. Yet, Frank knew himself well enough to know that he was rigid once he had decided on a plan. Not telling Maggie was the only change he was willing to make. Frank would not destroy his wife. He wasn't looking for a pardon; he was looking to square things. He wanted the self-respect he'd lost twenty-nine years ago. He felt Chris would want him to own up; that's why he had to stay with the plan. Caitlin made a lot of sense. He thought about the amount of money. A quarter of a million dollars might suggest a dot-com king with deep pockets, open temptation for further blackmail. Frank decided on one hundred seventy-five thousand dollars. That figure sounded more like the life-savings of Joe Ordinary than a guy who drank from champagne flutes. His next concern was what the hell he was going to tell Ryan Burns. How could he explain that he waited a lifetime to contact him?

At the cemetery on Sunday afternoon, Maggie wanted to ask Caitlin what she and her father were up to. She had heard them talking quietly to one another. Something was up, Maggie knew that much. She couldn't remember a time when the door to the study had been closed so often. As far as she knew, Frank and she didn't have secrets. He was trying to protect her, but from what? Caitlin knew what was going on, but Maggie would ask Frank if she wanted to know. Right now, the only thing that she wanted was her son back.

Nicolina wanted to grab Sophia and bang her head against a wall, but murder had lost its earlier appeal. The attempts alone had taken their toll on Nicolina, had made her feel like the failure her mother had said she would be. She attempted a different tack for now. 'You've done a great job with Monsieur's leg, Sophia. I don't know what he and I would do without you! I am so depressed about that young man; I still can't sleep. That's why I'm so glad that you're here. You're the best friend I have. I'm also very stressed with the case I'm arguing. It resumes very soon. Elsa is a lovely neighbour, but every time I step outside, she seems to be there waiting. I'm sure I'm not telling you anything when I say we have to be a little careful with neighbours, even with good ones like Elsa. On a lighter note, is there any chance of blueberry pancakes for breakfast, if I help out?'

Sophia got the message. *Don't go blabbing to Elsa!* She

began work in the kitchen. 'I will call you when they are ready.' Such a house of troubles, thought Sophia.

Nicolina called Walton again from the living room. 'Richard, is there any way you can learn if Kathryn Traynor is well enough to make court this week?'

'I've seen nothing so far to indicate Traynor won't attend.'

Nicolina found Sexton's number, dialed the first digit and stopped. The last thing she wanted to do was get Sexton's back up.

Raymond Lecours' indigestion went unabated. He was puffing on four *Cohibas* a day at the office in his blue upholstered chair; his cheeks were florid and his breath came in short gasps. From a few feet away, he appeared to have a rash on his face. Between the cigars, he was chewing Pepto-Bismol tablets. Everybody knew the trial was resuming; any sympathy was reserved for Kathryn Traynor. Lecours might have found great pleasure in Pastore's misery at first; now, on days when she sat close to him in the conference room, Lecours recognized that all spillage spread. The case would cause a stink he couldn't escape. When he looked at Pastore, he noticed she had developed a small tick at the corner of her left eye. *Damnation! Makes her slow and uncertain; that's what we really need right now! What in blazes are we to do if that evidence gets in and the court discovers we didn't disclose it? What will happen to me?* Lecours slipped out a fifth cigar.

Tim Traynor prepared dinner, even though Kathryn might not want it. 'Prepared' might have been a bit of a stretch. He'd bought quite a supply from Les Aliments

M&M. Tonight he was baking sole filets and boiling what they called a 'farm fresh blend', cauliflower, carrots and green beans. Beside the fish in the oven, stuffed potatoes 'made easy' were baking in Alcan heavy-duty foil. Weightier thoughts were troubling him. He hoped Kathryn was still sleeping. A flash of remorse surged though his blood, knowing he was about to trade a chance by Kathryn to improve her legal position before she lost her life for a humiliation he knew he'd survive.

When he tiptoed to the bedroom, Kathryn was wide awake. 'I feel much better, stronger every day, just as you said I would.'

Frank kissed Kathryn on the mouth. She tasted good, even this ill. 'Let me help you out of bed. Then, I want you to sit here for a few minutes while I set up the pillows in the den. I outdid myself tonight; hope you enjoy the dinner. It's full of protein, all good stuff!'

Because it was a daily routine, the den was ready for Kathryn in a minute or two. Tim noticed immediately that Kathryn was walking on her own. Actually, she might well have walked to the den without his help. 'Kathryn, this is the strongest you've been in days. Bravo!'

'I can feel the difference myself. Get that food. I'll be running around the apartment in no time.'

Tim was thrilled. He paraded the dinner, one dinner plate in each hand and set them down like any good waiter. Kathryn ate with gusto. Tim sat there, without touching his own meal, with a smile that went almost to his ears. To see Kathryn eat without effort or strain warmed his heart.

'I was asleep, but it seems to me I heard the phone, Tim. Who was calling?'

Tim's moment had arrived.

CHAPTER 58

CAITLIN SPOTTED MIKE'S car across the street from the neighbour's house, picked up her pace and slid onto the front seat. 'You're early!'

'I thought Sophia might decide on an early start. I didn't want to miss it,' Mike said. 'Have you figured out what to say to her if you get the chance?'

'As I was driving over here, I went over things. I'm hoping she leaves the house. You can pretend to bump into her and then, if she seems at ease with you, I'll join you. Then I'll go with the truth.'

'Your style.'

'What do you mean by that?'

'I like your style, head-on, no games.'

'Thought you were criticizing me.'

'Me? Never.'

'As we've already said, she's afraid or she has nothing to offer. If it's something like finding another place, I can help her with that and try the best I can to make her feel she doesn't have to be afraid.'

'Might work.'

'If she tells us something, we can't send her home if we take her evidence to Remay.'

'Let's work on that snag after we have the goods on the bitch. Right now, we're working with specs.'

'If I'm boring you, Mike, I can work alone.'

'What's up with you this morning? Lookin' for a fight, lady?'

Caitlin was not about to tell Mike she wanted more than a fight with him.

'Sorry, I'm edgy.'

'Shit! Get your head down. Sophia's just come out

on the balcony. All we need is the neighbour. You shouldn't have parked this close to the house.'

'Shoot me,' Mike whispered as he hit his head on the steering wheel.

'I can't look over too obviously, but I don't think she's going shopping.'

'What's up then?'

'She's sitting in a chair. Dammit! I know why she's not going far. The dog's hurt its leg. It's in some kind of bandage.'

'Not Monsieur Patate!'

'This isn't funny.'

'Try looking at things from down here.'

'Just a sec. She's taking off the bandage. I guess she wants to see how he walks.'

'Be brave, Monsieur!'

'A ten for his performance!' Caitlin lightened up.

'Bravo, Monsieur. My legs are cramping.' But Mike's head was resting against Caitlin's thigh and he didn't want any change there.

Caitlin could feel his breath; her breasts tingled. She did not want to change anything either.

'What's new, up there?'

'She has no purse; she's not going out today. We should call it quits.' Another front door opened. 'Shit! There's the neighbour I spoke to. Let's get out of here!' Caitlin ducked down to avoid Elsa and promptly bumped heads with Mike.

'Ouch!'

'Get up slowly and drive away. That neighbour can't see me!'

'I couldn't get up quickly, even if I had to.' Mike reached into the back seat and snagged his cap. With some difficulty, he got it on his head and eased himself back into position. He started the car up, never looked across the street, and drove away.

'The last thing I want to do is spook Sophia before we meet.'

'I honestly think we have a good chance tomorrow.'

'I'll be here, but I have to be home by the middle of the afternoon.'

'Where did you park?'

'I didn't; I took a cab. Thought you could take me home.'

Mike threw his left hand over his crotch, to keep things under control.

'You're blushing!'

'No, I'm not.'

'Your face looks like you just had a peel!'

'How about lunch?'

'It's not even eleven.'

'Breakfast?'

'Lunch it is. I haven't eaten yet. I feel like something bad, a burger loaded with ketchup and fries drowned in vinegar. Let's go to Nickels.'

'Chris said you were a health nut.' He regretted mentioning Chris, the second he'd spoken his name.

There was dead air between them.

'I guess Chris didn't know everything about me. Let's not go to Crescent Street; I don't want to see Winnie's.'

'Would you be brave enough to come to my place? We can order in. I wanted you to see it.'

'Mike Halloran, do you think you have a power over me that I can't control? Are you that full of yourself?'

'Jesus, I was kidding.'

'Now, who can't take a joke?'

Sophia was pleased with Monsieur's progress. She saw two young people in a car, but she turned her full attention to Monsieur. She did see Elsa. Sophia gave her a lovely wave and walked back inside with the pug. There was something to be said for anonymity; she did not need Nicolina to remind her of that.

For some curious reason, Elsa had made her think of her daughter. *She has not called though she promised she would. Perhaps she will never forgive me for something I did not do.* With some difficulty, Sophia bent and patted Monsieur.

He knew Sophia had nothing to do with his tumble and he knew who did. Monsieur could also tell a story about the slipper.

Riding up to the third floor together, neither Mike nor Caitlin said anything. Jokes eluded this situation. His knees were jelly; her stomach moved. When Caitlin walked into the apartment, she lost her voice. When Mike asked her if she wanted something to drink, she couldn't answer. Caitlin didn't pull Mike to her as she had that first night; she couldn't move. She worried Mike would hear her heart banging against her ribs.

Mike held out his hand. Caitlin saw the tears in his eyes, then the fierce desire behind them. What followed was a wet blur of need and sex, of anger and punishment. Late into the night, their blended bodies glistened and arched. Finally sated and remorseful, Caitlin rolled away from Mike.

For a few minutes, he didn't touch her. He pulled up the sheet and covered Caitlin. He waited for an hour before he spoke.

'Will you ever forgive me?'

'I don't even know what this is.'

'It's called love.'

'It's also called the lust of a woman who's been celibate for three years, give or take a few interludes.'

'You don't believe that, Caitlin.'

'Don't presume to know what I believe,' Caitlin leapt from the bed and began throwing on her clothes. 'He wasn't your brother!'

'Will you ever forgive me?'

'I'm not even thinking about you.'

'All right then, can you forgive yourself?'

'Fuck! Leave me alone! Didn't I ask you to go over a week ago?'

'I love you, Caitlin.'

She remembered her mother's forgiveness. Caitlin turned back to Mike who lay alone on the bed. She smiled down at him. 'I might,' she whispered. Then she ran out.

Mike knew enough not to go after her, until she got to the door. 'Caitlin, wait! You have no car!'

'Oh my God, I forgot all about my parents!'

'You know what, call them now. Then I'll drive you home.'

Caitlin grabbed the phone.

Frank and Maggie sat like stone statues on the divan in the living room. Both froze when the phone rang.

Frank stared at the cordless phone as though it were a gun.

The phone rang a fifth time.

'I have to take this, Maggie.' She covered both ears with her hands.

Frank took the phone. 'Yes?'

'Dad, I'm so sorry; I lost track of the time.'

'It's Caitlin, Maggie! She's all right!'

Maggie ran to the phone and grabbed it out of Frank's hand. 'How could you do this to your father and me, Caitlin? How could you?'

'Mom, I am so sorry. Please wait up for me. I'll be home in twenty minutes.'

'My mother hung up on me.'

'Get your stuff; I'll get you home in no time.'

'What wrong with me? I've just scared the shit out of my parents.'

'Maybe it's time you moved back to your own place.'

'Shut up, Mike, if you want to live!'

'All right.'

When they reached the foot of the driveway, Caitlin jumped out.

'Are we on tomorrow, Caitlin?'

'Wednesday's better.'

'Fine.'

As soon as Frank heard the key in the lock, he opened the door from his side. 'You had us so worried. We didn't know what had happened to you. Your car was in the driveway, so we thought you were home until you mother went in to say goodnight.'

'I'm so sorry. This won't happen again. Maybe I should go home.'

'We need you here for a while. In the future, call, and things won't get out of hand. Your mother's upstairs. I need you in top shape tomorrow night.' Frank whispered the last line.

Maggie grabbed Caitlin as soon as she got to the landing. 'I thought I had lost you too! Do you hear what I'm saying, Caitlin? I thought I'd lost you too!'

'Please forgive me!'

'I thought you were gone, just like Chris.'

'I'm not going anywhere Mom. I'm so sorry,' Caitlin wept.

CHAPTER 59

TUESDAY MORNING, FRANK was the first Donovan out of bed. Maggie slept soundlessly, worn out from last night's frantic anxiety. Frank didn't check on Caitlin. After a shower and shave, he disappeared into his study and called Bruce Strong on his private line. Though it was before nine, he knew Strong always got an early start. 'Bruce, just checking in. Are we on schedule for this afternoon?'

'Hi Frank. Haven't heard of a glitch on my end. Let me check here; should arrive by three this afternoon. You want the package delivered?'

'Not at my home, Bruce.'

'How about halfway, say, the NDG Park?'

'How will I recognize the courier?'

'We know each other, right?'

'I didn't expect you to do the grunt work!'

'No problem. Do you need any help with the package itself?'

'I have that covered.'

'Be careful, Frank.'

'I will be, and thanks.'

'I'll make the delivery by three-thirty by the baseball field across from the church.'

When Frank had hung up, he cracked his knuckles. Maggie hated when he did that. He was already on edge and perspiring heavily. The whole thing was beginning to feel like a B-movie with B-actors, and he had the lead. He felt worse when he remembered that he'd put Caitlin in the middle of his mess.

'Hungry?' Maggie popped her head into the study.

'Hi honey, not especially. Whole wheat toast and coffee will do me just fine.'

'I'm still wound up about last night, Frank.'

'Let's not go there. We've all made mistakes. At the moment, none of us are ourselves. Last night was out of character for Caitlin.'

'You're right. I was so afraid of losing her, but I still wanted to throttle her when she came home.'

'Makes total sense to me, Maggie.'

'I get your point. I'll call you when the coffee's ready. Are you all right, Frank?'

'Just tired, Maggie.' As soon as she left the room, Frank saw another glitch. What would he tell Maggie about tonight, even this afternoon when he left her for the pickup? He didn't want to lie to her. His plan today was his attempt to set things right. Yet, what if it began with a lie? Frank was beginning to learn first hand about tangled webs. What if something went wrong with the pickup at the park? What if he was pulled over driving home and the money was discovered? Frank began to bite his nails, a habit he'd beaten when he was eleven.

'Coffee's up, Frank,' Maggie called.

'Coming!' He hoped Caitlin would be up soon. Two heads had to be better than his own.

Caitlin was awake; in fact she'd managed only a few hours of sleep. *How could I have been so thoughtless? What in God's name is wrong with me?* She would like to have stayed in bed; she needed to rest, but she knew she'd better get downstairs. Her father needed her today. She made the bed with more care than she had used in a week, tidied her room, showered, blow-dried her hair, dressed in her best tom-girl clothes and headed down to breakfast.

'Will I be allowed any breakfast?' she asked her mother, her head hung at the right level for a penitent.

'Only if you're my daughter and very sorry,' Maggie quipped.

'Guilty on both charges.'

'You're invited then. What will you have?'

'I'd love a cheese omelette, but I'll make it myself.'

'Nothing doing! I'll have it whipped up in no time. Sit down with your father and eat. Orange juice?'

'Please.'

'There's enough toast here to feed an army. I kind of lost track. I'll get out the strawberry preserves.'

'What a memory!'

Frank was trying to get Caitlin's attention when Maggie's back was turned. Caitlin picked up the code and nodded. He felt better.

When Maggie finally sat down, she looked better. 'It's good to be together. I've missed family meals. Let's try to eat together tonight. I was thinking it might do us all good to get out of the house for a change. How about going to the Beaver Club tonight, Frank?'

His smile stiffened. He was found out before he'd even begun!

Caitlin saw his stress and came to her father's rescue. 'Mom, I asked Dad a few days ago to help me with something. I accept it's easier for you not knowing how I'm tracking information on the driver. But part of this afternoon and for a few hours tonight, I need Dad's help. We won't be home late. Can we do the Beaver Club tomorrow night?'

'Why aren't you leaving this work to the police?'

'They have other cases, Mom. I noticed another hit-and-run yesterday. I want to be sure they keep Chris' case paramount. Whatever information I gather, I send to the investigator.'

Frank grimaced as though he were sitting on nails.

'Frank, you look weary. Get some rest.'

Once alone, Maggie cautioned Caitlin, 'You and Frank have been so secretive. I hope everything you're doing is above board. I've never seen your father this anxious. I'm very worried about both of you.'

No one is in the right for any long period of time. Caitlin had read that statement a few years ago and thought it made good sense. Stalking Pastore and paying off Burns had seemed the right courses of action. Yet, both these ventures had sprouted dark tendrils that threatened innocent people.

'I'll do my best to keep us out of trouble,' Caitlin answered, trying to make light of things. 'If I don't get something substantial in a week's time, I'll let the cops do their thing.'

'I want my family safe, Caitlin. I can't bear another loss.'

'I understand, Mom. Don't worry.'

CHAPTER 60

BRUCE STRONG WAS a man who suited his name, a tough cop who'd worked his way up into the law. Instead of police blue, he now wore Italian suits, but each one bulged at the biceps. His steel-grey hair was close-cropped, with no attempt to hide the bald spot on his crown. He had the square jaw and teeth of comic book heroes. Though he'd made his share, it wasn't all about money for Strong. Sometimes, it was about *right* as he read it. He'd known and respected Frank Donovan too long for him to question his friend.

He assumed the money was a reward for information on the driver who had killed his son. The size of the amount concerned him. Money wasn't a problem for Frank, he knew that. Everybody had heard Donovan was rolling in the stuff. But Bruce knew, from experience, just how greedy people could become.

At three o'clock, he was sitting in his Hummer in front of St. Augustine's Church. That's how he knew the old place, even though it had fallen into other hands. He checked the trunk before he crossed the street. He saw Frank approaching from Marcil Avenue. In casual clothes, Frank looked younger. But, as he drew closer, Bruce saw the fatigue and age, etched in deep crevices.

'Trouble?' Frank asked, hoping there was.

'None at all. Left the stuff in the truck. I'll turn up Marcil. There's parking by the church. Pull up behind me and I'll transfer the money. This is none of my business, but don't get yourself in over your head. This is a lot of cash.'

'I've decided to go with one-seventy-five.'

'Better figure.'

'Do you need help?'

'I don't want to involve you, Bruce. You've done enough, I'm indebted. I think I can manage to get to Pointe Claire.' A gust of wind snatched at Frank's nerves, and he shivered.

'You all right?'

'Haven't been since Chris.'

'I understand. I won't keep you; let's get moving.'

The men parted. Bruce drove a few hundred feet up Marcil Avenue and left room behind him. In a minute Frank parked and flipped his trunk open. Strong would have done well as a criminal. The bag was switched, the trunk shut, before Frank had walked to the back of his car.

'You're all set. You never spoke of denominations, so I selected them for you, hundreds and fifties. One word of advice, get to the specified place early. Check it out. Be safe, Frank.'

'Thanks for everything, Bruce. I'm out of my league, so I'll take your advice.'

'Good luck!'

The men parted ways, and Frank drove home, feeling like Agent 007, minus the bravado and smarts. The first thing he did when he was safely inside the garage was to lock the door that led into the house. Then he lifted the bag from the trunk, opened it and began to count seventy-five thousand dollars to take out. What remained in the luggage was a safer figure. He counted it a second time, left the seventy-five thousand on the floor of the garage and ran into the house. He leapt up the stairs, grabbed a piece of luggage from his walk-in closet, and tore back down to the garage. He hoisted the money he'd give Ryan Burns back into the trunk and shut it. He then stuffed his own bag with the seventy-five thousand he'd left on the floor, carried it into the basement, looked wildly for a hiding place and found one in a storage space in the furnace room. In minutes, he was standing in the shower, blasting the spray. He dressed quickly and waited for Maggie and Caitlin, grateful to his daughter for keeping Maggie out of the house. Until he heard them, he lay on his bed, trying to loosen up, but failed.

He wanted to be on the road by five-thirty at the latest. Traffic along Highway 20 was bad that time of day. The Decarie Expressway was out of the question; it'd be worse. The back of his head was already wet. Food, that's what he needed. With only an hour to spare, he was grateful to hear Maggie and Caitlin. What if she'd come home too late? But she hadn't; that was good news. As Frank came down to join the family, he remembered that the money had to be switched to Caitlin's Beetle.

'Glad you're back! Do you have anything light and healthy?'

'How does sliced turkey breast, rye bread, lettuce and honey mustard sound?'

'Perfect, like you Maggie!'

'I'll have two sandwiches ready in no time. Salad?'

'No, thanks. But iced tea would go well.'

Caitlin was busy unpacking the groceries when Frank pushed his car keys into her hand. 'Let me help your mother; you've had her all day!'

'I'll leave you two alone.' She went out by the garage, stopped to look at the empty space and decided not to take it. Chris should keep it for a while longer. When the garage door was opened, she turned her Beetle around and backed it up as close as she could get to her father's car. She realized her weights had paid off when she easily lifted the bag from one car to another. Once the trunks were locked and the garage door closed, she ran up for a quick shower, the second of the day.

Frank tried to eat slowly, gagged and ran to the bathroom because what was going in was going out almost as quickly.

'Frank Donovan, what's wrong? Your face is white!'

'It's nothing, Maggie. I'm overtired is all. Let's promise one another to stay in bed till ten tomorrow.'

'You'll get no argument from me.'

'Good.'

'When are you going out?'

'In half an hour. We should be back by nine-thirty at the latest.'

'Whatever this is, I hope it's worth all the stress you're putting yourself through.'

'What will you do while we're gone?'

'I have Chris' photos; they're good company. I still haven't watched all the videos we took of the kids. I won't be lonely; I'll have Chris to myself.'

'All right, you two, stop smooching. We have to go, Dad.'

'Be careful, my two spies!' Maggie called after them as Caitlin backed out of the driveway. *Why did they take the Beetle?*

As soon as they got onto the Ville Marie Expressway, they were snarled in traffic that moved forward by feet. 'It's good that we left early.'

'Don't try anything fancy, Caitlin.'

'Calm down; I won't.'

Highway 20 was no better. 'I cannot believe people do this every day. A lot of them take the train.'

'Not from the looks of things, Dad. All of Montreal is on this damn road.'

Thirty-Second Avenue was bottle-necked as well. 'Never mind me; keep your eyes on the road, Caitlin.'

'Dad, you don't have to go through with this.'

'If I don't settle accounts today, I never will.'

'Not all accounts balance.'

'The ones that matter should, Caitlin.'

One hour later, they exited on St. John's Boulevard. 'Go to Hymus Boulevard and turn left on Stillview Avenue. I can find Norwood from there. I want to see where he lives. Then we can head to the park. Whatever you do, don't slow down in front of the house.'

'Elementary, my dear Watson.'

Ryan Burns checked the time often. At noon, he'd rushed home for a second shower so that Lindsay wouldn't suspect that something was up. His towel would be dry by the time she got home from work. He even helped with the dishes.

'What do you want, Ryan?'

'Nothing, Linds. Can't a guy help his wife out?'

'I wasn't born yesterday.'

'I won't touch that.'

'Smart guy!'

'Listen, I have to go out for a while, not long.'

'Here it comes…'

'No pub, nothing like that. I said I'd meet a guy I used to know for a few minutes. I'll be home by nine.'

'What about?'

Third degree again! 'I won't know till I see him. I'll be home before you'll miss me.'

'Who said anything about missing you?'

'Nice try, Linds.' Ryan took his wallet from on top of the fridge and forced it into the side pocket of his Body Glove shorts. He wore old sneakers without socks, but he grabbed a lightweight softball team jacket when he

left the house. Though the guy hadn't specified *where* in
the park, he figured he could spot another guy looking
for him. Like Frank, he wanted to be early, size him up.

Frank and Caitlin drove by the Norwood house
before Burns had left it. Nothing distinguished his
place from any of the homes on the street. They were
solid, brick structures with single car garages, simple
lawns with sparse flower beds, if any at all. Caitlin drove
around the park, up Seigniory Avenue, then left on
Stillview and left again into the Southwest One parking
lot. Caitlin was lucky to find a spot a few feet from the
exit. It was ten to seven.

'Dad, this is what I think you should do. I'll walk you
through the mall to the exit. It's small, but people get
mixed up with exits.'

'I can find my way around the country; I think I can
manage a mall.'

'Let's walk through it together.'

'Leave the money here?'

'We'll be gone five minutes tops.'

Frank followed Caitlin, past a deli, left at a ladies'
clothes shop, down to a Couche Tard at the end of that
section and out a side door on their right. 'There's the
park! Norwood's behind it on the far side, so Burns
should be coming in at that end. There are a few benches on a couple of paths. You can decide where you want
to wait.'

'I can handle this.'

'You look awful.'

'It's just the ghost of my past stepping up to the
plate.'

'Let's retrace our steps: left at Couche Tard, right at
the ladies' shop, pass the deli on the left and out to the

lot. I'll have the car running. Walk back quickly to it, and we'll get out of here as fast as possible. Don't prolong any conversation.'

'You're right.'

'Do you know what you want to say?'

'Beginning is the hardest.'

'It's five after seven; I think you should get going. I'll walk you through the mall.'

When Caitlin left Frank, he was close to hyper-ventilating. This was his showdown. The lightweight bag he carried was heavier that he thought it would be, and he strained to keep his shoulder from sagging. He stopped and looked back at the mall and tried to walk in a straight line from the door. He wasn't certain he'd recall the right entrance after he met with Burns. He walked under a huge willow tree that canopied his path, another landmark he should remember. He saw two benches, passed the first and took the second. He set the bag down on the bench and stood beside it. To his left, a few children played on swings, ahead of him, the baseball field was empty. Too early yet, he thought. Two or three artificial hills gave the park depth and appeal. A few adults walked dogs, or chatted while children played. Frank waited.

Ryan Burns watched him, certain he was the caller. His hopes sagged when he saw the bag. *Fuck! He's a salesman.* Frank saw Burns as he approached. 'You called my home a few days ago.'

'Ryan Burns?'

'That's me. Did you get me out here for a sales' pitch?'

'No, I didn't.'

'Well?'

'Twenty-nine years ago, we should have met.'

'Why didn't we? What is this? Are you a cop?'

'I'd like to explain. You and I were involved in a hit-and-run accident. I was the driver.'

Burns caught Frank with a fierce right hook to the jaw that knocked him to the ground. When he was a teenager, Frank had been a golden gloves boxer for a year, but he never saw the punch coming.

'You deserved that, buddy! A little late, aren't you?'

Two people in the park witnessed the assault, but did not come to Frank's aid.

CHAPTER 61

'DO YOU THINK you might be able to go to court with me this week, Kathryn?'

'I'm feeling stronger. I still have a couple of days; I'll see how I am the day before court. Was there someone on the phone, Tim?'

'I love you, Kathryn Traynor.'

'Who called, Tim?'

'Jen Sexton.' Maybe he wouldn't feel good later, but at this moment, he did. 'I think she should talk to you.'

'What's happened?'

'Let me call her. I have her cell number.'

'Hello, Jen.'

'Are you up for a visit?'

'I'll have to be. Tim tells me we should meet.'

It suddenly struck Jen Sexton that she'd need every minute she had with Kathryn. 'I'll be at your place in forty-five minutes.' During that time, Jen ran around like a madwoman. She raced home for the file, copied it, and sped to the Traynors'.

She straightened her blouse, tossed her head back and arranged a smile back before she rang the bell.

As soon as Tim opened the door, he saw immediately why men and women were attracted to Jen Sexton. When she smiled, Tim almost forgot the serious nature of her visit. Some people had it all; Sexton had more.

'Tim Traynor, come in.'

'Thanks; got here as soon as I could.'

'Kathryn's upstairs.' Tim led the way.

When she walked into the den, Kathryn lay on the sofa, propped up by pillows. She wore what appeared to be Tim's pajamas and a yellow sweater though it was too hot in the room already. The change in Kathryn was remarkable and sad. Jen felt every bit an intruder.

'I have a lovely wig that Tim bought, but it's not me. Sit down, Jen. Unrecognizable, is that what you're thinking?'

'Not at all, courageous and peaceful are what come to mind,' Jen spoke softly and quickly, wiping both eyes. She turned to Tim who was smiling down at Kathryn, 'You're both very brave.'

'Wasn't an option I voted for,' he answered.

Jen looked back at Kathryn and smiled, remembering. She could feel the blood rise to her cheeks.

'I'm not up for any shenanigans, you two.'

'Stop kidding, Tim.'

'Behave yourselves!' Without knowing why, he knew he could trust them both and left them alone.

'I like him, Kathryn. You have a good one.'

'I'm lucky.'

'Well, here's the story…'

'Oh my God! My cancer may be the result of exposure to the ingredients of Comitrixin? My office was too close to the lab? Foley's wonder drug is the reason I'm dying?' Tears streamed down Kathryn's cheeks; she rarely cried. It was a waste of energy.

'I think it is. There are problems with it no one dares to talk about.'

'Do you have proof of this, Jen?'

'I think I have enough to nix the IPO. The forgery and embezzlement charges were concocted to get you out of Foley. Here,' she said, pulling two sheets from the briefcase.

'This is incredible. I've been blaming myself for the years of lawn spraying. Foley's is the reason I'm dying! Is there anything else, Jen?'

'Pastore said she'd spread our affair around the office

and tell Robert. Tim knows a few of us at Foley's, so there's his end of the fallout too. Whatever you do about this, the decision is yours.'

'I wish we'd gone to different conferences.'

'I don't.'

'It's all so complicated, Jen. Do you have any idea how she found out about us?'

Jen couldn't tell Kathryn that Tim's humiliation was old stuff around the office; he sure as hell would have nothing to lose now. 'She wouldn't say.'

'What do you think would happen to your marriage if you told Robert?'

'He might well take the kids and leave me. He's had doubts all along, with reason, as you know.'

'Will you leave the copies with me?'

'That's why I brought them.'

'Next session, it's our day to present. If things go as well as expected, I may not even need this.'

'But you won't know till then, right?'

'I'll try to think things through; if I decide sooner, I'll let you know. But this is my life, Jen. That's bigger than any scandal. If you want to save your marriage, give some thought to confiding in Robert. You might be surprised.'

'I'm not brave, Kathryn; I never was.'

'Everything changes, Jen; I'm proof of that.'

'I'm a bleeder, Kathryn.'

'Aren't we all?'

CHAPTER 62

AS HE HAD when he boxed, Frank ran his tongue around his teeth. They were all still rooted in his gums. He braced himself for a kick that never came. Instead, Burns offered him his hand.

'You've gotta admit you had that coming! Now, get up before people see us and call the cops.'

Frank rubbed his jaw and got to his feet himself. 'I wasn't expecting that!'

'It was a surprise to me that night when you drove through the stop sign; I sure as hell wasn't expecting that either. Today, bad drivers skip stops and traffic lights. Back then they didn't.'

'That night, you didn't make your own stop either.'

'That's why I only threw a single punch. You were the adult in a car; I was a kid on a bike!'

'I know that.'

'Why did you bother to stop before you took off?'

'I wanted to go back, but I thought I could lose the job I was interviewing for. I didn't want a record.'

'I could have had a serious head injury or whatever and you just took off! I used to plan what I'd do to you if I ever discovered who you were. You're lucky I never did.'

'I've felt guilt and shame ever since.'

'Did nothing for me, did it?'

'I hope you had a full recovery.'

'Jesus, I was seventeen years old. I was a running back on our high school football team. We went to the semis that year, but the injuries side-lined me. The money from that delivery job was going to tuition and books. Lost that too. Had to work for a year before college and never finished because other shit happened.

And, thanks to you I have arthritis in my ankle and shoulder. Yeah, I recovered, but I lost things that mattered to me when I was young. The one good thing is that I'm a safe driver today.'

'I'm sorry for what I did, Ryan.'

'Why are you showing up after all these years?'

'I lost my only son to a hit-and-run driver. I figured it was time to square things with you, and I'm doing this for him as well.'

'Too bad about your son; I was lucky, I guess.'

'My son had no luck at all.'

'Is there anything else?'

'Yes, there is. I can't make the past up to you, but I hope I can try. In that bag, you'll find a hundred and seventy-five thousand dollars. I thought you might be able to make good use of my savings. My son would want you to be compensated, and so do I.'

'Is this some kind of joke?'

'No, it isn't. Check the bag.'

'Holy shit!' Ryan whispered through his teeth as he unzipped it. He quickly closed the bag. 'I never thought my luck would change. Doomed, that's what I thought I was. Holy shit, this is something!'

'I'm glad for you.'

'It was almost worth the accident. I really can't believe this! Holy shit!'

'Well, I guess that's it, Ryan. Best of luck to you!'

'What the hell is your name anyway? You told me, but I've lost it.'

'Michael, Mike to friends.'

'All right, Mike then. I want to get home. What can I say?'

'I'm glad we met.'

'A hell of a lot better than the first time! See you, Mike.' Ryan picked up his loot and left the park. *Linds is not going to believe this! Dave either. The first thing I'm getting myself is new wheels. Jesus, maybe an SUV! I'm going to blow fifty thousand on something I can finally have. No more second-hand jobs!*

Frank walked briskly back to the path, under the willow and across the street. He never looked back. He made a left inside the mall beside the Couche Tard and a right at the ladies' shop. His path was clear and he hurried.

At the Couche Tard, a man stepped out, blocking the entrance doors as he identified the guy tailing Frank about to open one of them. 'Excuse me. You can't go inside right now. There's some trouble.'

'Who the fuck are you? I need to get into the mall. My friend just went in there and we're together. Get out of my way!'

Dave Burns was losing precious time.

Bruce Strong took out his cell and feigned listening. 'It'll be open in two minutes, sir. You'll have full access then.'

'This is bullshit!'

'Watch you language, sir!'

'Fuck you!' Dave swore and ran around to the far door on his left that was a good five hundred feet away.

'All done, Cait. Let's hit the road.' The Beetle pulled out behind a van and disappeared down Stillview Avenue. 'No repercussions!'

'Dad, what's wrong with your chin?'

'A good right hook.'

'What do you mean no fallout? That'll turn into one mother of a bruise.'

'Small price.'

'What do we tell Mom?'

'I think we can manage to come up with something.'

Tailing Frank had been an easy task. Strong was satisfied with his work. One thing was sure; the money was a payoff, not a reward. Strong saw no point in alerting Donovan. He might need Frank's help some day.

'He must be in that van! He sure as hell doesn't look like a guy who'd drive a Beetle.' Dave shouted to himself, running wildly after the cars, trying to get a read on the plates. A cop he knew owed him for under-the-table roofing work. He might run the plates for him. Ryan had walked away with a bag. He hoped it was money.

Maybe there was more where that came from.

CHAPTER 63

JEN LEFT KATHRYN Traynor transformed, saddened, but buoyed. Courage in the face of death was the lesson Jen needed. Her own life began rolling in front of her eyes as she drove home. She decided to take the rest of the day off. The finality of Kathryn's life clarified her own. It was time for change. She understood why she'd given Kathryn the evidence. Even if she'd withheld the file, Lecours and Pastore would have found a way to fire her.

Once Jen was in the house, she was alone for a while before Ashley arrived home from school. The first thing she did was get to work on dinner, something she usually left for Robert. Each of her three children had only one word when they got home and found Jen in the kitchen, 'Wow!' Robert was suspicious.

The kids devoured the steak; Robert was not about to let his cynicism interfere with his T-bone and onions. After the dinner, when the kids had disappeared, Jen asked Robert if they could talk.

'Why am I not surprised?'

First, she told him about her visit to Kathryn's.

'Well, you've gone outside the family again. What else is new?'

'Robert, Kathryn had a right to know why she's dying.'

'We don't matter. I understand.'

'Robert, I'm a threat now because of what I know, so my position at Foley's is in jeopardy. I've found work with another company. I've made the contact. I begin in August. It's a good salary and a new opportunity,' Jen knew enough not to tell Robert she'd still be making a good deal more than he made.

'Why bother telling me any of this now? You're making all the moves without any input from me.'

'No matter how angry you are with me, this is the right decision for all of us.'

'I find it amazing you're such a hot shot in human resources and you take none of that expertise home with you.'

'You have every reason to be upset.'

'*Upset* doesn't cover it, Jen.'

'I have something else to tell you.'

'The drama queen.'

'I want to make our marriage work. I want a chance to start over with you, because I love you and the kids. Seeing Kathryn today, seeing her peace, made me real-ize that I have to grow up if I want to be part of this family.'

'I couldn't have written the script any better. Go on.'

Jen told him about Kathryn and the conference and Pastore's threat.

Robert threw his head back on the swivel chair and laughed hard and mean. All Jen could see for a full minute was his apple's apple. 'Shit, all these years, I've worried about guys and it's women you're into?'

'I'm not gay, just stupid.'

'Ah, so this is the tip of the iceberg. This is better than *The National Enquirer*!'

'Look, Robert, I've made mistakes, but I want to make amends. Change, so that I can be better with you and the kids.'

'So, I've been right all along?'

'It wasn't you; I've been selfish.'

'Isn't that line, *it wasn't you*, a cliché? Can't you do better than that, Jen?'

'I don't even want to know if you've been faithful. I love you, Robert; I always have.'

'You can ask me the fucking question. All these years, I've been waiting for you to see what you had with me and the kids. I should have done my own thing; I'd feel a hell of a lot better right now if I had.'

'Robert, I want another chance.'

'Another cliché, Jen.'

'People like me need them.'

'That's your best line so far.'

'Do you want me out of your life, Robert?'

'I'd like to send you to the moon. You have gall. Who do you think you are? I shouldn't have married you! Never marry a beautiful woman. That should be a label warning.'

'Do you still love me, Robert?'

'My misfortune,' he answered and he was crying and angrily wiping away the tears.

Jen began crying herself and went to him. 'I promise I will never hurt you this way again, if you say we can try once more.'

'What, are you thinking up other ways to hurt me?' he tried to laugh.

'Can we try again?'

'I can't promise you the future.'

'Now is good enough for me. It's good enough for all of us.'

'Well, at least, I made the decision, my first in years!'

Beyond the acidic pain, Robert began to hope.

CHAPTER 64

MAGGIE BEGAN PACING at a quarter to nine. Chris' loss and Caitlin's recent scare had left her with an anxious fear that no one she loved was safe. What if they'd been in an accident? Had she known where they were going, she might have been less afraid. Where were they? She walked down the driveway. There was no sign of them. Not knowing was worse than knowing. Maggie intended to abort her current mode of 'Don't tell me' because there were too many shadows in the dark.

When she saw the yellow Beetle, she waved at it with both arms.

'Dad, how are you going to hide your chin?'

'I was hoping your mother might be upstairs. I don't know what I'm going to do.' Frank turned his face aside and tried to smile, but he grimaced instead. 'At least, it's dark outside, Maggie won't see the bruise.'

'But, we can't stay out here, Dad.' Caitlin forgot and opened the garage door.

Maggie saw the empty space where Chris' car had been.

'Dammit, I shouldn't have opened the door. Sorry, Dad.'

Maggie ran to the empty space. Frank leapt from the car and ran after her. Caitlin got out and stood by the Beetle.

'Frank, someone's stolen Chris' car! Who could have done such a terrible thing?'

'Maggie, no one took it. I had it towed a week ago. I thought seeing the car would be too hard for you.'

'Why didn't you ask me, Frank?'

'I couldn't, Maggie.'

'That car didn't belong to you, Frank. It belonged to Chris! You had no business touching it. Our son sat in that car and drove it. It could have been a happy memory, something I knew he treasured, and you've taken that from me. What's wrong with your face, Frank? Did somebody hit you tonight? What are you and Caitlin up to?'

'I'm sorry, Maggie.'

'What have you been up to, Frank? Someone's hit you, and it can't be that woman driver you both pretended to be checking out tonight. Don't take me for a fool, either of you. You cart away our son's car; then you take off on a secret mission tonight and you come back the worse for wear. What is going on?'

'Maggie, let's go inside.'

'I'm fine right here. I'm asking you for the second time; what's going on that you can share with Caitlin and not with me?'

'Mom, I think we should go inside.'

'Did you know about the car, Caitlin?'

'Yes. We were trying to protect you, Mom.'

'Do I look protected right now?'

'Maggie, I should have told you about the car.'

'Yes, you should have.'

'Could we please go inside now? I need some ice.'

'I'll get it for you, but don't entertain the thought for one second that I won't demand to know what happened tonight. I don't ever want secrets between us, Frank.'

Frank was more afraid than he had been in the park. Caitlin and he followed Maggie into the kitchen where she filled two glasses with ice cubes, rolled the ice in a soft towel and handed it to Frank.

'Caitlin, this is between your father and me.'

'I understand.' Caitlin saw her father's jaw stiffen and he winced as she left the room.

'Can I make you some tea, Frank?'

'I could use a brandy.'

'I think I'll have one too; I have a feeling I'm going to need it. I'll deal with the headache in the morning. Let's go into the living room.'

'This ice pack will drip.'

'I'll fetch you another towel; let's go.'

Frank had barely sat down before Maggie began talking and questioning. 'I've loved you every day of our marriage and I am not about to lose any part of you. That's what secrets do, Frank. They reduce the person into smaller parts. We've just lost our only son; there are only three of us left. We have to hold onto one another, or we'll go our separate ways.'

'You said you didn't want to know anything, Maggie,' Frank said feebly.

'Tell me something, Frank. Did the driver who killed Chris punch you tonight? I want the truth.'

'No.'

'Were you gathering information on the driver tonight?'

'No.'

'That's what I thought.' It was Maggie's turn to tremble.

Truth can be as limiting as deception. When the illusions fall away, what remains is decidedly smaller in stature, visible and fragile.

'Something has been troubling you since Chris died, something more than losing him. It's eating you up. What's happened to you, Frank? I want to know because I want to keep loving you.'

'No, you don't Maggie.'

'That's where you're wrong. I have to know.'

'If I tell you, you'll leave me.' Frank looked at Maggie with a riveting stare, challenging her to back off to save them both. 'Maggie, please…'

'Tell me the truth, Frank. If we lose faith in each other, we have nothing.'

'I'm no better than the driver who killed Chris…'

Maggie shrank in her wing chair as the story unfolded.

'I stopped down the road. When he managed to get to his feet, I drove off…'

Maggie's fists were balled and she shook her head, trying vainly to deny what Frank was telling her. 'You just left him on the street?'

Frank barely heard Maggie's question because there was such pain in her words. 'I was afraid.'

Maggie herself did not hear much of the end of Frank's story; she'd stalled with the image of the injured teen, abandoned, alone like Chris.

Frank saw Maggie had stopped listening. He fell back in his chair, longing for her to say something, but she didn't. She rose unsteadily and left the room. When she was on the second landing, she opened Caitlin's door without knocking. Caitlin lay on her bed.

'How long have you known?'

'Not long, Mom.' Maggie said nothing after that and went to her room. Caitlin called Mike to be certain he'd be there tomorrow. *I can park anywhere I want to park. One way or the other, I'm going to speak to Sophia. Pastore's going to get what's coming to her!*

Frank waited, but Maggie didn't come back. Eventually, he got up, reached for the brandy snifters and emptied them in the kitchen sink. He spent most of the night in the study.

Around the time Chris was struck by the car, Maggie opened the door to the study and led Frank up to bed.

CHAPTER 65

WEDNESDAY MORNING, AT work, Nicolina tried to make eye contact with Jen Sexton to get a read on her. Each time they were close to one another, Sexton turned more attentively to the person speaking to her, blocking Pastore from their encounter. That could mean that Sexton did not want a hint of their collusion travelling down the corridors of Foley's. Pastore's exclusion could also mean that Sexton had betrayed her. When Raymond Lecours brushed past her earlier that morning beside the cafeteria, he looked very much like a lit cigar himself. Nicolina wouldn't have long to wait. She'd heard nothing from Walton. It appeared Traynor might well appear in court. The trial resumed Friday; she had two days.

Mike Halloran was surprised to see the yellow Beetle parked almost directly across from Pastore's house. He parked behind Caitlin and walked to the Beetle and slid in beside her. 'You're early.'

'Tough night, no sleep.'

'You're not afraid of being spotted by parking so close?'

'This has got to be the day, Mike. We can't keep playing this cat and mouse game. It's good you're here. You're blocking the neighbour's view if she comes out before Sophia.'

'Glad to be of service.'

'Is there something wrong, besides Chris? You seem down.'

'Family stuff.'

Inside the target house, Monsieur Patate had tired of prancing in circles in front of Sophia. He wanted to get back into the real world of sidewalks, hydrants, dogs, legs, shoes and store fronts displaying meat, bread and pastries. He ran for his leash, managed to pull it off the wooden hook, dragged it to the front door and waited for Sophia to take the hint. When she didn't come after him, well, he went looking for her. He found Sophia washing the kitchen floor. Did this woman ever stop working? If only he could speak human talk, he'd tell her that most of what she did, Nicolina didn't even notice. He'd be very happy to tell her that Nicolina had eyes only for herself. To show his impatience, he let out not one but three uncustomary barks.

Sophia's knees were sore again. It was the humidity she felt, that and old knees. Some days, when she scrubbed a floor, she was able to loosen up the pain. She knew exactly what Monsieur wanted. In fact, she needed fresh Italian bread and garlic to go with her Fettuccini Alfredo and shrimp. For a treat, after that heavy meal, she would buy lemon Granita, so she had her own reasons for wanting to take a walk this lovely morning.

'Well, Monsieur. It's time for us to be on our way. We have shopping to do! Now, just a minute, I must take the cane. One never knows.'

After Monsieur's tumble, he couldn't agree with her more.

When the front door opened, a shock of excitement erupted in the car across the street, but came to a complete halt when the neighbour walked down her driveway.

'Hello, Sophia. Have a good day!' Elsa called out.

A little smile softened Sophia's lips. It was good to see a friendly face. She also noticed that Elsa had not crossed the lawn to talk. Sophia felt new respect for her neighbour.

Elsa had decided on a more subtle plan of acquisition.

'Mike, we finally have our chance. Let Sophia walk to Monkland Avenue. We can catch up to her there.'

'Do you know exactly what you want to say? You better have it all mapped out. We could spook her and she might not want to talk to us at all.'

'I'm going to be short and to the point – it's too late for the slow approach. The media and press will soon end their coverage.'

'Let's take this slow. We don't want to overtake her before Monkland.'

Caitlin and Mike walked on the opposite side of the street, four car lengths behind Sophia. Monsieur looked back a few times, but he was more intent on the excitement ahead of him. It was good to be out, reassuring to know he could easily wait for the hydrant on Monkland.

Once Sophia turned right on the corner, Mike and Caitlin ran up to Monkland Avenue.

'Just a sec, Mike, I'm really nervous.'

'I'll talk to her first. She's shy and a little reticent; I hope she remembers me.'

'This has to work; I have nothing else.'

'Take deep breaths. Just do your best; that's all that Chris could hope for.'

Tears welled in Caitlin's eyes. 'I have to do better than best. All right, let's do it.'

Mike and Caitlin caught up to Sophia. Monsieur saw them first and parked himself in between Sophia's legs.

'Hello, Sophia. I'm Mike. We met last week. Do you remember me?'

'Yes, I have a good memory. Good morning.'

'I'd like you to meet my friend, Caitlin Donovan.'

As they shook hands, Sophia felt she had seen this young woman before, or she reminded her of someone else.

'It's a pleasure to meet you, Sophia. Do you have a few minutes to spare? I would like very much to buy you a cup of coffee.'

Yes, this young woman definitely reminded her of someone. 'I have had my coffee already and I have shopping to do.' *Why does she want to speak to me? I do not know this young woman.*

'Please, Sophia. I just need a few minutes of your time.'

Sophia took a step back and Monsieur followed her. She wished she had not come out today.

'Sophia, my brother was Chris Donovan.'

Sophia's face blanched.

'You must know that Nicolina Pastore was the driver of the car that killed my brother.'

'Yes, I know that.'

'I don't know how much Ms. Pastore has told you of the accident...'

'She told me that the police are satisfied it was a terrible tragedy. She has told me the young man, your brother, must have stepped out in front of her car.'

'Sophia, that's not true. My brother was struck when he was almost across the street. Ms. Pastore didn't bother to stop or call for help.'

Sophia's face darkened.

'Had she called the police immediately when she got home, my brother might have lived. She didn't call for two hours.'

What could Sophia say to any of this?

'I have evidence from her colleagues at work that she

drinks heavily. The police believe Ms. Pastore was drinking the night she struck my brother. She came home to sober up for two hours. Only then did she contact the police.'

Sophia took another step back, dropping her head.

'I need your help, Sophia. You are my brother's last hope. If you know that Ms. Pastore was drinking the night of the accident, you must tell me.'

'I am frightened.'

Caitlin stepped forward and laid her hand on Sophia's shoulder. 'I promise you that I will find you another place to stay. I will help you with the moving; you have my word, Sophia.'

'I worry about Monsieur.'

'Why are you worried about him?'

'He is not mine, but I love him. His owner is Ms. Pastore, but she does not love him very much.'

'If Ms. Pastore is arrested, Monsieur will go to the pound. You can claim him; I will take you there.'

Sophia began to cry. When Roberto died, she wept only a little because she was very angry with him, even though he was already dead.

'Was Ms. Pastore drinking the night of the accident?'

Sophia could not lie. 'Yes,' she whispered.

'Did she drink a lot that night?'

'Yes.'

Caitlin's tears flowed and she hugged Sophia. 'Thank you so much. You have no idea how much this will mean to my family. Will you be willing to say that to the police, Sophia?'

'I have said enough. I must do the shopping and I must go home.'

'But, Sophia, you have to tell the police what you know.'

'I must think; you must give me time to think.'

'What if Ms. Pastore drinks and kills another person, Sophia?'

'You are frightening me. Please leave me alone.'

Caitlin didn't follow Sophia. 'What do I do now?'

'Run up and give her your number. Then pray she changes her mind. You have nothing without her testimony. Just a sec, give it to me, I might have a better chance.' It took Mike no time to catch up with Sophia.

'Sophia?'

Sophia kept walking away.

'Please, give me a minute.'

She turned and Monsieur did too. 'Listen, I'm sorry we had to tell you in this way. But what other choice did Caitlin have?'

'It was an ambush.'

'That's true. But my friend is desperate. Her brother would be alive today if Ms. Pastore had just called for assistance in time. Forgive her. She needs your help; we have no one else we can turn to.'

'I have never spoken to the police. What you are asking is not an easy thing to do.'

'What if there is another accident? I'm sure you would feel awful.'

'Ms. Pastore no longer drinks. She threw all the liquor bottles in the garbage after the accident.'

That's why Caitlin couldn't find any in the house. 'She is involved in a big case. Did you know that she is arguing against a woman who is dying of cancer?'

'I did not know that.'

'Well, it's true. If she loses the case, she might drink again, Sophia.'

'Here's my number and Caitlin's. We will not tell anyone what you told us today. We will permit you to make up your own mind. Please, call one of us. We will help you with everything we promised.'

Sophia took the cards. Her hands shook when she turned away.

CHAPTER 66

CAITLIN TOLD MIKE she'd better get home. What she really wanted to do was to ask for a second opinion. The minute she was alone in her car, she called Carmen at work. 'Can you give me two minutes?'

'I can. I'm on my way to Kingston, so talk away.'

'Sorry, I forgot. Thought you were at the office.'

'How often do we listen to one another about work?'

'Too true. We should change that. Here's what happened…. Mike says we should give Sophia time.'

'He's right. If we push her, we lose her.'

'But this is ridiculous. She can put Pastore away. Can't we have the police subpoena her?'

'Of course, but she can pretend she doesn't remember which night Pastore was drinking.'

'Shit! I told her I'd help her find a new place to live. She's afraid of losing that dog, Patate, because he's not hers.'

'Monsieur Patate.'

'Fry, Patate, Poutine, who gives a flying fuck what his name is? I'll calm down in a minute and I'll give Sophia a few days.'

'Sounds more like the professor I know. Idiocy is my department.'

'You can't hog the best parts all the time. You're right and so was Mike. I could lose her testimony if I bully her. '

'You have what you want; you just have to wait for it.'

'Happy selling!'

'Thanks. Call you tonight.'

Frank and Maggie were sitting with their coffee in

the solarium. She wasn't ready to talk about Ryan Burns. 'We might have a problem with Mireille.'

Frank was too stuck in guilt to comment.

'She's been offered full-time work but she's giving us first dibs. The thing is I enjoy cooking; I don't want her full-time. She's a talker; I can't think straight when she's here.'

'You decide, Maggie.'

'Will you come to the cemetery this morning, Frank?'

'Are you sure you want me to go with you? You might be better off alone.'

'I think you should come; it's a place of healing.'

'Maggie…'

'I can't talk about that now, Frank. I've already told you, I want to remember Chris as much as I can. He's with me every minute, but it won't always be that way. You kept your secret for twenty-nine years. You can wait a little longer.'

'What time would you like to go?'

'After we eat.'

'Fine.'

Caitlin joined them but quickly decided not to get their hopes up before she had exactly what she needed from Sophia. 'Hi.'

'Hi, yourself. What can I get you?'

'Just cereal, but I'll get it myself. I want to ask you if you think you'll feel up to coming to my book launch in a couple of weeks. It's so hard to believe that I'll be one of the last authors to sign at the Double Hook before it fades into history.'

'Another sad loss for all Montrealers,' Maggie said wistfully. 'I used to have wonderful chats with the last of the three owners. It's such a delightful bookstore. Of course, we'll be there and we'll invite friends. You're the first author in the family, after all! It'll be good to celebrate something. I wish Chris were here to see his big sister!'

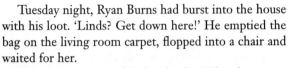

Tuesday night, Ryan Burns had burst into the house with his loot. 'Linds? Get down here!' He emptied the bag on the living room carpet, flopped into a chair and waited for her.

'Ryan, have you robbed a bank? What have you done?'

'It's a gift! Guilt payment!'

'What are you talking about?'

'Remember that hit-and-run I told you about, a guy hitting me when I was seventeen?'

'Yes.'

'Well, he found me and gave me this cash as compensation, one hundred and seventy-five thousand dollars!'

'Why now?'

'He lost his own kid to a hit-and-run.'

'This is our ticket to better times! It's wonderful! Better than the lottery!'

'Before you get ideas, remember, I'll share a good deal of it, but it's my money. I took the bumps and arthritis for it.'

'What about a week at a health spa for me, to pretty myself up for my rich sugar daddy?'

'You got it, babe.'

Dave appeared. 'Jesus, I almost had him. What the fuck?'

'You can say that again, bro!'

'You hit the jackpot, Ryan! Listen, I almost had the guy.'

'What are you talking about?'

'I tailed you and the guy who gave you this cash.'

'I never asked you to do that. You might have ruined everything, you shit!'

'But I didn't, did I? I followed the guy out, but he had some friend looking out for him.'

'Why tail him in the first place?'

'For the future, bro.'

'I have what I need right here.'

'When I see this cash, you needed me with you more than ever tonight.'

'What are you up to?'

'What if there's more where this came from? I saw two cars pull out. He was riding in a minivan, I'm sure. I got three numbers off the plate. I have a friend who might run them for me. A Beetle pulled out too, but that's a chick car. I got one number from it anyway.'

'If you weren't my brother, I'd knock your lights out.'

'What the fuck is up with you?'

'The guy was decent.'

'Shit, I'm supposed to figure this out on my own?'

'No, but you should have stayed out of this. I didn't need a tail in the first place.'

'You don't find it strange he had a guy with him?'

'Turns out, I had a guy with me, right? Dave, I swear, I'll kill you if you fuck this up for me! We're not black-mailers for Christ's sake. Grow up!'

'Case closed, and you're welcome!' Dave stormed out.

'Wait a minute, here's five grand for looking out for me,' Ryan called after him, scooping up hundred dollar packets.

Dave ran back to the front door, grabbed the cash and took off.

'You're welcome!' Ryan called after him.

'Five thousand for standing in a park? Why didn't you ask me?'

'He's my brother, Linds.'

'I'm your wife!'

'This isn't about you or Dave. Something is finally about me!'

CHAPTER 67

BY THE TIME Sophia and Monsieur trudged up the back stairs, they were both tired and stressed. There seemed to be a hundred little needles in Monsieur's right knee. Sophia felt worse. She sat on the top step and laid her bags on the balcony. Monsieur collapsed beside her. He was too tired to bark his complaint about his bum knee. He watched with envy as Sophia rubbed her knees. He tried his paw, but it wasn't much good. Sophia sighed; Monsieur panted.

Nicolina had lied to her. Somewhere deep down, Sophia had doubted Nicolina's story. What if Nicolina did drink again and drive? After Roberto, Sophia wanted to cook and she wanted peace. She looked down at Monsieur; he was looking lovingly at her with his blood-shot eyes, nuzzling her ankle. No matter what the young Caitlin Donovan had said, Sophia knew the truth about some things. There was a good chance she'd lose Monsieur.

When she was about to push herself to her feet, Elsa appeared.

'You look very tired. May I help you with the bags?'

Sophia was too worried to resist.

'I won't stay. Try to get some rest, Sophia. I had only one thing to say. If you're ever looking for a new apartment, I have one for you at my house. It's a bright, sunny bedroom on the second floor with its own bathroom. You can have it for two hundred dollars a month and you can have the run of the kitchen.'

'Run?'

'You can use it as much as you want.'

Things were happening too fast for Sophia.

Monsieur was agitated too. He hadn't heard his name mentioned. *Are you forgetting about me?*

'Thank you, Elsa. I must go in now.'

'It's something to think about, Sophia. I won't mention my offer again; just know that you'll be welcome.'

Sophia knew one thing for certain. If she left this house, she would leave it spotless with frozen packages of her food in the freezer. No matter what she had become, Nicolina had taken her in at a very difficult time in her life and she had Nicolina to thank for Monsieur. From her daughter, she had nothing at this moment to be grateful for. The stress tightened her knees further as she unpacked the groceries. That night she didn't sleep well at all. Even Monsieur cried a little. His knee was killing him.

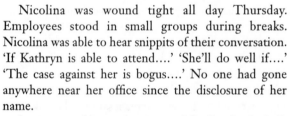

Nicolina was wound tight all day Thursday. Employees stood in small groups during breaks. Nicolina was able to hear snippits of their conversation. 'If Kathryn is able to attend....' 'She'll do well if....' 'The case against her is bogus....' No one had gone anywhere near her office since the disclosure of her name.

Lecours put his arm out to stop Nicolina in the hall. When he spoke, there was menace in every word. 'You're fully prepared for court, I trust? I plan to attend. You have everything riding on tomorrow.'

'Things are in place, Raymond.' *I really need him breathing down my back!*

'They'd better be, Ms. Pastore.' Without a word of good luck, he marched down the hall in a puff of cigar smoke.

He's ready to explode and I hope he does! She looked for Sexton, but she was conveniently out of the office. *This is a lot like going to my own execution.* Still, if Sexton kept her word, the case against Traynor should stand the way she'd set it up. How long could this woman go on living? Nicolina had to muster hope where she could get it. For the rest of her day, she huddled in her office. Nothing from Walton. What was this Traynor made of? She studied the case files for the thirtieth time. Trying to boost her morale, she remembered the cops hadn't called. That was something. At least, she could keep her focus on the case and not worry about another call from Remay. If things went well tomorrow, she was having a stiff Scotch. Enough of this sobriety! She left work on time and took the case papers with her.

Sophia felt the tension as soon as Nicolina walked in the front door, slamming it again. She made no comment about the aroma coming from the pasta.

'Don't even think of making me a coffee after dinner, Sophia. I have a huge day tomorrow. I can't be up all night.'

'Shall I serve dinner?'

'Of course, that's what I need, food and silence.' Nicolina shovelled the fettuccini and shrimp into her mouth without a word, devoured the garlic bread, wiping pieces of it in the white cream sauce and drank three glasses of Brio. The only sound at the table was Nicolina's slurping, something she did with every bite. On the inside, she could feel the pasta colliding with her nervous system and she knew not much of it would stay with her. Prickly fear travelled to her fingertips and toes. The inside of her thighs was wet with sweat. Her top lip glistened with perspiration. Abruptly, she stood up from the table. 'I have to take a short walk; maybe that might help.'

'Is this the big case?' Sophia asked timidly.

'What else would it be?'

'Take a good walk; I will clean up and take Monsieur out to the yard.'

Nicolina had already left the room. In seconds, she slammed the front door and she was gone.

Sophia said a silent prayer that Nicolina had not brought Scotch into the house. In this mood, her landlord was capable of anything. Once the dishes were cleared and washed, Sophia made individual packages of leftovers, wrapped them generously with foil and labelled them.

Monsieur had witnessed the food frenzy at the dinner table with a measure of indifference. He had stopped thinking of Nicolina as part of his family.

Nicolina stormed back into the house and marched upstairs. She hoisted both heavy bags onto her bed and spread Foley's case against Kathryn Traynor across her blue comforter. Was there something she might have missed? On her knees, Nicolina went from sheet to sheet, trying to memorize the facts. When she saw she'd forgotten something, she threw the offending sheet on the floor and read it word-for-word staring down at the paper on all fours. *This is ridiculous! I'm scaring myself. I'll soak in the tub; that might help. I need a drink!*

An hour later, a blotchy, wrinkled prune got out of the tub and left her hair for the morning. She gathered the papers in order, put them into their cases, lay awake under the covers and left a wet pool of sweat on the sheet when she climbed out of bed Friday morning. When she was dressed, she picked up her purse and cases and walked to the stairs on legs that didn't feel like her own. After three cups of coffee, she drove to court.

From behind a curtain, Sophia watched her go. Then she began to clean the house, beginning on the third floor. There were three bedrooms, a linen closet and a bathroom. This was a two-day job.

At the Traynors, Tim was helping Kathryn into a pair of blue pin-striped slacks. 'Easy does it, Tim. My balance is off.'

'I'll work as slowly as you want. Are these the right shoes?'

'Yep. I want the pink blouse; it shouldn't be hard to find. It's the only one I own.'

'Coming up.'

'I wish I didn't have to wear the wig.'

'Let's see what it looks like. And then we can decide.' Tim lifted the wig off the Styrofoam head and handed it to Kathryn and held a large mirror for her. Once it was in place, Tim was taken aback by the change. 'You're beautiful! I'd ask you to marry me all over again. I'm being totally honest, Kathryn, you look like your old self.'

She smiled. Kathryn believed she'd never see herself again, not the way she was before.

'Here, let's get you up, so you can see for yourself.'

Kathryn took a few seconds to take it all in, the clothes, the hair, the makeup, the hair mostly. 'I do recognize myself.'

CHAPTER 68

ALL PARTIES CONCERNED arrived on time. Nicolina worked on papers, whispering with Walton. They were both standing behind their table with an air of command and control that this was a 'done deal'. Pastore didn't bother nodding at opposing counsel. Raymond Lecours sat two rows back, his cheeks red and puffed with concern. Jen was dressed impeccably, sitting quietly on a witness bench, drawing appreciative stares from passers-by. At the moment, there were sixteen people in the courtroom.

At two minutes of ten, Tim rolled Kathryn to the plaintiff's table. Pastore stole a glance and was immediately depressed. Traynor appeared serene, composed, even determined. Her husband sat beside her. They too began to examine papers.

Shit! I thought she was dying! She looks better than I do! Nicolina glanced back at Lecours. He was looking at Traynor, rapping his fingers on his fist.

Of course, if Nicolina had taken a better look, she would have seen what Judge Martin Boulanger saw as soon as he entered the room. Everyone but Kathryn stood in respect. Martin Boulanger, hugely influential, had sat on the bench for twenty-nine years. He was a wiry, little Frenchman who was as tough as a bull and as honest as the first snow. He hadn't made much money on the bench, but he proudly wore his Swiss Army platinum watch, a gift from his daughter Nicole. Rarely did appeals on his cases stand. He knew the law and that's what he doled out.

What he saw when he looked at the plaintiff was a frail, courageous woman wearing a wig that made her face appear more gaunt because of its volume. In his twenty-nine years on the bench, litigants had died; lawyers had too, even a judge. However, never in his experience, did a plaintiff appear in court when he looked like this. Death had a way of organizing one's priorities. Boulanger saw too that Mrs. Traynor was holding onto the desk for support. He had a feeling he might not see her in court again; she wouldn't be up to it.

Boulanger brought the court to order and asked counsel if they were ready to proceed.

Kathryn's lawyer stood. 'Approach, your honour?' Kathryn felt Jen had understood that she had no choice but to present the new evidence. Jen's presence today validated her assumption.

Boulanger waved him to the bench and he submitted his documents with explanations. Pastore followed him. The judge put his hand over the microphone. 'I'll see you both in chambers. The court will take a forty-five minute recess.'

Tim squeezed Kathryn's hand.

Lecours had seen enough. He scribbled a note for Pastore and handed it to Richard Walton. 'Give this to Pastore without fail!' Lecours was chairing two board meetings of separate companies that day. He could not afford to miss either one of them. He'd be back in the office by four-thirty to deal with Nicolina Pastore.

Jen Sexton smiled with relief, happy he hadn't spotted her. In his state, he'd seen no one.

Inside chambers, Martin Boulanger read the documents very carefully. He had his two fingers at his temple and the others under his nose. He glared at Pastore and asked a single question. 'Were you in possession of this evidence before court resumed today?'

Before Nicolina could answer, Kathryn's lawyer submitted a courier's dated, signed receipt. 'Your Honour,

I also have a witness who will testify to the veracity of that receipt and the documents I have given to you today.'

'I was not entirely certain of the truth of these documents,' Nicolina managed to get out, but her words carried no punch at all.

'That wasn't your call to make. I will rejoin you both in the courtroom at the appointed time.'

Nicolina left first. Walton handed her the note as soon as she got back to the table. Like everything else from Lecours, it was blunt. *My office at four-thirty.* Walton took a break and Nicolina noticed she was quite alone in the room. Everyone else was out in the hall; she stayed put, listening to the ticking seconds of her life. This disastrous turn of events did not impact Nicolina's ethics or conscience. Plotting revenge on Sexton was a further waste of time. Lecours would get to Sexton. When the dizziness subsided, the pounding thoughts that repeated in her head were simple. *I will not be the fall-guy.* Though Boulanger's reappearance was indeed a fateful threat for her, Nicolina was far more preoccupied with shifting the blame to none other than the CEO himself, Raymond Lecours.

One by one, the interested parties filed into the courtroom. When he got back to the table, Walton discretely moved his chair farther away from Pastore's. Jen Sexton now sat directly behind the Traynors. Tim Traynor glared at Nicolina, but she ignored him. Kathryn herself was visibly fatigued. The recess had taken a toll on her stamina. Tim whispered something to Kathryn and she looked back gratefully at Sexton. She was very tired.

Martin Boulanger was punctual. When he began to voice his deliberations, his words were spoken with careful consideration and caution. 'Ladies and gentlemen, in my long experience on the bench, I have found that most attorneys who appeared before me have done their utmost to uphold the law; only a few have attempted to subvert it. In the case before the court today, I have grave misgivings that will require further scrutiny. If grounds for misconduct are found, appropriate measures will be undertaken without delay.

In case number PFR/14401-039, brought by one Kathryn Traynor against Foley Pharmaceuticals, I find for the plaintiff for the amount claimed, plus thirty thousand in moral damages and twenty thousand in punitive damages. I also give immediate leave for her to amend her suit to include negligence on the part of Foley. I strongly urge Foley to settle quickly.'

Pastore left the courtroom immediately.

Martin Boulanger descended from the bench and walked toward the Traynors. 'Good luck to you, Kathryn,' he said graciously and took his leave. At the mention of her name, Kathryn broke down and wept. For the past year, she had been referred to as the plaintiff, *her*, Traynor, words that had de-personalized her, reduced her to a cipher. Her cancer too had been indifferent, cold and ruthless in its own assault. With the mention of her name, Kathryn was a person again. She wept in gratitude. Tim bent and kissed her. 'I am so very proud of you, Kathryn.'

Jen walked around to the front of the table. 'May I kiss Kathryn now, Tim?'

'I guess I don't have to show you how,' he laughed through his own tears.

'You're so brave, Kathryn. I took your advice; I think Robert and I have a chance,' she whispered into Kathryn's ear.

'Thank you for risking what you did to give me the evidence.'

Jen knew she might not see Kathryn again. 'I'm just a phone call away night or day. Keep up the fight!'

'It's time for a private celebration, wouldn't you say, honey?'

'It feels so good to be me again.'

CHAPTER 69

NICOLINA RACED BACK to the office. *I'm going to nail that prick! He's going down with me because of something he told me to do! Can't wait till I see his face when I tell him what I have!*

She locked her office door and began replaying the tapes of all the conversations that dealt with the case. It might take time, but she'd find what she needed. She let go with a hearty snort when she recalled her conversation with Lecours. Drop the case, apologize, settle with Traynor and get out as quickly as possible. It was Lecours himself who had taught her to tape all conversations, especially phone calls germane to important cases. It was the CEO who had forced her to go on with the litigation. Lecours, she knew, would bluster this afternoon, blast her and fire her. He was not aware of the package she'd have waiting for him. She might not even need luck to walk away from disbarment. This time, she had the facts! All she had to do now was to find that goddamn tape. Then she remembered exactly where to find it.

At twenty-five past four, her phone rang. 'Monsieur Lecours is ready to see you, Ms. Pastore,' her receptionist said with obvious glee.

'Thank you, I'll be right down.' As Nicolina made her way to Lecours' office, the execs and employees stood watching her gauntlet walk from the doorways of their offices. A lynching draws attention. Nicolina smiled at a few of the mob as she walked by.

'Shut the door!' were the first words she heard from Lecours. 'I'll make this very brief. Your services with Foley Pharmaceuticals are terminated. I will give you the option of offering your resignation. You must be aware that finding future employment will prove much easier to secure if you resign. Of course, you might not even be practising law, Ms. Pastore. You are forced to wait for the court's findings on that. If you insist on a fight, I will begin work on your termination papers Monday morning.'

'Then, Raymond, I'll stay all discussion between us until Monday. I'm most interested in seeing the causes for my termination before I make my own claims. I'm sure you can appreciate my point of view.'

'Resignation is not an option then?'

'Most definitely not! I'll see you at eleven Monday morning, Raymond. That should permit you plenty of time to work up the papers. Have a decent weekend.'

Lecours felt blood throbbing behind his eyebrows. *Is the bitch that ignorant? I'll see to it that she never practises law again.*

When Sophia heard Monsieur's small bark and saw Nicolina pull into the driveway, she came downstairs as quickly as she could. Every room up there but Nicolina's and her bathroom were fresh and clean. On Monday morning, Sophia would get an early start on the second floor.

Nicolina unlocked the front door and ran past Sophia upstairs. Before she opened the drawer of her night table, she said a prayer. There it was; the Sony recorder she'd bought herself. She rewound the sixty-minute tape. Lying on her bed, she depressed the play button and listened, forwarded and listened, forwarded and listened. Then she heard the recorded words that would save her career! *Raymond, Nicolina, Forgive me for disturbing your Saturday morning…*

Raymond will piss his pants when he hears this! What

chance did I have to do my job properly? Lecours heads a com-
pany that brings in two hundred million a year. I'm an
employee, for God's sake. I had no choice but to follow his
orders. I'll be reprimanded; I accept that. But Lecours has
connections that he can bring into play to fix this situation.
With his ass on the line, this will all be taken care of. In the
end, I'll settle for a lump sum and I'll work somewhere else.
Or I'll stay!

Nicolina had to admit she felt a hell of a lot better
than she had several hours ago. She wondered what
Sophia was serving for dinner and she decided to find
out. Nicolina was almost anxious for Monday. Traynor
was a victim, but so was she – Lecours' victim.

Friday night, Lecours didn't sleep well at all.
Saturday night, he backed out of a dinner party. He had
no intention of sitting with old bores all evening.
Lecours couldn't figure out what annoyed him more,
the damages he was certain the company would face or
the blockhead arrogance of Pastore. He hated stupid
women, or men for that matter, who couldn't see that
they were beaten, outgunned, finished, out the door!
What was wrong with the woman? She'd blundered
through this case from the beginning to the end. First,
the forgery claim and then the *coup-de-grâce*. She'd be
lucky to clerk in a law office when the bar was finished
with her. On Sunday evening, he grabbed a cigar, and
his wife landed in the living room.

'Raymond, your health! Please, not in the living
room, the smell gets into everything.'

'Women! They're everywhere. Fine,' he growled.
'I'm going for a walk. At least I'll be in peace.' There
was a park a block away from his home and he decided
to head there. Crossing the road, he gasped, but lum-

bered on. Before he reached the sidewalk, sudden unremitting chest pain stopped his breath all together. He grabbed the centre of his chest but he fell hard, face down in the gutter of the road. Raymond Lecours succumbed to myocardial infarction. He hadn't even had the chance to light another cigar.

When he hadn't returned, his wife did not go looking for him. 'He's in another black temper. It's better for me, I regret to say, that I'm nowhere around.' His body was discovered two hours later by a cyclist, a kid on a bike. His wife's first reaction was relief; then she wept for the man she had once known a long time ago, long before the cigars!

Nicolina had no intention of taking things easy on the weekend. Saturday morning, she made extra tapes of the phone call. What a nasty thrill she'd enjoy handing Lecours his own copy. In a particular sense, she felt that he had more to lose than she had. He was in his sixties; he'd built a reputation, earned a fat salary and a six-figure pension whenever he exercised that option, plus a multi-million dollar package. She had heard seven million being tossed around.

The next assignment Nicolina undertook was to download the names and addresses of the recipients of her letter and tape. She wasn't going to rush this bomb because she herself wouldn't escape the shrapnel from this explosion. By late morning, she was hard at work on her letter. When she saw the personal severance package she'd set up for herself, Nicolina sat back and admired the half million she'd damn well make sure she got from Raymond.

Sophia cleared the breakfast table when it was obvious her landlord was upstairs working and had no intention of eating that morning. The basement was cleaned every day, so Sophia set her sights on the first floor. Monsieur moped around the house. These two women were no fun. What about his walk? What about the shops on Monkland?

Nicolina came down for a late lunch.

'How did the trial go yesterday?' Sophia asked timidly.

Nicolina was about to say that it was none of her damn business, but she changed her mind. 'It concluded abruptly. All parties were taken by surprise.'

'Were you pleased with the result? I know you have worked hard for many months.'

'You know what, Sophia? I think I am, strange as that sounds.' Nicolina had developed a grudging admiration for Kathryn Traynor. Survivors, both of them!

CHAPTER 70

ON MONDAY MORNING, Nicolina didn't give a hoot about the snide remarks as she made her way to her office. She had work to do. At lunch, if things went well for her, she might be walking out of here with half a million bucks. For the first hour, she typed furiously, edited and re-typed, until she liked what she saw. At eleven o'clock, she was still at work, cleaning up files, shredding and packing.

At eleven-ten, her secretary knocked on the door. 'Have you heard the news?'

'What are you talking about, Susan?'

'Raymond Lecours is dead. He suffered a massive heart attack last night. We just got the news.'

'Give me a few minutes; I have to compose myself.' Nicolina shut the door as quietly and reverently as she was able. Her inclination was to slam it shut and jump and holler, 'Yes!' She knew enough to behave herself. Every nerve ending tingled; her pulse pounded. In her head, she was shouting with gusto. *Can you beat that! Can you fucking beat that! Raymond said he'd work on the papers today; and the fucker will never get that chance because he's dead! Dead! Dead! Dead! Traynor and I have a lot in common; we hang on and we get through shit no matter what the bastards throw at us!*

Nicolina's smile was so wide it began to invade both ears. She picked up the phone and asked her secretary to get her Martin Boulanger's number. She knew any action the bar filed against her would take a few months at least, probably half a year. However, if she could set up a meeting after the funeral, she'd present the tape and the only version he was ever going to hear. Lecours was her boss; he had threatened her job if she presented this new evidence. She was also afraid Lecours would go through with his threat to blacklist her throughout the province. He'd told her he could with his influence and connections; she'd never get the evidence out. During the entire case, she had never been given a chance. Nicolina even thought of calling Sexton as a witness. Then she remembered her own threat about the affair and dropped that idea. Still, what a turn of events!

Outside her office in the business corridors of Foley's, comments became the occasion.

How sudden!

Tragic.

I saw it coming; he was a power keg! The cigars!

Will they hire from within, do you think?

Is there a promotion for me in this?

With somebody from outside, I might keep my job.

I can't miss the funeral.

He was insufferable!

A blowhard!

Good riddance!

Had Nicolina stopped celebrating and scheming, she would have learned Raymond Lecours didn't fare any better that she had in the admiration department. She had enough good cheer for herself and frankly, she didn't need anybody at the moment. The universe was unfolding as it should for Nicolina Pastore. In fact, she left work early and went to a beauty salon for a good cut. For months, she'd let herself go. It was definitely time for repairs. When she saw the results, she felt even better. Nicolina wanted to look her best when Martin Boulanger set a date for their meeting.

Alerted by Monsieur again that afternoon, Sophia scuttled downstairs before Nicolina got to the front door. She'd finish the second floor tomorrow.

CHAPTER 71

MONDAY MORNING, CAITLIN received one hundred and fifty book launch invitations and a copy of her book straight off the press from Geoffrey Smyth, her publisher. To get her nerves off Sophia, she sat in the dining room, addressing envelopes using her list of names. Maggie joined her because, for the time being, she was emotionally absent from Frank. He was in the study, reading up on the transaction he would work on in a matter of days.

'I am so proud of my little girl!' Maggie said to Caitlin, holding her book.

'Let's not go overboard too soon; Geoffrey says the work is just beginning.'

'I'm thoroughly enjoying seeing my daughter's work in print! I don't want to miss a second of this celebration.'

'Invite as many of your friends as you can, Mom.'

'They'll be there; don't you worry.'

Caitlin picked up her cell; it was Mike calling.

'Mom, I'll be right back. Relax for a few minutes.'

'Anything?'

'Nothing.'

'Be patient; I have great faith in Sophia. Do you want to get together tonight?'

'I think I'll work on the invitations for my launch.'

'Need help?'

'No. Give me a day alone, Mike.'

'Can't blame a guy for trying.'

'Tomorrow is already Tuesday!'

'Bide your time.'

'Easier said than done.'

'Agreed.' The rest of the day went well, at least when Caitlin wasn't checking her phone.

Even by Tuesday morning, Sophia had not made up her mind. She wanted the house in order to keep her options open. Monsieur got lucky with a walk; Sophia enjoyed getting out as well though she was wary of running into the young couple.

By ten o'clock, she was working on Nicolina's bedroom. Well before noon, she began on the linen closet, rearranging the towels, facecloths, sheets and other sundries. As she slid her hand under a pile of towels to straighten them, she felt something oddly familiar and pulled out a bottle of baby lotion. It fell to the floor; Sophia grabbed the wall to keep from falling. Her face drained of colour. Slowly she bent down and picked it up, hoping the bottle was still sealed, unopened. It wasn't.

'No,' she moaned deep down inside her heart. 'No.' She closed the closet door, took the bottle with her and hobbled down to the basement. With her heart racing, she found a telephone number and made a call.

Caitlin hadn't slept the night before, but she continued to work on the invitations the next day anyway. Her cell played that tune and Caitlin grabbed it. 'Hello?'

'Is this Caitlin Donovan?'

Caitlin raced from the room. 'Sophia?'

'Sophia Argento. I will talk to the police. I think that Ms. Pastore tried to kill me to keep me silent.'

'Oh my God! Are you alone in the house, Sophia?'

'Monsieur is with me; Ms. Pastore is at work.'

'I'll be there in twenty minutes and I'll bring Mike with me. Pack some overnight things. Stay by the front door. Make certain she doesn't come home early.'

'Where can I go?' Sophia was hoarse with mounting hysteria.

'You'll be with me.'

'I will wait for you. Please come quickly.'

'Do as I told you; I'll be there in no time. Thank you, Sophia.'

'Hurry, please; I am very frightened.'

Caitlin ran up the stairs for her cards and keys and raced back down. She poked her head into the dining room. 'Mom, this is an emergency. I'll call with the details as soon as I have them.'

'Caitlin?'

'I can't talk now, Mom. I have to go! I'll call Dad. Stop worrying, please.'

'Not again!' Maggie jumped to her feet and ran to the study. 'Frank, come quickly!'

Caitlin had already left and was backing out of the driveway when Frank ran out the door.

'Caitlin!'

'Dad, I can't stop. We have our witness. I'll call when I get there. That's a promise.' And she was gone. At the first red light, she speed-dialed Mike. 'Get over to Sophia's. She's in trouble. Please hurry!'

'Twenty minutes if I speed.'

'Take twenty-five and don't!' It was one of those days Caitlin caught every red light and she swore at each of them. 'What's wrong here, can't we synchronize lights?' When she turned up Harvard Avenue, she accelerated and then ground to a stop.

Sophia opened the front door, holding the lotion bottle. Monsieur greeted the pretty lady; he remembered her. Mike arrived before they closed the door and ran up to meet them. 'Why don't we talk in my car?'

Sophia was happy to get out of the house; she felt

safe with Mike and Caitlin. Monsieur came quietly; he behaved like the gentleman he was.

'All right, Sophia, tell me what you know.'

'Ms. Pastore was slurring her words and stumbling the night of the accident?'

'Yes. She almost fell even when she got home very late. Then she threw out all the Scotch bottles soon after.'

'That is exactly what the police need for an arrest.'

'Tell me about the attempt on your life.'

'She spread this lotion on the second stair. She knew I was the first one to climb them each day. Monsieur saved my life when he got ahead of me, but he fell and hurt his leg. If I had come up first, I would have fallen and maybe...'

'Thank God, you didn't. He's a brave little dog, isn't he?' Caitlin leaned over and gave Monsieur a good scratch.

Monsieur did a little pirouette for her.

'Did you pack some things?'

'Yes, but I cannot leave Monsieur.'

'Of course, you can't. Mike?'

'Call Remay.'

'Sophia, I'll just step out of the car for a few minutes. I'll be right back.'

Elsa was taking in the whole scene from behind her living room curtains. 'I recognize that young woman. She was here before. What are they doing with Sophia?' The neighbour would have run out, but she needed a cook, so the view from the curtain would have to do.

Caitlin was panicking and could not recall Remay's number. She called information and was immediately connected to Station 12. Remay would call her right back. Caitlin paced, and paced. Three minutes later, he called. 'We have our witness. We may have an attempted murder charge on Pastore too. The witness is her tenant. We need you here, sir.'

'Slow down. Am I speaking to Caitlin Donovan?'

'Yes.'

'The information you have is solid?'

'Yes.'

'What's the address?'

Caitlin rattled it off. 'We're together in a blue Sebring across the street.'

'I'm on my way. I'll have backup on call.'

Caitlin hopped back into the car. 'Investigator Claude Remay is coming, Sophia. He is the policeman on my brother's case.'

Sophia closed her eyes and bowed her head.

'Don't be afraid; he is a kind man and we're with you. But now, I want to call my parents.'

Sophia nodded. 'Monsieur needs a walk; she pulled out a plastic bag from her pocket.'

'I'll take him,' offered Mike.

Oh, did Monsieur complain!

'Let me try,' Caitlin said. 'I'll make the call at the same time.'

Now this is better.

Elsa pulled up a chair and got her glasses. This was better than *The Young and the Restless*!

'Dad, I'm here with Mike and Sophia Argento. She is the witness we've found. Remay is on his way. I'll get back to you. Tell Mom I'm fine. Don't get her hopes up yet.'

'I won't. Keep me posted, Cait.'

'I will.'

Remay took everything he needed and he was out the door. He did his job well, but he'd be the first to tell anyone, police needed public assistance. He used to wonder at what he could accomplish if he ever got to work a single case until it was finished, but he also knew he'd never find out. There wasn't enough money in the budget for dreams. He had no trouble spotting the Sebring. He got out, approached the car and rapped on the window.

Everyone inside jumped. They were expecting a squad car. Remay's was unmarked. Caitlin was the first out of the car. 'Monsieur Remay?'

'Yes. You must be Caitlin.'

'I am and that is Mike Halloran inside the car, a friend of my brother and a big help finding our witness.'

Mike left his car and they all shook hands. Sophia held onto the pug that was back in the car.

'You say the witness is a tenant?'

'She's Sophia Argento; she very nervous and she's the tenant.'

'Hello, Sophia,' Remay said, leaning through the back window.

Sophia nodded.

'Would you please step out of the car?'

Sophia's knees burned and throbbed and she winced with obvious pain when she stepped onto the sidewalk.

'What room do you rent from Ms. Pastore?'

'The basement, sir.'

'Well then, let's you and I go there. I'd like to hear your story. Caitlin and Mike, wait outside, please. This will take some time.'

Monsieur stayed with Caitlin, and he couldn't have been happier.

'What do you think, Mike?'

'I think we're good.'

'Me too.'

CHAPTER 72

REMAY WAS BOTH pleased and surprised at Sophia's recollection of events. He took careful, detailed notes and photos of the stair where the extent of the stain was still visible. He bagged the lotion bottle. He had one question. 'When you went to bed that night, did you by any chance come back upstairs?' That Pastore owned a bottle of lotion was nothing in itself, but Remay felt that motive and circumstance might go far in supporting the charge of attempted murder.

'In my nightdress? Never!'

'That is all I need for now, Mrs. Argento. If you tell me where your things are, I'll take them out to the car. You should not be in this house tonight.'

'Where will I go?' Sophia began to cry.

'Caitlin Donovan said she will find a good place for you.'

'Oh dear.'

'Now, Sophia, I need you to make one phone call to Ms. Pastore. Ask her to come home because there is an emergency.'

'I don't know if I can do that.'

'I will stand beside you. Don't be afraid.' Remay helped Sophia up to the kitchen because he felt she might collapse. He dialed Foley's and handed her the receiver.

When their fingers lightly touched, Sophia's were cold. 'Is Ms. Pastore there?'

'Nicolina Pastore.'

'This is Sophia. Could you come home? There is an emergency.' Sophia looked for Remay's assent and got it.

'What's wrong?'

'It's the gas. I smell gas.'

Nicolina remained in a good mood. Martin Boulanger had gotten back to her and she had an appointment with him on Thursday, the day after Lecours' funeral. 'I'm on my way.' Nicolina was in a grandiose frame of mind. She'd done a mental tally of all the things she'd successfully accomplished in the last few weeks. The light problem with her car had been quietly fixed, Remay had been put in his place, Lecours stood to face what she had on him, even though he had opted out by dying. All these things worked in her favour. A few employees had even nodded to her this morning, a sign they realized she was not about to be canned. She made certain her secretary knew she was off to take care of an emergency at home. That Sophia needed her help was another positive sign; Nicolina was back in control!

On Harvard Avenue, Remay was setting things up. 'Sophia, I want you and the dog in the house. I'll go back out and get him. Don't worry; you're not in any danger. I will meet Ms. Pastore before she enters the house. I want everything to appear normal.'

Sophia had balled both fists and stood rooted to the floor.

Stephen had joined his wife Elsa behind the curtains.

Remay came out front to pick up the pug. 'Caitlin, you and your friend are to remain in your cars until after the arrest.'

'Understood.'

Monsieur did not want to be back in the house, but he had no choice in the matter. He ran to the front door, even though it was closed and locked.

'I'm as spooked as I was when I was hiding inside that house.'

'Caitlin, forget that thought; it never happened.'

'I'll try.'

Twenty minutes later, nerves frayed. Remay was checking the time. Caitlin could feel rivulets of perspiration rolling down her underarms. Mike was rigid.

Nicolina turned up Harvard and drove towards her house. Once the gas problem was solved, she might invite Sophia out to dinner at a Greek place on Sherbrooke Street. She was feeling that good. Once she'd parked the car, she took her briefcase from the back seat and headed up the front walk.

Monsieur was back, barking behind the front door. He knew something was up.

Remay had quietly opened his door and caught up to Nicolina. 'Ms. Pastore?'

Before she turned around, she'd recognized the voice. Her blood froze.

'Ms. Pastore, you are under arrest for driving under the influence, manslaughter and failing to provide assistance at the scene of the accident that resulted in the death of Mr. Christopher Donovan on Friday morning, April 29, 2005. Another charge of attempted murder might also be filed. You have the right to remain silent, you have the right...'

'I don't have to stand for this! Have you even got a warrant?' Nicolina ignored Remay and tried to walk up the front stairs.

Remay had cuffs on her before she could say another word.

Sophia opened the front door and Monsieur ran to the edge of the balcony.

'How could you do this to me? I took you in!'

Elsa and Stephen rushed out to their balcony.

Caitlin and Mike crossed the street to get a better look at Pastore.

Stone-faced, Nicolina walked past them. 'Who the

hell are they?' she screamed in a voice that didn't sound like her own.

'That is the sister of the young man you struck and killed.'

'What should I do about Monsieur Patate?' Sophia called sadly after them from the top step.

Nicolina whirled around and shouted, 'Throw him on a barbecue for all I care!'

CHAPTER 73

WHILE REMAY HAD his hand on the top of Nicolina's freshly coiffed head, guiding her into his car, Mike walked up the front steps and helped Sophia out to Caitlin's Beetle. Elsa came blustering down the front stairs because she saw her golden goose slipping away.

'You can spend the night with me, Sophia,' she called to her, but Sophia was beyond hearing anyone for the next half hour.

Remay waved and took off with his suspect.

Caitlin walked a few feet away and called home.

Maggie hadn't left the phone and made a quick grab for it. 'Thank God, it's you, Caitlin.'

'Mom, tell Dad to pick up as well.' Caitlin was trembling and subdued and teary. 'Are you on, Dad?'

'I'm here, Cait.'

'A few minutes ago, Claude Remay arrested the woman who struck and killed Chris. Mike and Carmen have helped me all along, but it was the driver's tenant who was brave enough to give Remay the evidence he needed for the arrest.'

Maggie had not wanted to know anything about this issue, but with Caitlin's news, a knot of repressed anger loosened. 'I am very grateful, Caitlin. Thank you.'

'Cait, Chris would be proud,' Frank said.

'Mom and Dad, I have a favour to ask.'

'Anything.'

'Sophia Argento is our witness and she can't stay in that house. Pastore will post bail as quickly as she can. Could Sophia stay with us for a week or so until I find her a place?'

'Of course, Caitlin. We're both so very grateful for her courage.'

'Dad?'

'Goes without saying. Tell her I'll take care of putting her belongings in storage and sending someone to get whatever she still needs from the house.'

'She's adorable. She's seventy-four and vulnerable.'

'We'll try to help with that,' Maggie said with sudden energy and enthusiasm.

'She has a little dog, a character called Monsieur Patate.'

'I think we can handle a little dog,' Frank added.

'Great! We're on our way. Once she's home with me, can the three of us go to the cemetery? I have something I want to tell Chris.'

Frank had joined Maggie and they both answered together. 'That's exactly where we'd like to be. Come home, Cait.'

When Mike put his arm around Caitlin, she had a favour to ask of him too. 'I need to be...'

'When you're up to it, give me a call.'

On The Boulevard, Maggie and Frank were standing outside to greet all three of them. Maggie gave Sophia the warmest hug she could ever remember. Caitlin smiled. Frank carried Sophia's bags to Hunter's old room and then showed her the bathroom and other things she might need. Frank led Sophia to the kitchen. Monsieur was waiting for Sophia; he knew how to behave.

'Sophia, the kitchen is full of food,' Maggie told her. 'Feel completely free with anything you want to have. We'll be back shortly.'

'Dad, I'd like to get Chris red roses; can we stop at McKenna's?'

'Sure. Buy roses for each of us.'

When Frank drove into the cemetery, it was the first time the Donovans had been together there since the funeral. Maggie and Frank held back while Caitlin walked to the foot of Chris' grave. When she saw the marker, she broke down. 'I promised you I'd track down the driver who killed you, Chris, and I did. I didn't allow her to walk away.' Caitlin laid her flowers at the front of the plaque. Then she finally broke, and grief spilled from her heart. It was Chris' name on the plaque that tore her open. She didn't feel any better; Chris was still there. Around him, nothing had changed with the arrest, nothing. If she had clung to the notion that finding the driver would in some way absolve her own guilt, she discovered it hadn't. 'Can you ever forgive me, Chris?' she wept and her tears fell on the roses.

Frank and Maggie helped their daughter to her feet because Caitlin was in the place Maggie had entered the night her son died. 'Chris never stopped loving you, Caitlin. Love survives death. Let's go home.' Maggie was the first to leave Chris in the cemetery that afternoon. She saw that it was her daughter who needed her now. The family left together and drove back home.

'I had thought of cooking tonight, but I haven't the energy,' Maggie had to admit in the car.

'Don't worry about that; we'll eat out. Let's hope our home is still in one piece.'

'Dad, Sophia gave up hers to help me.' Caitlin filled them in on the story.

'She's quite a woman, Cait. At her age and in her position, I can't say I'd find it in me to take such a stand.'

When they walked through the front door, the Donovans discovered Sophia had worked her magic. Wonderful aromas drew them to the kitchen. Caitlin got there first. 'Guys, come and see this dinner!' Sophia herself had found an appreciative and grateful family.

Sophia and the family ate at the kitchen table that

evening, savouring every bite. From his dish on the floor, Monsieur chewed his food with the manners that befitted such a lovely home.

EPILOGUE

RAYMOND LECOURS' FUNERAL took place on Wednesday in Outremont. It was widely attended. The dead man had connections. The employees from Foley Pharmaceuticals dutifully attended just to be certain Lecours was really out of their lives. There were seven funeral limousines, a wall of flowers at the front of the church and hollow hearts in the pews. Lecours' funeral was as cold as the man himself.

Kathryn Traynor lived long enough to file the negligence lawsuit, but she lost her battle with cancer in the early morning hours two days later. The day of her death, she had been anxious, quiet, lost. Tim lay beside her that night and held her hand. Worn out with the day's work, he fell asleep. In the morning, he still held her hand, but it had gone limp in his and Tim could feel the first hint of a chill in her palm. Before notifying her physician, he held Kathryn for an hour.

Foley Pharmaceuticals did survive its legal woes. Comitrixin did not. Within a month, much to everyone's surprise, Foley's hired from outside the company, and the new CEO offered Jen Sexton an executive vice presidency. For the sake of their marriage, Jen declined the offer and took the new job she'd found for herself. Things were looking up for the Sextons until the day Tim Traynor called and invited Jen to lunch. She accepted. Nobody's perfect.

Caitlin's book was launched at the Double Hook Book Shop. She sat at the small table near the front window beside a pot of daffodils. For three and a half hours, Caitlin signed books; both floors of the shop overflowed with friends, and people lined up halfway across the entrance to Westmount Square until they could walk up the storied steps with the pink railing. Many of the friends who came had attended Chris' funeral, and Caitlin knew some of them came out of respect for the family. Maggie and Frank stayed beside Caitlin, handing her new books as she needed them. Sophia was there, but Monsieur Patate had to stay home and he sulked all day. Geoffrey Smyth shook hands with everyone and waited anxiously for the press. *The Gazette* reporter was punctual and professional. Everywhere, there was a sense of renewal. That day, Chris felt very close.

A photo of the family, with Caitlin signing books, appeared in the morning paper. 'This is a good memory, Caitlin,' Maggie said. 'We'll treasure it.'

'I hope you have an idea for your next book,' her father added.

'Frank, let's enjoy the minutes; the days will pass too quickly.'

After dinner, Smyth called to say they had sold two hundred and seventy-three books. While the family took a moment to appreciate the count, the phone rang again. Frank picked up because he was closest. 'Hello.'

'Frank Donovan, please?'

'Speaking.'

'I would have appreciated your visit more if you had been honest about your name, Michael.'

Frank turned away from Maggie and Caitlin. 'Ryan?'

'That's my name.'

'I regret that I wasn't completely honest, but given the circumstances, I felt I had to be careful.' Frank's heart muscle tightened.

Caitlin and Maggie sensed trouble and stood next to Frank.

'I guess I thought the whole purpose of our meeting was honesty.'

'Ryan, my name is Francis Michael Donovan.'

'Really?'

'Really.'

'Well, then you're forgiven. I'm at a better place in my life now. Some of that is because of you.'

'Thank you for saying that. I wish you the very best Ryan!'

There were tears in Frank's eyes when he spoke. 'Ryan Burns has forgiven me. That's something isn't it?'

Maggie took Frank in her arms, the way she used to before Chris died. 'You're okay in my books too.'

'Thank you, Maggie. A second chance is all anybody wants.'

Mike Halloran continued to see Caitlin, but he wanted to know where they were headed. The funny thing was that he understood Caitlin's hesitation. They met at Le Paris on St. Catherine Street, a small, distinctive landmark in the heart of the city. Caitlin had chosen the restaurant because she'd always felt it was one of the more romantic places in the city. At a small table with a white linen tablecloth, Mike pretended he was enjoying his pepper steak but all the while he was trying to phrase a question. Caitlin wasn't having an easier time with her delicious poached salmon with beurre blanc. Fine food doesn't calm a pounding heart. Mike spoke first. His words didn't come out the way he'd hoped they would. 'Do you think there's a chance for us?' He wanted to say, 'I love you and I know you love me.'

In the most simple of circumstances, speaking the truth isn't easy. Complete honesty in a relationship is a rarity, hampered by fear of loss. Caitlin began separating her salmon with her fork, knowing she couldn't say what she really felt. *What I'm feeling might be only lust. When I'm with you, I can't think; I can only feel.* Even she was disappointed with her response. 'Things are happening too fast to catch up to them.'

'Can we get beyond Chris? That's what I want to know.'

Finally, some honesty. 'I don't know if I want to right now.'

'In time?'

'I hope so, Mike.'

'Then, that's what I'll give you.'

'You're some kind of guy!'

'Only with you.'

'Let's see how we feel in a couple of months.'

'You've got it. Let's eat because there's hope and I'm starving!'

Nicolina Pastore didn't pass Go after her trial. She went directly to jail. However, Nicolina wasn't washing toilets or stuck in the laundry room. Like most criminals, she adapted quickly and somehow snagged library duty. She worked feverishly on her appeal and began studying the cases of the other inmates on her block. Finally, behind bars, Nicolina found the respect of her peers, something she'd craved all her adult life. It was reported that her only complaint was the food.

After the delight of that first meal, Sophia stayed on at the Donovan home, treasured, even spoiled. Maggie had set two house rules for Sophia: no house cleaning and no cooking on her bad days. Maggie did not want to take advantage of the older woman she came to love. Sophia disobeyed both rules. Her care and presence allowed Maggie the space to realize she wanted to go back to work in September. Frank surprised Sophia with an airline ticket to Winnipeg at the end of August to visit her daughter. Without the tension and stress of the Harvard house, Sophia's knees hurt less.

Monsieur Patate was sent to the best groomer in Westmount! The first thing he shed was Patate. From that day on, he answered only to Monsieur. Frank bought him a new, silver leash. His incontinence and other lapses were things of the past. He'd come a long way in his life, all the way from NDG to The Boulevard. Only those who knew the city knew how great that distance was. When Monsieur walked down Greene Avenue on his brand new leash with his fresh groomed hair, not a single dog smelled his humbler beginnings. His name was refined, his manners impeccable, his bearing royal. He had arrived and he was staying!

With the time Mike had given Caitlin, she and Carmen saw more of one another. Frank felt that Caitlin needed to get away, needed time on her own. He offered a week's vacation to both friends. Carmen worked two weekends to get the time off and was excited. 'I have an idea. Cuba's out. We don't want to go anywhere strange. The last thing you need is something new. What if we found a place in Miami? I was thinking of going a hundred blocks south of Club One, closer to South Beach. We'd lie on the beach all day. Nobody goes to Miami in the summer; we'd be safe,' Carmen enthused. 'Just think, Tony Roma's Carolina Honeys, baked beans, apple crisp; does it get any better than that?'

'Do you sit up nights planning schemes like this?'

ACKNOWLEGEMENTS

THREE SPECIAL FRIENDS have taken time from their busy lives to work on *Cutting Corners*. Where would we authors be without the generosity of such people?

Gina Pingitore has worked on all three books, proofing them on Friday nights and Saturday afternoons, each with the same enthusiasm she brought to the first. She also drew the first draft of the map for *Cutting Corners*. I will always be grateful to her.

Sandy Jarymowycz has a myriad of tasks to occupy her days, but found the time to work, like Gina, on all three books as well. She brought a keen eye and technical acumen to the book.

JoAnn Valente joined the team this year and spent countless hours, rereading the whole manuscript, designing ideas for the cover and fliers. JoAnn was a student in my first teaching assignment, and we rediscovered each other at a signing.

I would like to thank Jocelyne Dionne of CIBC for her banking tips, Jacques Gravel, a retired Montreal police officer, for his facts on police procedure and Kevin McNamee for his knowledge of fine wines. Thank you to David Klimek of *The Gazette* for his friendship and resources.

David Price is my publisher. I trust his editing and suggestions. It is my good fortune to work again with him.

ABOUT THE AUTHOR

SHEILA KINDELLAN-SHEEHAN is a Quebec born writer who winters in Miami. Her memoir, *Sheila's Take*, was published by Shoreline Press in 2003 to critical and popular acclaim. Her first novel, *The Sands Motel*, was published by Price-Patterson in 2004 and quickly became a bestseller. *Cutting Corners* is her second novel.

A Montreal detective novel by
new author Peter A. MacArthur:

Fat Jack

Peter A. MacArthur